THE WAY OF THE WARRIOR
RAINBOW WARRIORS

By Daniel Sioux Ranville

The Way of the Warrior
Rainbow Warriors
Cover and Interior Design, Editing by Daniel Sioux Ranville

ISBN-13: 978-0993604102 (Warchief Publishing)

Warchief Publishing
586 Lansdowne Avenue
Winnipeg Manitoba, Canada
R2W0H6
www.warchief.biz

For the sake of the children, seven generations...
Acknowledgements

Special beloved gratitude to Joyce Hayduk, the love of my life.

Special thanks to Wilson, my brother and brother Jonas, Thank you Natasha, Raven, Jurni, Sky, Anthony and Tanika. Thank you sister Roxanne for your singing, talent, your love. Thank you brother Peter, you have been encouraging and an inspiration. Brother Ben, thank you for being such an inspiration, for being tenacious and dedicated in everything you do. Thank you Anita and Wayne.

Thank you Carolina, Christina, Julian Gaelyn Jordan and Daisy. Thank you Jack and K.K., thank you Sophia most precious granddaughter. You are all the purpose of my life. Everything I do, I do it for you.

Thanks Rob and Sue, Norm and Tracy. Rob, without your work, I would never have launched this endeavor. Norm and Rob, you have become more than a brothers-in-law, but real friends. All the best in your book, *Careers for Kids,* Rob! Norm, standby, I may need your accounting expertise.

Thank you Sylvia Hayduk, Shelley and Wes Zilke.

Thanks to Dr. Alan Gutkin, Dr. Glen McCabe, Dr. Fred Shore, Dr. Chris Trott, Dr. Peter Kulchyski, Dr. Lori Wilkinson, for being the awesome mentors and teachers that your are. Your advice and counsel has been invaluable. Thank you Carl Stone, Dr. Bret Nickels and Kali Storm. Fred and Bret, I do believe you were the first teachers to have graded me an A in my education process, thank you for that, you may never truly know what that means to me. Because of it, I was able to launch myself into an entirely new dimension of existence. Without your guidance and encouragement, I would have remained a high school drop out with my public education experience to tell me what a colossal failure I was. I would never have come to the places I have seen and experienced presently. Dr. Fred Shore, thank you. Thank you. Thank you.

Thank you cousin Roxanne, Duane and Dave Shuttleworth. I heard your teachings in the dream world. This book would never be possible without your help.

Thank you Jules Lavallee for sharing your teachings, confidence and belief in me.

Joshua Mason, Johnny Einnerson, Derek Hart, Darwin Ironstand, you have been an inspiration. You are all true friends.

Thank you David and Kevin, you are a true Warriors! Thank you Sean and Danielle. You both showed me that it was okay to enjoy the moment, to be professional, to live life to the fullest. I will never forget our awesome times.

Thank you Uncle Wally. You accepted me for who I was and am. Thank you Uncle Gordon, for your work in our Metis land claims and how you showed me that I could contribute to the people in my own way. I wish you were here.

Thank you Danah Pochinko and Mike Bellehumeur, your friendship has been most awesome! Ron and Shauna Braun-Pepper, most wonderful. I think of you all often. I admire you. You're inspirational.

Thank you Charles Favel for the Fox and the Hound story. Thank you Darrel Stevenson for teaching. You have all sharpened me, made me into a better person. I am a lesser person without you all in my life.

Finally, thank you mom, dad, grandparents, aunt's uncles and all survivors of the dreadnaught that attempted to kill you. Your survival, resistance and tenacious courage are a living testimony to us all. The evil and corruption, powerful and almighty, though breathtaking, as very small children you resisted courageously. I wish you all a healthy and fulfilled life.

Thank you Kevin Bishop for being the first to recognize that I was a story teller.

Special Thanks to my first teacher, Jim Lavallee, I remember everything you taught me and I still practice Maskanas the way

IN LOVING MEMORY OF MY LATE COUSIN VANCE

The Way of the Warrior Rainbow Warriors

By Daniel Sioux Ranville

Table of Contents

Disclaimer

This book is a work of fiction. It is based on real events such as Canada's apology for their assimilation programs, Indian Residential School and abuses. All persons, characters are fictitious. Any resemblance to real persons, characters, living or dead, is purely coincidental. The author assumes no responsibility or liability for any and all alleged damages or loss associated with the contents of this book or third-party websites. This book does not offer advice or is meant to provide counseling. If you believe you need professional help, contact a clinical psychologist or utilize the IRS Crisis Line below. This book offers no legal advice; consult your lawyer, local Ombudsman, human rights offices, workplace harassment policies and human resources offices for clarification on legal issues.

WARNING

This book may trigger or invoke an emotional reaction, which may affect mental health. If this book distresses you, or someone you know, call 1-866-925-4419 to access the Indian Residential Schools Crisis Line.

Note: This is a culturally relevant work based in Aboriginal cultures and perspectives. Feel free to read this work as such. Doing so will enhance your comprehension and you will relate to the work in a meaningful way. This work, at times is written with a Metis accent, in English.

Prologue

Boozhoo!

Bakahn Maaengen, day-zhan-e-kah-zheese!

My spirit name is A Different Kind of Wolf. I am a *Lone Wolf Warrior*. I am Ogitchidaa of the Wolf Clan! My spirit guides are the Owl, Wolf, Buffalo, Bear and the Snake. I am one, among the many. I am a pipe carrier. My colors are all the colors of the Earth, like a hunter who wears camouflage or a snipers ghillie suit.

The Elder who named me said he watched, looked and listened to the spirits to learn what the spirits were calling me. He looked in the night sky beyond the stars but learned nothing. Then looked into the forest and trees and still learned nothing. Perplexed, the Elder looked into the Earth, the day sky, the water world, the rock world, the animal world, the sacred fire, and the like and still learned nothing. On the last sweat, of the last day of my vision quest, where I sweated four times a day, for 3 days, and on my 13th sweat, fourth day, the Elder looked again into the forest and thought he saw the brush move. It was like a wind came he said, and he thought my name was Wind, but he looked closely and saw something more. It was not the wind, it was a visual distortion set against the forest. As he looked closer, he could see the apparition move this way and that. And that's how the Elder learned my name. The spirit he saw was a wolf that could camouflage like a chameleon, against the colors of the earth. That is how I became, A Different Kind of Wolf.

As a lone wolf warrior my job is very dangerous. I am like a warrior scout that works on the fringe of the community, learning the ways and movements of the enemies. As such, I learn about other ways and cultures. I am entrusted as an Ambassador for the people that can work as a representative or liaison between the people and other family groups. I allow no one to see me, unless it is in the best interest of the *children of the earth*.

The gift I am entrusted, is the gift of *dreams*. Sometimes I interpret them. I definitely travel in them. So I am gifted with travelling in the spirit world also. I am a traveler.

I am also one of the storytellers. The Elders recognized that I have a superior auditory memory. When I am told a story, I can remember it up to the 97th percentile, usually on the first telling. I am terrible with names, unless they tell me their story, then I never forget a face. My wife says I have selective superior auditory hearing. I don't know what she means by that.

Maybe I learned this gift by having the genetic makeup of one of the traditional teachers from the ancient days. It may be that I play the guitar and can sing like the *Soggy Bottom Boys*. Hearing a note and then finding in fret or in voice, a process called ear training, only takes practice. In time, it gets better. Like all behavior modification, with time and practice we can get better at our gifts. It may also be that I crashed headfirst into a parked bus, a near death experience, while cycling. I will offer a more likely scenario.

When we were children, brother wolf and I would play in the rooms, on the floors always close to our parents. Sometimes other Elders would come in and they would talk. Most times, we cared not for what they said. It was when they hushed their voices as if in secret, that is when our ears would pry, stretching and turning toward what is being said like a wolf's ears. We listened very carefully because whatever was being said obviously meant it was in our best interest as children.

Are we doing something that could result in a severe and brutal beating and should we move our play to another room or are we safe? Children watch and listen far more intently than many would ever know. It turns out, it was against the law to talk about our traditional ways and teachings. That is why the Elders would hush.

We kids thought we were in trouble! So we listened very closely.

So the Elders tell me all the stories and when I tell them back accurately, I become like a living encyclopedia that can recite the stories, traditional teachings word for word.

When I was a small boy in public school, I missed a lot of education. It turns out that it was not my doing that caused delays in my educational experience. Though many of them blamed me for it throughout my childhood. It was their racism, ignorance and the like perpetrated against me by a few racist teachers and others who would rather remain silent as bystanders. During these experiences, I was told that I was some sort of retarded person that could not be taught anything. I recall teachers who would simply ignore me in the classrooms.

One school had me sit in the library for a couple months coloring while all the other kids sat in their classrooms. Consequently, I made no friends and as an outsider among the children of that school, the students subjected me to open ridicule during the recesses and lunch times. Combined, I was blamed for being unteachable, retarded and just plain stupid.

Frustrated with me, they said I was lazy and they dismissed me. So for a long time, I thought I was stupid and retarded. But when I went back to school as an adult, trying to get away from a life of gangsterism and terrorism, I met teachers who would teach.

I told all my friends I was heading East to Montreal and instead I went West to the Mountains. I disappeared myself because in the gang world, you don't just leave, you disappear or they disappear you. A few years later, when the turnover rate in gangland changes names and faces as some die, disappear or go to jail, I returned to a fresh Winnipeg, as an unknown. I found myself slipping back into gangland so I decided the one place no one would find me is back at school.

I went into university as an adult, tested as a possible candidate for dyslexia as my reading and comprehension was very low. Nevertheless, because teachers would actually teach, I was able to overcome many educational barriers. I got my first A letter grade ever in my whole life, in the whole wide world at university!

This encouraged me so much I caught the learning bug and found myself spending hours in the library. Even when the funding ended and I could no longer afford my university education, I would spend most of my time reading and learning, writing at the public libraries and I would rummage for free books, buying many at book exchanges. I attended, as many free lectures as I could that were made available to the public. I brought my cameras and recording devices along. And with permission from lecturers I collected and recorded lectures and discussions. If I was not allowed to record the proceeding I brought my superior auditory memory and I remembered what I heard, to the 97th percentile.

I discovered that it was not that I was retarded, it was that these teachers who were non-Aboriginal had come from families who were taught they were superior to us *natives* and that we inferior folk could not be taught and so they did not bother with us. I discovered that the so-called superior kids also were failed in public schools. This is due to in-group biases, favoritism, public relations or other such delusion, having been pushed through and passing them with whatever willy-nilly grades they were given by teachers. Teachers had and still have the power to do that!

It turns out grading a student in the public education system is all relative. What one teacher considers an A for effort, another would consider a letter grade of C. Then when the child leaves the school that grade at an A moves to the school where they grade them a C. How we, as Canadian citizens, would tolerate such colossal failure of our children is what this book describes. Anyone can discover these truths for themselves, but it would require you work your schedule around Saturday afternoon football, Hockey Night in Canada or the latest episode of Desperate Housewives. It also requires courage to look at things disturbing in hopes of correcting them skillfully, informatively.

I discovered many of my classmates had become a nation of ignorant white people who could not be bothered with education, books, writing, thinking and the like. Yet, many of them now held offices, positions of power delegating wealth, status and opportunity to their friends. When all along, I was taught they were superior, since they were coddled so much in our early school years, I assumed they were veritable geniuses in adulthood. I discovered quite the contrary!

Many could not understand the use of *big words*, philosophy, mathematics, logic, sociology, psychology or any other academic discipline. What happened to the bright young minds that I always thought were far more educated than I? Somehow, the table has turned!

Because they were doing so much better than I was academically in our early school years and later, they developed wonderful careers, got mortgages, bank loans for cars, I believed white people were superior! I was in awe of them. I wished I were white! That's the place you want to be, is white!

Somehow, in my quest to try to understand what the big difference was between them and us, I ended up blowing past many professional white people in my late twenties and thirties with just a few books!

While a late bloomer, I learned that I was simply playing a role, earlier in life as a gangsta, ascribed to me by a dominating culture based on white supremacy and I discovered that it was all a bunch of horse manure!

Today, my intellect is stunning and intimidating for many, even threatening to some. Some discriminate against me because I am an intellectual. They think that I think I am better than they are. They project this on me. Meanwhile that is the last thing on my mind! From their perspective, they feel threatened.

I can see through all the lies and deceit, corruption and aggression. I can see the insanity that plays itself out in the media, politics, governments, cultures and motivations including the stupidity of greed. It turns out that I am not the one who is retarded as taught and I today, can provide a comprehensive and coherent answer for all of it.

The reason why I wrote this book is to let young people know about the forces of oppression they face hoping the heads up will help them make appropriate preparations. This is also for non-Aboriginal young people who also face oppression, as they watch helplessly the wholesale destruction of our planet, inequality and human rights violations. Many young non-Aboriginal people leave their homes of opulence, throwing off their riches to become squeegee kids begging for change, *and change*, in many of our urban centers.

It is abundantly clear that young people can see through the smokescreen and are born ready to address the issues. The gift the young people possess will save us all from self-destruction. They will save the children of the earth, for the sake of the children, for seven generations.

Sadly, today many young people are born into a hostile, violent, aggressive world that is armed with dogma, ideology, racism. Some situations are more challenging than others are. Many young people are running from fox-hole to fox-hole in the midst of a constant and unrelenting bombardment of explosive and incendiary shells. There is not enough cover for young people while machine gun, sniper and rifle fire suppress them from achieving their objectives. Kids are competing with each other for a place to sleep out on the streets every night.

Meanwhile, there are predators that spend their leisure time searching for a fresh new victim because they are aware most people can't be bothered with these issues. Those who do care can only do so much.

Sadly, many young people, mostly Aboriginal kids, and women do not survive, are never found are either missing and/or murdered.

The children and grandchildren now abuse elders. Whereas in the old days we held our Elder in great respect and high regard.

We are assimilated into a great corruption behaving like the individualistic cultures of North America, where they send their Elders to be abused in *Old Folks Homes*. These agencies resist accountability. Transparency is discouraged, but in a delusional sense, they say they are accountable and transparent, and many believe them.

The Elders who gave me my name told me I am unique. Different, set apart from other wolves. They asked me about my life and they learned that I had experienced something contrary. I had several near death experiences. Apparently, it is a sacred thing to come back from the dead.

I explained at age nine one of the other little warriors pushed me off a tire tube into Lake Manitoba. I could swim, but I was pushed in such as way as to lose my sense of direction. I swam down instead of up. I was not ready so I didn't have a chance to catch my breath and I drowned. I saw the silhouette of a Warrior coming to rescue me.

Later, I jumped a fence, which broke, and I fell on a fence post, which stabbed into the back of my leg. I lost a lot of blood. I just missed a major artery or I would have been dead in seconds.

Later, I saved a life by intervening in an altercation. I stopped a gunman from shooting another by standing in front of a sawed off shotgun. No shots were fired and the other man was able to run away while I remained to talk the gunman into a healthier decision.

Still later, I drove my bike into a stopped bus headfirst and was unconscious suffering massive soft tissue damage with several dislocated ribs. This makes it very difficult to breath.

I also fought off the flesh eating disease when bacteria infected me after surgery. The bacteria entered my spinal chord and I got spinal meningitis as well. That was a six-month fight to the death.

But early in my childhood, I was about three years old and I had the whooping cough, Bordetella Pertussis. I had a coughing fit, which lasted long enough for me to stop breathing and I fainted. I was later dead as a result but was revived by my father.

The Elders agreed these events have the breath in common. They said Weendigo is stopping me from speaking. They have attempted to take away my breath. I have a story to tell that Weendigo does not want me to tell, they said. They encouraged me to tell it anyway.

So I want to tell you a story about all that I have seen and heard. Like I said, I do not remember the names of the people in the story but I can tell you with great certainty about what happened.

Introduction

PERCEPTION

Someone approached the podium to speak to military personnel and high ranking officers, Police, Corrections, Sheriffs, Probation, Fire Department officials, city counselors, politicians, social workers, government officials, bureaucrats, principles and vice-principles, teachers, child care workers, executive directors of social services agencies both private and public, university students and youth, youth at risk, religious leaders, career counselors, trades and apprenticeship representatives, union leaders and administrators, moms and dads from all walks of life and the young teens they brought along with them, medical doctors and nurses, insurance agents and their representatives, even Elders were all present. A hush came over the crowd that now stood before this lone wolf warrior. The sound of people shifting in their chairs as they settled into their seats echoed across the auditorium. As all quieted and all eyes piercing toward the lone wolf warrior a most riveting and thought provoking tale was presented.

First of all, I would like to thank all citizens for rising up to demand more for the sake of the children for seven generations, our great city, provincial and federal governments for providing sponsorship for this event, recognizing the importance of the challenges we face. Our most valuable resource, children and youth require our attention more than ever before. Our governments have engaged an extraordinary acknowledgment together, for the sake of the children, for seven generations. It is good to see that our country from ocean to ocean is now and forever committed to being a child-centered society and requesting specifically, for our traditional knowledge, as we have been child centered since time immemorial. It is indeed a most unprecedented cooperative collaboration!

I was 38 years old when I discovered my perception was a bit off. During my life, from the time I was an infant, into my childhood, elementary school years, playgrounds and swimming pools, teen years, young adulthood and later adulthood, I had interactions with many children and adults. I learned many things along the way. I was a Metis, born into a Metis family, in Canada, one hundred years after the great Riel Resistances. I was friends with many Portuguese, Ukrainian, Polish, Polish/Ukrainian, Italian, French, Czechoslovakian, First Nation, Metis children. I was able to learn a great deal from these experiences. I learned about the different languages, cultures, customs, of different people. There were dances, song and music, stories, histories, lifestyles, religions, beliefs and even superstitions! It was a rich childhood in the sense that I experienced many wonderful people and their cultures. But it was not to last.

As I grew older, the Fox and the Hound principle came into effect. I could not understand it but my "white" friends no longer wanted to have anything to do with me. My Metis friend, explained to me the story of the Fox and the Hound, friends in childhood, but later, because of the established ways of Foxes and Hounds set by culture, they became enemies.

In addition to my own cultural ways, as repressed as they were by the Canadian government and society, I learned more about what it meant to be white rather than to be Metis. So I thought I was white for a long time. I had no idea that we develop our perception, personalities, identity, and connections to reality. I did not think of life this way. It was all a simple, natural process of the way things are. It was my world. It was how I attempted to fit in. It was how I connected with my reality. It was how I saw reality. It was how I came to understand and believe in these realities. Oh how I came to believe in them!

Perception is powerful medicine. How we perceive our reality affect our interactions, life chances, quality of life, life choices. If someone, insidiously constructed a smokescreen for my perception by telling me stories, teaching me what I should believe in, whose religion is right, who to hate and why I should hate them, my mind, and my brain would make neural connections that would facilitate these beliefs. When stimulated, these neural connections would fire off precisely as they should stimulating precise locations of my brain, stimulating my perception of reality with all learned beliefs, providing me with understanding of any given situation.

If I were a soldier in combat, I instantly know what to do when I come under fire. If I were a football player, I know precisely how to behave in that culture. It gets more complex when you add racism, stereotypes, identity, and history, environmental background the dominant cultures, oppressions and the like all of which children learn. It is delusional to think we can prevent our children from learning these belief systems no matter how hard we try. The more we shelter our children, the more revealed the forbidden fruit becomes. Life becomes challenging to navigate under these confusing conditions. After a lifetime, our beliefs influence how we perceive and thus how we interact and the outcomes that are produced by the choices we make.

If we are healthy and balanced, our experiences are likely to result in better quality life and chances. This is likely due to our ability to perceive reality accurately and interact more effectively because our perception gives us accurate information that we process using our mind.

Alternatively, if our perception is incorrect, unhealthy and unbalanced our experiences are likely to result in a poor quality life and chances.

This is why racism and other systems of oppression like poverty, poor education, religion, abuse and violence are so insidious because they contribute to the development of poor perception, resulting in unhealthy choices and risky lifestyles. This in turn contributes to individuals both privileged and underprivileged to comprehend the reality of the situation with a less than accurate perception. It may be that both lack the cognitive energy to consider all of the variables in the equation. Rather, they are simply getting from A to B with as little resistance as possible and sometimes, frustrated both have run-ins with each other.

Perception is the manner we perceive our reality so we may derive meaningful experiences to interface with people, places and things. We derive knowledge, wisdom and understanding, allowing us to comprehend our reality and life experiences.

Our perception can influence the knowledge that is passed on to the next generation whether correctly or not. Perception influences the next generation's ability to perceive because perception influences reality in the first generation and passed down inherently through role modeling, culture and teachings. Our children are watching us closer than we imagine if we imagine at all and they will base their own behavior on what they witness as a truth. Adults can corrupt a child simply through role modeling behavior. This is a truth.

Another truth is that of wiring. Our brains are bio-mechanically engineered through a series of neurons that include ganglions and dendrites to say the least, all of which is manipulated by hormones, energy levels, genetic materials and the like. Genetic material of course will manipulate development due to various circumstances such as environment and thus genetic material will lay dormant in some cases, while in other cases activate. The neuron/s collectively facilitate comprehension. When a new concept is learned, the neurons will reach out to each other and share information that facilitate a learned concept or belief system. We have seen images through various media of brain cells sending and receiving electrical signals stimulating parts of our brain. Various behaviors or stimuli will stimulate various parts of our brains facilitating our comprehension or understanding of what, we are in that moment experiencing.

When we learn a new concept these neurons reach out to each other and make neural synaptic connections and this helps us remember what we learn. In terms of perception, our learned belief systems can make connections with other belief systems that may be dysfunctional. Our wires can get crossed in a way that does not promote accurate perceptions and belief systems. Nevertheless, these connections are made, for better or worse and we attempt to navigate our reality with what we have in terms of neural synaptic connections that affect our perception of reality.

A person developing in a safe and secure, loving environment free to express themselves without punishment may be more likely to develop into a more secure person later in life and that may help facilitate successful outcomes for that person. While someone who develops under systems of oppression, insecurity, unsafe and unloving environments may be more likely to develop into an insecure personality type with a greater likelihood for less successful life outcomes.

There are of course exceptions and variations to both of these scenarios due to culture and dynamic life experiences but these principles are well founded in scientific research which is peer reviewed and duplicated, making it sound empirical research.

Various substances can influence our perceptions. Lack of food substances, lack of water can create hunger and dehydration. These will influence how we perceive our reality. Drugs, alcohol and other mind-altering substance will have an affect on our ability to perceive reality as well. A hostile and abusive, environment and conversely, a friendly, contented environment will also have influences on our perceptions. Cultural environments will affect our perception as our culture provides the expression of emotion appropriately and sometimes inappropriately. Finally, we are able to tune out perceptions. If we are focused intensely, we can tune out perceptions such as noise, light, pain, and other variables including witnessing other people's suffering.

Certainly, those generations before us who suffered at the hands of government agents and religious clergy through diverse tortures will affect perception development in both the tortured and the torturer. On the one hand, the torturer perceives the victim deserving mistreatment for various reasons as moral justifications, dehumanization helps reduce guilt or shame in the act of torment and produces ability to torture. Some who are unable to perceive the feelings of others have no problem whatsoever torturing others they are uninhibited or less inhibited. Such individuals, sociopath's, psychopaths and anti-social personality types, fail to recognize verbal, visual cues or may have developed a personality that justifies torture. They may even derive sadistic pleasure in the act of torture.

Bullying, as we have seen in the news recently where new laws against bullying are considered, is a form of torture. The torment young people face while some bullies derive sadistic pleasure in the act of tormenting their victims have produced suicide and suicide pacts. The victim's perception and learned perception is affected in the act of torture. The victim may perceive others as dangerous, learning that danger is imminent. Hypervigilance or danger wariness may be heightened in a victim. In short, a victim's perception of reality may be altered to the point where accurate perception is difficult to attain due to the proximity of learned incorrect perception in consciousness or awareness. Sometimes the problem is within inches of our noses and we do not see a problem. Although, some may faintly perceive that a problem in perception exists.

An alcoholic or drug user will often have problems perceiving the link between their drinking or using habits in tandem with relationship and other problems associated with substance abuse. Additionally it may be the drinking and using itself is a symptom of underlying problems imperceptible to a user and abuser or those around them. Thus healing from suffering may require time to perceive layers of poor perceptions that contribute to an unmanageable life and unnecessary distress. This is because the belief systems, values and priorities are activated by neural stimulation in various parts of the brain, processed within millionths of a second. While in the moment, and under various conditions of influences, our consciousness or awareness of what it is we are processing may appear to make sense. It is in fact, a complex dynamic of various dysfunctional belief systems working in tandem producing dysfunctional awareness.

Think about this for a moment. Whose job is it to take the garbage out in your home and why? Notice the thoughts that immediately enter your mind as you begin to try to answer this question. Notice the beliefs, the value systems the priorities that enter your mind. Notice how your cultural mores begin to influence and justify your answer. Notice your beliefs about gender no doubt play a role in your mind. This is undoubtedly a complex dynamic of multi-variable factors in an equation that must be processed in such a way as to produce a sum. Right or wrong, your final equation will result in whether or not you are sleeping on the couch tonight.

There was laughter throughout the audience. Some murmured to others in a matter of fact way, while others in hushed, hesitant voices. There was a stir and a debate that ensued and the speaker allowed them a few seconds to process the example. The point was made.

In my own experience, I was asked how much I drink at a given time. I explained that I would attend the local liquor store and purchase one 40 oz. Whiskey, one 26 oz. Whisky and a small flask of liqueur for my coffee in the morning. This was a typical and rather tame, quiet weekend of drunken debauchery. At the time, I was in therapy with a clinical psychologist for personal problems of perception, though I did not know it at the time. I only knew that something was amiss. The therapist was astonished at my alcohol intake. I was amazed that she was so astonished, because from my perspective I did not have a drinking problem. I was able to drink as much as I wanted and could still get up for my responsibilities on Monday and throughout the week. From my perspective, I drank no different from any of my friends and they had worse problems than I did. Not impressed with my line of thinking, my therapist said, "It depends on who you ask. If you asked me or my friends compared to yours, to us, one or two in one night of the week is more than enough". From my perspective, only a privileged person thinks like this. They have spent a lifetime in healthier environments and so they do not perceive alcohol as a good time. Some of us less fortunate perceive alcohol as a way to enjoy oneself by enjoying the effects of alcohol over an evening, maybe two. But for some, holy, two weeks! Months!

To one who abuses substances, this line of thinking makes no sense. For some of us, one is never enough and neither are twenty. My therapist had her work cut out for her. She had to change my perceptions so that I would understand and comprehend my reality in a healthier manner. This would be difficult because my role models in the consumption of alcohol were heavy drinkers, some "alcoholic" or addicts. I also lived in an environment where this behavior is acceptable and normal. My community and family with inter-generational reinforcement had contributed to form my perception. I also did not believe in alcoholism, I still don't.

Anyone who considers another an *alcoholic* perceives the person this way using a set of morals and ethics judgmentally, from a Judeo-Christian perspective. This in itself is cognitive dysfunction.

These values and beliefs are not anyone's culture except for the Judeo-Christians or those whom they assimilate. To label someone using this perception is to engage in a *cultural imposition*, something Dr. Emma La Rocque describes in some of her papers on Indian and white relations. *Cultural imposition* has transferable qualities herein where one perceives another using only their cultural mores, belief systems as dysfunctional as they are, imposing them judgmentally. I am not sure if Dr. La Rocque would agree but that is how I understand and use the phrase, *cultural imposition* in many of these cases.

Alcoholism comes from two born-again Christians who beat themselves up by abusing substances in tandem with clearly dysfunctional belief systems. The only help available to them at the time was the Judeo-Christian faith, which in itself is replete with dysfunction, child abuse and child sexual exploitation. So *alcoholism* is a judgmental label developed out of severe conditions of dysfunction. I do believe in *substance abuse* though. One can use too much alcohol so that it begins to affect one's life in a negative manner. To be successful in changing my perception, my therapist faced overwhelming odds that needed courage, strength and perseverance. The very same thing many of us face and need.

Those of us who survived difficulties face overwhelming odds when we are attempting to help our community and family. *Physician, heal thyself* is the first challenge. Many Elders must recognize they have been affected by the oppression they faced as children and be sure they are in the process of healing themselves. We all must realize this truth. We must heal ourselves before we can be of service to others.

In sum, perception can develop within each of us derived from our teachers in our family, community and environment. Our perceptions are often diverse compared to others. There is no one way to perceive reality. There are unhealthy ways and there are healthy ways to perceive reality. Substances, environments, cultures, beliefs can affect our perceptions, opinions and attitudes, even education are examples of substances that can affect how we perceive. Egocentrism can affect our perceptions. In my situation, alcohol may have created problems for me it may not. I had difficulty perceiving illicit substances and my abuse of them was associated with my personal problems or if my personal problems contribute to heavy use. I could not see that I abused illicit substances or the reasons why I did. From my perspective, I used moderate amounts compared to some real problem drinkers and users that I knew. I was the responsible one!

That said I had no idea that I was seeing the world from the perspective of a small child, probably aged three to seven years, trying to survive a fearful and volatile world. As a small person at those ages, I was abandoned and neglected by my parents and family objectified me. Mother frequently beat me abusively, and father ignored that because he was there physically, but in other ways not present. His perception did not allow him to see any problem with child abuse. He probably thought it would do me some good. Nevertheless, I was a child and I could not process what I experienced and so, I had many unresolved issues or I had resolved them using the imagination of a child. This would prove to be problematic later as a child's perceptions and cognitive development run contrary to acceptable social norms.

These instances combined, contributed to how I perceive my reality. I was neglected and verbally abused and berated by many schoolteachers, hiding from the dreaded Children's Aid Society, most schoolmates bullied me, brutalized by certain police, and faced discrimination because of my appearance as an indigenous person. Consequently, my life chances were seriously undermined by a dominant culture who saw themselves as the norm and me abnormal being an Ab-original.

The speaker laughed aloud but no one else did.

As I developed into a bigger person, my perceptions remained that of a child because the trauma of childhood blocked proper healthy development of my personality and perceptions. In many ways, I matured into a responsible young person and eventually into an adult.

I functioned, however I was doing so with the perception of a small-frightened child in many ways I behaved childish, immature and irresponsible, impulsive and lacking forethought of the consequences of my actions.

I had a debilitating belief that I was unlovable, an ugly, filthy, vile, disgusting person that people would find easy to hate. I felt rejected. Others who believed this about me projected these onto me, thus treating me as an object, a thing. I projected that to others as well. Consequently, I was afraid of people. This vulnerable position made me open to exploitation by other abusers and bullies. Somehow, they could see that I was afraid. I discovered some liked me but only because they could get something from me and I could get something from them. This is called a co-dependent relationship and I had no idea this was unhealthy. It was all I ever knew.

I did not know that in this type of relationship, I objectified myself. I had no idea that I was a person with low or no self-esteem and I came to believe the things I was taught about who and what I was. I learned and accepted beliefs of myself in a dysfunctional way. I lived my whole life with this other part of me operating subconsciously and I had no awareness of this phenomenon of dysfunction. Not surprisingly, it served me well as a terrified child surviving repeated horrific trauma, brought about by Colonization, Racism, Discrimination, Christianization, Assimilation, the so-called *Riel Rebellion*, as *Dr. Fred Shore* describes, the *Forgotten Years*, The Diaspora of Metis, Indian Residential School (IRS), Post-IRS in the 70's, 80's and today AKA, our public education system.

I was born of parents who had almost no parenting skills, who may be psychotic or at least within the range of psychopathic behavior. This is not their fault. It is a direct result of a traumatic and horrific history that is and remains a part of Canadian identity and culture, economically, politically, socially. It is imposed upon all of our families and communities, it is not just an *Indian* problem, though that is how it is presented in media. Nevertheless, even without knowing my own history and legacy, I continued to perceive my reality in this way for many years. My reality was normal. My beliefs normal, from my perspective. At some point in my life, I could see that I was having problems but I was unaware of what they were. All I knew was that "white man stole my land and I am the enemy of white man from town" and this is the perception that I operated from, my entire life.

I automatically assumed that no one liked me, even if friendly to me. I was always suspicious. I hated myself and I hated life, as it was a hellish life from which there is no escape until the final moment of death. These beliefs contributed to self-sabotaging behaviors. For example, while in job interviews, I would blow it by speaking my mind. I had assumptions of conflict occurring why not speak my mind. I would become combative. In jobs, I would begin to see instances of racism, which were in fact real, and I would posture defensively, aggressively. I would be fired or I would fire myself believing sincerely that I was justified in my behaviors, that they were authentic. I was always insecure. I believed that I was nothing! I was worthless. I deserved nothing good. I lived my life like that. I had a "hit me" look and I wore it openly everywhere I went. I did not feel alive unless someone took a shot at me.

When things went well and I started to feel this foreign substance called peace and serenity, happiness, I would sabotage it because these things were unfamiliar to me and I was uncomfortable in its moments. I believed I was not worthy. I was unaccustomed to a good and deserving life so I did not allow that for me. If our relationship was going well, I would sabotage it by saying something mean and hurtful and then I would laugh and say, *just kidding*. For me, my safe place was in misery. I had to be suffering. I had to be hurting because it's all I ever knew, it was all I was comfortable with on a daily basis. Happiness, safety, security, stability, those were foreign to me and I was not secure with that. Meanwhile, I was trying hard to be all of those wonderful, beautiful, wholesome and healthy things and to have them in my life.

Talk about neurotic! On the one hand, I wanted life to be wonderful and on the other, I didn't want life to be wonderful. Professional people would call that "confused". I'll say!

Another perception remained or developed as a child within me. I knew that I was missing something and I would not be deprived of it. At first, as a child, I wanted to be a *Campbell's soup kid* with a *Leave it to Beaver* lifestyle, I thought it was toys and a happy family, safe stable and secure, like the *Brady Bunch*. I thought it was a good woman, kids, a car, a Harley-Davidson, a home, love and all that stuff.

I worked hard for that but none of that mattered in the end. I needed to understand and comprehend my life because I never had a good one. I craved knowledge because I believed that it would help me to understand my world and I could better predict future events. I was motivated in this way. I was insecure and I never had security or stability before so now I crave control.

Having had no control in my childhood I came to believe that I had to find ways to make my own security. I had to control my environment including people places and things. I have a god complex. I became egocentric. I controlled relationships, people, and knowledge. I have control issues.

It makes sense because I was operating from the perspective of a child trying to survive a hellish nightmare where I was not in control but at times had to take control. However, the methods in which I would find control were dysfunctional and I would never know it. If I were to be punished, I would control its administration. This is a living nightmare. The very same nightmare, my parents and their parents had to survive and the previous generations before them. I also learned later that this nightmare comes from the dominant culture that now imposes itself on everyone. No one has escaped its insidious nature. Some just have less abuse than others.

I realized all this in therapy. So now, I have to unlearn everything I have learned. I have to disconnect the neurons that promoted dysfunctional thinking, beliefs and perceptions. This is difficult because these neurons seem to reconnect overnight while I am asleep. And so the next day I have to persevere another day in attempt to disconnect these stubborn neural synapses which facilitate poor habits, these belief systems. It is not impossible to change these biologically engineered neural connections, it just takes time and energy, readiness and willingness to unlearn dysfunctional behavior in spite of triggers.

People who appear to like me, probably do like me or love me and no one is out to get me. When paranoid, I can remind myself there is no need for that. And I can think about what triggered the paranoia, consider the trigger, resolve it and carry on. Not everyone is racist against me. Even if they are, that is their problem not mine and I wonder what horrors are in their own life that facilitates such a debilitating belief system that do not promote harmony and peace. I tend to be more compassionate towards people who are problematic in these regards, more aggressive as I have intimate knowledge of what has contributed to personality development, probably better then many of them.

Admittedly, I am not the best at this practice as those who know me well will be able to point out for anyone. But today, I do not beat myself up when I make a mistake. At least I am aware and making the most of it. Tomorrow is another day to try again. I hope that over time, even as I have learned this dysfunction, unlearning it daily, and learning a new way, making new neural connections and strengthening them daily. Life can be wonderful if I allow it to be.

I do not have to be self-sabotaging in my successes. I do not have to assume the worst and I can assume the best in people, places and things. I know that I love my family and my community. I know they love me. I can be secure, not insecure. I do not have to be in control, but rather, I can live and let live. In a way, I am in more control than I ever was by changing my perceptions and beliefs about my reality to something empowering and more accurate. There is, in this moment, a universe of peace, tranquility and harmony that is infinite, real and tangible and I can have that any time I want.

The perception that is in my story is the perception of an abused child, self-abuse, morbid reflection and insecure perspectives. This does not undervalue its content but rather reveals a great deal about IRS legacy, Canada and Aboriginal people and communities. We are all engaged in this life together. We are all colonized, assimilated, and many at one time Christianized.

The Spanish colonized South America and many indigenous people no longer speak their original language but rather speak

Spanish or variations of Spanish and also have Spanish names. The Spanish also colonized the Philippines and today much of the language spoken and surnames are of Spanish influence. I am of Metis descent and I am no different from many others who were colonized and assimilated.

Colonized by the British Empire I consequently lost my original language and today, my surname is Francophone, while I speak English. Much of my identity comes from the Metis culture as well as those other influences. Where do you fit in this picture be it a non-Aboriginal person or an Aboriginal person, an Elder, a Helper, a Warrior, a citizen, a teenager, a parent, a manager, CEO, banker, social worker, teacher?

If you are a teacher, conventional or otherwise, the least I would hope that you gather from this is that you are often teaching kids that are as I was. I was beaten and abused, traumatized and it seemed that no one loved or cared for me and I became unwell. I tried to reach out to those who turned out to be bystanders and they dismissed my complaints as if I was no matter or concern. They even accused me of lying and being a shit disturber. Have compassion for your troubled students as they are so young trying to understand their world. Do not favor those who give you no trouble but rather, reinforce even more so, those who are vulnerable and troubled. The ones who are strong are already capable, they need attention but only sometimes, the ones who are weaker need your attention the most. That is the Way of the Warrior.

The crowd was receptive and they seemed to understand. There was a break and many gathered for wine and cheese, snacks, cakes and tea or coffee. Many spoke to each other with open hearts and minds. They were all willing to work together for seven generations, for the sake of the children.

Chapter 1

THE GAG

It is forbidden to speak on these matters, absolutely forbidden. These matters have always been for those in high places, mighty places, seats of authority to manage. We common folk have not the wit to discern the complexities of this way and that and so they tell us, they guide us. It is expected of us to confess any confusion we may have with our priests. We are to confess. Anyone who tries to speak on that which is forbidden is immediately arrested, tried and convicted by judgment. One who would so dare to speak on these matters is branded a fool, an idiot, and lunatic. They would be institutionalized and treated for a psychological disorder and their rights would be taken away entirely. They would be subject to total control by agents of the institution. They would eat when told, sleep when told, and awaken when told. For them, it is a privilege to see the sun. This has been the way of it for ten thousand years.

Throughout those years, there would be varying brands of priests in high places, locked away in high ramparts and bastions and towers. Of recent, the academics have vicarious control over all rulership. Should anyone cross them, they are charged with authority to dismiss anyone's talk with contempt. Their hands raise and flick anyone away that does not agree with them or would jar them or bust them. They look away and laugh bemused as their faces sneer in contempt, one side of their mouth raised offering cheek.

In spite of all that, we will now speak of these matters now as the prophecies are being fulfilled and it is obvious the time is right. Let the scoffers scoff, come what may, we will speak of the great councils and all the preparations that were made to begin the healing journey. Ten thousand years ago when the great corruption came, sacred medicine was offered, ceremony, and then visions were given to the *children of the earth* and prophecies were made in answer to the great corruption. There are now signs and wonders even the priests cannot ignore. The Elders are back with the people. They have come out of hiding deep in the forests, miles upon miles away from the Indian agents and RCMP who would, as

1

part of their duty, arrest them. The Elders, once outlawed all over the world for ten thousand years have come back to the people.

When the great corruption came, the people lost their faith, they lost their way in the face of great adversity, chaos and mayhem. The people were sorely misguided placing their faith in the priesthood who led them into order using whatever means to justify the ends. But I am not judging them, I do not blame them. It is what it is.

It was the priesthood that rose to great and lofty heights with promises in leading the people out from the dark ages, a time of woe and sorrow. The priesthood brought us order where there was no order. Though not everyone agreed, the priests should be given such a charge over the masses. How could it be that only one group would have absolute power over the people when it was always, since time immemorial that the clan teachings brought harmony, peace and abundance for all? The priestesses resisted. For ten thousand years, the priestesses resisted and their resistance was put down in a most hideous fashion by the priesthood. There were many "witch" hunts and "witch" burnings and the smoke of their pyres rose into the night skies for ten thousand years. The smoke clouded the moonlight and starlight, the stink of it was most displeasing. The filth of the whole affair was not welcome in the eyes of the great mystery.

So it would appear, the conflict over the great corruption that came upon us all was a conflict between the priests and the priestesses, between male and female, if there is such a thing. Some said it was a conflict of class struggle between the haves and the have not's, the proletariats and the aristocrats, the common folk and those in high and mighty places. Whatever it is, there is no doubt that a great conflict exists between great powers mysterious and terrible in all of its glory.

I have been dreaming since the age of 3 autumns. My first night terror was of a small dark cubbyhole, a space above the stairs of our home. As I was crawling down the stairway, I could see that something was hidden in the shadows of that small crawl space above the stairs. I could hear it smelling the air, breathing heavily searching for me. Whatever it was, I seemed to know that it was going to devour me, to tear my little arms and legs off and to eat them.

It reminds me of how, as a child I used to tear the wings off a fly and its legs. Why did I do that?

I knew I would die if I did not avoid the terror in the shadows. I somehow understood that this thing that should not be could not be reasoned with. There was no bargain that it would accept. It would accept no negotiation. It was purely hungry and would do anything to fill its belly. I was helpless and terrified and I did not understand what was happening to me.

I wonder if that is what the fly felt when I captured it.

I walked warily past the crawl space and I heard the low growling of this predator as dreadful as it sounded. I was to walk very carefully so as not to allow it to detect me. I have had many dreams since then. They were all very mysterious.

Chapter 2

THE DREAMS

Young people from different walks of life have recognized that something strange is happening in their lives. These young people do not know what it is but they know that it is there. It troubles them. They are confused by it. They talk about it with each other. They dream about it. Strange dreams, visions of decrepit filth, bile, putrid waste material of human feces and urine permeate their nocturnal imaginations. In their dreams, they see people walking in the filth acting as if it isn't there, but it is because these young people can see it. Those who see the filth tread carefully. They try not to touch the oppressive slime while stumbling through dark corridors in their dreams. Always walking, searching for a way out of these apparent sewers, which present as their high schools, social services agencies, doctors offices, neighborhoods and homes. They keep their hands in trying to avoid touching anything so as not to be infected and they walk carefully down dark hallways, locker rooms, change rooms, showers, and waiting rooms stepping over giblets, death and debris. In the dim lit corridors, filth is everywhere. In every dream, they cannot find a way out of the darkness.

What does it mean they ask when they awaken? Why do the dreams recur?

Young people see predators in their dreams. The tall people with the eyes completely blacked out. These visions frighten them. They try in vain to reason with the predators but they cannot be reasoned with, they do not bargain, they only want one thing, to consume the dreamer and to possess them entirely. So the young dreamers run as fast as they can but it's never fast enough. The predator catches them and holds them. The predator takes delight in the fear the young people experience, watching the shaking, trembling, absolutely horrified dreamer with its cold blackened eyes as it presses down. The predator does not smile, it simply is utterly horrific because the young dreamer knows the predator has no feelings, emotions, morals about the young dreamer. The young dreamer feels objectified and knows that to the predator, they are just another victim. There is no resistance, no one to save them, they are totally confined and there is no escape.

The fear makes their heart pound in their throats and they feel their eyes bulge out of their heads. The predator has them and they cannot move a single muscle as the fear incapacitates them. Like an animal, the young dreamers wet themselves in fright. Try as the young dreamer might, they cannot move. Just as the predator moves in for the kill, the young dreamer makes one last desperate struggle to escape and they find themselves suddenly awake and sitting partially up in their bed totally horrified. The young dreamer hears the cackling laughter of the predator fading back into the subconscious as they awaken more sharply.

Young people do not want to go back to sleep after experiencing such horrors. They fight to stay awake no matter the cost. They will do anything so they do not have to visit the horror that sleep brings. The horror of it fills them with dread for days because the experience is very real for them. They are confused by it.

What does it mean? What is the thing that should not be?

Then one night the young dreamers are caught at unawares once again and they are asleep. As they drift deeper into the horror of helplessness they begin to hear the predator approaching in a matter of fact way. The heavy booted or shoed steps sound against the hallways and walkways approaching their home as if it was business as usual. Closer the sounds of heel-toe, left-right, step-step and the rustle of black slacks, rain coat in tail, as it approaches in the night air. Still closer, the predator draws near like a tormentor to the victim of torture who must recant or confess. But what do we confess? We would confess if it would make the terror and horror end.

To the tormentor, torturer, predator, it is business as usual, as they make their arrival to the door where the ceremony of torture will take place. The victim, the young dreamer is frozen in fear and struggle as they might, they cannot move a single muscle. The young dreamer is helpless and defenseless.

Suddenly, the predator stops and tries for the door. As if to make fun of the young dreamer, the predator turns the doorknob as if it cannot open the door or rattles the keys to the room as if they cannot get in. The young dreamer does not know that the ritual of torture began when they fell asleep, with the sounds of the footsteps approaching. Sometimes, the young dreamer awakens just in time to avoid the night terror. But still others may not hear these footfalls, they only realize all too late that something has just sat down upon their bed and they can feel the bed sink inward as they roll over slightly in their sleep. Yet they are too weary to see what it is. It is the night visitor who has come to terrorize them. Sometimes the evil presence reaches out with its long, bony, claw like hands to grope.

Sometimes the young sleeper is aroused, the terror knows just when their victim is aroused, and at that moment when pleasure is stimulated, the rape begins. Mammaries and genitals are squeezed and torn away and breasts and genitalia are brutally violated with excruciating pain. Still at other times, the night terror sits upon the victim's chest to press their hands over the mouth or throat to choke the victim. The victim, the young dreamers resist and they try to speak in great terror to stop the horror of impending death, but they are not allowed to speak. Speaking is forbidden. Sometimes the night terror will take the form of an old hag, a witch who is known for her over sized felt hat and ragged cloths. She smothers with her hands or her genitals by sitting upon the victims face, what foulness! The terror, the horror, the helplessness of it all!

What does it mean? Why? Why me?

Still, in another dream, the young dreamer navigates through city streets, forests or roadways lost. Lost, terrified and alone, they seek reprieve, refuge, safety and security from what they know approaches. It is only a matter of time. As they maneuver in various directions, they curiously look around and make mental notes, landmarks, a tree, a building, and a streetlamp. As they continue on their journey, they notice that people also walk among them. Upon closer examination, the young dreamers notice something strange about these people. The young dreamers begin to wonder about what it is they see. As the dreamer considers the individuals that present themselves in this dream, a sense of paranoia grips the dreamer and they are alarmed.

At that precise moment, all the individuals turn and look at the young dreamer as if to smell the aroma of the young dreamer's thoughts, as if they hear a faint whisper, they bend an ear. The young dreamer realizes these are not regular people. The young dreamer must hide their thoughts even from themselves so that they do not betray themselves amongst an entire city of predators.

Suddenly the dreamer can hear strange sounds, murmurings and whispers in the air of their nightmare, unclear sounds approaching. There it is the rustling sound of vicious guard dogs searching frantically in the cold windy autumn evening. They are searching relentlessly seeking out the young dreamers to arrest them, capture them, and torture them and to eat them!

Wolves begin to howl throughout the city in the night air. They are calling to each other. What are they saying? What does it all mean? Vampires begin to bare their teeth, salivating like Pavlov's dogs trained to prepare for a meal at the sound of a bell. Fear grows in the young dreamer and they struggle to suppress it. They cannot give themselves away to these monsters. They must appear fearless. Try as they might, the monsters move in closer to inspect the young dreamer up close and real personal. They look at the young dreamers chest searching to the left and to the right, breathing and moving curiously and inquisitively up to their face and finally into their eyes. The young dreamer is frozen stiff and totally surrounded by empty cold husks. One wrong move and it is all over, but the young dreamer must move or they will be discovered. If they move too quickly or with a sense of urgency, it is a dead giveaway. The young dreamers must regain control of themselves. Slowly, the husks move away searching elsewhere or carrying on with whatever it was they were doing in the first place.

Now is the time to begin to journey once again but the young dreamer knows they must do so very carefully. Suddenly, across the street they look and see the tall predator mirroring the dreamers every move, the tormentor also looks up at them. It is the great and gruesome captain of these vile and putrid creatures, these demons. The young dreamer is now wondering if they have been discovered. The young dreamer recognizes the empty shell, the shallowness, the lack of depth in the thing that is across the street staring at them.

There is no soul, no personality, no connection it is empty, void of any understanding. The dreamer wonders if it knows about the real identity of the young dreamer, that it is not one of them, that the young dreamer is desperately trying not to be turned. The young dreamer wants to live free and independent from these things. The young dreamer does not want to become a werewolf or a vampire, a zombie.

The young dreamer is desperate to maintain their identity, their soul, their personhood. The young dreamer must be in control. Control is a must as they do not want to be used by this great evil to do its evil bidding even as these other husks have been turned to the will of the great corruption. The young dreamers do not want to turn. The young dreamer thinks harder wondering if they are given away in the darkness and suddenly the King husk nods its head and smiles knowingly they have their prey. Strangely though, the young dreamer remains.

The predator simply looks on and curiously, the young dreamer wonders why the demon does not strike. What is it waiting for? What does this all mean? The young dreamer awakes.

In another dream, the dreamer is on a bus looking out the window. Suddenly the dreamer is not quite sure what was just observed. Were those two cops shooting someone in full public view? But the bus driver keeps driving, oblivious. The dreamer looks around to see if others observed the same thing. No one seems to notice. Creeped out, the dreamer looks out the window again but this time observes total chaos.

People are ganging up on other people, mobs, beating them savagely, brutally killing them, stabbing or bludgeoning them to death. People are running wildly, some chasing, others escaping to chase after another victim. There is death everywhere. Terror is everywhere. Blood and screams of horror and everyone else on the bus seem oblivious to it all. Raping, murdering, killing, torturing, maiming, children, women, and the elderly it is all utterly horrific.

Then the dreamer becomes aware that someone on the bus is staring at them with dark cold eyes. They smile at them knowingly and nod, guessing what the dreamer is thinking. Is this the thing that should not be? Yes. Now the whole bus is aware of the dreamer and they all turn. The dreamer wakes terrified, horrified and feeling dirty.

The young people dream these foul, loathsome dreams and more. The young people are aware that something is twisted, corrupted, turned inside out but they do not know what it is. The young people simply know they want no part of it. The dreams and the nightmares, night terrors, remain throughout their childhood, teen years, adolescent years, twenties and into their thirties. Some have seen the apparitions, the shadow people, the little girl with jet-black hair and ragged, torn black dress, bare footed she presents herself to little girls but they never see her face. Some never get away from their horrors and they die with them in old age or in some unnatural manner. They fear death by its insidiousness.

It is a strange phenomenon that young people all over the world are sharing these nightmares. It is unexplainable. No one knows why young people are developing under these conditions of great stress. No one can explain why young people are staying awake late into the night that their circadian rhythms have been altered. More and more young people are afflicted with these strange night terrors and no one knows what it means.

Many said that it was just dreams and others said it was a sign of the times. Many people grew very wealthy exploiting this terrifying phenomenon. Some talked about the *Zombie Apocalypse* and *alien invasions* speaking of signs and wonders that Mother Nature was fighting back. Some said the *Illuminati* were responsible, you could see the signs in every music video or photos of the white house or parliament. Others said it was religion. No one really knew what it was because for many thousand upon thousands of years they were not allowed to talk about it. So they spoke in secret, through nursery rhymes, and poems in spite of the laws forbidding them from speaking of the great corruption. Only the priests could make sense of it.

They said it was the Devil and his evil minions, the demons who wanted to take possession of the people. They said that salvation could only be had through them and their religions. Though many were confounded because they prayed with great prayers and much supplication, much faith expressed in their gods and angels but no salvation would come. They were told they were not being faithful enough and so they completely gave themselves to the church in hopes to find relief and still, no relief would come and so with great effort, they would exert their faith to no avail. They gave money and volunteered their labor throwing themselves blissfully, faithfully into the arms of the priesthood. Still, their religions did nothing to give them reprieve from their fear and night terrors. They were like sheep driven off a cliff.

Books written and movies were made about it. Young people played video games about it, went to these movies and they read the books alarmed by the striking similarity to their nightmares. Some young people agreed, yes, it was all just nightmares and nothing more should be made of it. Some made light of the matter, creating fantasy even, dungeons and dragons they called it. Still, others argued that it is important to consider that something else was occurring, that it was too important to dismiss. And so, some young people went to the movies to be entertained while others went to discover something new about their terrors. Moviemakers and story tellers had learned through interviews, research and data collection gathered on the phenomenon, that this information can be exploited and capitalized upon. Something was wrong about it all and young people knew it.

THE POWER OF YOUTH CLANS

Parents and caregivers notice their younger ones were up all night long on Facebook chatting, arguing and engaging in online bullying. It was a growing and widespread phenomenon that many capitalists and later, governments would take advantage of with advertisements or with politicking. Young people did not want to go to sleep at night fearing the worst horrors would visit them. Many young people would remain awake for days on end texting, sneaking out, visiting the comfort of their friends in camaraderie.

Young people were no longer getting their regular and natural stimulation through traditional play.

Texting became a global phenomenon that enhanced group affiliation and socialization where traditional age-old barriers like racism and genderism would be deconstructed. The adults began to see their young people forcing social changes faster than anything seen in world history. The 60's were a time of change and young people led the way this is not in doubt. The new millennium would be known for its revolutionary changes to traditional institutions and dogmatic adherence to the old order. And it will forever remain undeniable that young people lead the way.

In a way, that is how it has always been. Empires have always exploited the tenacious courage of young people to further their own causes throughout history in a most insidious manner. Young people were rewarded, called heroes. Child soldiers are not a new phenomenon, it is just that the West has not been privy to child soldiers as openly as we have seen in parts of Africa lately.

Empires throughout history exploited young people. The Nazi's utilized German youth inappropriately and the *Global Imperial Church* would do nothing when they allowed thousands of young children and youth to Crusade against their enemies in the Middle Eastern countries.

Children and youth have always led the way to social changes. Today, it is known that young people are the largest consumer of goods in any population and advertisers present their wares to young people rather than to parents and adult caregivers. Capitalism has flourished as electricity consumption increases from the use of television, Ipods, Ipads, computers, and other media devices are in high demand. Advertising has invaded every aspect of privacy and even Google who started out so friendly sharing its technology free is now growing increasingly invasive with privacy issues.

In many instances, these are nefarious and insidious exploitations while at the same time, young people are aware of the great power they have always held and they are using it for positive change! Young people resist a power that manifested itself as a predator in their dreams and even as they resist, the great corruption maneuvers to outflank the young adversaries and so the conflict continues like Yin and Yang.

This phenomenon brought a group of young people to visit The Elders. Some were called to seek the Elders through dreams and they travelled many miles over land and sea. Bushido, Wushu, Maori, Metis, Jaguar, even Celtic Warriors were arriving to seek guidance with the counsel of Elders. After all, how can people share the same dreams?

TOBACCO

It was the young Aboriginal people of Turtle Island who began to notice they all share the vision. And so they gathered together at first in small groups of friends of two or three. The gatherings became larger as more and more young people learned that they were not alone in the night terror. The young people began to share first with close friends because it was apparent to those who knew each other best, that something was wrong. Because they cared for each other, they asked each other what was the matter. This is the first lesson in the Way of the Warrior, to be aware of each other's burdens and to be available to assist when needed. And this is how the Way of the Warrior returned to all people around the world.

In their discussions, some described those gifted with "travelling" in the spirit world. It was described that some could interpret the meaning of their dreams. All that was needed was to present Tobacco to the gifted person. This is what a group of young people did when they discovered they had something terrible to manage and that they needed help.

This is the second lesson of the way of the warrior, to stop, look and listen and in awareness, to recognize that something is wrong. In recognizing that something is wrong, the warrior must identify the wrong. It is important to examine the wrong thing until it is clear that the thing that is wrong can be adequately addressed and remedied. If the warrior needs help with addressing this thing, the warrior must recognize they need help. In this recognition for the need for help, the warrior cannot be misled by cultural and societal expectations of individualism, the false teachings of the *brave* and *courageous hero*. Rather, the warrior must realize they are stronger when many arrows come together and bind themselves as one, united in a cause.

It is the teaching of humility that helps those warriors appreciate the strength of many. The Wolf Clan holds the traditional teaching of humility and the teaching says that no one is greater or lesser than the other is. The best that we can achieve is equality. That is how this group came to The Elders.

And what a strange group they were. Young people sharing a nightmare, each had unique talents, skills and abilities. No, they were not the Avengers, or Fox Force Five. They were young people on a journey and they met at a crossroad. The timing was right, the place was right, and they were ready. Without readiness, no change will come. And so it appeared that it was meant to be.

One young warrior was chosen to present *Tobacco*. It was said that the protocol is, *Tobacco first*. Tobacco is sacred medicine, most powerful of the four directions medicines. It is a symbol that binds the person to The Elder in a contract. If The Elder, as presented accepts the Tobacco, the adventure begins!

The Elder said to the young warrior that the Summer Solstice is ending and the winter equinox will begin. All the preparations must be made to usher in the new season. There will be a vision quest with sweat lodge ceremonies and sharing circle, an offering to the spirits the ceremony ends with a feast. This offering is to be presented in the forest. It is a plate prepared first, and offered first, to the spirits before any feasting begins.

It is important to abstain, if they could, from all substances that interfere with the ceremony four days before and after, but its best to begin preparations of that nature a month prior.

The Elder said coffee headaches during a fast are the worst! It is better to wean oneself off coffee over time than to cut oneself off cold turkey. There was a bit of a chuckle from the Elder when this was mentioned because the Elder knew that many nowadays, don't listen very well and many do not follow protocol.

Chapter 3

ORIGINS

The young people began to arrive one by one to the sacred site. They felt alone and unfamiliar with where they were. While the day was beautiful for autumn, the air clean and fresh, and the sky bright and blue, a bit cooler but winter had not yet arrived, everyone tried to get cozy. They were on the prairie. It was vast and open, with a lone tree to keep them company. The grass had been prepared, Tobacco was offered first and then the *Grass Dancers* would come.

GRASS DANCERS, WAR DANCE'S, WARRIORS AND CLANS

Whenever the people would come to the prairies the Grass Dancers would dance over the prairie tall grass pressing it all down to accommodate the ceremony. The ground firm beneath their feet and the warm autumn wind rushed through them where they stood.

The young people noticed that the Elder was not alone but was with a great council of Elders and they were all dressed in sacred regalia. Medicines were burned and could be smelled in the air. Among them were very impressive looking Warriors dressed ready for battle.

There were some that were very large Warriors both beautiful and striking, powerful in stature and they had very keen eyes. They stood ready and alert. They were called the Bears.

Bear Clan Warriors are in all shapes and sizes, but most often, they are larger in stature. Their size is deceiving while it appears they lumber clumsily here and there, one would do well not to piss off a Bear Clan Warrior! They strike as fast as lightening! Onlookers, hunters and passersby, caught mother bears on video. Once alerted to any threat a mother bear will go from zero to sixty kilometers per hour, which translates, into fifteen meters per second or up to fifty feet per second! Though a bear is a large animal it can and will move swiftly when motivated!

Bear Clan Warriors are no different! Gentle and fun loving they are, quick to laugh and they always encourage those around them, often visiting, travelling to family groups and communities always to encourage everyone, lifting everyone's spirits, they are powerful medicine people.

Bear clan warriors are very patient with others, gentle and graceful. I watched one poor chap pushing a Bear clan warrior's buttons repeatedly, incessantly until a swift and colossal reaction emerged. I don't think this was the reaction anyone close by was expecting least of all this poor chap. Instantly dark and thunderous clouds appeared, fast as lightening, instant as wind the Bear Clan Warrior charged and gripped this young warrior powerfully and gave him a healthy serving of humble pie. It was like the button pusher became a rag doll being effortlessly thrown and tossed about like a piece of meat. I saw legs, head, neck, and arms swing wildly, even the skin on his face was pulled by inertia, as this clumsy chap couldn't react to tense up quickly enough. If the Bear Clan Warrior wished it to be so, the younger one would have been dead long before he knew what came upon him.

But the Bear clan warrior was trained in the Way of the Warrior and only fed enough humble pie to release the dumb one back to his feet.

Visibly shaken, eyes widened as if shown what the future reveals and all answers to all riddles and mysteries disclosed, the little man staggered away breathing heavily.

There were other Warriors there too, smaller in stature but no less impressive looking than the large Warriors were. These Warriors worked in groups. These were called Wolves or Dog Soldier Warriors. Wolf Clan Warriors are excellent for stealth missions and communicate together effectively. They are strong, muscular and swift and they have excellent endurance. One would suppose the character *Wind in his Hair*, from the movie *Dances with Wolves* was a suitable model of the DOG SOLDIER WARRIOR if one needed a visual reference.

There are also LONE WOLF WARRIORS who do not travel with the pack, even as some wolves are lone wolf. They follow no one. They go where they want and they hunt on their own. Sometimes, the lone wolf will come across another group and they will play with them for a while, but when the playing is done, they go on their own way again. They are very friendly. In the Wolf Clan Warrior system, the Lone Wolf Warrior is given a very dangerous mission. They are to be trained in all the ways of the people in a most serious fashion. Their job is to scout along the peripheries and borders of the peoples boundaries and territories. It is very dangerous work, *knife work*, it is sometimes called because their gift is stealth, to remain hidden in the shadows.

Knife work is really a tease other Wolves cajole the Lone Wolves about, because it is believed that if one must use a knife, it means they are ineffective at their work, they are not doing a good job and their gift is obviously not stealth.

To take a life is no small issue, as family always misses the person taken and many Warriors will come looking for signs. If they ever catch a scout alone and at unawares while a loved one goes missing it would end in tragedy for everyone.

Lone Wolf Warriors are to remain invisible to nearly all and few can detect them, unless of course it is another Lone Wolf Warrior. They watch and they wait and while they wait they learn about whom they observe, are they friend or foe? Because the Lone Wolf Warriors are often gone to scout the borders of the land to keep the people safe, they report to other Wolf Clan Warriors of their findings. And so they are knowledge keepers. They know many languages and because they are very bright, they represent the people as an Ambassador! Therefore, they must be culturally competent! They must be able to adapt to change so they represent the people appropriately, they must respect other people's ways by knowing them, and they must be able to practice them, without prejudice.

The Lone Wolf Warrior will sometimes allow themselves to be seen by the people and at other times will observe for a long time learning. They are highly respected and mysterious individuals. Their medicine is very powerful as they are peacekeepers, maintaining harmony. The civil chief and war chief rely upon the lone wolves heavily when leading the people. They make sure no one crosses their healthy boundaries to throw everything out of balance.

One time, a single lone wolf warrior, working as security for a company found herself surrounded by five enemy. Because she was trained in the Ways of the Warrior she was able to fend off the enemy. Using a Tiger Claw martial art in self-defense as one enemy advanced, all five were picking themselves up off the floor shortly thereafter. All five thought twice about attacking again. They all left with their tails in between their legs.

There are of course other Clan Warriors, the Hoof Clan, the Eagle, Owl or Martin Clans, all are gifted all are powerful in their medicine, traditions and teachings. All are Warriors! All have unique gifts.

Hoof Clan are often very tall and slim, they are healers, very gentle, kind, loving and caring people they are. When they look at you while listening to your talk medicine, their eyes are piercing, penetrating as if they see your true self and see how you fare. They are always feeding you and they are great hosts for a good feast! Wolf Clan and Bear Clan Warriors are the law enforcement officers and military of the people. They are very committed.

THE IMAGINARY INDIAN

Warriors are misunderstood nowadays. When people think about Warriors and especially with regard to First Nation Warriors, they may make the mistake of stereotyping Warriors as bloodthirsty savages bent on death and destruction. This is a common misconception a prejudice of the Warrior. It is a way to dehumanize and objectify Warriors. It is a form of corruption of the truth about Warriors and their ways. There is a reason for these stereotypes to exist and it is to control Warriors by discouraging their ways, their resistances to disrespectful encroachment on the people and their territory, their way of life. These imaginations are cultural constructions of the mind based on stereotypes, prejudices and rumor. They are baseless imaginations, entirely delusional and is a dysfunctional trick of the mind to imagine Warriors in such a way. Europeans do not know what a Warrior is! They have never been among the people long enough to know the truth about what it means to be a Warrior! And those who have were never taken seriously when they attempted to speak the truth! They were dismissed as "gone Indian" or "turned Injun"!

The other stereotype about the Warrior describes a noble savage, "one of the good ones" people like to say when they project their imagination on Warriors. They agree, the cause is good, the savage has noble, even likeable qualities that any "civilized" person would have. But they often say it's too bad those Warriors and their ways have no place in the *civilized* world. The noble savage Warrior stubbornly maintains their old traditional ways and they do not know what is best for them, they need management!

These kinds of stereotypes are lies. They are imaginary versions and stereotypes based on dehumanization for the purpose of objectifying the Warrior. The reason is to create propaganda about the Warriors. This propaganda serves to elevate the esteem of the one who gazes upon the so-called savage.

Also, there are those who do not understand the difference between a war chief and a civil chief. Because of the misunderstanding, the lies they have been told about the ways of the Warrior, and the lies they have been told about themselves, it was very difficult to change their perception of Warriors. They stubbornly resisted the truth and relied upon the lies, the stereotypes and the racism. It conveniently maintained their sense of self worth, esteem by looking down upon others.

They would not understand that in times of war, it was a war chief who took the leadership of the people and the civil chief stepped down. The War Chief was now the leader of the people and when the war was over, the War Chief would step down and relinquish power back to the civil chief. The reason they did this was that it is understood that some Warriors are better at leadership during times of war while other Warriors were better at peacetime leadership. All leadership must be based on consensus in order to maintain harmony.

The Elders who stood there are the most respected group as they have the stories and the teachings which they share with everyone especially during the long cold winter months by the warm fires. This respect is not to be mistake for status or power and authority, it is simply respect as no one or one group or clan is more important than the other is, they are all equal. They know the medicines and they are aware of the seasons and the times and changes. They maintain balance and harmony with ceremony, songs and dances. They have been around over many summers and as they enter their winter stages of life, they are very knowledgeable. They have the most experience in all matters and their counsel is gravely important to the people.

They are virtually walking encyclopedias! They know of literally thousands of medicines in plant form, mushrooms, seeds, bark, root and thistle. They are indeed mighty Warriors even in their older years, they are highly revered by the people and how the children do love their Elders!

In turn, the Elders appreciated one specific group whom The Elders relied upon for unanimous decision-making. That group was the circle of *Contraries*.

CONTRARIES

Contraries are very powerful, the most powerful of all circles that contribute to the political leadership of the community. The only other circle that has even more power than the Contraries is the circle composed of those who have the ability to create life inside them. This is not to be confused with gender as gender does not exist in the psychology of the children of the earth.

Contraries are also known as the sacred clowns. We all know that laughter is the best medicine and the contraries know about this medicine the most. Contraries are powerful Warriors and healers. Contraries are often made up of young people between the ages 12 to 30. They love to do everything backwards. One of the most undervalued gifts young people offer us today in our modern world is the ability to see the hypocrisy and corruption that is in many adults. Teenagers are quick to point out the hypocrisy of their parents or society. This is powerful medicine and the Elders have recognized the importance of it.

After all, why wouldn't an agency, corporation, department, or government that offers services and representation to citizens, not want to be accountable, open and transparent? If they have the integrity, why would they want to hide things from the people? If they have no integrity then it is easy to see why they hide things from the people and they offer many excuses for their delays and stall tactics in being open, transparent and accountable. They are and should be ashamed of themselves. Young people can see this. It does nothing for the spirit of young people when leadership has no integrity. Integrity is essential.

That is why, when a decision needs to be made, the Elders send the idea to the contraries and they will tear holes in the fancy ideals of adults, pointing out the hypocrisy of it all. If the contraries reject the ideas that are presented to them, the Elders must revise the concepts until consensus is reached. When consensus is reached, you can bet that the contraries have ensured that the ideas for the people are in the best interest of the children, for seven generations.

Contraries are risky. They take risks. They love the thrill of new experiences. They will climb trees and mountains. They will challenge each other in a one-up competition for honor. They show us there are other ways to do things. They are full of fresh ideas. They are very committed to proving these ideas do work.

Risk is the gift they have to offer the rest of the community as many people can become complacent. The contraries challenge complacency and they dare to stand up to others many times their size. Contraries do not follow the established rules, not because they are naturally anti-establishment, it is because they are challenging us to think outside the box. Contraries are always creative, looking for new ways to do things. They are uninhibited by psychological barriers that would stop others. Where others see a barrier, contraries see opportunity to gain honor. They are great teachers.

Contraries teach us to grow, to develop beyond what we are comfortable. They challenge and strive. They are the only group that can drop out of high school and still have research skills that will rival any Ph. D. If contraries get the idea to research into something that interests them they focus and maneuver, unrelentingly until they are satisfied they have learned what they needed to learn. They can learn to build atomic bombs in their basements if tenacious enough and some have! Others will learn computer hacking skills embarrassing the pentagon when they hack into the most secure computers of the world. There are no words big enough that waiver them. They don't say, "oh that's a really big word I better put this book down and stay ignorant". No, they Google or find a dictionary and they persevere through their research until they gain understanding. They are very gifted.

Have you ever noticed some who present as abnormal to the flock? They have their hair fashioned different. They wear different cloths. They talk different. They behave different from all the rest. These are trendsetters. They are contraries who understand that in order to be the most creative they can be they have to abandon culture and society entirely as they cannot stand being the norm, conformed. The next year or the following, followers begin doing what the contrary had started ahead of all the rest.

The contraries can get a little too powerful though. Their medicine can be a little too much. For example, the contraries, when gathered together in their clan systems, groups, they can cook up some good contrary medicine that others would find overbearing. They get all rowdy and loud, they start swearing and saying inappropriate things. They laugh too loud. Rowdy and rambunctious they dismiss authority, laughing at it. So when things get out of hand, the only other circle that can overpower the contraries is the circle of power, those life bringers.

Have you ever seen a group of teenagers gathered and notice how rowdy they get? Though many will try to control them, they actually get rowdier! Then when the aunties come, they suddenly sit down as if a great power has entered the room and sat them down using invisible forces. The aunties with their stern looks and thunderous voices of power, somehow manage to humble the contraries in an instant.

Suddenly all contraries are sitting quietly, hands folded and in between their knees waiting to be released from the spell.

The Elders, love the contraries!

You don't see this in contemporary society so much. In fact, because contemporary society is patriarchal with a value system favoring hierarchy and authority provided to them by their religions, they devalue youth. In fact, on the contrary, the whole system values the father, paternalism and everything is based in paternalism, patriarchy and hierarchy. Contemporary society is contrary to a child-centered society like the Way of the Warrior is child-centered.

The young people were greatly astonished at the impressive and most prestigious site that was presented before them. They even felt a bit insignificant that such a production would be prepared over what they now felt was a small concern. As the young people approached the Elders, a lone Warrior began beating upon the drum four times, rattles and whistles were sounded, bells rang out and cymbals crashed in a great clambering, cacophonous chorus and there were many war cries. Then the lone Warrior began singing a chant. While the singer resonated most triumphantly, the Elders smoked their pipes. The Elder later explained to the group of young people that the sounding of the drum was to invite all of the good spirits to join them in the sacred circle. The Elder said the medicine that was in the air was protection medicine and evil spirits cannot stand its sweet loving aroma. The song was an honor song welcoming all that is sacred.

The Elder noticed a very young person was among the group. This person was about 3 springs. The Elders were astonished that such a small one was among them and they said it was a good day and very sacred that such a wee one would feel so at ease among them. This new development makes the ceremonies all the more powerful when the little ones are present.

THE SACRED FIRES

The Way of the Warrior is to keep the sacred fire burning bright. The sacred fires are the children and they are the sole purpose of everyone's life. It is why we are all here! Some nowadays ask what their purpose in life is and they search for years. The sacred fire is the purpose in the lives of the Warriors. That is why the people are child centered and everything they do is always about the sacred fire, and the saying is, "for seven generations, for the sake of the children"! The sacred fire is our future and every decision we make, how we choose to behave depends on that future.

Today we understand the power of role modeling behavior. We understand that children learn by watching and listening to caregivers. The Elders have always known this. The Medicine Wheel technology, the Seven Sacred Teachings, The Traditional Stories, The Ceremonies, The Traditional Ways, Aboriginal perspectives, philosophy, teachings, ensure they are for the sake of the children for seven generations.

Every decision we make in the present affect the Sacred Fires for seven generations. Thus, the traditional ways and daily regimens of the people are strictly followed and reinforced with ceremony throughout the day to help maintain the philosophy of seven generations for the sake of the children. This does not mean traditional families need to be religious, fundamentalist, with authoritarianism. A traditional family is not so cold and regimental. On the contrary, a traditional family is warm and loving, balanced and harmonious. A traditional family is aware that children are watching and learning from the Elders and so every measure is taken to protect the children from corruption.

When a traditional person collects a medicine bundle or is offered a pipe in a traditional pipe ceremony, these are not for the adults, the women, the contraries or the sinners that need salvation. Traditional warriors understand that the bundle is not patriarchal, paternalistic, hierarchical, and authoritarian like the Christian faith is. The traditional bundles are not for the father only. If all has been done correctly for the sake of the children for seven generations, there is no need to carry a bundle for these groups. The bundle is for the sacred fires.

The sacred fires are most powerful in medicine. They are pure, sacred, innocent and fresh from the great mystery. We benefit greatly from their powerful medicine. They purify a home and everyone instantly heals from all worries, corruption, adversity and fear. Notice how everyone's behavior changes when presented with a little bundle of joy. Notice how endorphins begin to flow in a great surge through our bodies as we enter a home where there is a sacred fire. How they warm us and keep us, uniting us bringing us all together to hover over the sacred fire. What fear and trepidation when we carry the sacred fire and we are instantaneously careful with the sacred fire as we embrace a newborn. What an honor it is to hold and love our sacred fire.

And they bring us so much joy and love as they grow into their own. They teach us and we are made better by them. They purify us and we remain to tend our sacred fires even unto death. They are our purpose, we are child centered and everything we do is for the sake of the children for seven generations.

You don't see this so much anymore. Today we are patriarchal, paternalistic, hierarchical and authoritarian. We don't care for the sacred fire. We tend to neglect the sacred fires and many children are aware of that fact.

We often send our children to daycares tended by people do not have any cultural competence, care and understanding of the diversity of our children and they try to be all things to all children. They will even impose their cultural ways on our children, forcing them to pray to their gods, they will even abuse our children.

The nanny state oppresses the parents now by giving them fines for not sending their children to school or daycare without proper nutrition. They say parents are neglecting their children and behaving irresponsibly and they cannot or will not consider their own oppression does nothing for the sake of the children for seven generations. The nanny state oversees the parents every detail now and parents are arrested and humiliated by police and social workers. Children are apprehended now. They are placed in foster care when they should be with their parents.

We understand that some parents need help, some are neglectful and we are learning more about the role of mental health in our societies. Some children do need to be apprehended. But the oppression of parents does nothing for the children, for seven generations. We care more about our fathers whether they are the great white fathers, the almighty dollar, church fathers and we do not think about the sacred fires, for seven generations. We think about what we can get now, we destroy our environments, and our families are divided, twisted and corrupted and children compete for attention in the home. It is very sad.

Then a group of Bears began singing and drumming on a large sacred drum and they sang a sacred song while the Wolf and the Bear dancers began to dance a traditional War Dance. The War

Dance is also misunderstood, fueled by the stereotypes of the Warriors. The War Dance is not a display of savagery bent on bloodthirsty revenge! It is done to prevent a war!

Remember, all things happen first in the spirit world. It is ceremony that facilitates change in the spirit world first. The War Dance is a ceremony, meant to facilitate change so that no war occurs and both groups have a war dance ceremony to prevent blood shed believing that this mutual expression, done in spirit first, reveals the outcome. This is how they know if they should go to war. However, the dysfunction of insecurity, instability, things being out of balance and harmony, tends to play tricks on the mind and people do not understand what they see. So this War Dance is not to prepare for war, it is meant to prevent one!

In one long progression of song and drum beats all the Warriors ended the sacred entrance in three quick beats!

SACRED LOCATIONS AND LITTLE PEOPLE

There was a certain location in the middle of the prairies that had special significance. The Elder described the area as very sacred because the little people inhabited it. The little people are very sacred spiritual people who are very small and usually only the very little children can see them. It is believed that very little children are fresh from the spirit world, not yet corrupted by this world and can still see and understand many sacred things. It is said that the very small children can see the little people and will often play with them.

It is said that parents and caregivers must take care to ensure the children stay close by at all times. If parents and caregivers do not take precautions the little people may invite the very little children to come live with them. Thus, it is a good idea to keep a close eye on your little children when going about your daily duties. It is also said that some little people can also be tricksters and so it is best to show great respect to the little people and to be very careful not to offend them. The little people often like shiny things, sweets and treats and these offerings are worthy to the little people. So if you see what appears to be a very sacred place where the little people live, it is best to show great respect and to leave an offering if you can. In the very least, it is a good idea to say a prayer of respect for the things we do not understand.

It is also said that the great beast can transform into that of the little people and will mislead the children away and their parents will never see them again.

Also, some of the people have the spirit of the little people, and we call them, little people even though they are grown adults. Some adult little people say things like, "I am a child at heart" or they love the children and are always encouraging them in their potential and in their gifts. They love all that is little people, they love Christmas, birthdays, cake and treats, gifts and toys. These very big little people are very sacred.

The Elder continued to address the young people earnestly and with great encouragement.

The grown ups and young people often do not understand the significance of the little people as presented by the very little children the Elder said. However, the Elders seem to understand what the very little children are describing. It is a strange universal phenomenon that Elders and very little children often have a sacred and special relationship and it is not understood why. Perhaps it is because the Elders are close to the spirit world as they prepare to begin the journey back to the great mystery and the children of the Earth have just arrived. In any case, it is a naturally occurring phenomenon. The very little children seem to be curious about Elders. The very little children are drawn to Elders and often ask many questions of the Elders and they talk in a very sacred way. This relationship is pure and sacred and is seen in every culture around the world.

The Elder went on to explain to the young people that in certain places, they will notice themselves become lighter, as if something is lifting them off the ground and yet their feet remain firmly planted. What they experience is the sacred spirit of the great mystery that provides insight to the person who arrives in a sacred way to that area. This is the doorway to that other sacred world. There are other areas around mother earth that are like this one and each has a different phenomenon. Some people can experience it while others cannot or will not. It is said that those who remain among the will not's long enough, eventually become the can not's. The Elder chuckles a bit, thinks about this bemusing humor, and wonders why it is both funny and not funny, it is a great mystery.

The Elder explains to the group of young people that the other sacred places among mother earth take the form of a brook or a meadow, stream, a lake, a rock or a tree. It is customary to come to those sacred places and offer Tobacco, prayers and thanksgiving. Theses sacred places are powerful places to conduct ceremony and healing.

It is said that when the great corruption came to the other sacred places of the world, at other times, the corrupted would place their own alter on that sacred place to corrupt it. So wherever there is a church, synagogue, hospital, school, university, major corporation even city, you know that this was once a very sacred place but the great corruption has placed their alter on top of it. It is said that when the great corruption began many moons ago, the ones described in young people's dreams, those demons, were all once warriors much like these young warriors. Unlike these warriors, they are now ghosts lost on their way to the happy hunting grounds. They became corrupted in this world having lost their way. It is not that they will never get to the happy hunting grounds, it is just that it will take them longer to find the way.

Some may think of this as punishment but it is not, it is a consequence. The Elder explains the dream the young people are experiencing has been around for a long time and all the Elders were aware of it, they have all had it. The Elder explained that they could not intervene because they were told, long ago, that one day, the young people would recognize the shared dream and would present Tobacco on the issue. The Elders said they have been waiting many generations.

MATERIALISM, SPIRITUALITY

Everything happens first in the spirit world, the Elder said. Then as the spirit world is, the physical manifests itself. Today, we call it energy. All life and all matter is made up of energy. There are only two kinds of energy, positive and negative energy. Apparently, science tells us that this energy consists of many great waves, like waves on the lake, river or stream. Or as the sound waves of thunder, the sacred drum, singing and chanting, even hip hop and heavy metal. This energy, if it could be seen appears to the eye much like waves upon water! Even as waves upon water have the potential to do anything and go anywhere, so too these energy waves have the potential to become anything as they manifest into physical items. Until these energy waves are observed by someone, they remain as potential. They have the potential to become anything. They become something upon observation. When observed, these energy waves collect other particles through a process of attraction that formulate into material. These particles of matter attract to each other in such a way as to produce the material world we know.

However, scientists are finding that all matter does not actually exist in a physical sense, as we humans are not able to experience it in truth. In truth we see and perceive matter, as it can be felt and touched, we can sense aroma, or we experience the sounds. However, this is simply perception with attached beliefs about what we perceive and it is not exactly what we think it is. It is simply a collection of energy, waves, potential, electrical impulses perceived through our senses. It is energy, traveling to various regions of our brain, translated, in order to comprehend our so-called reality. But the truth is, we never actually experienced the reality in the way we think we did, it was all in our head! Where did the reality come from? It all comes from the great mystery, like a river that flows we either flow with it or against it.

Star Trek, the Elder says, has something called a *Holodeck*. It is a phenomenon where reality is simulated much as many video games are now. The difference is that reality is not projected on an LCD screen, it is simply light, projected onto force fields giving it texture. That is how Holodeck technology works.

Our bodies are like the Holodeck. Our body allows us to interface with reality, as it is perceived through endless energy waves. The great mystery is the potential that projects reality for our brains to interpret along with what we learned from societies, traditions, beliefs, cultural practices, stories, imagery, icons, symbols, languages, all give us the meaning with which we interact and take meaningful experiences. Nevertheless, our lives are still lived inside of our heads because our experiences remain physical manifestations that are converted back into energy, which is interpreted inside our head through electrical stimulation. Nothing real has ever occurred. It is as though life is but a dream, but whose dream?

And so it must be that our real selves are simply spiritual manifestations of the great mystery, that infinite field of energy potential where all life and reality originate. We are all one, one and the same.

Therefore, we so-called *Indians* always were practical people and we have always known what science now teaches us about physics at the sub-atomic level. We have always described these kinds of principles as spirit and sacred. Although we never took a dogmatic religious approach to our spiritual beliefs, rather we took a pragmatic approach.

It was a common way of life to exist in balance and harmony with this truth with a sincere belief that all is sacred all are connected. And so it is that the Elders have observed and passed on knowledge to the children of the Earth for eons and eons, until the great corruption came. The Elders could actually see this great mystery for what it truly is, an infinite energy field with endless possibilities. What it gave us was everything we could possibly ever need in abundance! This knowledge was shared with everyone in the communities. This was common knowledge at one time.

It was a common thing to observe thousand upon thousands of plant life and vegetation and to be able to identify all of them by name and to speak of its healing or deadly qualities.

The Elders observed the turtle who had a runny nose. They watched which plants it ate during the time it had a wee bit of the sniffles. The Elders learned the healing qualities of such a plant through this observation.

The Elders knew that it is wise to learn from their brothers and sisters, the winged ones, the two legged and the four legged, those that creep those that crawl, those that swim, the tree world, the rock world, the sky world the star people and the children of the Earth. Yes, the star people used to visit regularly but since the great corruption, they have become shy. All are sacred, all balanced, and harmonious. Even the newcomers to Turtle Island described our home and way of life as though it were a great garden in a place called Eden.

They said the trees were giants and the fish so plentiful and large, if one were to reach over the side of their boat, they would have a catch that would sink them on the spot. Others describe their great ships to have run aground by copious amounts of fish in the oceans. It was our teachings of respect through medicine wheel technology that produced this abundance. We never took more than what was needed, it was never necessary. But that was not to last.

THE MEDICINE WHEEL, BALANCE AND HARMONY

The Elders have always seen the wisdom of the medicine wheel, the circle of life. The thinking and the development of the brain, in all of its intricate neural connections, memories, stimulating various emotions, mental reactions, and belief systems would certainly be different from those affected when the great corruption came.

Scientists tell us the brain develops outside of the womb, and the brain adapts itself to the environment where it develops. So the difference from one versus the other is that one groups brain will develop in an environment where the great corruption occurs along with all of its consequences. The other brains develop in environments of abundance, in a philosophy of harmony and balance. The great corruption that came changed all of that for the children of the Earth when it arrived to Turtle Island.

The children of the Earth were no longer living in balance and harmony. Where once, all were equal and no one was greater than the other or more important than the other, now all of that was gone. The children of the earth became corrupted and were placed beyond help because the corrupted took away the medicine wheel.

Instead, they introduced religion and advised we place our faith in gods and prophets.

The Elder again chuckles at what appears to be the irony of the attitude toward the traditional and healing ways of indigenous people and what science is only now discovering. There was a time when some people thought they were superior to the children of the earth. It now appears those who thought they were superior are now dining to a healthy serving of humble pie. But the Elder did not want to gloat, but something was indeed funny about the whole affair.

Perhaps it is the irony of how some scientists still use terms like *hunting and gathering people* when describing indigenous people. Scientists describe indigenous traditional ways as *animism*, comically, dismissively, like they do in cartoons where trees talk and animals are cute cuddly creatures. It is no different an attitude where an adult listens to a toddlers story of little "imaginary" playmates. It is as if many people expect us to grow up and grow out of our belief systems of so-called *backward* and *superstitious* ways. It is a form of supremacy culturally imposed upon indigenous people by a white supremacist culture.

And so everything first begins in the *bzzzzzzzzzzt*. Oh, hold on the Elder says, I have to check my Facebook. Everyone bursts out laughing as the Elder reaches to check the messages before turning off the phone.

And so everything first begins in the spirit world and a good Warrior learns how to reinforce first in the spirit world. If the Warrior is unsuccessful in the spirit world, in reinforcing and applying remedy with medicine, prayer and ceremony, only then is the Warrior required to apply remedy in the physical.

Why ceremony, medicine and prayer? It is because we tend to rely too much on what our minds tell us and so we can become biased on our own mental uses. Without ceremony, we become *mental*. So our traditional ways clear the mind and all of its constructions of reality, beliefs and worries. Once our minds are cleared, we can then see things, as they truly are, a proper use of the mind. Some are better at this than others, but we are all in the same boat and that is what makes us all equal. Ceremony gives us remedies.

These remedies can include the use of ones mind to discuss things in a peace pipe ceremony, or other traditional talking ceremony that allow two or more minds to come together to find common ground. The use of violence is the absolute last option available. It is and should remain to be rarely used because if a Warrior is truly effective in applying remedy, things should never be reduced to violence. There is only one reason one should apply the remedy of violence and that is when there is a clear and immediate threat to oneself or others livelihood where a reasonable person believes they or their loved ones are threatened with imminent danger or death. We have a Jaguar Warrior here with us today and we know from their teachings that it is considered clumsy to have killed another person and if you do so, your Warrior ways are ineffective. We don't go straight to killing enemy. The Jaguar Warriors have come all the way from the south on the Medicine Wheel, travelling from their ancient Aztec homeland to be here with us today. And the Elder pointed to them and they were indeed very beautiful to behold!

COUNTING COUP FOR HONOR

Like the contraries, Warriors would engage in on-up competition to gain honor. Rather than seeing who could kill the most enemy, the original wars were fought by counting coup.

Warriors would sneak up to enemy and tap them on the shoulder. This would steal the honor away from the enemy and the Warrior would run as fast as they could. If they got away unscathed they would gain honor. If the enemy caught them, they would beat the living shit out of the Warrior, if they could, to get their honor back. This would force the Warrior to stand and fight the enemy in combat. But there was never any need to kill anyone. It was enough to compete for honor.

Things are different today. The little warriors that are on the street having been inundated by the great corruption have all things twisted in their heads. They think it is honorable to murder people. This is not the Way of the Warrior. This is the way of the corrupt.

It is not the fault of these little warriors, it is directly and causally related to the great corruption that came to Turtle Island, bringing with it their assimilation, cultural impositions, judgmentalism, racism and oppression.

If we consider that everything begins in the spirit world first, and we are properly trained in the Ways of the Warrior, we should be able to see adversity presenting itself first in the spirit world. This is not to say that we can see, whenever we want all things in the spirit world at any one time, but if we are trained properly and we are great warriors, we can see many things far off. Consider also that we are children of the earth, we need help, and so we rely on our brothers and sisters and all our relations to guide us. We are very poor and wretched creatures when we rely too much on our minds, on ourselves, but our minds are a great gift from the creator. That is why we must be trained in the Way of the Warrior, to be given our spirit names, our colors, our clans and our teachings. When we know who we truly are we can begin creating our sacred regalia.

SELF-RESPECT, RESPECT, REGALIA, COLORS

The Elder continued our regalia are a spiritual and sacred manifestation into physical reality meant to tell other Warriors from other family groups and clans who we are from a distance. They can read our story when they see our colors and clan symbols embroidered on our regalia. What they see, they understand is spiritual, sacred, as they are aware that physical reality is our way to interface with other spiritual creatures and what they see is spiritual and they accept it as sacred. Those observing us in our regalia can become acquainted with us, our spiritual selves and they are comforted that we wear our identity with confidence and we are not trying to hide anything. We who are properly trained in the Way of the Warrior invite friendly balanced and harmonious relations rather than to threaten and intimidate, we help rather than exploit and take advantage, and we support each other rather than bully others. We who are trained in the Way of the Warrior learn how to establish healthy boundaries for ourselves and for others.

First for ourselves, so we do not cross our own healthy boundaries and then for others, so we do not cross theirs and they ours. Our healthy boundaries are built upon the foundations of self-respect. You cannot give respect if you do not have self-respect. Self-respect is balanced self-love, it is that part of you that you have struggled to defend against abusers and bully's, those who are corrupted. Everyone knows that haters be hate'n. We often do not understand why they do that. When we have self-respect, we love ourselves enough to say no more! We have drawn our lines in the sand and we ask them not to cross that line which is our healthy boundary. Come what may, we stand our ground and sometimes we are willing to die rather than allow our abusers to victimize us. We who are trained in the Way of the Warrior have faith in the great mystery that provides us with everything we need and we are satisfied with what is offered. We offer thanks rather than resentment. This is very sacred. It is not corrupt.

The corrupt version is one that is over-confident, with false pride, arrogance and rooted in fear. It is constructed in the mind of the corrupted with many false constructions, manipulations that belie the person into corruption and their thinking becomes dysfunctional. They tell themselves many lies, which they come to believe as truths. They know they do it. You cannot hide from yourself for long. The lies always catch up. The corrupted warriors wear their colors to threaten and intimidate others and they belong to the night terrors that the young people are dreaming about. They are not wholly lost, they are just wandering a bit too far off. They are in fact the very little children who have been lured away by the great beast and have grown up and developed in the midst of other victims of the great corruption, in dysfunctional environments they learn dysfunction, long into adulthood.

We Elders believe that our people who are *Children of the Earth* were always Warriors but became a warrior culture when the great corruption came. We were spirit traveling among that great mystery and became material. In becoming material, *spirits in a material world*, just like that old song by Sting! The Elder forgetting how old they are, looks on and notices everyone is too young to remember Sting. The young people look at each other and back at the Elder with blank stares and eyes blinking. The Elder smiles and chuckles as good medicine begins to flow from within producing a good laugh.

The Elder used a different metaphor, one more relatable, the recent Star Trek movies, returning to theatres seemed appropriate. When we became materialized, the Elder continues, kind of like the *transporter room* on the *Enterprise* that materializes people from the planet below to the ship above…and now the young people understood what the Elder described. We are spirit first and we materialize here on this planet as spirit, knowing and seeing spirit in all things. We understood that all is spirit. But something changed our perception. We became too attached to our physical universe, relying more on physics rather than balance and harmony with the medicine wheel technology. We believe we are now being born into corruption and it's not how it used to be. These are confusing times.

WARRIOR CULTURE, BORN INTO WAR

Our Warriors are now like paratroopers who would courageously jump out of airplanes deep into enemy territory and they knew as soon as they jump enemy below would attack them. If they managed to survive the jump, they knew they would be assailed from all directions. It did not matter where they went, they would encounter enemy. Enemy everywhere. That is how the Children of the Earth are now born! And so the children of the Earth had to be born Warriors! This is how a Warrior culture came to be.

The Elder became thoughtful at this description, apt and appropriate as it was, the Elder recalled the great wars and all of those experiences of warfare. The doctors and nurses would treat the wounded and all who placed themselves in great peril and risk. All of those thoughts flooded the Elders mind. However, this time, the young warriors that stood before them understood with clarity what the Elders described and they respected it for what it was even though many of them never experienced war.

The sun was climbing higher now and its warm rays were a comfort and they new it would only get hotter throughout the day. Flies buzzed and birds called out to each other. The Elder smiled. Suddenly, in the moment, a fresh breeze and clean crisp air brought back awareness of the peace and serenity of the moment. The war was over.

It was not because the parents and caregivers were not loving or supportive. It was not that the environment was not peaceful. They were born into war and so they would not let themselves relax and be at peace. For too long and for too often they remained ready for the fiery darts to pierce their skin and knock them to the ground where they have seen so many never get back up again. Now they could not turn off the readiness for battle and the imminence of death followed them wherever they went. The great corruption that came had pressed the people too hard and many children of the earth were lost. They were driven away from the sacred and their minds had been twisted, corrupted, they never had time for ceremony anymore because the corruption had them obsessed with hunting and gathering, and they were locked inside their heads. They lost faith in the great mystery that always provides what is needed. They took control and in so doing, they practiced a life without faith. They lost trust in the great mystery that provides. Without faith and trust, they became insecure and developed control issues, a dysfunctional mental process that has consequences.

The young people who have lost their way can be found and restored among the people once again but only if they are ready to be restored. Without readiness, there can be no lasting change.

The Elders now looked hard at the group that presented themselves before them. With great admiration and fascination, they wondered if these young warrior initiates knew what they were getting themselves into, no matter, the bet was placed and here they were. Change was in the wind and no one was walking away. The Elder explained that the group would be left to themselves for the time being. Upon return, the fun would begin!

Chapter 4

THE MEETING

Before entering the sacred plain, one young person spoke about how they always knew there was something not quite right with the system but never could articulate it. Generally, they were all able to follow along with what the Elder spoke about. It made sense. They could see the practical implications of this great mystery and this warrior way and the resistance to the great corruption that came. That was why some grew their hair long when the system positively reinforced and rewarded short hair for boys and long hair for girls. It was their way of protesting the system. Others got tattoos and faced discrimination for the rest of the corporate lives. Gender markers and racism in the classroom meant inequality when cultural icons and other cultural constructors like cartoons, television, storybooks, parents, and video games emphasized equality, sharing and caring.

Well, maybe not video games said some laughingly.

Many describe seeing these and other things that did not add up to them or did not look quit right. While other young people said they could see how some little kids would learn to "play the game" in our public education system and they would be allowed to get away with everything. Teachers would deliberately change the story around in favor of one child, look the other way or lie in attempt to protect *one of their own.*

They describe the abomination that presented itself to them on a daily basis. They were disgusted by it. These young people could see inequality, hypocrisy, at a very young age and they developed under frustrating conditions with little to no supports. They describe resentment toward the abomination because the system loved itself, it protected itself, it felt entitled to everything and it was dismissive of everyone who would not be assimilated, who would not conform, fall into rank and file, play the game so to speak.

These young people saw the system and those attached to it had entitlement issues to the point that it could not be argued with. The people and their system were always so self-righteous that it was never wrong. How could it be, when they have all the answers? Some words they used to describe these individuals were "dogmatic", meaning they followed dogma, which usually describes religious devotion to a creed or teaching, system of beliefs. Dogma in itself is not so bad they said, but when these beliefs get twisted, contorted, crooked, bent, as in bending the rules just a little bit, can lead to terrifying results which harm everyone involved.

Dogma can blind a person to the evil they do in the name of righteousness, some said. Many described being forced to attend Sunday school and Church when they were little children. Here they learned about god, Jesus and all them 'postles who talked about love and loving thy neighbor, abhorring evil and abominations to the Lord. They talked about right and wrong, good and evil. This is where they learned to think in hierarchical dualisms, meaning a set of dualities such as good and evil, hierarchically stratified into ascending and descending lists. You, me, us and them, the good and evil in each of us, the physical and spiritual aspects all of which are assigned varying roles of importance and all conform to these hierarchical dualisms for better or for worse. Some are better, while others are worse and we have the right to judge pagan, barbarian, savages, especially if we are saved through Christ Jesus, apparently.

Dogma teaches us that if we are saved and others are not then we are better than they are. We have a set of teachings that confirm our superiority and they come directly from god. We developed moral justifications for our choices. We developed concepts such as progress and backwardness, technological progress and Stone Age tools, civilization and savagery/barbarism. All of these provide us with a sense of superiority, a place that we perceive others and place judgment based on all of these concepts of duality. Since the beginning of so-called civilization, we have developed societies based on these principles, which include authority figures who justify their entitlement to speak on these matters, to teach us morals and ethics simply because they say they are prophets, ordained priests and ministers, Bishops and

Cardinals. These were our religious leaders who were very important to societies and people.

Authoritarianism said others, describing a free book made available online by *Dr. Bob Altemeyer*.

Others agreed saying they *morally justify* their behavior. That is what these young people described witnessing at very young ages growing up in our Canadian public education system and they said it was an abomination!

Others said that it was not only the public education system that is unfair, full of people who are *willfully blind* to their own behavior, describing a book by *Margaret Heffernan*, there are other systems that behave like this too.

The justice system, when even after the Aboriginal Justice Inquiry occurred and presented recommendations, very little was done to address those recommendations, they said.

In Saskatchewan, there was the Neil Stonechild Inquiry and again, there is no indication anything is being done to remedy the situation.

RACISM, WHITE SUPREMACY AND SYSTEMIC DISCRIMINATION

Racism and discrimination in the workplace everyday disguised as joking, just *blowing off steam*. Employers, supervisors who do not understand the complexities of racism inadvertently or insidiously become spin-doctor's, soothsayers advocating on behalf of white supremacy. They speak skillfully, softly, soothingly about the harm a grievance can do to another who is hard pressed as they try hard to work their careers. Employers are telling their staffs that are offended by these outright racist remarks that there really is no racism, that someone is probably just letting off steam and we should let them.

They justify the racism by getting the victim to empathize with the bully and all the problems these bullies face daily and once the victim empathizes, they agree it is acceptable to let off steam now and then, that it is not worth it to take these jokes personally. Or is it?

While being subjected to the twisted truth, the forked tongue that whispers sweet nothings to the offended thought of their own career and its consequences appear in their imagination. They may wonder if they can get any support from other staff, they look to the left and to the right in their imaginations and they can see how some will look down, pretending they don't see, others will walk out of the room. They realize many do not have the fortitude to stand up for what is right, they would rather fall into rank and file in willful blindness. Not even their Christian faith, love thy enemy as thyself or neighbor would motivate them in righteous indignation.

They think about their own mortgages, car payments, private school budgets, taxes, renovations, and trips to Vegas or the Bahamas. They wonder if it is really worth it to complain, or should they just go back to work and reassure their bosses how much they understand and that they won't be back, they even thank their bosses for helping them from the crippling disease of taking things personally. The boss replies, "that's what I'm here for".

One person asked the others, why is it acceptable to talk about white people as if it is not racist but the "N" word is totally unacceptable? The term "white" is a racist term that refers to a racial group and if racism is outlawed, then why are we still using it and why do "white" people find the term acceptable?

Another answered this befuddling query by saying, "white" represents the establishment, the system. It is a place of power, wealth and status. It is the authority over everything. So why be offended at that? It was established as such in the mid 17th century to privilege the "white" man over and above others. It was done by a series of philosophers who utilized Darwin's theory's about evolution, twisting them, contorting them, corrupting them so that it would appear that races of men exist. The "white" man was promoted to be superior to all other races. This was promoted in cultural writings and literature at the time.

Racism was written into the constitutions of the day in all nations. Racism was written into the socio-economic and political systems ensuring white supremacy would stubbornly remain for hundreds of years. People would be born into these systems and would be socialized within them becoming cultural products of racism. This would be all they ever learned and all they ever knew. Changing the system would be very difficult but many warriors found ways to resist this insidious systemic racism of white supremacy.

It is important to mention that not all white people are insidiously white supremacist. In fact, if they knew about all of the complex dynamics of their behavior they would be very eager to change denouncing white supremacy. Many white people did not ask to be represented by their ancestors, culture and heritage in this way. Many white people feel they were misrepresented. In fact, that is what is happening presently and it is youth that are leading the way.

Today we have television, which is losing its grasp on people, sports keeps television alive today. But we also have the Internet and our cell phones which promote culture. Back in the olden days, they used books, novels, the printing press to get news and information out. *Edward Said* describes this process in two of his books, *Orientalism* and *Culture and Imperialism*. He said the West considered itself the best, dismissing all the rest.

"Hey, you made that rhyme, that aint no crime, your a poet and you did'nt even know it" said a foolish one laughing. Everyone else chuckled a bit, others smiled but most would rather continue listening without interruption.

Believing you can always find laughter even in the most serious moments, the young one said, "You guys are too serious", not happy at all with the grim nature of their gathering.

The West promoted itself as the most cultured and most important of all other groups in the world as promoted by British and American scholars mostly. They promoted the culture to influence the people into thinking that as a race, the "white" man was superior to all. This sense of superiority provided *moral justification* to harm others, as others were not really considered human at all. Anything not white, and specifically, not British male were low on the totem pole so to speak.

If they are not human, they can be objectified, toyed with, enslaved and abused as they do not really have feelings anyway, they are not like us. That is how slavery of "black" people was considered appropriate during the time of the *Virginia Company* and the American South.

The Virginia Company is best known through the story of Pocahontas, a British construction of a tale written from a British, patriarchal, racist, imperialist, perspective for British people not entirely accurate to the true events. In the book, *Invention of the White Race, by Theodore W. Allan* the white race was a construction that took time to create using laws and moral justifications all of which occurred around the Virginia Companies businesses. All of these self-aggrandizements, fabrications and manipulations of philosophies, later became lies, which privileged the "white" man to make laws in their favor.

Their socio-economic, political, and cultural systems all have racism embedded within them that perpetuate racist doctrine presently and continues to privilege the "white" man systemically.

This is now known as systemic racism, a white washed phrase for white supremacy. It is often seen in police service and justice, most apparent and recent was with Manitoba Health. Health Sciences Centre staff allowed an Aboriginal man to die in the waiting room. Without so much as to take a moment to check on him while he was waiting 34 hours to be seen by medical staff.

It is said, some thought he was "sleeping it off", and perhaps meaning they thought he was just another drunk Indian passed out. There is no mention of an indigenous person working in the hospital emergency room that night, suggests systemic racism and overt racism is playing a role in this tragedy. This is even in the face of a known culture of racism in Canada. But many would rather delude themselves by saying they are not racist or even acknowledging that racism may be part of Manitoba Health culture. The fact that there are copious amounts of research and documentation to indicate Manitoba Health is racist. Aboriginal people have the poorest access to health, the poorest health and the highest death rates and they die sooner than everyone else in Canada. No, this wouldn't indicate a culture of racism exists with Manitoba Health. Many are delusional.

There is an official report said another, that the emergency room staff are hurt by allegations of racism. Apparently, many staff at the adult emergency say they give charity to the Main Street Project. As if that would excuse them of racism or consider the fact that, this very statement makes assumptions about Sinclair's ethnicity and those who would make use of the Main Street Project.

Somehow, they make several connections with regard to Sinclair. That he was native, passed out, sleeping it off, homeless, even though he wasn't homeless, barfing, staying warm in the emergency room, mumbling inaudible sounds, that they buy meals for people that make use of the Main Street Project. It is presumed that these people are like the several assumptions noted in the official reports, native, drunks, passed out or sleeping it off, homeless Indians.

And yet they all deny being racist, continued the other. They are even viscerally hurt by such an accusation.

Another added, I wonder how many of those non-racist staff have asked for cultural competency training, advocating for equal access to health services, when it is generally well known among health professionals and service providers that Aboriginal people in Manitoba and across Canada do not enjoy the same service as "white" people. If they are not racist, how could they allow the system to perpetuate racism, subtly or overtly if they are so viscerally offended at the notion of them being racist? If they are "allies" of the "natives", how does their silence in the face of continued racism, in a culture of racism, inequality, prevent such a tragedy?

Another joined in, do you think the staff at the emergency room scheduled in the shift that allowed Brian Sinclair to die, do you think their reaction was similar to Senator Pamela Wallin when she said everyone was persecuting her? Her reaction was visceral and defiant saying she was a victim of a kind of a witch-hunt.

They all certainly denied involvement into the allegations made against them, answered another.

And they were so hurt, said another!

They could not or would not fathom they had done anything wrong, replied another. Perhaps they have entitlement issues.

Then someone else spoke up saying, I am sure there is more to the story than what we read in the newspapers. It should all come out in the inquest.

Another with a deep loud authoritative voice said, I have no faith in the inquiry, I have seen the Aboriginal Justice Inquiry produce nothing and there are others, not to mention the Royal Commission on Aboriginal People. Racism has been in the system since the Virginia Company you say, it is written into our Canadian Constitution through the Indian Act, it is part of the socio-economic and political systems and therefore, part of our culture. Anyone who would suggest they are racist are either delusional wearing rose colored lenses or they are in denial. Racism pays! It paid in the 17th century, throughout history and it pays today. All you have to do is remain silent and look away then delude yourself with moral justifications.

Remember the news reporting a white woman, Lisa Gibson who murdered her two kids and the media called it a mental health issue citing post-partum depression. But a few months before that, Samantha Kematch and Nicole Redhead were reported as a killers in a half-truth, grossly ignorant, accusing, report in the National Post. The Lisa Gibson and Sarah Witzel cases, Witzel didn't kill her child, but did report as diagnosed with post-partum depression both white woman, both report as excused due to mental health issues. They didn't know what they were doing.

While Kematch and Redhead are presented most unflatteringly and as bloodthirsty, pagan, barbarian, savages, and grotesque giant children who clearly had mental health issues are reported as though they were fully aware of what they were doing. The media focus directly on Kematch and Redhead and others behavior and lifestyle. "Kematch and Redhead were each born to violent drinking mothers and raised, if it can be called that, in the familiar triad of aboriginal dysfunction of this country — amid violence and poverty, sexual abuse and a fog of alcohol and drugs".

That's a triad asked someone?

The media portrays a favorable excuse for civilized baby killers who are white, victims who fell through the cracks in the same system, victim's inasmuch as their children. Gibson was presented most favorably as a victim of a terrible mental disease, of how things can go wrong when the mind plays tricks on the person. There is even an outpouring of public support for Lisa Gibson where vigils and public memorials were held. Gibson was presented most favorably as a victim of a terrible mental disease, of how things can go wrong.

The media is less favorable when it comes to Aboriginal issues. The pagan, barbarian, savage images of Indians are relied upon heavily in the case of Kematch and Redhead. These kinds of sensationalized stories focus on behavior as if lifestyle choices of Kematch and Redhead were inherently consistent with Aboriginal people, "in the familiar triad of aboriginal dysfunction of this country — amid violence and poverty, sexual abuse and a fog of alcohol and drugs". These images do nothing for children of the earth or ethnic relations in Canada. These kinds of media representations, distortions of the facts produce reaction in people, they feel morally justified in thinking savages should be locked up, and the key thrown away, it's a burn the witch mentality.

The failure to point out how white supremacy, racism, and all the other issues we are here talking about play a role in the lives of Kematch and Redhead is racist propaganda. Maybe the truth is not what readers of the National Post and most other media want to read about and so we get the twisted, corrupted version that fits our constructions of reality. If the truth were told, maybe we will come to understand the complexity of the issues rather than relying on the same old.

And yet it remains ironic that many failed to see any of this hypocrisy. In the least, no one wrote about this dichotomy. How is the mental illness of Kematch and Redhead compared to Lisa Gibson any less excusable, favorable in the deaths of their children?

All of these situations were tragedies and all stories describe the hell and the horror of declining mental health either through post-partum depression or through intergenerational effects of European colonization, invasion, war, disease, starvation, genocide, Canadian assimilation policy and paternalism, racism, Indian Residential Schools, a failed education system, white supremacy and competition for scarce resources. Stereotypes are at the root of this hypocrisy. It is a perpetuation of the belief that Indians need managing, they don't know what's good for them, they need the white man. It is also the maintenance of racist beliefs that alleviate white guilt and shame for absconding land and relegating other humans to their death march and death camps.

THE IRONY OF RACISM AT OSBORNE HOUSE

It is ironic that Osborne House, in Winnipeg, run by non-Aboriginal people who serve a predominantly Aboriginal clientele would provide the usual remedy of paternal tutelage over those who are presumed to need managing. In this case, the remedy is to raise funds for exploited and vulnerable women by means of satisfying patriarchal demands in exchange for funds. This certainly makes sense to a non-Aboriginal group born and raised in white privilege, socialized and enculturated in patriarchy, paternalism, hierarchical authoritarian stratifications based in racism, who live in privilege with all the accoutrements of status, wealth and power. A strip show really that exploits vulnerable women who feel the need to work in this industry to earn a living and at least they were paid, makes sense to white supremacists. How ironic that this expression in the exploitation of vulnerable women would benefit the exploited and vulnerable women who would receive treatment by the white do-gooders.

And they cannot or will not see it said others listening.

Why would such a privileged group care to use critical analysis of their actions when their very position privileges them to have all the solutions to the Indian problem or any problem? This perspective would be apparent to any educated person who cares to consider the dynamics of racism and oppression. However, the problem originates with a racist, British, colonial and patriarchal group of businessmen. This has privileged Euro-Canadian colonizers since immigration to Turtle Island began. The collaborators continue to benefit. Many feel entitled to everything mother earth has to offer and the sense of entitlement is complete with near total lack of respect for the indigenous groups that were here before colonization began.

The ignorance of racism exists because most have no idea about its origins, how it works, and its purpose. Because racism affects my loved ones, our children, and me, I chose to study racism in depth, with some university training, but also with good old-fashioned libraries and bookstores. I have found many non-Aboriginal people have little to no concern about the insidious nature of racism and have no desire to discover how it harms the racist and the objectified. I believe it is because the racist place themselves in a place of privilege and power that is ego and ethnocentric. This makes it near impossible to acknowledge that any problem would exist with them. That is because the problem is a mental one. Since we use our minds, it is impossible to tell when our minds become dysfunctional. It is not until we run into many problems that we become aware that our thinking, perspective is off center.

While the Canadian Constitution forbids racism, the system of racism is embedded in our economic, socio-cultural and political systems and is clearly apparent in the Indian Act. This is why racism is so elusive and difficult to remove from our minds and societies. We are forced to utilize it in daily economic practice. The constant reinforcing image, narratives, cultural constructions have influenced children in development, reinforced in early adulthood and throughout adult life. Racism permeates our societies so much that we are blind to it even as it is in plain sight. Anyone who would say they are not racist are ignorant, hiding it or are in denial of it. The best we can do is to acknowledge it, and get help for it. For me personally, I got help from a therapist for nearly five years this October on a near weekly basis in cognitive behavioral therapy and I highly recommend it for anyone who can admit they have a problem with racism.

Racism has harmed all societies globally. Not one group has been untouched by hate crimes and crimes against humanity. Every society will experience inter-generational effects of racism for seven generations, as it has been seven generations of abuse. Unless one gets help, our usual remedy has been to exact revenge against our oppressors which only results in a racist reply resulting in a downward spiral in group relations. The lack of trust is like putting out fire with gasoline. It is a negative feedback loop.

Over the centuries, we develop plenty of reason to lash out in self-righteous indignation the moment we are given the opportunity. Feel free to visit the opinion columns of any media forum. This too is reinforced culturally. Consider the recent media comparison of the women who murdered her two children in a bathtub and it was discovered that she had a mental health condition with over 100 supporters complete with an overnight vigil. Meanwhile, Phoenix Sinclair's mother who also and clearly has a mental health issue is demonized. I do not need any inquiry to tell me why Brian Sinclair died in the hospital after being ignored for over 34 hours. I do not judge those who perpetrate racism, I understand it is due to ignorance, a failure of our public education system and our system in general. In fact, I pity those who are hateful because they must have endured horrific experiences that would facilitate such vengeful hatred. We are becoming aware that the priest have not just sexually assaulted Aboriginal children, they exploited white kids too. Hockey coaches, teachers of both genders are being arrested and charged with sexual abuse and interference. Apparently many kids tried to tell their parents and caregivers but like us, they were hushed, silenced, beaten and told to stop telling lies! However, a full debriefing of the origins and history of racism is necessary complete with cognitive behavioral therapy and no visit to the Canadian Museum of Human Rights will ever provide such a debriefing so long as the word "genocide" continues to be denied and that denial is bought by the Canadian government. Nevertheless, no amount of revenge will help the situation. Compassion and grace under fire is what provides integrity to remain in the face of open adversity.

I agree that Minister Eric Robinson was not being racist, but was rather answering racism within the racial context of the situation. Robinson simply projected white supremacy back to the group of white supremacists who were busy reacting with a *burn the witch mentality* all of whom vociferously pointed their fingers at Robinson aghast that an Indian, the same Indian who plays the race card would be racist! How they ran around like chickens with their heads cut off gleefully, blissfully screaming like pagan, barbarian, savages, justified at the apparent racism. They almost looked like their own version of a war dance complete with a war whoop with senseless drumming and dancing! They were totally unaware of their own racism.

When one identifies racism within its context, such as white supremacy, religious and race based authoritarianism, patriarchal and paternalistic tutelage, the only language that is available in identifying the issue is racist language until there is a readiness to agree to abandon racism. But that is not the case with Osborne House and the conflict with the phrase "White Do-Gooders". It is not Robinson's system, it is their system of white supremacy, of the great white father knows what's best for his little Indian children. Because of the way our society is arranged we will not get rid of this problem likely for seven generations. We live in two worlds, a racist world and a non-racist one, one we apparently endeavor to exist. To think a non-racist world is readily available is delusional especially in Canada. Rather, it is an ideal to which we work toward and the best we can achieve is equality.

Apparently, even white people say that using the term white in reference of a person's race depends on how the word is inflected in a sentence. They tell me white is more of a concept than a racial identifier. I believe this is the perspective of the place of privilege described earlier with reference to being white. Even the Winnipeg Police Service requires people to use racist terminology to identify people by their race (white, black, native, Hispanic). Therefore, if Eric Robinson needs to apologize, then so does the WPS as it offends me to have our police service rely upon racist descriptions that undoubtedly influence the type of service we get? Feel free to attend WPS's "gang awareness" training they provide to social workers and probation officers. Eric Robinson correctly identified a racist situation of white supremacy, the "white man's burden", to manage with paternalistic tutelage the "Indian problem", within its context and addressed the situation appropriately and academically and he need not have apologized for it.

Rather an apology should come from the board of directors of Osborn House and should be directed at Robinson, the vulnerable women at Osborne House and all Aboriginal people in Manitoba for not being properly trained, educated, to stand with integrity, transparency, accountability in the face of scrutiny. Rather they tried to cover up. Why? Why do they all try to cover up? It's because they all operate from this mindset of white supremacy, the "white man's burden", to manage with paternalistic tutelage the "Indian problem", New Directions, MacDonald Youth Services, Manitoba Health, WPS, and any other agency that is run by an over-represented population of white people serving an over-representation of Aboriginal people. Robinson was right, they really are a bunch of white do-gooders, and that's using their own racist system of white supremacy to describe their behavior! The other reason why they cover up is because they do not want to take responsibility for their actions. Responsibility is a mature grown up thing to do. Rather, they are immature would rather blame and cover up in shame and they should be ashamed!

I believe Nahanni was correct in questioning the appropriateness of the fund raising strategy. I wonder how this was culturally relevant, appropriate and safe for the participants of Osborne House. I wonder if the staff at Osborne House are culturally competent and what kind of training is provided to ensure staff are culturally appropriate and relevant. I think about what vulnerable people would think when they see that it is good policy, good fund raising initiative to make use of patriarchal demand for titillation and pussy. To continue to perpetuate the objectification and sexualization of women. The very issues that placed many of these women within the care of Osborne House in the first place. This is like the children of Indian Residential School going to a priest for help because someone was diddling them in their sleep. "But who my child, who would do such a thing"? I wonder how empowered staff are at Osborne House to be able to raise concerns about the well-being of participants of Osborne House in the face of strict authoritarian style leadership and command. In child and family services, dominated by over representation of Aboriginal people requiring services, I wonder about these questions and more when our mandate and legal duty is to do what is in the best interest of the children. Do not forget about the great assimilation programs that were the solution to the Indian problem and how that has affected the survivors of Indian Residential School and the children of survivors. How ironic, probably the best example of irony one can devise!

I lost my language, I thought I was a cowboy or at least Mexican; I was educated in an outdated public education system that has not changed since its inception over a hundred years ago. Moreover, the same model Indian Residential School was developed based on the British industrial schools for orphans, we had developed that same public education system using these barbaric models of assimilation. I believe I have met only one mostly non-assimilated indigenous person and even though he endured pure hell, his identity remains. I believe there are very few non-assimilated Aboriginal persons, but our resistance remains! I wonder if this fundraising strategy, this service is in the best interest of the participants of Osborne House or is it another assimilation program for which we should be so grateful. Do we need to start our own Osborne House, one that is staffed with culturally competent people, that deliver culturally appropriate services?

The White Man's Burden revisited continues unchecked, unchallenged at every bastion of white supremacy in our society, and yet we continue to resist and we are not alone. There are many ethnicities including those of Euro-Canadian descent who throw off the racial constructions of reality with a shrug. We have been calling them allies. Devolution has only served to pass the white man's burden onto many of our child and family services as assimilation has affected many Aboriginal people. Again it doesn't matter who runs the system it is still a system of white supremacy, founded in racism, legislated with racist ideology by white supremacists.

Yet, should we choose to empower Aboriginal people to use the system to end racism, with stronger legislation to protect the whistleblower, faster, efficient human rights investigations, faster more accountable grievance procedures for parents who have children in care, better supports for support workers, with more people demanding transparency, accountability the system would change. But that would mean the middle class administrators would have to demand more from the rich upper class. If the middle class enters the territory of the lower class and there is no more middle class you have a recipe for revolution! But the administrators need more funding and yet the gap between the rich and the poor grows wider. I believe it is not just the system that is harmful but rather some of the people who are part of the system are part of the problem as they collaborate in hopes a few small crumbs drop from the wealthy tables of the elite upper classes. And we should demand more because we deserver better than this. The Human Rights Commission, Ombudsman, and other government offices, when utilized, can be a powerful ally for the people. But there can be no collaboration between the agencies. How do we ensure there is no collaboration? The truth of the matter is to have the CEO of Osborne House address her own racism within its racist context of the white man's burden if she can and to apologize for the conflict of interest which she has demonstrated.

She was never acting in the interest of the Osborne House agency or its mandate to provide care services to a vulnerable group. She was only thinking of how the ends would justify the means. Then she could apply her remedy any way she wants at any cost over and above anyone's best interest. She would rather protect herself, her career at any cost. Therefore, the irony of racism is clearly apparent. Moreover, this comes from the useless, good for nothing, dirty Indian as the white people referred to me in public education. Yet, I do not see them educating themselves and talking to you in this respect. Therefore, it is ironic indeed!

Anyone who wishes to study the phenomenon of racism need only Google search as a few good articles and videos exist online too, said some. It's not the best research method but it's a start. It may get you interested enough to get a library card and take out some books.

Well hang on, someone said from the back, I can't even keep up with all the big words I have to look up, paternalism did you say?

The better thing to do is to read books about this outdated way of thinking. Nowadays you can get a library card and download your books onto your devices, said others.

The young people gathered were mostly young high school students and others were in their first or second years of college or university. There were a couple young folks struggling with their education and they knew it was because of racism in the public education system dominated by an entirely different culture that remains indifferent to discriminating issues. The only problem was that they could not articulate it succinctly and cohesively.

In other words, they knew what the problem was, they just did not know how to express it in words. They also believed no one would listen to them anyways, no one ever cared before so what makes anyone think they will start now? Still, others wrote lyrics, rapping about what was important to them, what they valued and the hypocrisy they witnessed and how it made them feel.

Poetry is what it comes down to, others agreed. The sad thing is, they do not get the sense anyone is listening or if they are, they misunderstand.

Another interjected, I had a teacher in high school, in Winnipeg. I knew he didn't like me from the moment we met. I could tell ya know, I seen it a thousand times before. It was the way this dude talked to me, he wouldn't look at me and he was always rude. He used to say to the classroom, "hey everyone, *Smith* isn't here to learn, we all know that, so ignore him like he isn't here". And so I was ignored.

When I handed my assignments in, they were marked low and I was being failed. So one day I figure, you know what, I'm gonna win this mother fucker over. I don't know what I gotta do, but I gotta try.

So we had this big assignment, worth 30 percent of the entire grade. I set out to get the highest grade in the class. I studied for weeks. I done all my research. I had a good presentation. And when the day came and we presented to the class. I got a C plus.

He read the grade aloud to the class as I was sitting down at my desk. Two dudes in class started laughing openly, the teacher pretended not to notice. I wondered what the fuck are these guys laughing at? They told me they were trying to guess each other's grades and so-and-so guessed closer than the other did and they were surprised at how close they came. I guess they knew about

Mr Pricks racism, being racist themselves. I think what they were really laughing at was how I was just treated.

Anyway, I was broken after that. I gave up. Funny thing though. I did this science project the year before and won a place in the provincials, over hundreds of students across the city. Did I get a poor grade cause I was stupid? No! I knew what I was up against.

You can't win in this kind of war. You have to prove yourself to these fuckers and in the end, it's pointless. You can't prove nothing to these mindless, ignorant pricks. I had to leave and do my own thing.

So I learned later, that this is what is called, being pushed out of school. I wasn't quitting, even though I quit, I was pushed out! I always looked at white people with suspicion after that. I stuck with my own kind too.

Then another young person stood up saying, I was about twenty-two years old, I worked at a restaurant. I was a server. The owner was *white*. We were talking about Aboriginal issues and I didn't know a whole lot about it but I did say that I was planning to attend university. My boss said to me that I was *one of the good ones*, that he didn't think I would waste the funding opportunities on drinking and drugs like some of those others. I thought it was a compliment! But one of the others pulled me aside and told me I could file a human rights complaint for what he said. I didn't understand what the problem was so I told them I thought it was a compliment and left it at that.

My boss' sister used to supervise me. One day, a group of Neechi's came in for dinner. She tried to sit them down in some other section. They insisted they wanted to be served by me. I felt special but I knew why. They also told me they would rather be served by one of their own, that I was the first brown face they ever saw working there. I said I thought so and thanked them as the feeling was mutual and they too were the first brown people I saw.

Later on that night, I was berated by my boss' sister for talking with the clients too much.

I was harassed by these two a lot. But I had rose colored glasses on or some damn thing, maybe it was cuz I was so far away from home and needed the job? But I defended those two to the rest of the staff until the boss fired me for failing to call in sick. I guess I gave them the right to fire my ass but it wasn't because I failed to call in sick, that was their excuse, but these were white supremacist racists, the most insidious kind.

I remember meeting his son. He was about my age. His son, was adamant that he was not like his father. I wondered if he meant the racist part because he kept going on and on about his dad has all these ideas and he does not agree with any of them. He went on and on, to the point it was overt, obvious, you know what I' sayin'. I guess this kid was resisting the racism. Or he was scared I might attack him, catching him at unawares in the mall. Maybe he felt threatened having concocted all these images of pagan, barbarian, savages. I wonder if he is still resisting.

Some research indicates kids like him end up returning to their father's conservative beliefs, as they get older, replied another. I would like to think we are not the only ones resisting out there though.

Yah well, they are all racist to me. Every last one of em, okay well maybe not all of em, said the other.

I was fostered by a family. They were good to me, a good home. Stable and in a good neighborhood. But you know what, I could tell there was some favoritism going on. The dad favored his daughter and she could do nothing wrong. Even though I was a little kid, I understood that ya know. I couldn't expect anyone to pay attention to me all the time. So I accepted that about my foster parents. They took good care of me so I let a lotta shit slide.

They got me into hockey. I really enjoyed that and I did really well. I was moving up the ranks and I started getting a lot of attention. I think I could have been an NHL candidate. I was doing good in school, not the best grades but I wasn't failing. I was doing well as a kid and because I had a routine, a schedule I was staying out of trouble. I was exercising everyday. I was sleeping at night and waking early in the morning for practices, even on weekends! I'm old now, but I remember when I was just little, between the ages of 8 to 14 hockey was my life and loved it! I remember it like it was yesterday.

Then one day it all stopped just when I was about to make a breakthrough into the Triple A league. My foster dad didn't like how I was beginning to outshine his daughter.

I did something bad, my foster dad took away all my hockey equipment for the year, and he would not give it back. I think that was when I started to lose focus. I started smoking and that's a bad thing for a hockey player. So, I was losing shape and I couldn't keep up anymore. I lost my drive and so my grades began to fall too. I was getting depressed and I didn't like what was happening to me. I wanted my hockey equipment back.

I was getting stressed and one day this white kid was drawing something at his desk and a bunch of other kids were gathering around and laughing. Someone asked him what he was drawing and he said, *him in 2 years*, pointing at me.

I went over to look at the picture and I saw an image of a dirty drunken Indian with a smoke in his mouth, wearing a black leather jacket.

How did he know! How did he know I would be smoking and losing, dropping out of high school? How did he know that I would be a welfare bum on Main Street?

Anyway, he was laughing at me a couple years later and I was getting pretty tired of his bullshit so I punched him in the face. Well the teachers grabbed me and the police came and arrested me charging me with assault. That's when I got on this thing they call *the track* in Manitoba justice. The never-ending cycle of breaching, arresting, breaching.

My probation officer was a pissy little white kid who had no idea where to find the north end. I gotta tell ya, it was humiliating to have to subject myself to the authority of this little piece of shit! Here I was a big tough Indian that did over five years hard time! And I had to report to baby face with the rosy cheeks.

He was so incompetent, so sheltered that he was never out of his own neighborhood before. So he couldn't find my house in the

North End when he tried to come visit. So I came to him. But I was late and he breached me. That sent me back to jail for a few more months. Then I got out and the same thing happened for the same stupid reason. Finally, my life spiraled out of control and things were getting worse.

I think it was all because I was never really accepted in my foster home because my foster dad was white, his daughter white. My foster mom was my aunt and she was Metis but she couldn't defend me all the time.

There was this time when the Triple A league in Winnipeg was against an all-native hockey team from up North joining the league. The whole league! Parents and players were totally against this native team from joining the league! They had these petitions going around and everything!

They played a couple games against them and the all-native team were way better players, they were all superior players by far. But that's not how all these white people saw it. They said things like, "Those aren't hockey players, those are goons" and they said, "Those are blood thirsty savages". They said, "They don't want to play hockey, they just want to fight, their not in it for the sport". I guess all those cushy little white kids didn't like the body checks.

They either imagined that since they were playing against natives, they could expect savage and barbaric hockey since the stereotypes of the Indian suggest that we are bloodthirsty, pagan, barbarian savages. Or they didn't like being outplayed.

It got so bad that year that it was hitting the news about parents fighting in the stands and spilling out into the parking lots after the game. It was a race war on ice.

It was racism and they all denied it. Racism was on both sides. No one accepts responsibility for it.

My uncles said the natives really were playing way too aggressive but I asked them if that really was true, was their statistics to support that allegation or was it the stereotypes that fueled these race based allegations?

They assured me racism had nothing to do with it, the natives were barbaric on the ice. And that's how they described the native team too.

It was hard for me to witness this as a native person because I was confused. I didn't play for them, I played on the Triple A team. They wanted in. They didn't get in. Why? I think it was because they were native. They had to appeal the decision a couple times in the face of strong opposition from nearly every family in Winnipeg and who were signing petitions. But they finally won and got into the Triple A league but they had to argue and fight for it. You know what, I saw that and I knew what that was all about, racism.

I understand what these Elders are saying about seeing things first in the spirit world and then taking appropriate action in the physical. It's like hockey. You have to see where the puck is long before anyone skates with it. You gotta be there before anyone else is. If you're a goalie you gotta make your move before they take a shot cuz that puck moves fast. If you're a defenseman you gotta be able to stop with the puck on a dime and be moving before anyone can see what you're doing. If you're the forward trying to take the puck away from that defenseman you gotta be able to anticipate those kinds of moves on the player you're watching.

Why would my uncles utilize these racist terms to describe an all-native team? It seemed ironic that natives would be racists against natives. Can that really happen?

Then another shared their experiences.

My ma used to beat the shit out of us for not behaving in public or if we whined in public, pining for her to buy us something, a toy or something to eat. My brother and I got some pretty serious beats if we didn't keep up while shopping, she walked very fast. She would say, "fuck man, what's your fucken problem man! Are you fucken stupid or something? What the fuck man"! It was as if she did not want to be out in the public, in front of so many white people. That's all we saw back then. White people, everywhere you went, white people surrounded you. Not like today. Now we have all these Hindu's, Phillipino's and all these immigrants coming here a lot.

She was embarrassed, ashamed of herself and she thought we were purposely trying to embarrass her in front of all the white people. I guess she felt so insecure about what white people thought of her that she made a point to abuse us in front of them all as if looking for their approval, kinda like how you said you gotta prove yourself to these assholes. She would grab our faces and pull our cheeks, yank our ears, or slap us up side the head, or take us back home and beat us with the belt or willow stick until we were nearly comatose. All because she was sure, the white people were staring at her in public, thinking things about her and us, that we were bad kids and she was a bad mom. She hated taking us out shopping. She hated us and them and even herself.

I don't know what her problem was.

It's probably because they woke up and did'nt eat their wheaties said one! I know my ma gets all pissy if she misses breakfast.

Possibly, said another, we don't know what these people are going through. But they are miserable! Eating, sleeping, reading, education and exercise, all help promote a balanced lifestyle. But many of the dudes we're talkin about are not balanced. Clearly, they are all fucked up inside!

Someone else said, I guess we really can't take it personally then. If they can't manage their own behavior for whatever is going on in their lives then it really isn't about me at all! Many agreed and nodded in acknowledgement to each other.

I had no idea I was doing that!

Doing what?

Taking their bullshit personally!

Well yah, said another. From what I understand by listening to these Elders, we were born into misery! If you have to defend yourself from birth, even before you are born, as some mothers are so unwell fending off oppressions, then ya, many will be out of balance and harmony because of this miserable existence. Then I guess you get used to taking things personally. I guess many learn that they must have done something bad or they come to believe they are inferior, worthless, useless good for nothing *Indians*.

Indians are from India, said a Rajput Warrior quietly listening to everyone.

Yes, we know said a person of First Nation descent. They call us *Indians* because of the racial thinking of their day, they could not or would not understand our identity. We were brown you were brown. To them, we were Indians even if India or Hindustan was thousands of nautical miles away by boat.

They call us Indians too said a Metis person. I guess it's because we are brown too.

Not all of us, said a blonde hair blue eyed Metis warrior.

RACISM!

But it's not about YOU! It's about THEM!

Whatever they are going through is making them miserable. So when you come along rapping about racism they get all bitchy and they tell you to get over it! we're all fucken miserable they say!

Jesus! said another gathering an epiphany. I guess I wouldn't wish my worst situation on anyone then!

What do you mean, others asked.

Do unto others someone said.

Walk a mile in someone else's moccasins said another.

Haters be hate'n.

Everyone laughed a bit about the whole affair. They were very thoughtful.

While the Indian, or native is born into war like the paratrooper example, the white man is born into privilege and a sense of superiority and it is so permeating within their belief systems and perceptions that they are not even aware of their own biases. They will often say things like they are fair, they treat everyone reasonably and they would never discriminate against anyone! The staff at HSC in Winnipeg would be an example of that kind of belief systems.

Not every white person is born into privilege, replied another.

I come from a racist white trash family, alcoholic father and wife beater, floozy mother, older brother a drug dealer, in and outta jail. It's pretty fucked up. Same as you folks, we had cops come in, take my little sister away to the CFS. We starved. I don't know what it was about us. But we didn't have it any easier than lots o you folk.

Hmmm, replied another. Maybe racism and discrimination did to your family what intergenerational effects of Indian Residential School did to ours. Maybe your dad was raped and abused by the priests and nuns too, at least it might explain the alcoholism and wife beating. What kinda white are you anyway?

My mom is from Hungry and my dad is Ukrainian. I dunno, maybe, I never really looked at our family history like dat before.

Then another added to the conversation.

I had one person tell me they were born into a small town rural Manitoba, the most racist town you could be from, they said to me. They said they turned out okay. But that person had no idea how racist they were! They just thought that because they could be in the same room as black people, Indians, rag heads or sand niggers, it means they aren't racist. They fail to see all the beliefs, privilege, cultural influences, methods of oppression that work to justify the delusion of thinking they are not racist. They truly believe these things, they do not see the other influencing factors working in the back of their minds. They can't even see how insecure they are even as they sit in a place of privilege!

These other influencing factors, they continued, they come from their culture, their stories, which appeal to their children, their laws, ensure racism is firmly embedded within their systems of power. Their beliefs in the superior nature of their culture and society affect how they navigate reality with this sense of superiority. These beliefs are passed down through successive generations through their culture of stories, religion, laws, and their beliefs of "civilization" and "progress" which include justice and fairness. So they think they are being fair, when in fact, they are not. They remain willfully blind to their dysfunctional thought processes. They ask silly questions like, "would you rather prefer if we all go back to the stone ages without showers and transportation, energy and all the accoutrements of modern comforts". They justify their privilege and greedy land grabbing, Empire building with these tangible goods as if they cannot live without them. Their denial of inherent racism to themselves and to others keeps the corruption intact. It is a stubborn system that remains within the psyche of the "white" man.

Not just the "white" man said one! This is a system we are all born into! We are all perpetuating the racism.

I guess that's why my uncles defended the racism in the Triple A league. They must have been born into a white supremacy society and came to believe in their racist belief systems.

I guess that's why my ma beat the crap outta us in public. Maybe she came to believe in her inferiority as a Metis woman but tried to prove herself to white people.

There is a theory called the Stockholm syndrome. It describes how some people when held captive by an abuser along with all of the rituals of torture, terror and indignity the victim attempts to control the situation by relating to the abuser. Children who are kidnapped may come to believe their kidnapper is an uncle or a daddy. Kitty Genovese after being kidnapped and held ransom by terrorists became a terrorist, which is where the theory of Stockholm syndrome originates.

Many children who went to Indian Residential School became Christians later in their lives even testifying how wonderful their experiences were. Many defended their abusers vehemently! Many preached against the traditional ways of their own culture trained by the priests it was devil worship. Some just collaborate because they benefit from white supremacy.

They cannot see the alternatives and other options available to them continued the group, as their development in their culture privileges them to believe in their righteousness, and many Aboriginal people collaborate with it for the same reason. White people are superior and natives are inferior. White culture makes them ethnocentric. They cannot see past their own ethnic and cultural constructions of reality. They are firmly ensconced, dug in, fortified in their beliefs about their life and reality. They are so completely locked inside their heads with psychological constructions of reality that make sense to them.

To us all said another!

This is because as they develop under such conditions of privilege their brains form neural connections that facilitate memory, which facilitates beliefs about themselves and others in the world.

Did you ever notice when you read a bedtime story to a child, they never understand the story, and caregivers have to explain it to them with their cultural values imposed upon the children. These values are positively and negatively reinforced. These memories are given meaning through culture and society. These neural connections stubbornly remain intact, which makes it difficult to change. Even if they become aware of racism and its inequality and even if they do not wish any part of it, they find it difficult to escape the foundations of their development.

It is their memories that become stimulated in certain regions of their brain invoking belief systems and then behavior that seems natural to them and because it seems natural, they repeat the undesired behavior. They are oblivious.

Though many prayers are prayed, unless they treat the root causes of dysfunctional belief systems by understanding psychology, prayer never works, nor faith. Then they wonder why they keep doing what they do not want to do. They are not aware that change takes time, effort and commitment. They are not aware that biologically, their neurons stubbornly reconnect while they sleep in its natural attempt to return to equilibrium, balance and harmony no matter how dysfunctional it may present. When they awaken, they must be aware that a new day dawns with new challenges to change undesirable behavior and they must remain committed to change. Just like Warriors are committed to their duty!

You can't really blame some of them when we can see that it is ignorance that is part of the problem. They were born into a world that privileges them, that promotes them as a group some said.

They are born and raised in environments that promote racist attitudes. Google search it and you will find videos where these little kids are spouting racist slogans of white supremacy at the age of two and dressed up in Ku Klux Klan suites! These little kids don't know what they are doing, they are totally innocent! They are being taught and then positively reinforced into ignorance by their white supremacist parents who were also born into white supremacy, were raised in white supremacy and became white supremacists! It is all they have ever known for generation after generation, in their schools, cultures, politics, religions all rooted in racism.

Your talking about intergenerational affects of racism, said another making sure, they were following the gist of the talk. So that's what you mean when you say they were born into this mess, that they learned this throughout childhood, throughout their miseducation. Many of us too were raised hating *white man from town*!

The truth is, we don't know anything about anyone at any time, replied the other. Our stereotypes are not reliable. When we are out in public, we may encounter those folks who may look like they fit the constructions of reality such as the stereotypes we were taught but we don't know anything about them. We don't know about their life experiences and stories. That is a plain fact! So recognize that Jack!

Don't say it, said another to the foolish one!

What, I wasn't gonna say nuttin replied the younger one!

But how can they change unless they become aware that change is necessary, when their belief systems tell them there is nothing wrong with them, some wondered? If this is why our system is repeating generation upon generation indignities and inhumanities how do we stop the cycle.

Another person went on to explain, a scholar named Porter wrote a scathing report called *The Vertical Mosaic*. Porter said Canadian society was hierarchically stratified based on ethnicity or race as it was once and is still sometimes called. In other words, "white" people like the British and the French occupied the highest and most powerful positions in Canadian society. Other "ethnic" European groups like Polish, Ukrainian and Czechoslovakian people who are considered "white" but not as white as the British or the French, benefited from the racist policies in the very least because of their off-whiteness. Many even anglicized their names so it at least sounded English. They could at least hide from racist reprisal relying on the color of their skin.

Russ Gourluck described the British establishment's attitude of the day, had considered the "Slavic" people were "the scourge of Europe" in his analysis of the history of Winnipeg. He showed in his book that Ukrainian people were ghettoized as they were separated from high society demarcated by the railway tracks and main street underpass. There were other ethnicities as well, Polish, Jews, Hungarians, Italians, Greeks and others but it was clearly dominated by Ukrainian people at the outset.

So in other words, Polish, Ukrainian and Czechoslovakian people were considered at the time, garbage races. They were the "N" word of Europe asked some younger ones in the group.

From a racist perspective, which many British and French people came to believe, answered another, yes.

Remember Edward Said's work on Culture and Imperialism? Well he said literature was also *vertically stratified* based on racism, making a similar statement to Porter's Vertical Mosaic. So we have a hierarchically stratified society according to Porter, including its literature, story telling, cultural transference according to Said.

Others listened intently at the gripping conversation as they attempted to process the information sincerely. Many listeners had never heard such talk before. Nor had they cared to hear. Nor were they ever included in such high matters meant only for very important people. They thought themselves lowly common folk. It was indeed a rare treat for them to be seated with this unique group of initiates. They were not asked to leave so they felt somewhat comfortable, included.

Just then, someone spoke up saying, perhaps they thought that they deserved it.

What do you mean another asked?

One of the things bystanders do when they witness such brutality is to engage in mental acrobats, which relieve bystanders of guilt and shame for doing nothing to stop the inhumanity. Bystanders will convince themselves of racist justifications by dehumanizing people with mental processes of dismissing the others humanity, calling them apes, or animals. They will do this in dangerous situations, like when there are mass killings occurring throughout the city by mobs armed with machetes. That is if they don't decide to participate. Even in less open situations like the Manitoba Health question, is there a racist culture operating or not? Many bystanders will convince themselves if there is racism there, it's not with them. They diffuse the responsibility.

But its not like we're accusing them of Nazism though, replied another. If they make mistakes why not own up to them?

We don't know how many mistakes they are making or how often, was the reply. You would need a forensic team, which should include a clinical psychologist to investigate.

The Manitoba government would never pay for something like that, others replied.

They would if the people demanded it!

In the case of indigenous people, the children of the Earth of Turtle Island, they called them savages, uncivilized, barbaric people, ignorant and retarded. Many teachers would not bother to teach the children in the Canadian public education systems because teachers were taught they were superior and Indians could not be taught and so they never bothered to try.

This is still occurring today, many said.

And so, if the oppressed did nothing to stop their own oppression, it would appear to the Eurocentric gazer that they brought it on themselves?

Yes, a very simple-minded conclusion that dismisses a complex dynamic of multi-variable equations that are beyond the wit of the ignoramus.

Eurocentric geezer?

No, Eurocentric gazer!

Everyone laughed at the foolish one.

Ethnic cleansing was a term used at one time, concerning the "Slavic" races, as other groups of the day believed they were "cleaning" their own lands of "garbage filth", as they put it. They believed they were purifying their absconded land of savages.

The truth is the many bystanders could have intervened usually long before any harm came to anyone, Brian Sinclaire, Phoenix Sinclair, Neil Stonechild and all the missing and murdered women. Brian Sinclaire had several bystanders intervene but they were powerless and helpless to get anyone to notice a man, clearly in distress. And still, no one came, why do you suppose that is. Phoenix Sinclair had several opportunities to intervene but still, no one took appropriate action. Why do you suppose that is? Canada is a culture of white supremacy, founded in racism with all socio-political and economical structures having racism embedded within them. When Canadians realize that and accept that, they can decide if they want to continue living in a society with competing marginalities.

Competing marginalities, ask some?

It's a feminist topic but we are using it in reference to other marginalities like when ethnic groups compete with each other for access to power, wealth and status, replied the other.

You mean Porter's Vertical Mosaic where the white European groups like the British enjoy the highest and most powerful positions, then the French, then European groups like Ukraine, Poland, Germany, Spain, Italy, Greece, Belgium, Turkey, Czechoslovakia, Hungry, Romania, Bosnia, Bulgaria, Portugal, Russia?

Then the darker, blacker people of the African states at the lowest end, someone else added?

And then even lower than all of them, First Nations groups added others.

And then at the lowest, Aboriginal women still, others added.

And at the absolute lowest of the low, Aboriginal children, said others.

It's interesting how Europeans like the British and the French think they are the founding groups of Canada when in fact, Aboriginal people, First Nations, Metis and Inuit people are the real founders of Canadian society.

It's all a buncha horse sheeit, said another. Nothing would have happened if it were not for the treaty making process and all the help given to the settlers by indigenous groups.

Like Thanksgiving, asked someone.

It's beyond thanksgiving.

Another described that Europeans believed these "Indians" have no concept of god or the savior Jesus and thus were called heathens and heathens were enemies of their gods. An enemy of their gods meant they were not saved and it was a Christian's duty to Christianize them and if they would not Christianize, it is better for them to die or to be killed rather than live as a heathen. They are trying to build gods kingdom here on earth. Anyone who would not convert was considered antichrist.

Why do you say, "Their gods"?

Because there are so many versions of Christian beliefs, each one has their own version of god and so they have many gods. Each sect believes *they* are the chosen ones of god. They say the others are heathens, unsaved, fallen short of the glory of god. Which one is right, we will never know. They are all right from their own perspectives, but at the same time not one of them are right from their own perspectives.

Such extreme thinking is common among fundamental religious people. And so many Christians at the time believed they were doing God's will by killing and murdering and assimilating many children of the Earth.

And they were all doing it, asked another?

Pretty much, they replied.

In the case of the Ukrainian people who evacuated from Europe after 1870, because they were severely abused and beaten, starved, murdered, raped and deprived of all dignity, bystanders looked at them with contempt or disgust. Their racism and religion caused many religious zealots and racists to blame the victim. That happened to them upon their arrival in Canada too!

Orthodox Christian churches were built and many Catholic's and Anglican's were not happy. They would have preferred to see more steeples being constructed rather than onion domes, everyone hated to see synagogues being constructed. The Mason's were the only ones who enjoyed all the work, they said laughing.

Why, asked the young teen.

Their belief systems tell them oppressed people like Indians, or the Slavic's, deserve what they get. Operating from a place of supremacy, of judgment justified by religious beliefs they swiftly pass judgment in anger and visceral hatred. If your not one of us, your one of them. If you're not with us, you're against us. If god be for us who can be against us. Morality, ethics, good, bad, right, wrong, evil, righteousness all come from the church fathers, patriarchy, paternalism, hierarchy, authoritarianism.

If they don't want to get with the program then they deserve to have their land taken if they are not using it the way *the establishment* would, for industry and war. They deserve to be punished if the oppressed do not work the land. They deserve to be placed into re-education camps like the Indian Residential Schools. And many figured that if Canada was intensely focused on the *Indian problem*, they were not focused on the Slavic problem so many said nothing, pretending nothing was happening. They see no evil, hear no evil and speak no evil. Many believe they brought it upon themselves. Both Indians here in Canada and Slavic's who escaped the brutality of nation building in their own homeland were blamed for their own misfortune.

They believe since they are not saved they are doomed to their fate, when all they have to do is confess that Jesus is Lord their suffering will stop. If they don't confess they are not worth saving, they are the devils children, antichrist enemies of god. The Anglicans hated the Catholics and visa versa both hated the Orthodox churches so who does an Indian turn to for salvation?

Why do they have to confess that Jesus is Lord, asked someone?

Christianity is the program. You need to get with the program. This program has all the answers. When you have all the answers and you are with the program you conform! You got the Christian work ethic, god does for those who do for themselves, you are saved so you can judge others based on your religious perspective, you have a hierarchy to rely upon, a community of like-minded people. When you are a Christian, you are no longer an Indian, the two programs are not compatible. You can't pray to your spirit guides and Jesus at the same time in the churches. No, you gotta get with the program.

The questions continued, why is getting with the program so important?

TREATIES

Then a First Nation person answered. If you are not an Indian anymore, you are more willing to give up your treaty rights. The treaties are our official contract between Canadians and Indians where Indians offer up all this land in exchange for certain rights and privileges. It saved us a costly war and bloodshed. But your treaties ensure you have a right to live on your land base with government supports. White people get to live on this land within their own systems of paying taxes that support this agreement. These treaties are meant to last for as long as the sun shines and the rivers flow.

But many Canadians are encroaching on the last little pieces of land left to us. They build dams and hydro development projects, golf courses, roads, oil and gas projects. All of this disrupts our lives as these projects disrupt the lives of wildlife, ecosystems and environment. White people do not understand we are all connected even to the environment and our relatives, the winged ones, the four legged's. If you disrupt that, you disrupt us and if you do that, you are not honoring the treaties, which are a constitutionally legal agreement. When we Christianize, we are likelier to give up those treaty rights. We don't want to do that! Those treaties were meant to protect our children, lives, livelihood, culture, languages.

We struck treaty with the understanding that we would engage with the newcomers on a nation-to-nation basis, as equals. We understood that we would share in all land and resources, politically, economically, strategically. That is how we have always struck treaty. Treaties were sacred, spiritual agreements, not simply legal contracts on paper. We operate from a spiritual, sacred perspective, not a physical, mental one. Our perspective includes the physical, mental, emotional and spiritual aspects of the medicine wheel where none is more important than the other is. The British patriarchal system of the day operated from the same aspects but it was corrupted by greed, a collective sense of entitlement and white supremacy, which undermines the medicine wheel and the treaties. They did not want to share. They never do.

Christianizing the Indian has been a part of the assimilation policy since colonization began. They have always wanted to turn Indians into white people. This way, there is no special relationship, no treaties, nothing to protect indigenous identity. They want us to be a part of their slave system so we too can pay taxes and support the great white father. They say, "c'mon, we all have to do it, what makes you dirty Indians so special"? They want all the land and they don't want to pay the rent!

It's all very confusing, because I know Christians who are still Indians and still live on the reserve. I guess it's a long slow process of enfranchisement where eventually the Christian will leave the reserve and all that is Indian to become part of the flock.

Don't you mean sheep, said another being facetious.

Or at lease collaborate said another.

You don't need to be Christian to collaborate replied another. You just have to be assimilated. But Christianizing is part of the whole process of assimilation. Christianity is the father of assimilation.

Apparently, the psychopath thinks like this they said, listening intently and with great interest, making many connections. Psychopaths are lazy, they get everyone else to do things for them and they love to control others in a superficial sense of superiority with delusions of grandeur. They would love to occupy the highest rungs of society. They would feel entitled to the public coffers. They would be hurt if you questioned their entitlement or accuse them of racism, hurt to the point of reacting in visceral rage. How dare you!

Eh what's that others asked. What is a psychopath?

THE PSYCHOPATH

A psychopath is a person who does not have the ability to empathize, they cannot experience feelings like emotions, grieving, even pain is dulled, suffering, guilt, shame, remorse, happiness or some other emotions we all take for granted are dulled. They are somewhat fearless too!

They are not brave or courageous in the fearless way we understand fearless, they just do not experience fear in the same way we do. As for shame and guilt, they do not experience that and they explain away a victims impact statement by saying they should not have placed themselves in a situation where they can be taken advantage.

If they steal an Ipod and other things from your truck, they would laugh at you the victim and blame you! The psychopath would say that if the victim was stupid enough to leave their doors unlocked then they deserve what they got, to have things stolen from them.

Psychopaths are best known as serial killers, but many either are not caught in their murderous deeds yet, or they function normally in society, pretending to be normal, mimicking the behavior of normal people. But they are not normal. They are anti-social and yet because they are so good at mimicking behavior at reading what other people expect of them, they meet others expectations if it will get them what they want, if it is worthwhile. And so that is how psychopath's blend in society. They may not even be aware they are different. In fact they don't think anything is wrong with them. Rather, they see others as though they have problems of weakness.

You would be surprised how many psychopaths there are in the world! Apparently, the West is particularly good at producing psychopaths!

They say psychopathy may be due to raising children without proper support and attachments to caregivers and community.

Without proper attachments, the child does not connect and the neurons do not formulate or develop neural connections, which would bring meaning to any sort of connection to the human family. It is their disconnection to people that gets them into trouble. They could care less about anyone else but themselves. They are self-serving, self-centered. To them, it is nothing to be a baby killer or a granny groper. They care less about other people. They only see people in one way, if they can get something out of them or if they can't. If they cant, they have no use for you.

Many psychopathic people who work for corporations appear to function normally in these environments because of the competitiveness, ambition, selfish drives that are common in climbing the corporate ladder. But not everyone out there is a psychopath.

I was going to say something about this earlier but never had a chance. A psychopath is like your great beast you are all talking about, a psychopath is a chameleon. They blend in with society only because society is a means to an end, survival. They are social loafers, liars and manipulators, they are the full embodiment of laziness as they will do as little as possible get what they want. They always manipulate the systems and the people in them to do things for them. Some are ambitious, self-indulgent creeps that will do and say anything to get their way. They will even feign a suicide or fall in love with someone if they thought it was worth the effort. They are master impersonators. They become your best friend, changing into the very ideal person you wish you knew but don't. They become the full embodiment of your wildest imaginations! They only do things if it serves their own self-interest.

Jesus! I know people like that!

Yes, you probably do!

I dated people like that!

Perhaps, but you don't really know until you know. Many express they feel a coldness and it's an unforgettable feeling.

Yup, that's my ex!

That's how I feel when I leave the *farewell* office.

Holy fuck! I think I am a psychopath said someone and everyone turned around to look at that person with great curiosity, alarm and wonder was in their eyes!

Relax, your not, they replied

If you were a psychopath, you wouldn't even be here. This would be too boring for you. Plus if you were and were interested in these goings on, you would have said nothing and would hide in the crowd, anonymous. You wouldn't give a shit about our nightmares. In fact, you wouldn't even be scared of your own nightmares.

Anyways, it sounds like we are describing a psychopath when we talk about abusers and oppressors either en mass like a culture of vultures or in individuals.

Another continued, the oppressors have a belief system called the Christian work ethic that tells them that god helps those who help themselves. It is a simple belief system that makes sense in a simplistic way, but if it is not critically analyzed, this belief can be very dangerous.

But they do not appreciate critical discussions that question their authority and that is why speaking of such things are forbidden.

It's the same with the psychopath said the other. They don't like it when you question them. They prefer you didn't. They feel affronted, or offended. You don't want to affront them!

What's affront eh my darling? What's affront?

Affront means to challenge, insult, disrespect, or otherwise to offend them. Once they feel dismissed, you have triggered them.

They have a sense of entitlement to power and authority, they believe they are very important people and all others shouldn't question their authority or intentions. They already feel empty inside, as if they do not really exist and what does exist is unworthy, ugly and repulsive to them. They believe they must have people, places and things to show their power and authority. Like teenagers who believe they are superior to others being in a popular crowd the psychopath finds it important to be among a certain crowd. Symbols of power, wealth and status like cars, people, houses, neighborhoods, restaurants, are very important to the psychopath as it should be enough to keep the common folk, the rabble away. When they see themselves or you point out to them their empty soulless selves, they become so agitated, enraged they will objectify you, they will elevate themselves above you and as an object, and you deserve their wrath. Psychopath's take special offense to your disrespect in a way you really do not want to experience.

In the study of psychopathic serial killers, it has been found that a psychopath projects their life experiences onto their victims and they capture, torture and murder their victims in an elaborate ceremony based on self-loathing. They ritualistically express their morbid self-reflection onto their victim. They do to them what happened to them as a statement of punishment. They are very dangerous when affronted. They will wait and watch for an opportune time to take you out and they never forget!

I'm sorry you were saying before I rudely interrupted?

Oh, that's alright, you were just helping us understand the importance of challenging authority and arresting the psychopath. I was saying, if you were caught speaking against the church systems of the day, you could be branded a heretic and you could be excommunicated from the church.

Some of you might be thinking, big deal if I was excommunicated, I would just go live somewhere else. That kind of thinking comes from your foundation into western individualized belief systems, that you can make something of yourself. Except in those days, excommunication from the church meant you no longer had any rights and privileges, you turned your back on god and Jesus and all them 'postles. You could be burned at the stake for your heresy, or you would be tortured on the rack or placed in the Iron Maiden.

Iron Maiden! Alright, said an older one imitating Bill and Ted, characters from a movie in the eighties. That one got really strange looks from everyone.

The other continued speaking authoritatively pointing the finger up in the air, pointedly saying, so do not mistake what it means to turn your back on the establishments, the authorities, the institutions of those days or even the modern ones today. The Christian work ethic and other beliefs about "Slavic" people go back many thousands of years. The oppressors in Europe would have seen their quick defeat as a sign of their inherent superiority over "Slavic's" and reinforce the inferior position of the so-called barbaric savages, Ukrainians and Polish, Czechoslovakian peoples of Europe.

The fact that Ukrainian people would even rise up against their oppressors would be seen as the insolence of a child who would not listen to their parent. Back then, they believed that beating a child with a stick would bring a child back into the path of righteousness. They quoted a scripture that said if they spared the rod, they spoil the child. So it was this belief, that it was in the best interest of the child to beat them back into the paths of righteousness. Meanwhile research shows that anxiety disorder is likelier in children who are subjected to corporal punishment.

To beat children into submission was a common form of assimilation. They took this belief to the Ukrainian people and if they would not be managed paternalistically, they would suffer. They would say the Ukrainians brought it on themselves. In the same way that a spousal abuser beats their spouse, they say they brought it on themselves, that they made them do it. Is that not correct with your line of thinking on psychopaths and abusers?

They deflect responsibility for their own choices and actions onto the one they abuse.

They do not take responsibility and to this day, Holodomor is denied, others added.

In Canada, Canadians continue to deny that genocide occurred here even though we know there are no more Beothuk.

Beothuk? What do you mean Beothuk, others asked?

Canadians think *Indians* are one homogenous group. Canadians use an *out-group homogeneity effect* projecting their imagination, stereotypes onto Indians. They do not recognize diversity of people that are the original inhabitants of Turtle Island. So they do not think the Beothuk are worth mentioning in the question of whether or not genocide occurred in Canada. The Beothuk were a group of people or race of people if you ascribe to racism. The Beothuk were victims of genocidal hatred. They were annihilated.

The oppressor dehumanizes the oppressed. Once they dehumanize, of course it is easier to harm people. They call them savages utilizing racist terminology and beliefs that justify their superior position. They blame the victim for their predicaments. They believe that if they do nothing to stop the violence and oppression, they must deserve it. Where do you suppose they would learn that concept?

CHILD ABUSE, SELF LOATHING, SELF DESTRUCTIVE BEHAVIOR

Abused children have commonly reported that they must be bad if they are continuously being beaten viscously and savagely by their abuser, said a childcare worker.

In their under-developed brain and cognitive belief systems, they don't have the experience yet to comprehend the complex dynamics they face in life. So children can only relate to the concepts taught in their cultural environments.

In this case, a religious one that teaches punishment for those who do evil things, bad things. Therefore, too many small children who are abused violently may come to believe they must have done something wrong to deserve this kind of poor treatment. Small children believe they must be very bad children and that is the only answer available to them, which makes sense of the violence they develop. They get this garbage from their religion. We are taught this in Sunday school. We read about it in children's books. It's in cartoons.

A Metis Psychologist among them interjected saying, this belief system children form amidst violence and abuse, that they deserve it because they must have done something bad and therefore, they are bad, turns into a problematic belief system later in life.

If small children come to understand that they have done something wrong and they are bad, they try harder to be good. Try as they might, they cannot stop the cycle of abuse they face in their lives. Over time, they come to believe nothing they do or say to their abusers stops the abuse from occurring. The problem is more complex when the abuser apologizes, presenting sincere remorse, maybe even believing they are sorry and if this is a parent, the child forgives and repeatedly forgives.

Children need to attach in a healthy, safe, secure, stable and loving environments. They long for caregivers and family to accept them. If they do not attach in a healthy way they live with *attachment issues* for the rest of their lives unless some type of healthy intervention occurs.

They will have many challenges in society if they do not form healthy attachments. So in their innocence, they wish for abuse to stop, they long for healthy attachments. This is why children are so forgiving of their abusers. They are too under developed to understand the complex dynamics they face so they form unhealthy attachment styles in hopes of adjusting to their abusive, cold unloving environments. This is the origin of dysfunctional belief systems like being willfully blind. Many grow to be willfully blind to unhealthy relationships when they are older.

I am beginning to see why Harper's apology is so important, someone said.

Yes, said another, if insincere, it would trigger thousands. Plus add the concepts of paternalism, patriarchy, hierarchy, authoritarianism, just like our nuclear family is set up now. There are many belief systems, constructions of reality that play a role in everything we do.

So they are confused by the apology, the love and then the visceral hatred. The repeated and cycles and patterns of abuse cause them to lose hope that they may one day find reprieve and so they often wish they could escape. Some will escape into books, others art, others sports and others work. But so long as they continue to escape from abuse or the belief that they deserve to be abused, because they come to believe they are bad, their escapes are only temporary solutions. They do not last. Eventually, their escapes no longer provide reprieve. Their self-loathing and visceral hatred and fears manifest as a tormentor that follows them, searching, unrelenting they are hunted, persecuted. They are very hard on themselves when they make mistakes.

The child comes to believe they are bad. Nothing they do or say will change that. So they believe they deserve to be punished. When they are grown older, and the punishment stops, they find new ways to punish themselves because they cannot accept they are good people. If their logic tells them the punishment stopped, they must be doing something good. But that belief runs contrary to what they came to believe about themselves in their development. That is that they are bad. So, if they are bad, they believe they need to be punished to reinforce what they have come to believe about themselves. So they do or say things that bring about punishment.

They behave inappropriately and become *anti-social* as they lost trust and faith in authority figures, seeing their hypocrisy. Then they are back to what they are familiar with, they are back to what they know, they are relieved that nothing has changed.

They are not aware of it, but they crave punishment. These poor young souls have difficulty if there is no abuse in their lives, they cannot adjust to peace, harmony, tranquility and life vicissitudes. Their brains have developed neural connections that only allow for constant abuse. They cannot possibly imagine anything else because they have never experienced anything else. That does not mean that they can never experience life without abuse, they just need help acclimatizing to peace and harmony. It takes time and it is a work in progress.

Unless they get help or access to psychological services, their belief systems tell them they are bad and so they deserve punishment, they have accepted that about themselves. This belief system is referred to as self-loathing. Their experiences of abuse and their beliefs told them they must have been bad and they cannot seem to stop the abuse from happening means they must be stupid! Well what else can it mean? Everyone it seems is telling the poor child they are stupid, useless, good for nothing, drunken lazy, *Indians, Niggers Newfies*, or whatever other derogatory descriptions there may be, and they will never amount to anything.

They hear it at home, at school, in the streets, from family and parents and in future relationships.

Parents and caregivers ask their kids if they are stupid or they say that they are, outright! Other parents don't have to say anything, a stern look of disapproval is meant to shame the children. Parents convey worthlessness and inferiority by using sarcasm when talking to their children.

It sounds like the psychopath who objectifies the victim, interrupted another. The psychopath abuses the victim in a ritual of abuse. So too, the parent ritualizes the same abuse they went through as they express that ritualistically on the child!

For example, continued the other, when parents ask young ones if they prefer to live in a mess such as a messy bathroom or bedroom it suggests young ones are too stupid to know any better.

We watched one father in the car next to us abusing his son asking him if he will grow up to be a *sissy* and when his son started to cry he then proceeded to call his son a *cry baby* and a *little whiney girl*, a *suck hole*, and escalated to calling his son a *fag*. His son was probably about four years old. And this was a white man exclaimed another! But that is his culture, he probably is doing so thinking he is saving his child!

How do you think young ones would feel if they understand their parents thought of them as useless, stupid and ignorant? After a while, many would become sick and tired of their parents and will want to run away.

We know of one parent whose spouse left her and all four children moved to four corners of the earth just to get away from their controlling mother another added.

Many white people talk like this to their own children believing they were the spawn of Satan or under demonic influence in sincere belief their children are led astray! Children hear these statements all day long throughout the most impressionable years of their life! They do not understand why they cannot stop the abuse and so it must be that they continuously bring the abuse upon themselves. They reason, using the cultural and social constructions that have been made available to them, that they must be repeating this behavior because the abuser was right! They are stupid and they bring it upon themselves. So the small child learns to hate themselves as they come to believe they have brought this abuse upon themselves repeatedly.

Parents should be aware of the power they have over the minds of young ones and should not abuse that power. Young people have indicated the power parents have over them even in their twenties, thirties up to their sixties! The mind is difficult to change once it has learned concepts and this can be seen in many adults as they continuously work to impress their parents, constantly trying to prove themselves. It is futile. If a parent cannot accept their children for who they are that is the parent's problem. Such barbarism, such savagery, backwardness is clearly linked to religion, authoritarianism, paternalism and patriarchy. These do nothing for the spirit of the child.

So now, the children have learned they are bad, they are stupid and they bring trouble down upon themselves and so they begin to learn to hate themselves for repeating the patterns of abuse. In a strange way of self-expression, their anti-social behaviors are really, just rituals of their abuses, which they are not allowed to talk about, it is forbidden, absolutely forbidden, even to themselves, so they express it ritualistically, sub-consciously.

Untrained observers only see what they observe and without education, they ignorantly make assumptions about the person they are observing that facilitate cognitive dissonance, the devaluation of something valuable, the person. The stereotypes, the racism the learned cultural superiority that is readily available to explain away the complex dynamics of the behavior observed cause the observer to lose appreciation for the person they observe. They will then blame the victim with racist thinking and project stereotypes onto the victim. This dysfunctional behavior then perpetuates racism and stereotypes. But many deny they are racists because they are not educated enough to consider the complex dynamics of multi-variable algorithmic equations. They prefer shortcuts.

The Eurocentric gaze described by Said and others suggests those in the West, white people are born into a world that prepares them with a sense of superiority. From their perspective, they are not required to understand what it is they observe. Rather, they say things like, "it's common sense" in reference to behavior. They have established ways that make sense to them from their perspective. When they observe behavior from this Eurocentric perspective, selfish and self-centered, egocentric, culturally constructed, constricted, narrow view, they automatically elevate themselves above the other/s. They become self-righteous, and they are judgmental.

Let me provide you with an example. For a long time social work, education, justice, police, medicine, and other professions were and sometimes still are dominated by white people, meaning, the vertical mosaic described by Porter. The British at the top highest-ranking positions, the French below them and other European groups are below them. This is a racially stratified hierarchical system. This is a collective cultural group. They have ways that make sense to them if they are in their own land bases, countries, nation states. But what if we take that social worker and place them in Afghanistan or Mauritius? Do you think the same "common sense" constructions of reality will apply? No! They don't because these white people are now in a totally different culture, land base. It would be arrogant of such people to set up a social service and apply their Western cultural values on the people of Mauritius. Mauritius people have their own common sense values that may not make sense to the white people of the West. And yet, that is the precise problem with service delivery from white people in Canada who apply their common sense ways to Aboriginal people, where they fail to recognize diversity under the term Aboriginal and in so doing are obviously applying ethnocentric values on diverse groups as if they are applicable. But do they see it? No! They can't!

They don't even care to understand what the term Aboriginal means.

They spell it in lower case, and then they say ignorant things like, "First Nations and aboriginal people" or "Aboriginal and Metis, not realizing that Aboriginal refers to the three constitution groups, First Nation, Métis, Inuit people. Inuit is virtually non-existent in their psyches. So how can you have First Nation and Aboriginal people? That's like saying, Aboriginal and then repeating First Nation, Métis and Inuit. It doesn't make sense. And yet, for those of us who do understand what they are saying or trying to say, it is clearly apparent to us they are ignorant. It speaks volumes to us when we observe their behavior. It tells us they don't even care to know about the diversity within the term First Nation or understand the identity of Metis or Innu people. Why? Because they don't have to, they believe they are superior to others in every way, that they are entitled to know everything, and anything they don't understand is just stupid because it's not *common sense.*

Law requires medication be accounted for at all times when working in a residential care facility. The white people know this. However, because of the way white people have governed our country, we are now experiencing a severe labor shortage and so we have to import labor through immigration. We now have immigrants arriving from all over the world that have no idea about Canada, its racist history or its western values of white supremacy and authoritarianism. So they may not have any idea they have to follow the law and record medication dispensing and accountability. In their own countries, this may be totally acceptable.

But now we have a white kid who is a manager of an agency that provides support services with a residential care facility.

This white kid has never been outside of their rural farming community before and has no idea what its like to be from African nation states, or Middle Eastern nation states. This white kid could care less about what's going on *over there.* But the white kid has to manage a group of recently arrived immigrants who have escaped persecution for their beliefs, or civil war after bribing many officials are now trying to make a go of it here in Manitoba.

These recently arrived immigrants may have no idea that law requires them to record medication counts. So the manager is confused, confounded and perplexed as to why he can't get his staff to follow the protocol. To the manager, this white kid from town, *it's common sense!* So this white kid would fire the shit out of everyone if he could but they are unionized. Frustrated, he applies the Eurocentric gaze and remains stupefied by the cultural disconnection. His place of privilege affords him the ignorance and there he remains in his little box, prepared for him by his culture, totally self and morally justified.

This white kid is more likely to promote or hire those he can relate to, those who share his common sense. Anyone who is different or difficult is likelier to be passed over. But he will tell you he is not racist. No, he gives everyone a fair shake. He believes in justice, righteousness, Jesus and all them 'postles.

Who do you think is the slave and who is emancipated, liberated and free? The one in the box, or the one who can see the box from the outside? The one in the box has a whole system of common sense. The one outside makes no difference because they are not the one in power.

Then another spoke up.

I remember calling the Mobile Crisis Line once. They hung up on me. They accused me of being abusive. Because I was abusive from their perspective, they felt morally justified to hang up on me. Admittedly, I was not in the best mental state but that was because I was in a fucken crisis for fawk sakes!

When you are in a crisis and you call a crisis hotline you are asking for help. But if the other person is failing to help you then things spin out of control. The feeling of helplessness that overwhelms your senses demands action. It appears the person who hung up on me was having a crisis too.

Hanging up on a person in crisis, reveals they are running away as well. The fight or flight response to stress demands them to make a choice.

It appears the Mobile Crisis Line requires attention as it is not as reliable as we think it is. Perhaps MacDonald Youth Services the service provider of the Mobile Crisis Line needs to provide reinforcement and support for their support staff so that their Mobile Crisis Line is reliable. However, I wouldn't hold my breath. Again, it would take more funding for administration, funding the rich and powerful do not want to share.

When we discussed the situation with their managers at the time, we got lip service. When we followed up with them, they stopped returning our calls and eventually we went away. Many told us they had given up on calling the Mobile Crisis Line anyway.

Someone said, I guess it's kinda like going to the priest for help eh?

That is when we realized this is a second rate service like most of the social services in place in Manitoba and we all seem to find it acceptable. It is a service rooted in religion, patriarchy, paternalism, hierarchy, authoritarianism. They believe they are doing us all a favor, they have all the answers, they are not aware of their white supremacy. There is no public outcry. But that's probably because of the learned helplessness we have all shared developing in this second rate country that has roots in racism complete with entitlement issues and white supremacy. We learned to be helpless in the face of abuse, from our parents, our society and we had no one to turn. We come to believe there is nothing we can do to stop the abuse.

What do you mean by *white supremacy*? Do you mean the Ku Klux Klan asked someone nearby?

No not the KKK, I mean the system that we all exist, the little box we are told to live inside. The box or the system is based in white supremacy, they believe they are superior, they have salvation through Christ, their god is white, Jesus white, the 'postles are all white. The church is built upon white supremacy. The governments, nations are all based in white supremacy. The legal system has racism embedded within it.

The KKK are racists based in white supremacy that's true too. White supremacists that I describe are those who say they are not racist, wouldn't want to be, but those who bought into the program that privileges white people, that convinces them they have all the answers. They may say they are not racists but they *are* white supremacists, it's systemic. They are not insidiously racist but their ignorance makes them racist in many ways. They operate from a place of superiority, racism. That is white supremacy. If they knew they were behaving like the KKK, they would seek help for their white supremacy, racist ideology, cultural influence, privilege, discrimination.

To clarify, many of these folks work in social service agencies and our public education system continued the other.

White Supremacy was so busy privileging themselves they failed to notice the destruction of people, dismissing, objectifying, and blaming them. This caused many Warriors to stand up to the white supremacists and point out their racism. But it was too late. White supremacy left behind a white supremacist system for non-white supremacist, feminists and others to manage but it doesn't matter who manages the system. It was founded in racism and anyone who manages it maintains white supremacy.

Cultural competence and certifiable training are required to provide crisis intervention, not just a soft reassuring voice replied the other! There is something happening here. Try not to be distracted, try not to give yourself excuses to ignore what's going on. You have to notice the event. Be sure that something requires attention. Don't make excuses for white supremacy as if no one can do anything about it. Stand united to end the system. Do not collaborate with it, don't let yourself be bought off. Have integrity. Just because you're the only one that seems to notice systemic racism otherwise known as white supremacy and others are pretending they don't see it, shake them up. Ask them if they want to join you, they may actually want to help and are just waiting for someone to motivate them.

Then you have to interpret the event as an emergency. Don't let the problem go unaddressed. Make sure you have done something. Make sure others have done something too. Call them on it. Follow up with them.

Then take responsibility. Just because you may not know all the issues and how to articulate it you can still point out that you are offended by white supremacy. If you need to get some help then call some people and point out what offends you. Get some reinforcement. You don't have to stand alone.

Then you have to know what to do to help. Decide how to help the situation in the best and most noble way. If you think about costs versus rewards just know that there is a higher reward for doing the right thing and that you may regret not doing anything for the rest of your life. Or you may tell yourself all kinds of lies, which lead to more lies to remedy the guilt or shame you may have for having done nothing. If you're worried about what you look like there are two things to think about. First, who cares what other people think of you. If they think negatively of your activism that's not your problem, that's their problem. You can't control what others think of you and it shouldn't matter. What you can control is what you think of yourself. That's really what should be important. Don't let other peoples opinions of you affect how you think of yourself. That's dysfunctional. If you have self-respect and value for yourself then it shouldn't matter what others think of you. Second, you are likely to be regarded with honor for being the first to recognize the issue and taking initiative! A person who takes initiative is always appreciated because that is what leadership is all about. When you take initiative and take action then you can coordinate others mobilizing them strategically to stand up to systemic racism, white supremacy.

Then intervene. Don't be afraid to rock the boat to shake em up! You would be surprised how many people want change so much and it's so much easier when you have help.

The social service agencies, the public schools, they all came from the Indian Residential School. That's how they developed their education systems here in Canada. The Indian Residential School developed from the old English Industrial Schools where they would apprehend orphans on the street and force them into these residential care homes like little orphan Annie or the other kid, "please sir, can I have some *moar*".

Oliver Twist, said another.

Oliver Twist, replied the other.

So we have a system and networks that reinforce the system that is based on assimilation, the breaking down of a persons identity through coercive tutelage, torture. It is based in religion, justified by charity, patriarchy, paternalism, hierarchy and authoritarianism and as such, it is a dysfunctional system that morally and self-righteously justifies its existence, it manufactures consent, wealth and power. It is a system that favors the white man from town and those who would collaborate with it.

Those who collaborate with it are part of the problem and not the solution. They are indoctrinated like cult members to follow without any critical thought. They apply a superior perspective, a Eurocentric gaze and they are judgmental toward those who either are not assimilated or do not fit their constructions of reality. They hang up the phone or they remain stupefied sitting in ignorance but comfortable as their delusions tell themsselves how superior they are. And they reinforce each other in these delusions!

This system really comes from the old churches when the Catholics reigned supreme. It is well recorded the church would find ways to make peasants offer gold to save their souls, placing them in even more vulnerable states.

Indulgences, cried another.

Indulgences, replied the other.

The early church fathers exploited the vulnerable, the uneducated, the less sophisticated, the poor, making them even poorer by selling them indulgences in hopes they could buy their way into heaven faster. Utter nonsense.

Meanwhile, they wanted to build bigger and grander churches!

Everyone came to the church for salvation but many were not allowed to read the Bible for themselves! They were not allowed to question the authority of the church and the church fathers. They would be excommunicated if they tried that. The church had total power and authority, even more power than Kings of the whole world.

This pattern of authoritarianism would be passed down intergenerationally. This model would be the model for Empires thereafter, Kingdoms, which would then become nation states, all run by devoutly religious men and they forced women and children to fall in line or they would be kicked out onto the streets to starve. They learned to do this from the church fathers that would withhold food and rations from the people and then sexually exploit them in return for a meal. If they didn't like it, they would be excommunicated and that was a death sentence. This pattern would continue to the present. There are not enough checks and balances in place to protect vulnerable children involved with the law. What's to stop a probation officer from making deals with vulnerable young people in exchange for favors. How can we be sure people in authority who administrate to the poor and the oppressed wont take advantage of the situation?

Today we have all these white people who believe they have the superior way to live, they have all the answers with their beliefs in salvation, Christianity, the work ethic, progress and civilization. Why wouldn't you want any of this they say?

So now they have all these child welfare agencies, social services, public education systems, run by white supremacists who truly believe they have all the answers! They offer a pittance and act as though they are doing you a great favor.

They are like the Nazi soldier who offers Sophie, in *Sophie's Choice*, the option of keeping her son or her daughter, but not both. The soldier explained that since she is not a Jew, she had a great privilege to choose which will live and who dies. An abominable situation, she chose to let them take her daughter. Otherwise, the Nazi's would have taken both children to die. They set themselves up like they are gods administrating who gets what and how much they get and it's based on racism.

Ethnicity, said someone from the back.

Racism, replied the speaker. Ethnic stratification based in racism.

These rituals are really just a cry for help, they are trying to tell us what happened to them and they want help, to be saved, liberated, and emancipated as they are imprisoned by the system from the abuse, confusion and torment. They are lonely, unsupported and afraid. It makes them angry and dysfunctional, helpless and harassed, not all of them, just the ones who bought into the program and those who resist it but also benefit from it at times.

Maybe that is what "white" man is saying in their entire wild and bazaar behavior! Maybe they are describing what happened to them!

Yes! Think about it another said!

Throughout history, "white" man once lived as the First Nations, has been colonized, proselytized, oppressed and assimilated! First, it all started out as city-states then Empires! Ancient Mesopotamia, Catal Huyuk, Sumeria, Egypt, India, Isreal, Greeks, Romans, French, British, Dutch, Portugal, Spain, Germany all were Empires that had to undergo colonization, proselytization, oppression and assimilation! Britain alone underwent numerous invasions and colonization.

The British present themselves superior to everyone else but the truth is they are no better than anyone else is and in fact, have only replaced themselves as that which they hated for centuries, their oppressors. They are now doing the oppressing! Furthermore, white people were colonized and oppressed by black people, so much for white supremacy! How did that happen?

It sounds like we are saying that oppression and assimilation is like an abusive relationship. The abuser mistreats the victim and in the case of the British Empire started out no different than we Neechi's, but over hundreds of years and multiple invasions and colonization's, they convinced themselves the lies of their colonizers, that they were savage, barbaric, heathens and they needed to civilize themselves, Christianize and assimilate their own family groups. They literally locked themselves up in a mental prison with apparition bars they call culture, deluded with constructions of reality that have them convinced the prison they are in is really an Empire. They have locked themselves away inside a dark place and are afraid to resist. Then they proceeded to repeat the patterns of abuse on others, their children and then other groups. The people of the so-called or formerly called, United Kingdom, what do they call themselves nowadays anyways?

Just as someone was about to answer the historian, someone impersonated "The Rock" yelling aloud, *IT DOESN'T MATTER WHAT THEY CALL THEMSELVES* and everyone laughed!

Anyways, the Romans also had their own version of the paternalism, patriarchy, religion and Roman-centric gaze and called the people of that island savages! Imagine that, the great and mighty British were savages! With all the raping and enslavement, they are not even the pure race they think they are, and they went around believing in their racism, that they were the master race!

Master-bator more like it someone said and they all laughed!

The Romans too believed they were saving the Britons from their uncivilized ways, their barbarism, and their savagery. The Romans truly believed they were doing the people a favor! But even the Romans underwent so many invasions and colonization's themselves, they too were nearly wiped out!

I guess after several hundred years of invasions, which included brutal rape, starvation, murder and mayhem, the people of that Island began to develop their culture in their own environment of instability, insecurity, lack of safety and proper attachment style. They must have conformed under conditions of duress, having undergone their own rituals of torture, coming to believe in their own worthless identity and accepting the assimilation conditions as presented! They too must have become a Warrior society!

They certainly became a warring society with infighting, with much bloodshed, and certainly with their own concept of what it means to be a Warrior society, but they were not like our Warrior society. Ours is very different.

Then a deep Thor sounding voice entered the conversation. It has the potential to become dysfunctional but I think that is why we are all here today, said an Anglo-Saxon Warrior.

When you speak of resistance against the great corruption, we too have a resistance movement and we have maintained our old traditional ways over many hundreds of years, like you, hidden underground. Not all of us are wholly consumed! We have our own Elders back home. And they call them witches or witch doctors, gypsies or *the old ones who know the old ways* they say in reference to our Elders.

Wartime is a very hard time for everyone. Wartime requires everyone to be united and anyone who is not with the group is a traitor or collaborator. No one trusts anyone. People must conform as the situation demands it. It is very difficult to remain neutral. The enemy says that those who stand by doing nothing are traitors too. So the people are hard-pressed from both sides, the people can only run away from the madness, they become refugees or some choose sides, win or lose. The parents demand their children fall into line and if the children learn too slowly they are beaten to speed up the learning process. But your right, your white kid from town could care less about that, their privilege affords them ignorance.

Then others gathered in, surely, people know about all of this and many began to murmur. There was growing excitement among the group now and many came to say hello to the Anglo-Saxon appreciating their resistance to the great corruption.

This is not something the British monarchy and those who still pay homage to the Royal throne care to admit said the Anglo-Saxon Warrior.

The Royal Throne, someone says laughingly and everyone joined in laughing as they remembered how their families refer to the toilet as a Throne. Even the Anglo-Saxon laughed because he felt comfortable among freedom fighters and shared the same perspective of the bemusing humor. The Anglo-Saxon continued.

Well they became a Warrior society and then some! They managed to affect the modern world!

They cannot and will not see that it is their oppressive behavior, creating the predicaments many colonized find themselves, others agreed.

It may be they capitalize on the problem they create paying people to fix it, and then tax them, replied another. And so the charity institutions of the old days received public funding through charity and taxes collected to address the "Indian problem", which includes Metis and Innu people.

The Metis and Innu are included in this "Indian problem" because racists, who often do not think they are racists, cannot escape their racist beliefs. For these racists, The *Indian* includes Metis and Innu people, even though ethnically and culturally these are very different people. It escapes them that diversity would exist even among the term *Indian*. They are not even aware that "Indian" is a word that originated in racist times and comes from a racist mindset projected on to the diverse First Nations, Metis and Innu people. The term "Indian" best serves the "white" man in the enactment of the most racist piece of legislation in the history of Canada, THE INDIAN ACT.

THE INDIAN ACT

What's the Indian Act eh my darling? What's the Indian Act asked the foolish one. But the foolish one asked a very good question indeed!

Sitting alone by the fire, a *Lone Wolf Warrior* dressed in traditional regalia, war paint and had many strange tattoos. All over The Lone Wolf's body were written the names, places and symbols of all the victims of colonization in Canada. On the left arm, close to the heart, Helen Betty Osborn, on the right shoulder, where the upper cut and powerful right hook roll up, J. J. Harper, over the chest Stonechild, and belly, *Starlight Tour.* Brian Sinclair and all the names of missing and murdered women. RCMP sexual harassment and their alleged, neglect with Robert Pickton, as well as Ashley Smith, among Corrections were all tattooed in such a way as to tell the story of indignity, inhumanity and gross misconduct. Children's names were tattooed on muscular arms, chest, hands, legs and neck, such as Phoenix Sinclair and Jeffrey Baldwin. All written in script and calligraphies "gangsta" style. The Lone Wolf Warrior had the official emblem of the Aboriginal Justice Inquiry tattooed across his chest overwriting the emblem, was a circle with a line crossed down the middle indicating the deceit of the emblem. There were the victim's faces so well known to Canadians through media photos all tattooed over his body. Derek Huff a former Edmonton Police officer who stood against many in the Edmonton Police Service for their silence toward Police Brutality, was inscribed too in honor of the resistance. With a *never again* attitude, The Lone Wolf wore as a testimony against oppression, as a personal protest against abusers, racists, ignoramus', memorializing the fallen, as a living expression of hope and resistance.

The Indian Act, foolish one, is at worst, the enactment of modern slavery expressed at its fullest legislated power in Canada, at least, the Canadian government would say it is meant to be paternalistic.

Paternalism is where the government acts like a paternal parent to *his* little Indian children. A group of "white" men decided to ensure the Indian was well under the scrutiny and power of "white" man from town! Without consultation with those whom they had just struck treaty, without representation of Canadian people, without any "Indian" present, they made a law that meant "Indians" would become wards of the state.

Being wards of the state, Indians could no longer buy or sell anything without the permission of the Canadian government. Not a cow, crow, crop or arrow could be sold without the permission of the oppressive Indian Agent, usually of British descent I might add!

Even when we starved, crops we worked with peasant style farming common to feudal systems, hoes and rakes, all wasted because "white" man from town would not buy from Indian's or we could not sell it even if we wanted to.

Apparently, we were too successful being better farmers than many "white" man from town. So they took away all of our tools and gave us hoes and rakes to work with, but still, we were better farmers. So they did everything to prevent us from participating as equals in the Canadian system. And so much for the lazy Indian stereotype to, we were better at most things than they.

The Indian Act, foolish one, gives them all the power to do whatever they want to Indians. They could amend it so that a road or golf course could be built in reserve land, which makes the term "reserve" pointless if they keep encroaching upon it.

We could not leave the reserve without permission from the Indian Agent, this was called the pass system. Indian agents directed band councils, when they had no business doing that as it was not in their jurisdiction, but they did it anyway.

They even made it against the law for a lawyer to represent Indians for land claims. In the past they would never consult with First Nation people because they did not have to, lately, they must consult in some cases. We expect changes to Indian education, which the government says is revolutionary, but the government gets the final say about it, and though they may consult, they do not have to take anything we say about it seriously. In fact, they still get to manage us as if we are their little Indian children, which is called paternalism, as if we need a great white father who knows best. We do not get to govern ourselves.

This is modern day slavery. Just a few laws need to be changed and Canada will be able to exterminate Indians legally, just as the assimilation programs, and they are doing that right now. The Indian Act allows them to do so, and it's all legal. They changed laws, made amendments so that our language, traditional teachings, culture, could be exterminated, acts of genocide.

They did that to Jews in Poland, where it was illegal for a Jew to sit on a park bench. Just a few changes and Canadians will collaborate with the military, police, justice, in rounding up all of us and transporting us away from the cities and townships, to begin their exterminations. Schools will be used to process us, camps will be erected to hold us, and our children will legally be ripped away from families, never to be seen or heard from again. Social workers and civil servants will collaborate in processing and administrating justice. We have seen it before, we see it now and it can get worse, with just a couple changes to laws.

Is that why the Idle No More movement started, asked the young one.

Precisely.

There are new laws made in Manitoba recently, reminiscent of the laws passed in Warsaw Poland, in World War Two, forbidding the Jews from sitting on public park benches and later Jews were not allowed to be in the park at all.

The Manitoba government is funding programs that have social services collaborating with police. These services identify which families are at risk and service providers will intervene allegedly to provide support. Another law they are considering is one that will allow food and beverage services, residents and others to collaborate with police in identifying gangland homes and gangsta's.

The public will be able to make a phone call, the police will come and remove the suspected gangsta from the premises, and they will be barred. Or the house they are at will be banned from having alcohol. Clearly, these laws are similar to the oppression of Jews in Warsaw Poland.

Much like Harper's *get tough on crime policy*, which takes a pre-emptive, first strike policy against gangsta's. They cannot and will not see these laws have the potential to infringe on human rights, discriminate against groups, will serve to further oppress the people who are victims of our corrupted society, those who are in poverty the most, the children. The reason is apparent in Dr. Bob Altemeyer's work on authoritarianism. Even though we point out the conflicts clearly apparent in the Bible, they cannot or will not see it. The same goes for the situation of oppression and white supremacy. They cannot or will not see it.

Because of the Indian Act, we do not have the same rights as many Canadians. The Indian Act is used to whittle away our treaty rights and we have to fight to get them back! Our leaders have debated them successfully arguing our treaty rights and in law, their own laws could not protect their delusional sense of superiority. The courts have been in our favor time and time again. Yet, this Indian Act remains to thwart all of our efforts to be free from the paternalistic tutelage of white man from town. It is only recently the Nisga are allowed to own their own property and to sell it or rent it.

But how specifically does the Indian Act stop us from being free? I am Indian and I live in the city, free to do whatever I want!

Bah! You have to give up treaty rights if that's how you choose to live. They change the laws so that if you live in the city, you pay by giving up something. Just like these gun owners. They want to own guns they have to be willing to give up the right to live free from police infringing on their right to privacy. The police are allowed to enter their homes without a search warrant.

It is the same for those who leave the reserve. You have given up some of your treaty right. If you're not doing so yet, you will have to pay taxes. This is a violation of treaty rights, as First Nations should not have to pay taxes. But they allege you give up some of your rights when you move to the city. Suddenly your treaty rights are encroached, just like how they encroach on the land. They only exist on reserve or at least that's what they want, to whittle away what little you have left. They will take your soul too if you let them.

This is called enfranchisement. They want to take away all your treaty rights so that you have nothing left and you become a white man, paying taxes to support the great white shark, I mean father.

The people chuckled a bit at the facetiousness of the Lone Wolf Warrior.

Specifically, because we are wards of the state, we are considered vulnerable people and the government has stripped us of our right to own property, to buy and to sell, for many years. It is the government that decides how much money we can use.

Remember the news, foolish one, the Attawapiskat financial and housing problem where the Chief and band council declared a state of emergency in their community. It was the Indian Act, which prevented the Chief and Band Council from being able to meet their housing needs.

Many are not aware that because of the Indian Act, there needs to be a bureaucracy, an office or group of offices to oversee the management of the law. So white man from town created the department of Indian Affairs. This is a massive group of offices that has hired thousands of "white" men from town to oversee the administration of the Indian Act.

These "white" men from town have no cultural or linguistic understanding of the diverse groups of so-called *Indians* and so they have no idea what "Indians" need or want. They only know what they think Indians need and want based on their own self-righteous paternalistic ideology of white supremacy. Their beliefs systems, as some of your are describing, do not allow them to think outside of the box they create for themselves. They are not even aware that there really is no such thing as an "Indian problem".

They have no clue they have ascribed remedies to a problem that does not exist! And so, many thousands of "white" man from town have been applying these remedies, meanwhile, they are being paid top dollar for their work in the department of Indian Affairs.

They change the name every year, so I have no idea what they call it now, but for me, it is the department of Indian affairs. Some say, Northern Development, others call it whatever they call it.

Just then some yelled out, *IT DOESN'T MATTER WHAT THEY CALL THEMSELVES!*

Yah some cried out!

Howweeneck! Lets see eh, be quiet and listen, others said!

For me, it is a bureaucracy of "white" man from town getting rich on the "*prison industrial complex*" as Angela Davis describes in the U.S., for us, it is called the Indian Act and Child Welfare Services, Public Education, Social Services, Indian Affairs, and the reserve system here in Canada. All of it profits the white man from town.

Indians are objectified, ghettoized, administrated by an expensive bureaucracy that lacks transparency, accountability and Canadians blame Indians for it as if it was an Indian problem. When in truth, because the government has a special interest here, the rank and file Canadian citizen has no business with the Indian Act and treaties. They must defer to the authority.

Since 1876 when it was first enacted, generations of people were given careers in this department all of them, "white" man from town. It is the operating cost of this overblown pointless bureaucracy which is their answer to a problem that does not exist, which obscures the real culprit from accountability, the "white" man from town and their yachts, summer homes, higher education accessibility, modern homes and vehicles, fancy cloth's to maintain their delusional sense of wealth, power and status.

They say we Indians have special status and many argue we should not have any special status that we should all be equal but they are ignorant. If anyone has special status, it is these delusional ones who think their money will buy them respect and self esteem. The cost to their belief in status, power and wealth and their insatiable appetite for these things is never a price too high! It is not Chief Spence, as the media and other white supremacists believe, it is they themselves!

By the time the money reaches the band office, and the money is in the hands of Chief Spence, there is nothing left to work with! And so the First Nations offices and the people are left with debt they inherited in a vain attempt to meet the people's needs. Debt comes from paying for "white" man from town's, town houses and town cars as everyone, not just Indians have their hands in the cookie jar! But it remains convenient to blame the real victims, those left with what is left over after everyone else has helped themselves.

This is not just with Indians and reserve system funding. It is in every facet of our society where financial irregularities exist, which is wherever financial management exists! Not just Indians, EVERYONE is helping themselves to money. From the board of directors, to the Executive Director on down to the support worker who rounds up the mileage to get just a few bucks more out of the proverbial cookie jar. There is corruption in the Senate, in politics, in government, bureaucracies, departments, divisions, among office personnel and it is rampant! Even the great and powerful Deloitte and Touche LLP could not fully disclose the real financial issues present. Their wording was carefully crafted so as not to bite the hand that feeds them.

If there were no Indian Act, Indians would be free to govern themselves free from paternalistic tutelage of "white man from town". If we rid ourselves of this Act, we not only free Indians, but we free all Canadians from at least one piece of corrupted law which clearly has racism deeply embedded within it.

"Oh", said the foolish one.

Though many ignorant white people and other ethnicities, which should be grateful to Aboriginal people they have a safe place to live rather than their own war torn countries which they escaped continue to blame Chief Spence!

They conveniently forget they have their own smokescreens, unaccountable leaders in their own politics and governance. 2013 will forever be known for its corruption and poor management, from the RCMP sexual molestation of female officers, racism apparent in the Pickton case, Police brutality across Canada, systemic racism run rampant like Manitoba Health, Quebec mafia corruption to the senate and the prime ministers office, to Mayors of Winnipeg and Toronto making the news and the now defunct and but if not corrupted, then totally incompetent police at East St. Paul Manitoba. All of this should be no surprise to anyone. What is surprising to me, said the lone wolf, is that they will likely forget 2013 white corruption and recall Attawapiskat, Idle No More movement, Elsipogtog resistance movement as a bunch of terrorists, bloodthirsty savages, criminals with a *burn the witch mentality*!

I remember a friend told me they found ten thousand dollars in an envelope that was inside a box at work. Apparently, no one missed it. It was unaccounted for with a strict accounting system.

How does one find ten thousand dollars just sitting around an office?

It would appear someone was lining their pockets! Someone at that agency figured out a way to make money disappear without being noticed.

That's not an Aboriginal agency either! One could surmise the amount of corruption permeates throughout society and is not just another Indian problem, but rather it is a social problem.

Recall in Manitoba the Middlechurch scandal. One wonders what is going on across Canada. A simple Google search would provide anyone, should they care to enquire as to the extent of corruption that is inherent in Canadian society. There's lots of scandals occurring, lots!

Let's not forget, continued the lone wolf, Canada is among the top wealthiest nations in the world! That means this is as good as it gets! If there is an elite group that is manipulating everything, Canada is among them.

Throughout all history, there has always been a class system of the poor, the middle class, administrators of welfare and policing and the upper class, royalty. Canada being among the top rulers of the world means Canada is royalty.

The average income is apparently 35 thousand a year. The poorest is under 20 thousand. The highest 140 thousand and up. All approximate guestimates. Yet, our politicians who make at least a hundred grand a year plus any bonuses they may legitimately and legally receive, sit among the very elite of Canadian society with their income as much or as nearly as 400 thousand dollars a year! Yet, they are being caught more and more with their hands in the cookie jar, and for what, an additional ten thousand? Is that worth the effort? I mean really!

Everyone was thoughtful for a few moments.

Is it just me or has Canada become entirely corrupt lately, the lone wolf continued liking the attention.

Every time yous kids go to school, each day, every time yous study and get A's in classes and subjects, every time yous stay out of trouble, every time yous kids volunteer to help your community or get a part time job somewhere while you go to school, get involved in extra curricular activities, like band and drama classes, is an act of resistance and you are a revolutionary! Every time yous teenagers stay in school, no matter how hard white supremacists make it for you, you are engaging in acts of resistance. You young parents, who face poverty, but rise above it are freedom fighters. All yous young people, young adults, when you learn to be responsible, take responsibility for you actions, choices and decisions, yous are resisting against the power of the Indian Act. When yous young people go to bed early and wake up fresh to get to your *pointments*, yous are freedom fighters! Revolutionaries. Especially when yous get help and resist the gangs, yous are REAL WARRIORS!

If yous are in gangs and selling dope to your own people, even as I once did, yous are engaging in acts of treason against your families, yous are collaborating with the white supremacists! Oh nothing could be better justification to the white man when he sees you selling dope, he says, "See, I told you they were bad". Oh they love seeing that, they laugh and they say, "goood, goooood, we weren't wrong see, look at them, savages"! But many of yous do not understand this truth. So do not take this personally, it is not said to be judgmental or mean spirited. We are all aware that the great corruption has confused everything. Think about that!

The lone wolf warrior continued to look on into the fire introspectively, wondering if anything got through.

Though the victims of human atrocities have spoken out against their oppressors, it was always met with visceral reactions of denial, much like that of a spousal abuser or child abuser would deny their abuse, continued the group.

The new phrase en vogue these days is to "defend themselves rigorously" against allegations. But in Canada, the evidence is clear! Historians, time after time have written page after page about the injustices and the lies Canadians tell themselves about the true nature of their nation building. There have been the Aboriginal Justice Inquiry, the Saskatchewan Justice Inquiry, The Royal Commission on Aboriginal people, all legal documents all empirical pedagogy. These documents are no longer questioned in its presentations, though many have tried in vain, they are clearly reaching. In spite of its clarity, the Canadian people continue to use these mental acrobats to deny their involvement and in doing so, they perpetuate the oppression of Aboriginal people. The longer bystanders look on and do nothing, to intervene in obvious assaults, oblivious and willfully blind, they sanction and approve of oppression. It is as if they are telling the tormentor that it is just and acceptable to continue to torture their victim in full view of public spectacle. This is all in spite of a multi-billion dollar industry of research.

Likewise, in so doing, they ritualistically say this too happened to me, they also say we should get over it, it happened already!

BACK TO THE SLAVIC RACES

But it is also noteworthy that it was the "Slavic" races, in this racist system, that advocated for equality as they were the primary immigrants and consequently, voters across Canada.

Public outcry as Dr. Fred Shore describes it caused the Alberta government of the day to treat with the Metis people and Alberta.

To this day, Alberta is the only province to have done so another cried out alarmingly!

But still, racism exists among many Ukrainian people presently all across Canada, replied another.

Those Ukrainian's must have forgotten their own history, being in a place of privilege here would make the horror of oppression in their own country easy to forget, said another.

All other provinces, namely Manitoba a province created by Metis, where Metis people are from, to this day, refuse to acknowledge the Metis and especially oppressive toward Aboriginal people.

The public outcry came from Ukrainian people said one Metis.

They would see Metis families along the roadsides starving and begging for food. It was an unbearable sight and so the people cried out to their governments to address this indignity, this inhumanity.

Surely, the Ukrainians saw in the Metis that which they fled in their own countries, said some.

Surely, the Metis triggered many Ukrainian people, said others.

Either that or they were sick and tired of being asked to give charity in the churches and pulpits, said others.

The Canadian government gave in a little as they reluctantly eased their punishment on Metis people for their resistances, as Canadians demanded the punishment to stop.

Punishment, cried some?

Paternalism, cried others, patriarchy!

To this day, if you compare any situation across Canada regarding Aboriginal people and the oppression they face, Winnipeg, Manitoba has the worst conditions of oppression.

In Winnipeg, there are the worst conditions of poverty due to poor education, access to health services and social supports. It is not because of the old stereotype that Indians are lazy, though that is precisely what "white" man from town would have you believe! No, it is due to a lack of financial resources made available to Aboriginal communities in a fair and equitable manner that is transparent and accountable. It has been shown repeatedly over the years that most of all financial resources made available in the public education system is made more available to communities with "white" kids. The South end of Winnipeg, where most white kids live, gets more funds than the North End of the city, where many Aboriginal kids tend to over-represent. The South ends of the province of Manitoba, where white people over-represent get more than the North, where Aboriginal people over-represent.

This is undeniable and anyone who cares to do the research will find this to be an accurate representation of the reality of racism in Canada.

You can Google it if you want they said and many took out their devices and were now taking notes.

There are even videos online that are available another interjected.

We are being punished because the *Riel Resistances* occurred here many said!

They take care of their own, others cried!

Many wondered if this could really be true! Are the Canadian governments and Canadian people really punishing Aboriginal people for their part in the great resistances? Can the false history of the so-called Riel Rebellion we learned in our public education system be affecting non-Aboriginal people on how they perceive *natives*?

There was much whispering and growing murmuring now. Connections were being made.

But how do we address this situation many asked. How do we reason with that thing which privileges itself in status, wealth and power while it justifies itself to the people as the savior in all of its self-righteousness. How do we bargain without collaborating with it when it will not bargain *unless* we collaborate, conform? How do we negotiate with those who refuse to negotiate? How do we resist the great corruption that is all around us? How do we escape the terror and the horror? Many were afraid.

That is why they came to see the Elders. We see this beast in our dreams!

I have these flashbacks, said another. When I hear a song from the old days, when I was a child, or on some certain days when the sun shines just so, or when a wind blows, or the path I am on reminds me. I suddenly remember many sad things that happened. I guess I must have heard this song playing when I was trying to sleep or when I woke up after a late night party.

I would get myself ready for school and as I left, I would have to step over the bodies of all these people who were passed out on the floor. I would have to go to school without any breakfast. I went to school like that a lot. It was normal. When I came back home for something at lunchtime, no one was awake. I remember wondering if they would still be there sleeping when I got home. I also remember wondering what the point was in coming home for lunch when I already knew there was no food or parents at home. For a long time I guess I was being triggered by songs. I would be instantly transported back to sad times, I would even lose touch with reality for a few seconds and whomever I was with would have to call me back.

I would blink and wonder why they seemed so concerned. They told me that my eyes went glossy and distant and I froze into a position, staring blankly and they said I was unresponsive when they called me. I didn't know I was doing that either! When I was stressed out, bills, kids, relationships, I would ruminate and I would flashback. It made me very depressed. I would lose hope. I guess, for many years I lived in hell and in terror from the racism around me, the racism I lived through, the racism my parents lived through and their parents. I guess I was living in hell.

I had no idea it had nothing to do with me. I always thought it was something I did, that I deserved this shit. I felt like I didn't deserve anything better.

And I remember walking home from school in grade seven, as another joined in the conversation, I would get these jitters the closer I got to the house. Going home meant presenting myself for abuse. I had to prepare myself mentally and it was unnatural to present myself for the ritual of torture but it's all I ever knew, all I had and I had no other place to go. I would look to see if the curtains were out of place. The closer I got I would listen for sounds. I think I was scouting, to make sure all was clear to go inside the house. I remember walking up to the door and looking inside first, to make sure everything was all clear that everything was in place. When I opened the door, I would open it, quietly. I would look at the expressions on the faces of everyone in the house, searching for signs that all was clear. If I got any notion anything was wrong, I would turn around and head right back to school. If it was okay, I would walk quickly to my room and close the door behind me and I would stay in my room until it was time to eat. For a long time, I had forgotten that I did this. Then one day, while in therapy, I learned this is where my control issues originated. I also had this same ritual on my way to school too as I felt a lump in my throat thinking about how I would have to face bullies and bully teachers.

I guess I developed a ritual to protect myself and for a long time, I had to live a structured, predictable life where everything had to be in the right place so I could feel normal. If anything was out of place I would be irritated. I would get agitated and increasingly aggressive. It was like something would come over me, a dark foreboding cloud. People describe it as moody, others say it was intense, others said I gave off bad energy and it made them afraid.

Sometimes I would walk for hours after school. I found a couple favorite spots. These special locations were kinda like the one we're on now. They were sacred to me. I was often healed there. One was on Matheson where they put up a synagogue. When they kicked me off the grass there, I would walk over to a small museum just down the road where a Metis person once lived. But they kicked me out of there too sometimes so I would go on the swings, in the park beside it. Both were sacred spots.

Later, I would go for these long walks around my neighborhood and I would look at all these beautiful homes. They looked so Brady Bunch. Clean yards, a nice garage that was full of tools, motorbikes and other off road vehicles and a boat! I would sometimes see what's going on inside and it looked so warm and cozy inside. Even in summer, it looked so Christmasy. One day while walking I saw where one of the kids I go to school with lived, inside wearing a warm cozy sweater. He just promptly got up, walked over to the window, and slammed shut the curtains on me. I kept walking.

I was always observing, from within, always within, peering out like a small child seeing things for the first time. I walked a lot of miles watching how beautiful and most wonderful others lived. I was hidden inside, scared to show myself, terrified.

The whole city turned out to be my land in the end and I shouldn't have been kicked out in the first place.

Maybe that's why we all feel so insecure, piped up another. Maybe we learned that we were worthless, undeserving, useless people, in my case, Metis. Abuse was at home, then at school, and in the streets, at work, in business, abuse was everywhere! The teachers, the drunks, the lack of parents, the whole of Canadian society, totally oblivious of my suffering and if we spoke up, we were made to feel ashamed, we were shamed, they said, *shame on you*! Shaming, shame, judging me, judgmentalism, racism, conformism, over-policing, guilting me, to shame. Fuck I hate it when people say shame on you! Shame on them! SHAME ON THEM!

Bug eyed and with visceral hatred they would point their fingers at us, at me. They would blow their hands and rub them off as if "cooties" were on them and laugh calling me a dirty Indian, even though I was Metis. I learned to hate Indians for that, even though I didn't even know what an Indian was. I sure hated them! I hated them all, blacks, whites, nips, flips, paki's. It became debilitating after a while. I couldn't even leave the house anymore. It was as if I had done something shameful and I had to cover myself up and hide from people. But I don't really know what I did that was so shameful other than being born. Always, I tried to hide from peering eyes and pricking ears. They judged me, I was guilty, and I was ashamed of myself. I was ashamed of having children. I was ashamed of my own children! I was never allowed to speak of these things and when I did, I would hide in shame as if I did something that was very bad, forbidden! I would hide, scared at home hidden in my room waiting for the all clear.

It's kinda hard not to take things personally, said one, about the age of 15 summers. Agreed said another a few summers older.

It's not easy, said an older one. When I was younger, I hated going into a mall too. It felt like people were staring at me, like they were thinking and talking shit about me. When I was at home, watching a movie with my family and a scene would come on and I would laugh and say something about it, everyone would hush me. I just thought, *Holy*! Then I felt totally rejected, pushed away, discarded even hated. Sometimes, when they teased me, I always thought they were hating me, picking on me. My brother would walk up to me and slap my foot while I watched TV if I sat with legs crossed on the couch. Or he would pull my sock half way off. I always thought he hated me and this was how he showed it. Maybe he was showing his love but I was young and I didn't get it, I thought it was something else. I asked them to stop, but they thought it was funny and so with all that laughing going on, it was hard for them to stop, hard for them to see me suffering. I wonder....

The same thing happened in high school. The bullies would find my buttons, push them and it would piss me off! They laughed when I chased after them. They told me they loved to get a rise out of me. They had no idea they were adding to my suffering that I had from home. I'm glad there was a guidance counselor that I was able to speak to for a while. It really helped otherwise I might have hurt someone or myself. But I had to stop talking to him. Apparently, he would have to report what I am saying to the authority, as that was the law. I didn't want to bring the house down, but I should have. Things were getting pretty serious there for a while. Then I quit high school, found sex, drugs and rock-n-roll. I turned gangsta!

Speaking of "deserve", said another. All this talk about worthless and good for nothing reminds me of a whole life of being a doormat for everyone. I let one partner walk all over me, humiliate me. Then I was with another, years later and it was so wonderful, I couldn't even adjust to it. I began to sabotage the relationship. I didn't think it would ever work out cuz I was too fucked up. He didn't deserve to get hurt by me anyways, I woulda fucked it all up in the end so I may as well get a head start on everything. I didn't want to hurt no one, least of all the one I love. I remember wandering around the house feeling like it was all a dream that I would wake up soon. I couldn't sleep until about 2 hours before I had to wake up. I carried on like that for about 3 years. I'm still in a relationship, but we managed to keep it going, through thick and thin. I guess that's love. I guess I never felt like I deserved anything good in my life.

Whenever something good came along, I sabotaged it. I couldn't adjust. My normal was to be miserable. Anything that set me outside that normal was too foreign to me and I could not adjust. Though I knew I was supposed to live a better life, I only got so far. I only allowed myself to get so far and then I would sabotage it. I know now that can't be normal. I need help to adjust to new normal's that would benefit me. I guess I can't do that on my own, not yet anyway.

One who identifies as a Celtic Warrior shared saying, they grew up in Ireland with British rule over every aspect of their lives including British soldiers in the streets with machine guns. The British called the resistance, the Irish Republican Army, terrorists. It was all very confusing. Politics, religion, Catholics versus Protestants at the dinner table every night, oppression in the streets and alcoholism rampant with child abuses from the church and state as well as neglect and abuse from parents and caregivers occurred daily.

As the Celtic Warriors spoke, it was all reminiscent of Canadian colonization. Many marveled at the "white" folks who spoke of colonial oppression and racism in their homeland, and even here in Canada.

THE ROMAN PERSPECTIVE

Gallia includes Celtica, Belgica, Aquitania, (Southern Europe, France, Spain to Turkey) Celtica (Ireland, France, lower UK), Germania (Germany, Ukraine, Poland), Gallia were all geological locations inhabited by family groups of three to ten or more, very similar to First Nation, even in culture, originally. However, in Europe it was the Roman's who invaded, colonized, Christianized and assimilated those tribes, explained the Celtic Warrior. The Roman Empire wanted slaves so there were many raids, much horror of war for many hundreds, thousands of years. They were not interested in land and resources like Europeans today. We had to develop among the horrors, similar to the descriptions of many First Nation people. Alcoholism, mental health issues, turned our parents and caregivers into mean spirited people with the crazy eyes.

And there was no clinical psychologists to help with irritation, agitation, abuse and controlling people, helplessness and self loathing. The person you went to for help was likely the same person that abused you, fucked you, raped you. If it wasn't family it was a priest. It was like they would beat us so that we would be controlled, beaten into submission. It was a common thing, almost normal, why would anyone complain about normal things. We too were raised in dysfunction. There are many of us who have been resisting since the beginning too and many of our own people have turned against us, a type of civil war. It is very sad, very lonely for all our children.

RELATIVE SUFFERING AND DECOLONIZATION

I guess we all grew up feeling helpless. Some got it worse than others did and nothing compares to the suffering I endured. It was hard for me. But maybe I should be happy I didn't get it any worse, said another young initiate whose voice faded into mumbling, surprised for even speaking up, finding the voice.

Just then, the Lone Wolf Warrior with all the tattoos joined in, I think it's important for you to at least acknowledge your suffering. We lose sight of the problem if we all compare how much we suffered. All of our suffering is meaningful. We have all been through a lot. It is not a fair world sometimes Don't be too quick to dismiss your own pain and experiences out of a sense of guilt for what others went through. It's better to empathize and share the pain with grave respect. That's why you wouldn't want to wish your worst day on your enemies. When you realize that your revenge is futile, that it only adds to more suffering, then suffering and inhumanity will never end. It's not easy. It's a work in progress. With time and commitment, we may just make our contribution count. Right now, you are all still learning. Your priorities are all fucked up. Your values are all fucked up. You are like soldiers who have shell shock or soldiers who panic on the battlefield.

You are all hysterical, confused and running around out in the open, exposed and vulnerable. You are all easy pickings. Many who should be here are not because they would rather sleep in because they have stayed up late on Facebook or playing video games or using. They are the lost ones that need our help. But many of us have a long way to go because our priorities are all fucked up, we don't value what we should be valuing and we devalue what we should be valuing! That is because we have not fought hard enough for the things that we deserve, that is ours by rights and we have not won our lives back. We have not decolonized yet!

First, we must gain ground up here, in our minds, and here, in our hearts and to take back that which we have always protected, that sacred self. They will colonize not only your land, but your body too and they will enslave us all. So, we do not value ourselves because we have no appreciation for our self worth, dignity and self respect. Some are not even aware they have to fight hard to win back their own bodies, and then they can be more effective in fighting for their homeland. But until we stand up and win back lost ground, only then can we appreciate what we have worked so hard, only then can we learn to prioritize.

And some of us, have fought hard and because they do not appreciate what they have, they do not value what they have protected, they cannot appreciate how far they have come! Many have been trained to value material things, when these things do nothing for our spirit. Many have been trained to devalue their money because they have grown up in poverty, they have never had money before so now when they get it, and they spend right away. That's a welfare mentality! But that's not because of anything that is inherent in us as people, it is because of the world we were all born into, the training and education we have all received. It has fucked us all up! Yous kids must realize the gravity of the situation yous are all in!

With that, everyone was very thoughtful. Connections were being made. They were learning. Hope filled their hearts. Before this day had arrived, many were simply confused about the whole affair. They had accepted that there was nothing anyone could do, least of

111

all them. Many of them had accepted what they were taught about themselves, that they were useless, good for nothing, no good people. But now, things were going to be different. Inspiration was burning deep inside. They felt positive change coming.

Chapter 5

CEREMONY

And so, *everything happens first in the spirit world*. That is where we are going the Elder said to the young people who were now seeing more clearly into the meaning of their shared visions. The Elders could see that there were still many unanswered questions and many different perspectives needing different explanations. The young people were eager to learn. The Elder asked if everyone was ready and only one piped up saying they were born ready! The Elders and experienced Warriors laughed knowingly at the arrogance of the young fool, innocent as it was, it would soon be answered with great clarity. The young fool looked around nervously noticing no support for silliness, yet still tried to save face. Awkwardly, the young fool at first low, then in a crescendo of notes mixed with laughter the fool exclaimed, *Mmnnnleeeaaaahhhhh-ha ha ha haaaa*!

SAGE AND THE VISION QUEST

One in every crowd thought the Elder as he walked away slowly, smiling gently and silently over the incident. The Elder called the young people to smudge first and then to follow now as they walked into the sacred area where they were to fast.

The rules were simple. There is to be no talking to anyone whatsoever. There was no food or water available for the next four days and four nights. That is, save for a small half pint bottle of water given to each person. Some refused it, while others took it for safekeeping. The Elder explained that it was medicine for their Vision Quest. The Elder said they may need it, and they may not, but at least that it is there for them should they require it. All were to suffer and in their suffering, they were to cry out for a vision. The Bears and the Wolves sang and danced late into the night while other Bears and Wolves took their positions scouting and protecting along the perimeters. They would report throughout the night.

A bear and her cub were seen along the rivers edge and two owls spoke to each other before dawn. Both went off to their nests was one Warriors account. They would sleep in shifts. It was all very serious Warrior work and no one played any jokes about it, not once, ever.

When morning came, it came early for the young people, earlier than usual. Some were not used to fires and smoke. Some having lived on the Rez their whole life, had never even met an Elder before or knew what they do. Others came from the city. A few were not even Indians. Some were of Jewish descent, others called themselves "muts" or "mongrels" as they claimed to have no idea who or what ethnicity they developed.

Perhaps they meant to say they do not really ascribe to any ethnicity or rather this opinion may be an indication of their self-esteem or worth, because of their racialized environments. Mut or mongrel is a reference to a breed of dogs. The association with mut or mongrel seems to have an identity rooted in racism, when referring oneself as if they were a breed of a dog, even as racists referred to Metis as half-breed, as if Metis were two breeds of two dogs. Clearly, half-breed was not meant to be a compliment, but rather rooted in ignorance.

Others were of Philippino descent, and others Irish folk and still others, English. Some had no idea why they were there other than the fact they said they would try anything once.

They were all silent now and walking around in the hot morning sun wishing for their coffees and their bacon and egg breakfasts. Some thought about waffles and others wished for a muffin. All the young people wandered and wondered on that sacred prairie grass all day long silent and quiet. All that day, they no longer saw the Warriors who would remain off in the distance, out of site, watching over them. Even the counsel of Elders would come and look in on the young people during their fast that day, careful not to disturb them. The young people may not have known it, but many great Warriors carefully guarded them. These young people were special, they would have a vision, they would share with the people, and healing would come.

Great care was taken, every measure ensured healing would come.

But first, they had to sacrifice themselves, giving themselves over for the sake of the children, for seven generations. They gave up the comforts of their beds, their distractions of gaming, television series, air-conditioned bedrooms, smart phones and androids, tablets, computers, socializing, drinking, using, and all the comforts that high society offers.

They are now hot, sweaty and grimy having no showers or access to water. They are sitting silently underneath the lone tree huddled together trying to find shelter from the hot sun. Even as the sun moves across the sky, East to West so too the shadow that looms before them, West to East and they are following it carefully, sharing it, without a word said.

In all of the strangeness, someone has to pee and it's strange because peeing runs contrary to the concept of maintaining hydration. Yet, everyone affords each other the privacy and dignity of the act, again silently and without a word spoken. What wonder to behold the humanity, the dignity and the respect as they are united in a cause. No one had to teach them any specific religious teaching it was intuitive. Even the fool knew better.

That night all dreamed strange dreams. They were vivid and in color. The sounds were clear and bright. They saw images of beings and things talking to them. For one, a horse walked right up and started talking in clear English and another spoke with their dead grandmother. Streaks of wind flashed across the night sky, South to North visiting the dreamers and spoke ancient words of wisdom. Zeus, God of the Greeks stepped down from mount Olympus and sat among the young people dreaming, just listening to their dreams. A black cat walked across the field that night and shivered in the cold night air. No evil came to them because the helpers had laid the ground with protection medicine.

CEDAR

Cedar, South on the medicine wheel, when placed on the ground creates an infinite barrier for the visionaries so that evil avoids crossing it. Evil cannot stand the sweet loving aroma of this powerful protection medicine. Their nose goes dry and they begin to sneeze and their eyes water. It is said that when a person claims to be allergic to the medicines, it is not the allergy in the scientific sense of the word, but rather it is revealing the ignorance and the corruption which evil has attached itself to the person. Demons can't stand the smell of traditional medicines burning, the person can. When such individuals learn more and are more respectful of the medicines, they are cured of their allergies miraculously.

The next day was hotter than ever and more than ever, they thirsted. They had no energy left to wander or wonder much. Again, they shared the shade of the lone tree on the prairie. Grimier and sweatier they huddled and perhaps it was because they were so thirsty and tired, they did not talk at all. They barely looked at each other. They felt they did not have to anymore, they were connected to all things.

They were connected to themselves, each other, the earth and all that was in it, the moon and star people, the night sky and the sun. They were connected to the star people and all things throughout the universe. They felt everything. Even sounds could be felt. Light could be felt. That day, they saw water in the air all around them. As they looked out into the prairies, surrounded by tall prairie grass they felt as though they could breath it all in and exhale peacefully, calmly and gently. So they did, they lived precisely in the moment and though they did not know it, they were practicing mindful-meditation, the ability to let go all dysfunctional mindfulness and be in the moment. All thoughts and worries, fears, frustrations and morbid reflection were gone. They breathed deeply all day long. They were very sacred.

In fact, they did not know it but this is precisely how all Warriors once lived, before the great corruption came, all day long, every day, in the moment experiencing all the great mystery offers. It was ceremony that gave them this ability to be so respectful even in the face of colonization, Christianization and assimilation. They were balanced and in tune, harmonious with the medicine wheel. They had a sense that all was sacred and they were able to think clearly and concisely. They could see the spirit in all life, even in the grandfathers, those so-called stones that were heated for the Sweat Lodge ceremony. They could see the spirit in the tree and the prairie grass and the Tobacco medicine and the earth they walked upon, all was sacred. Even every breath they took which gave them life. This was worth it, this was worth saving for the sake of the children, for seven generations. No wonder so many gave their lives for their culture, these traditional ways. No wonder the children of the earth resisted the great corruption!

The fire was kept by helpers away in the distance and they could smell the medicines and the smoke. The sun again moved East to West and the shade, which they took shelter again, West to East. The Elders watched and saw the young people moving with it. The slightest touch of sunlight could be felt and they strained to stay in the shade. It was global warming that made this autumn feel like a longer than usual summer. For the first time flies were seen in the high north where they were never before seen and so, strange things are afoot and things out of balance.

They were graceful and beautiful in the hot sun. The Elders saw that they were not alone.

When the third night came upon them many had reached out to their bottle of medicine. No one drank the medicine in one fell swoop. Many had a half sip just before bed. There were others who were unsure about the protocols and so they watched and observed. Some observed the First Nation and Metis thinking they knew what to do when in fact, because these traditions were most savagely and barbarically outlawed by the Canadian government for several generations, they had no idea about what to do. On the contrary, it was the Samurai and the Wushu, the Celts and the Anglo-Saxon Warriors who had more of an understanding about what was occurring.

How they dreamed that night! Their dreams were more vivid than before. It was as if they had not even fallen asleep but rather closed their eyes and were in another world, other dimensions, other times and places. One woke to the sound of a great Owl calling from up yonder and was suddenly awake, alert and upright on the ground. This one was not afraid, but rather perplexed. Why was that sound so loud and clear? Again, it was heard but no one else was awake. Slowly reaching for the water medicine and taking a swig, relaxation came and soon more visions. The owl is a messenger.

The next morning and still hotter than ever all were clearly exhausted, famished and very thirsty. Although they were grimy and clammy, no one stank but instead smelled like April fresh downy or bounce in the drier. The young visionaries could see that the Warriors had returned and they looked mightier than ever before. Perhaps it was their weakened state or they were very sacred but when they looked upon the Warriors, they saw magnificent looking people and they were awestruck.

It appeared that preparations were being made. There was some hustle and bustle. All the young people saw someone new among the counsel of Elders. He spoke with them at times and laughed with them. This tall man was dressed funny, as if ready to enter a sweat on one-half, while on the other, ready to go to the office. He had a towel in his hand. He walked among everyone talking and laughing, asking many questions. It seemed dumb to ask so many questions when it appeared that he already knew the answers for most. Most of the Warriors ignored him, as they were very busy. Then the heat wave came upon them and they began to make their way to the beloved tree. Silently they waited in desperation.

Suddenly the tall man approached the young people but stopped short of the Cedar barrier. "Whoa! I don't wanna cross that" he said laughing aloud. Apparently, he must have come from another community hearing about the ceremony. "How is everyone doing" he asks them? No one spoke. "Oh yeah that's right too eh, your not supposed to talk to anyone I guess". Still no one spoke. The tall man laughed kicking at the dirt on the ground at his feet. He strode along the Cedar barrier telling stories about his first Vision Quest. The tall man did not like that no one was talking to him. Every now and then when he asked a question or looked for acknowledgment, the tall man saw that no one was listening or watching and he would scowl disapprovingly.

"How many days now" he asks? "Third" said the foolish one walking over to the edge careful not to cross the cedar barrier. The tall man laughed so hard the Elders looked up to see what was going on. "I see you drank most of your water" said the tall man laughing, always laughing. The foolish one looked at his water bottle and was encouraged by the fact that only one small sip was taken from it. The foolish one said "yah, there's not much left eh. I don't know if I'm gonna make it eh" smiling. The tall man returned the smile with a smirk in contempt. The others watched disapprovingly at the foolish one.

What the hell does he think he's doing they all thought as they watched him talking away. The tall man looked hard at the foolish one with a huge grin on his face he knelt down and sat cross-legged to face the young one. His eyes were keen and bright and very inquisitive to the foolish one talking as if nothing was the matter. They spoke a lot of nonsense, the weather, and the experiences. When the tall man asked the foolish one what he saw in his visions, the foolish one did not answer. The foolish one only stared long and hard at the tall man who was now looking down on the foolish one with that same huge grin. They understood one another. The tall man getting up to face the group said, "what about the rest of you, what did you see? There was a pause, what's the matter? Cat got your tongues he said laughing aloud. No one said a word. The young one as if released from a spell swooned and felt a headache coming on. "Hellooooo, anybody home"! "ANYBODY HOME" this time his voice was loud and hoarse and his eyes became black as night and then in an instant he became his old self again, laughing and laughing. Instead, they wondered why is this person talking to them when surely this person is aware of the rules. Who is this person? Why is he here? Why are the Elders and Warriors letting him talk to them? All were annoyed.

It was the foolish one who looked on with the tall man and they both laughed at the group. The group did not understand the relationship that presented itself before them. The group of young people wondered if this was some sort of trick. Was this a spy? Is this spirit? Should we be afraid? The foolish one and the tall man laughed again as if knowing what they were thinking.

The tall man said, "If your wondering if you should be afraid, you should be" and he laughed and laughed. "You are all probably thinking that I am some sort of spirit" he said and laughed at them. The others, astonished tried to appear unconcerned. "I remember my first Vision Quest" he said laughing and grinning. "By the third day you will all be half in the spirit world and half in this world.

You are all nearly dead now. We are all watching! Waiting"! The group looked on at the two who laughed and laughed. "We shall see, we shall see" said the tall man as he walked away laughing.

The group looked and they saw the foolish one appear to feign in the hot sun, swooning. Two young people walked out of the shade and helped the foolish one back to the tree. They gave the foolish one a sip of medicine and then another. The foolish one slept nearly all that morning.

THE SWEAT LODGE

Thereafter the Elders came to the group and asked them to follow along the Cedar path to the sweat lodge. Be very careful not to cross over the Cedar the Elders told the young initiates. As the group of young people followed along, the Warriors looked upon them wide eyed and astonished because they could see that this group of young people are now very sacred. One by one, they entered into the sweat lodge. The foolish one wondered how this could be done after three days in the hot sun? How and why would I allow myself to enter a sweat lodge to sweat out what little hydration is left in me? Why am I doing this? Why is my body moving and why am I not stopping myself? I go to my death. Still, the foolish one entered the lodge asking all of these questions.

The helpers heated 28 stones in a sacred fire, these hot stones are called Grandfathers. After seven grandfathers were heated by the sacred fire to the point of glowing red hot, the helper brought them into the lodge one at a time and they were all greeted by the Elder who said, *Ah boozhoo Nokomis*, meaning greetings grandfather. "Door"! shouted the Elder. The helper pulled on the tarpaulin and sealed the group inside. It was now pitch black save for the soft red glow from the grandfathers in the center of the lodge. The lodge was heating up!

The foolish one could not see the hand that was brought up to the nose it was so dark. The Elder explained the history of the Sweat Lodge Ceremony. They were now back in their mother's womb, the womb of Mother Earth! When they leave, they will be reborn and have been cleansed by Mother Earth's sacred water.

The Elder handed out rattles for everyone. Then the Elder led the group with a song, which was chanted aloud four times, and the drum and the rattles kept the time for the song. When the song sung after a long time, the lodge got hotter. Speaking uses physical properties like a rattle when shaken makes spiritual properties and this is how we communicate back to the spirit world. That is why we have rattles, drums, whistles and chants. The Elder had what is called medicine, which was then poured over the grandfathers, and a great and tumultuous reaction occurred where hot gasses suddenly filled the lodge and the steam of it was very hot. It was so hot that some thought they were on fire. Others felt cold like ice frost had suddenly come upon them. Moaning and groaning could be heard as the medicine was poured over the grandfathers. Great suffering was occurring now. Many were gasping for breath. Others inhaled deeply and calmly knowing all would be well. More medicine was poured and more hot vapors could be heard steaming and crackling in reaction to the grandfathers. And then the Elder stopped pouring the medicine and he gave a teaching while everyone listened.

Maybe the grandfathers, these red-hot rocks represent the seed of men as it enters the womb. Maybe the water medicine represents the life bearers' ovum and the sounds and crackling represent the union of birth even as they sit and relive their own birth. The Eagle screamed and rattles were sounded. Someone yelled, from inside the lodge, "SEMAH" and outside could be heard a faint response, "okay"! Still the heat was unbearable and many began to panic. The Elder sounded the drum and asked everyone to share something from the heart. Even though some were afraid, they would die in the lodge and wanted tearfully and dearly to escape, they all managed to sit through a sacred sharing circle in the lodge. When all had finished sharing, the Elder called, "DOOR"! Suddenly, the door opened and light burst into the lodge and everyone blinked trying to adjust to what they just experienced and the light. They looked at each other with great wonder and surprise. Sweat poured from their skin and steam rushed out of the lodge relieving the young people and others from further suffering.

"Bring in the grandfathers" and the helper brought in seven more glowing red-hot grandfathers, this time bigger than the first. The procedure was repeated, visions were given, and it was very sacred. This was repeated two more times with a total of four doors on the medicine wheel beginning in the East and ending in the North. Each door had seven grandfathers. Each door was very sacred and represented each direction and all the teachings that attend those directions including the animal totems and medicines. It was relentless for some, cool for others. Everyone had their own unique sacred and spiritual experience. It was a private affair while shared as well. Some saw visions, others didn't know what they saw. That can happen too! Sometimes, when we see something new, we do not understand it and there are no words to describe it. If someone never saw a doorknob before, may never know how to use it. Children are like that, they seem to have trouble opening doors or they accidentally lock themselves into the bathroom and they need help getting out. If you never saw a light switch before, how would you know how to light the room? So it was for many first timers as they did not understand what they were experiencing but they could appreciate its sacredness.

The Elder led the group of young people out of the lodge and the Warriors guided them back to their sacred place for the remainder of their Vision Quest. Again, there was some relief in the shade of the tree.

Later that day, the Elder came back for the group and led them on another Sweat Lodge Ceremony, then again later in the afternoon and still again in the evening. In all, there were four Sweat Lodge Ceremonies that day, all attended, and everyone was very sacred.

That night, the young people reflected on what they experienced. They wondered if what they imagined, their visions, were real. The dreams were so vivid! Sounds were crackling like fire! Color flashed like lightening across the night sky in the dreamer's dreams. Emotions of wonderment and excitement at flight and travel were surreal. The journey was coming to an end. In the morning, they would be prepared. But how the moon shone that night as they had never seen its light so bright ever in their lives.

And so for the last night many dreamed dreams and saw visions. They were encouraged that they had all made it and without as much suffering as they had imagined. Many had marveled at how strong they were. They came to know they had strength, courage and downright tenacity in their characters. It was wholly new for them. They knew now they would make it to the end. But who was that strange tall man that came to them many wondered? The Elders seemed to know him because they seemed to remember they had seen Elders talking to him. It was a strange experience indeed!

Some woke early wondering what the plan was. Others slept in not caring. Yet one by one, all were awake as the hot morning sun greeted them. None spoke but all seemed relieved. They waited patiently for their leadership.

The Elders stood by the fire, Warriors walked about this way and that gathering water and medicine, more firewood and family and friends began to arrive. Containers of food and drink were delivered and a great feast was prepared. The Elders visited and met many people instructing them the feast would soon begin. All visitors were instructed to wait in the community center. It seemed to take forever that the ceremonies would take the next step for all participants. Everyone was eager and very excited. Serious business was afoot.

The Elders came to guide the young people to the fire near the Sweat Lodge. Everyone thought they would sweat one more time and so, they mustered up the courage for one more sweat. Just then the Elder said, "we won't sweat today". The Elder looked upon the group and with great wonder in his voice and exclaimed, "Ah ho! You are all just radiating"! The Elder looked on and was very thoughtful. The young people returned the gaze confused by this observation and wondered what it was the Elder saw. Still they looked upon each other as children wondered about other children they see for the first time. Eyes blinking they smiled upon each other and laughed.

After four days in the sun, it was clear the shade did little to protect them from sunburn, if that's what it was. Their skin was clean, crisp, clear, and bright red. Their eyes were wide and they blinked with enthusiasm. They smiled at the old Warrior gently and with great courage. It was obvious they were very much alive and well. If one looked closely enough, they would see a multi-colored aura radiating like a rainbow around these young warriors. These were the Rainbow Warriors spoken of in the prophecies! They were those who would come to save the world from its own self-destruction. For now, only the Elders knew about the prophecy of the Rainbow Warriors. The Elders had long foreseen it.

You have all travelled in the spirit world and you have seen many great and wonderful things. Soon the time will come when you will share with the community what it was that you saw. Some of you will remember, and others will remember many days later. Today, for those of you who will share, the community awaits. The spirit plate has been prepared and delivered by our great Warriors. Soon your fast will come to an end. We the council of Elders have watched you all very closely, the Warriors too have shared their observations with us. We have all seen many great things. Then all were given their colors and their spirit names and they learned of many teachings about their true spirit self.

THE WAY OF THE WARRIOR IS THE WAY OF HONOR

The Vision Quest is a rite of passage for young people. It is generally administered by the Elders when a young person is ready, on, or about the age of nine. However, times have changed. Because the Canadian government and the religious establishments of the day saw to it in their assimilation programs, our languages, traditions and ceremonies were outlawed. We resisted these laws banning us from practicing our culture and ways of expressing who we are at first but many died at the hands of the authorities who arrested our Elders and Warriors. When there is no ceremony or tradition, our children of the earth rely too heavily on the mental part of the medicine wheel, and they would develop out of balance and out of harmony. Ceremony and traditional teachings help us maintain balance, by clearing our minds, our mental side to see clearly the spirit world where all things begin. This is why many warriors died.

They would have their head shaven to be shamed and then they would die, usually in jail. It was a hard thing for a Warrior to live under those conditions. Many lost hope because they could not find their way and they could no longer identify with who they were. The authorities projected shame and guilt upon them. They used torture, abuses, insults and they looked upon our great Warriors with contempt, disgust. The torment was too much and many succumbed to death while others remained to live in self-destruction, reliving their tormented experiences. For those who would resist, they would choose death over slavery. This was the Way of the Warrior when colonizers and settlers first abducted our Warriors to force them into slavery.

Back then, many African people were taken from their homeland and brought to Turtle Island as slaves and they too were great Warriors. But they could not get back to their homeland and so they were made to survive here with us and many were adopted into our tribes if they could get away. But our Warriors would rather die or die trying to run away from the slave drivers. Even if our Warriors were captured and sold into slavery, they refused and resisted slavery and would rather be beaten to death and often they were. For those Warriors who would resist by surviving, it was as if they could not speak of the horrors of their experiences and so, their behaviors told the story as they ritualistically relived their horrors. They would engage in self-destruction even as the slave masters attempted to destroy the Indian in the child. The slave masters continue to do this today to our Warriors even before they are born. Our Warriors are born fighting and resisting even in the womb. Long before our babies are even born, or even thought of, they are fighting and resisting with no rest. That is the Way of the Warrior!

We Elders believe those Warriors who are trying to tell us what happened to them through their destructive behavior cannot describe the horrors of war. There are no words, just deep, guttural, throat-sobbing tears come up. We Elders believe that these Warriors are not allowed to speak of their horrors because the new culture calls them wimps. Some of our own Warriors call each other wimps. And so there is no safe place for Warriors to talk and to heal.

We once had a great Warrior ceremony called the *SHARING CIRCLE* and it was outlawed. What a wonderful ceremony too, it is the most intimate and interactive display of community, family and healing. Our Warriors used to find healing in the talking circle but now they call it "gay". There was never any "gay" in our culture. We didn't say things were "gay" as if to devalue something or someone by pointing a finger and saying, "gay". If they mean the two-spirited people, they are are sacred Warriors, we were all equal to them, and they are held in great honor and respect. Now someone has spread lie about our family and our ways. Our Warriors have a Judeo-Christian believe system that genders people, hierarchically stratifying them based on gender, devaluing a whole person for their lifestyle. We Elders believe that inside every Warrior is the spirit self that cries out in anguish like a baby will cry to let parents and caregivers notice they require comfort. But some people who see our Warriors crying out for help today are called "babies". They say, "quit your crying you big baby". For us Elders, this kind of talk is disrespectful because we are a child centered people and the baby which is in all of us, are greatly respected. This is a hierarchical stratification based on paternalism, the father and it devalues our sacred fire.

Those little babies are our sacred fire that we are to tend at all times. Babies are sacred. All of our activities are entirely devoted to our babies. They are our purpose in this life.

If you look around and observe closely you can see that our relations, the two legged's, the four legged's, the winged ones, those that fly, those that crawl, those that creep, they all have babies. Life goes on. We all deserve a chance at life. That is why we continue the circle of life in this way. That is how we all have come to be. Something must be happening somewhere that has allowed us a chance at the gift of life.

Now our Warriors are delusional in thinking the Sharing Circle is "gay" or for babies. They deprive themselves of one of the most sacred healing ceremonies and all the people of the world would benefit once again from the Sharing Circle. It is talk medicine and it is good!

In the Sharing Circle we have a talking stick that we pass around and everyone can listen carefully to the one holding the talking stick. Everyone listens carefully, formulating thoughts, processing information and considering many things. As the talking stick is passed around, new speakers who have already considered many things present new thoughts and ideas. They add to the discussion, which brings additional thoughts and ideas to process. This ceremony can go on for hours, days, weeks, month's years! We have developed patience and listening and considered many things is a great honor for everyone as their minds are trained in these ways. It is not uncommon for someone to pause before speaking, to gather their thoughts before speaking. It is not uncommon for everyone to grant someone the time to pause and reflect. This consideration for the one who is taking things seriously is important it is polite for everyone to use the time for oneself to reflect. When the white man saw this pause during our discussions he was very inconsiderate, talking out of turn and without the talking stick. He would think he knew what we were thinking and he would finish the talk for us. He was very impatient and we have never seen anything like it. Since childhood, our Warriors were trained in decision-making, discussing medicine, traditional teachings, philosophy, spirituality, nature, governance, promoting peace and harmony. Our people would have been educated with this sacred ceremony. If there were no other tasks, no "hunting and gathering" as the white man calls it, there was always a sharing circle occurring somewhere in a teepee or by a fire. Today everyone is turning the TV. on, browsing the internet, a kind of Sharing Circle, but not quite the same, there is no discussion no interactive proceeding. It is not sacred. Our Sharing Circle is very sacred. It is not to be disparaged with white man's beliefs about sacred people and our sacred fire.

Some say that a great struggle is occurring. They say that there are several levels of life and reality. They say we have come from these other places, other universes, other realities. When this one was created, it was because we won the great struggle in the other universe and when we did so, we pushed the enemy back and now we are here. Instantly a big bang occurred and here we are.

We Elders believe that it is that great mystery, that physicists call potential, what some Wushu Warriors call, the force. It is like the waves upon water and out of those waves, anything can happen. It is very sacred. We Elders have grave respect for the great mystery. We Elders have been observing, watching, listening and experiencing the great mystery since time immemorial.

All that time we have shared, our knowledge, our traditional and healing ways, the Way of the Warrior, and we pass it down generation to generation. The Way of the Warrior must be experienced. That is what you young people have done these past few days. You have experienced the great mystery. There is more! Much more! Never rest on your laurels, never be content with what you know, never allow your sacred water to stagnate, stir it up, shake the boat, always be open to learning new things. Do this to the end of your days.

SWEETGRASS

Never say never, said the foolish one trying to be funny. No one laughed. But the Elder understood and simply reached over for Sweetgrass and lit a wooden match to burn it to produce soft, gentle healing.

It may be the foolish one was experiencing profound emotions at that moment and it seemed inappropriate to attempt humor, some will do and say very inappropriate things under stress. One young Warrior was watching Schindler's list and could not help but burst out laughing at the scene where a soldier casually fired at innocent people shooting them in the head using a snipers rifle. It was not because this scene was so funny rather it was because that Warrior had never seen such barbarism, such horror that the body took into itself grave negativity and was not able to cope with its poison. The only coping it could utilize was hysteria and the Warrior began to laugh hysterically, shaking violently and then to cry ashamedly.

We use Sweetgrass to heal difficult emotions.

Many of you will remember this experience for the rest of your life and it won't do you any good. Others will become religious zealots. Others will remain balanced. That is okay. There is no right or wrong way as a Warrior. We are all a work in progress. We do not judge! Who can judge? No one is better than another is. The best that we can do is equality. There is no wealth, status and prestige in the Way of the Warrior. Those are delusions. You will have to unlearn everything that you have learned about life and reality in order to come to the truth about life and reality. All that you have learned is delusional. All of you will struggle with this teaching. You will struggle and make many mistakes. That is okay too. We all make mistakes. To err is human someone once said. We do not judge someone when they make a mistake. We look for signs of improvement, no matter how small and we tell them, we can see them changing in a good way. Plus, we are all in the same boat, we are all a work in progress. No one is greater than the other is and we are all equal. We all have our gifts. We reinforce each other with them! Tobacco first, if you need to ask someone for their gift to come reinforce another! That is the Way of the Warrior!

Come! We will talk more. And so the Elder led the young Rainbow Warriors to the showers where they quickly washed up and readied themselves to feast.

First, each was given a banana to eat. The Elders knew that the electrolytes in the banana would prepare their bodies for the feast they were about to enjoy. They also drank water. They did so with great restraint and a newfound respect for the power of this great medicine. Though the Elder did not instruct the Rainbow Warriors to talk, it was generally understood now that they could do so without any worry about protocol.

The talk was mostly about great relief to have water and a piece of food. The Anglo-Saxon and Celtic Warriors were amazed that they too once had similar ceremonies before the great corruption came to their islands. Some exclaimed the hotness of the Grandfathers in the sweat. Others were grateful they were spared a sweat on that day. When they were all ready and assembled, they came into the community hall where a whole community of people had gathered hearing that the Rainbow Warrior prophecy was fulfilled!

Chapter 6

THE SHARING CIRCLE

And so it was the dreams that young people everywhere, from all over the earth were sharing that made things strange. How is it that people can have the same dreams over and over again? Why does the sky speak? Why is it always night? Where are these places we visit? What is the meaning of the terrifying visitor that comes to smother our breath? Do we see the past or is this the future many wondered.

Many young people came from all over the world to visit an Elder and a council of Elders and to inquire about the meaning of all these things. Many of these young people were not First Nation or Metis or Innu, though representatives from these diverse groups attended as well. They came from different cultures and different lands from far away. Many were trained already in their own Warrior ways. Still they came to speak their hearts to the Elders in hopes of finding the answers to many riddles and to learn and receive instruction. All were equally attending to the wise counsel all for the same reasons, hoping they could share the answers with family and loved ones back home.

Many had found they got more than they expected. They were all very satisfied with their experiences. They said they now know who they were for the first time in their lives and that this crude material was not who they were. They understood that it was certainly a part of who they are but their bodies and faces, shapes and sizes were not the sum total of all they were as they were taught to believe. They realize now they come from some place known as the great mystery where infinite potential can be realized. They became aware that the universe was really just a mass of energy, which science tells us and the Elders have always known since time immemorial. They came to know that spirit expresses itself through them and all life, all material, that all is sacred. They understood these mortal bodies they inhabit are simply an expression of spirit. Many came to believe that their religion had the final say about spirituality. It was a book with all the answers anyone ever needed to know and there was no need for

Sharing Circles or discussion. The priests, nuns and other clergy trained, ordained would administer spirituality to ignorant people. Many preferred said they preferred to have a discussion that could go on for a lifetime where no one was admonished for their freedom of thought on the issues. The liked the idea they could speak their mind in a forum that would allow discussion where they are not ashamed of themselves for asking questions and considering many great mysteries. They preferred this model of education rather than public education which is a hierarchically race based authoritarian system of oppression that administers to children oppressively they said. They understood its origins were in slavery of children replete with abuses of all manner and sickness. They said not much has changed.

The discussions all were engaged in stimulated much thought. Those who travelled from far away lands and cultures were well rewarded, as many answers to many riddles were discovered.

They learned the origins of "civilization" with its accompanying principles of "progress", "development", "production", "salvation", and more, all of which are cultural and psychological constructions for the mind. They understood that many of these cultural constructions have nothing to do with their own cultures, but rather were imposed upon their homelands by the power of corrupted cultures. They described stories they heard, books they read, movies they saw, foods they ate, prayers they prayed, histories they discovered, people they met, advertisements, politics, philosophies, teachings, products, manufacturing's, fashion, media, were all elements of cultures that imposed a way of living and perception.

These influences are really just little boxes in which people are born into, developed inside of, expected to think inside, must fail to realize there is an infinite possibility outside of that little box. They understood it was all an expression of power that influences the development of the children of the earth. They came to understand that it was a form of corporate slavery. It is a prison for their minds, a phantom prison of apparition bars.

All understood that it is wise and good to share each other's cultural elements in a respectful way, but they understood the differences of public relations and propaganda. The latter is far more insidious and creepy in nature with elements of manipulations and crafty devilry. In the old days, cultures shared with each other respectfully.

It was known that Columbus did not "discover" Turtle Island, but rather he was lost and the people saved him and his crew. In return, Columbus sent word about the ways of the people and the abundance they shared without want or greed. Then the great corruption came and changed everything.

It was known that the people of Turtle Island travelled to what is now known as Europe, Japan, Indonesia, Australia and all others lands. Currently, history writes in their favor and they cannot or will not fathom the idea that it was the people of Turtle Island that enriched the world with their teachings and traditions. The Way of the Warrior, for the sake of the children, for seven generations.

Recently, someone rowed a boat from Turtle Island to France claiming to be the first North American to do that. Well, from a Eurocentric, North American perspective, that could be true, but you would have to be inside a little box to consider that. From a Turtle Island perspective, this is nothing new. That little box has them claiming fame and many accolades are offered.

The people who live inside a little box cannot or will not consider that indigenous people travelled out of Turtle Island. They cannot consider the fact that if two-legged's can row a boat here and a North American can row a boat there, they cannot or will not imagine the possibility that a child of the earth can row about too, and across great oceans! No, they are too white supremacist to consider that.

The little box that controls everyone, tells them, people sprang out of Africa, but they cannot or will not accept the concept that the children of the earth actually came out of Turtle Island. It is this culture of white supremacy that is a mass neurosis, psychosis as Deepak Chopra refers to it as.

Many understood that the night terror that visited them in the dream world was unidentifiable in the waking world so they awoke or attempted to stay awake to avoid the nightmares. Many found safety in consciousness where the demon may not find them. This reinforced their reliance on the mental states and comfort states, which is delusional and contrary to sacred law and medicine wheel technology. They described the night terror as a thing that could not be reasoned with, you can't bargain with it, there is no negotiating, as if it was in a constant and incessant state of furious rage and anger, it is selfish, self centered, ego-centric, careless, evil as old as "civilization" itself. They learned this dream, this terror has been around for over ten thousand years and many generations of Elders have known about it. Prophecies were given and it appeared they were now being fulfilled and many were encouraged.

SYSTEMS OF OPPRESSION

The great beast was seen throughout history. Some said that it was patriarchy, or a system of government, which empowers men, relegating women and children to submission. Patriarchy is male centric they said. This paternalistic attitude oppressed women and so many who called themselves feminist believed this was a source of the conflict where the great beast lives. They argued for the equality of women.

Others said capitalism was the source of conflict where the great beast lives and so many argued for the equality of capital or money so everyone could meet their needs with paper.

Still others argued there was a class conflict between the proletariat and the aristocracy, between the rich and the poor.

Empire, many said was the source of this great conflict where nations would build themselves a great empire, which gave them a source of wealth, power and status.

Finally, others argued that it was secret societies, the elite upper classes, the illuminati or the masons.

They understood that all of these were sources of conflict and much of it did explain their shared visions of horror and terror.

Noam Chomsky describes the process of manufacturing consent from the masses, for the purpose of hegemony at any cost. Imperialism was the source in which the great beast lives they said.

They said the people are a great beast that must be controlled by manufacturing consent. However, we are learning the beast resides in the hearts of people known as *Authoritarians* in a type of demonic possession. But it's not demons that posses authoritarians, it's ideas.

According to Bob Altemeyer at the University of Manitoba, authoritarians are people in North America, who are very aggressive, submissive to authority, fervent believers in the system and are willing to aggress against anyone or anything that the authority tells them and they do so without any critical thought whatsoever. They can be mostly found in fundamentalist religions that are patriarchal in nature, emphasizing an authority figure, such as the father with at least a "mommy and daddy" knows best belief. They are born into such a hierarchical structure and all their teachings are based on hierarchy. Authoritarians will even aggress against members of their own church, country, and constitution if someone told them to, so they do not have devotion to groups or creeds, rather simply to following authority. Authoritarians are forgiving towards authority figures that are caught in a scandal or breaking the law.

These would include, police who beat up an alleged criminal wrongfully, military personnel who attack non-combatants or citizens of an enemy of the state, political leaders who are discovered to steal money from the public coffers. They are entirely devoid of compassion even when someone makes an honest mistake a poor choice under conditions of duress. They are quick to judge and execute vigorous punishment completely justified in their execution even gleefully, hysterically aroused doing so.

Dr. Bob Altemeyer says no one should be surprised to learn that some defend crooked leaders caught in scandal. The surprising thing is that authoritarians are often devoutly religious. But their love and deference to authority supersedes all other rules and logical thought even within their religious books. They will twist and contort gospel and scripture to suit their authoritarian personalities. They remain willfully blind even when Dr. Bob Altemeyer pointed out conflicts. But all they said was that there was no conflict. So they are okay with breaking any rule or law so long as the authority says it's okay or if it was an authority figure, they defend authority.

The most important thing to authoritarians is to follow the leader. It's not the holy books or scripture that is important to authoritarians it's the relationship between the *authoritarian follower* and the *authoritarian leader*. Authoritarian followers must obey and everything else is secondary. Authoritarian leaders know that it's easier to use holy books and scripture to justify their leadership as they claim to be gods representatives here on earth. They will lie and twist the scriptures to meet their objectives. The only thing authoritarians may not do is attack themselves when authority tells them to attack people who fit their description. It appears authoritarians do not self-destruct but they can deconstruct, if they want. Authoritarian personality types are indeed an intriguing mystery.

Noam Chomsky apparently describes authoritarians, as does Dr. Bob Altemeyer as the most direct threat to democracy. In consideration of Canadian policy of paternalistic tutelage eloquently described by *Noel Dyck, What is the Indian "problem" tutelage and resistance in Canadian Indian administration* in other words, the great white father and furthermore; *Dr. Bob Altemeyer's Authoritarianism*, where Dr. Altemeyer describes authoritarian followers and leaders cooking up authority and unconditional, reverence to it. We now have the connections necessary to understand Canadian patriarchal and paternalistic attitude and beliefs through religious and political ideology, which continue to oppress Aboriginal people, other ethnic groups and their own white people as well.

Many said this is similar to a bullying relationship. It is an abusive relationship. It is a co-dependant relationship. They said the psychopath or sociopath is the bully and the victim attempts to control the abuse and both are delusional. They say this is an Indian and white relationship, a treaty relationship in Canada, a modern treaty even as Metis and other First Nation are negotiating with this beast, as if one could negotiate with this thing under conditions of inequality and after being tortured and assimilated.

Many said you must be saved through the blood of Jesus and the Beast is in fact the Devil, a roaring lion that goes this way and that seeking whom to devour. They said you must repent and be baptized in a holy spirit and god of the bible would protect you from this beast. Even as they make these bold statements Islam says Christians are infidels in fact everyone who is not with Islam are all infidels, enemies of god.

But here we have one that said they were baptized and did repent and exercised absolute and total faith in everything for the god of the bible and still they were terrorized in the wee hours of the night. They said that even as they were terrorized, they would pray with great prayer and much supplication, calling out to Jesus with great power and authority chanting repeatedly, "the power of Christ compels you! The power of Christ compels you! The power of Christ compels you!" and the great beast would just laugh at them. They could not understand why Jesus would not come to help them. It worked in the movies. And there were many that described these occurrences. So they were mighty dissatisfied with the idea of repentance and salvation from the great beast.

In total, they were all describing great horrors throughout history, of a terrible conflict that cost many lives in all generations where the children suffered the most in every situation. There was great inequality between many groups. It was apparent that feminists did not fully agree with the class system, the class conflict theories failed to consider racism and feminism, and the same went for racism, capitalism and religion. All of us are now attempting to reject racism, the theory that races of people were hierarchically stratified based on racial superiority taking shortcuts to problem solving. We learned that racism or white supremacy is firmly embedded in capitalism, classism, religion and even feminism, whether anyone likes it or not. You don't even have to be white to be a white supremacist. You just have to defer to authority and the great white fathers who allow scraps to fall from the Kings table where brats and dogs quarrel and you will be rewarded in this way. It seemed the beast is well disguised in this phenomenon or at least had many heads in one body. So they said conflict, aggression, hatred needed to be answered with love.

Still they were confused and wondered if they had it in them to love those who would burn down their homes, rape their children and loved ones, murder and maim them, torment them into submission. Having been born into dysfunction, learning about revenge and honor killing and other dysfunctional belief systems being trained since birth to be aggressive many wondered if this is possible even with faith in Christ or Islam. They wondered if this option was even sane! So they remained confused.

Many discussed that fear and insecurity have corrupted the hearts and minds of many. Having been raised in an authoritarian setting where the lower ranks must defer to authority, means one must devalue their own identity under abusive conditions. The breaking down of identity in such individual's means pent up aggression increased likelihood of anxiety disorder all building up over the years and resentment develops. This would contribute to their aggressive tendencies looking for every self-righteous opportunity to aggress against others, projecting insecurities and racist imaginations. They would have been taught that aggression, judgementalism is the only way to control others in hopes of developing a utopian society based on assimilation with a *Borg* mentality. "Resistance is futile".

The bottom line here is that such processes use the dark side of the force to attain unity. Fear, hate, anger, suffering and resentment make people insecure. Insecurity permeates every aspect of authoritarian personality types in their belief systems, experiences and perceptions. Authoritarians mostly and others who are insecure would rather conform, fall in line, fall into rank and file, to obey. This way they can feel a sense of control over their lives and their abusers, masters and authority figures who make all the decisions. They are afraid to rock the boat, their anxiety and anxiety disorders cripple them. They don't like it when revolutionaries stand up, speak out, question authority and create disturbances. They think such disturbances will bring great wrath and furious anger down upon them and so they over-police everyone, especially dissenters. They are oppressed and they oppress those below or beneath them in the hierarchically stratified society.

The Rainbow Warriors were led and then seated in the front of the community hall. There was a microphone and large sound system setup as hundreds of people arrived from communities all around to meet those spoken of in the prophecy. They even managed to Skype the event in real time so other Manitoba communities could see the Rainbow Warriors.

The entire community had filled to capacity and it was very dangerous to have so many in one room. So the Bears and the Wolves set up two large screens and more audio systems for those who waited outside. They pointed out the fire escape routes in case of emergency. Now everyone could hear from the Rainbow Warriors and they could see them all fresh from the spirit world. They shined bright and there was indeed an aura of rainbow colors upon them that could even be seen on screen. These were indeed Rainbow Warriors!

The Elder stepped up to a microphone provided in the center of the hall and began to speak. The Council of Elders were seated all around as it is customary to offer seating first to Elders. The Elder spoke about the prophecy of the *White Buffalo Calf*. This prophecy marked a significant change in the times all the people were experiencing. The White Buffalo Calf signaled events that would prevent the destruction of the *children of the Earth* and of all their relations. The prophecy spoke of great terrors and horrors, a great shift in the medicine wheel meant the world would suffer greatly and perhaps even die. However, the appearance of the White Buffalo Calf meant the world and the Children of the Earth would be spared. The Elder described these prophecies in great detail.

Then another Elder from the great council spoke.

Another Elder came to describe the Rainbow Warrior prophecy, which was always known to be a part of the Buffalo Calf prophecy. The Rainbow Warriors would come to lead many generations of people in peace, harmony and balance in the medicine wheel. Many people would follow the ways of the Rainbow Warriors who would teach the Children of the Earth the good roads to travel. This balance would renew and replenish the Earth with great respect for all life including those that creep, those that crawl, the winged ones, the two legged, the four legged, the tree world, the sky world, those that swim, all our relations, from all directions on the medicine wheel, for seven generations, for the sake of the children. This translates into forever. The Rainbow Warriors would save the world from total annihilation.

And so it was that two major prophecies were fulfilled. Several Elders came to speak to these two prophecies all they knew and when all the stories were told the people understood that the prophecies were fulfilled and all were encouraged. It was now time to hear from the Rainbow Warriors.

One by one, the Warriors spoke of all they had seen and heard in the spirit world. Some described things they did not understand and they said there are no words, they could not comprehend it, nor fathom what they experienced. They only knew that it was very sacred. When they tried to explain it, it sounded irrational.

They described visions of a time long past when there was peace and harmony a time before the great corruption. They said fate is a strange thing because when all is said and done, you really would not want things any other way. They said they hope that people would take comfort in that. What presents as a challenge, hardship, sorrow, loss, grief and the like, the great mystery seems to find a way to provide. They understood this is a great mystery many would find unacceptable. Nevertheless, they described something about asking the great spirit *to grant them serenity to accept the things they cannot change, the courage to change the things they can and the wisdom to know the difference*. In the end, fate, as it would seem would provide us with something and in time, we would understand we wouldn't want it any other way.

Others described visions of what would be in the future should we not have the courage to change the things we could change. They saw buildings collapsed and in decay. A way of life gone forever. They saw people wholly consumed, wandering aimlessly and under the control of some powerful force. It was a very discouraging image.

All that was discussed caused a great stir among the people.

Finally, a Lone Wolf Warrior, chosen to represent approached a microphone and spoke these words for the people. The Warrior identified as a Metis person of historic Red River descent and could describe the vision through the history of the Metis people.

"If we could read the secret history of our enemies, we should find in each life sorrow and suffering enough to disarm all hostility". Longfellow (1807 – 1882)

Analyzing the history of Canadian colonization and settlement, the colonizer and the colonized reveal the participation, struggle and resistance of Metis people. This evaluation reveals triumph and glorious testimony to the strength, character and resistance of Metis individuals against Canadian empire. Metis determination reveals a legacy of awareness, patience and self-direction in the process of decolonization and resistance. Metis people will teach Canadians the profundities of self-respect, character and integrity. Counting the cost of Metis resistance reveals a disturbing examination of the power and authority, the abuse and self-entitlement of the colonizer and later, the settler. Meanwhile Metis people resist and remain steadfast in their identity believing that a relationship with all nations based on mutual respect and determination is possible. Times are changing. Canada accepts its history and commits itself to reconciliation. This could never occur unless there was resistance.

We have spoken of many great mysteries, which inherently examine colonization, its purposes and intentions. This establishes the direction the colonizer initiates with respect to the colonized. Colonization comes equipped with moral justification and ideology allowing people to harm others with total disregard to their humanity. The result produces widespread abnormal behavior in tormented individuals who experienced colonization, the aberrant behavior is transferred intergenerationally. Barnes, Josefowitz, Cole, (2006) Residential Schools: Impact on Aboriginal Students' Academic and Cognitive Development, examines the outcomes of those who survived IRS. Those who raise a family after experiencing severe trauma without mental health support present their trauma to family and community, transferring it through communication and role modeled behavior. In all the literature reviewed, consideration to historical context of colonization and assimilation including Metis is presented linking Indian

Residential Schools (IRS) and mental health outcomes. An examination of the effects of transference on children of survivors reveals dysfunction as obvious consequences to IRS. How does transference affect these children? What is the magnitude of the consequences in the tormented? The literature reviewed suggests dysfunction, dysfunctional beliefs or dysfunctional cognitive behavior, dysfunctional relationship/s, alienation with oneself and others are the outcomes. Dr. Vaknin provides detailed descriptions of the process of torture and assimilation providing comprehensive understanding of the tortured psychology. This has direct application to Metis experiences of assimilation through IRS. Blackstock, Trocmé, Bennett, (2004) in Child Maltreatment Investigations Among Aboriginal and Non-Aboriginal Families in Canada examines Aboriginal child apprehension in the Canadian childcare system. Barnes and Vulcano (1984) look at school self-acceptance measures as determinants of academic outcomes in comparison to mainstream Canadians. Rojas and Gretton, (2007) in Background, Offence Characteristics, and Criminal Outcomes of Aboriginal Youth Who Sexually Offend consider youth sexual offenders as a direct consequence of IRS. Lavallee and Poole (2010) in Beyond Recovery: Colonization, Health and Healing for Indigenous People in Canada and other literature reveals mental health models predominantly western in approach are not as successful as culturally relevant ones. The literature reviewed supports expanding traditional Western approaches with culturally relevant traditional healing methods. Finally, it is essential to examine the present status of Metis resistance and mental health and the consequence of conflict between Metis people and Canadian empire. Diabetes and mental health statistics are presented most accurately in, A Profile of Metis Health Status and Healthcare Utilization in Manitoba: A Population-Based Study (Marten et al. 2010). Peter Menzies, (2007) Understanding Aboriginal Intergeneration Trauma from a Social Work Perspective provides a unique case study of alienation and homelessness identity directly related to IRS and intergeneration transference. The literature reviewed shows Metis psychology unanimously under-represented, under-reported and under-researched exists in regards to colonization and IRS. The research takes advantage of the term Aboriginal, which is a term, meant to describe the three constitutional groups including First Nations, Metis and Innu. However, the literature takes advantage of the term Aboriginal, but it usually refers to First Nations. It seems that many believe that Aboriginal people are First Nation people. They are correct, but Aboriginal people are also, Metis and Innu people. The under-representation of Metis in these studies is a shortcoming in this literature review. There is almost no Metis specific research. Logan (2007) We Were Outsiders: The Metis and Residential Schools are among the most recent attempts to document and present material with Metis and IRS. There is an obvious need to research Metis psychology in the face of colonial context and resistance to assimilation.

Succinctly, Metis people are culturally distinct, resilient throughout history and remain presently. Metis history including colonization is notable at the time of Canadian expansion into Western Canada. This includes a declaration of nationhood, negotiating the terms of Canadian expansion, a provisional government, the Manitoba Act and the creation of the province of Manitoba. Unfortunately, overwhelming settlement and changes to the Manitoba Act after 1870 resulted in the erosion of terms negotiated, land lost and displacement of Metis people from Manitoba in a great diaspora evading apocalyptic catastrophe. Imperialism (Sprague 1992), racism among other concepts such as patriarchy and religious ideology are identified sources of souring relations between Canada (Sealey 1975, Sprague 1988, Shore 1997).

Canada wanted to remove Indian title to land so that accessing resources developing power and wealth appeared legal (Chartrand 1991). After negotiating treaty with First Nations people and establishing Indian reserves, Canada developed assimilation policy under the auspice of the Church and British imperialism, the two main authoritative establishments of the day. Racism fuelled the fire of segregation and assimilation (Allen, 1997). Canada justified itself for its part in honoring terms with Metis people and then simply neglected their well-being. This pressured the Metis to attend IRS. The combination of neglect, ethnic removal from their land base, discrimination and finally IRS attendance resulted in multi-generational torment reciprocating into personal and community dysfunction. The impact of those outcomes, like transference are apparent throughout the literature.

Canadians were aware of human rights violations against Aboriginal groups and Metis people during assimilation policy implementation. However, these considerations were and are dismissed in the media, "miniaturized" as secondary to the goal of removing the "Indian" and in our case, the Metis from land and resources claims (Kunz, Fleras 1997). If Metis resistance is Canadian conscience, then the media is that devil on the other shoulder whispering moral justifications. Public outcry produced a Metis Betterment Act 1938 and land was set aside for Metis people in Alberta (Hatt 1985). While the province of Alberta is progressing along humanitarian lines, Canada reinforced racist notions by enacting laws to prevent legal action that would intervene in human rights abuses (Sinclair, 2011, talking with Aboriginal Law Students Association, University of Manitoba on IRS). The Metis experience was experienced by colonizing settlers immigrating to Canada themselves fleeing corruption in their own homeland. The corrupt forces of Imperialism and assimilation in motion, Canadian culture projected false beliefs and perceptions of "Indians" as "pagan, barbarian, savages". Additionally, colonizers own internalized assimilation and colonization experiences including self-loathing were projected onto Metis people (Saul 2008, Vaknin 1999). These ideas and lack of resistance to corruption made it easier to dehumanize Metis people and allow human rights violations to occur. Canadians participating as bystanders, benefitting from land loss and ethnic removal from their land base allow corruption to prevail even presently. Canadians were and still are taught they are doing Metis people a favor (Sinclair 2011, Milne 1995, Flanagan 1983).

According to a recent analysis of Metis mental health, Metis people in Manitoba are similar or higher in prevalence of cumulative mental illness compared to the general population. "Provincially, Metis had a similar five–year period prevalence (i.e., not statistically significantly different) of cumulative mental illness than all other Manitobans (28.4% vs. 25.9%, NS). Cumulative mental illness disorders include residents who received treatment for one or more of the five following mental illnesses: depression, anxiety disorders, substance abuse, personality disorder, and schizophrenia". (Martens, et al 2010). According to the Manitoba government mental health website, "In Canada, mental illness is the single largest category of disease affecting Canadians (CAMIMH, 2000). One in 5 Canadians, or up to 20% of the population will experience a mental illness at some point in their lives, one in three will suffer from a severe and persistent mental illness (CAMIMH, 2000), and one in eight will actually be hospitalized (Submission to the Commission on the Future of Health Care in Canada, CMHA, 2001). If we add family members who carry a major burden of care, the figures of those impacted by mental illness in Canada would be multiplied 2 or 3 times (CMHA, 2001). Timely and appropriate mental health services are critical to Manitobans' health. When mental disorders occur, they have an immense impact on individuals and families". (http://www.gov.mb.ca/health/mh/index.html, last accessed, 14/04/2011). Overall, the cost of poor mental health on society is intimidating and staggering because of its subtle and overt presence in our communities. Research indicates that if these issues are not addressed the consequences we face will repeat, deteriorate and contribute to significant financial cost and loss of life.

Logan, (2007) establishes Metis attendance at IRS despite Canadian government policy to the contrary, disallowing Metis attendance. Logan agrees with the notion that Metis resistance is a shared history as she quotes Howard Adams, "Imperialism is a complex and murderous procedure. After invasion and the holocaust, there are a number of succeeding homicidal actions before the Aboriginal people are exterminated or imprisoned. All Indigenous people of the [European] colonies suffered the same fate: Canada, Australia, or Africa. The Indians and Metis of Canada were no different. Canada probably had better public relations affairs than the other colonies. This is why Canada's history suffers from the greatest distortions and falsehoods of imperial nations". (Adams in Lutz et. al, 2005). Howard Adams work, Tortured People (1999) inspired these discussions.

History records European nations endured their own colonial experience and assimilation considering Roman imperial expansion, ethnic identity formation and nation building processes and of course Imperialism. Again, assimilation and ideology often change the meaning of colonialism into a cognitively acceptable notion of civilization and progress (Saul 2008). Logan presents the "victors" in this struggle between the colonizer and the colonized. Clearly, that Metis resisted and survived such horrors maintaining their identity and culture is a statement of victory. All nations survived colonial experiences. The difference between the colonizer and the colonized lay in the choices the two groups take with respect or disrespect to each other especially with regard to sharing wealth and power in a mutually respectful way. Resistance also means the colonized should resist the iniquities associated with assimilation especially with regard to corruption and they have done well for over two hundred years. In the early days, the British would have given gifts to Chiefs attempting to corrupt them (Allen, 1997 pgs. 85 note 46 and 265), to make them dependent on European industrialization, to control them. Gifts of corn, meats, metal pots and other trade goods were given and yet to the astonishment of the British, the Chiefs would give everything away to the community. Corruption only becomes evident after the implementation of IRS when assimilationists had direct access to the children. Consequently, some Chiefs and other Aboriginal leaders are not what they once were, but that is the power of assimilation or, corruption.

Assimilation is the process of breaking down identity to re-create a new one. The goal of torture is to break the will of the person so the tutor can rebuild a new character (Vaknin, 2007). Assimilation in the context of IRS establishes a case for torture. These definitions are in line with the United Nations Convention Against Torture (http://www.hrweb.org/legal/cat.html, Part 1, article1.1 last accessed Tuesday, April-12-11).

"For the purposes of this Convention, torture means any act by which severe pain or suffering, whether physical or mental, is intentionally inflicted on a person for such purposes as obtaining from him or a third person information or a confession, punishing him for an act he or a third person has committed or is suspected of having committed, or intimidating or coercing him or a third person, or for any reason based on discrimination of any kind, when such pain or suffering is inflicted by or at the instigation of or with the consent or acquiescence of a public official or other person acting in an official capacity. It does not include pain or suffering arising only from, inherent in or incidental to lawful sanctions".

The Metis confession is to admit that being Metis is not good, being "white" is better. This notion creates a division, an identity crisis and causes one to question the validity of their identity. The process of splitting and fragmenting identity and personality begins. This process is damaging and has lasting effects transferable to following generations. In IRS the languages are suppressed, but after 1885, the languages and other markers of Metis identity were already well under oppressive regimes. Metis identity was ethnically cleansed from Manitoba by "Orangemen" (Shore, 2001).

It is noteworthy, that the bystander effect seen throughout the literature on IRS may be due to fact that Canadian assimilation programs were so horrific. The power of the Children's Aid Society so widespread that no one dare stand up or speak out against these policies. As seen in Jane Elliot's blue eyes/brown eyes experiments with adults, it is better to sit quiet while the tutor or tormentor is focused on another pupil. In this case, Canadians would remain quiet while Canada assimilates. Perhaps the threatening and intimidating experience of watching the tormented produced the acquiescence of the bystanders, encouraging the confession to end the violence (also seen in Jane Elliots, A Class Divided and Vaknin 1999). The literatures on the bystander effect certainly suggest as much (Latane and Darely, 1968). Assimilation policy appears to contribute to participation of bystanders noted in victims' stories of abuse in public education systems. Teachers would openly ridicule Metis children for their Aboriginal identity (Keith, 2006). Every act of oppression served as an essential component in the Canadian policy to assimilate.

An analyses of immigration policies (http://www.cic.gc.ca/english/pdf/research-stats/facts2010.pdf) reveal many Canadians would have endured their own fate through their own colonial experiences. Many immigrants would have endured their own oppressions and abuses. Many are known to have fled their own racialized oppressive regimes having lost their own land and access to natural resources and subsequently power and wealth (Gourluck 2010). They would have lost their own ability for self-determination. They would have fled to Canada. What they would find is no different from what they fled. The only difference is that the government is focused on "savages" and so, they would agree with assimilationists, that the confession is the only way out of abuse.

Throughout assimilation, coercive tutelage (Dyck, 1991) or torture, the victim personalizes the abuse, as every point of contact is associated with pain and suffering over identity. The result causes the victim to question their identity, wonder what is wrong with them, what have they done to deserve to be treated in this way. Abused children often cannot make sense of abuse. Internalization of abuse develops the child-like understanding that they deserve abuse because they must be bad kids (Bradshaw 1988). Victims of torture in older people are no different. Victims of torture internalize their abuse sometimes assimilating (Forward 1989, Vaknin 1999). A case in point is the psychological phenomenon known as Stockholm Syndrome where victims develop attachment to abusers perhaps attempting to control their abuse (Vaknin 1999). The swing of a stick, belt, whip or other torture device as it contacts the skin invigorates the nerve endings causing a violent reaction of fight or flight in terror. The results are similar in shouting abuses, threats and intimidation. Even a passing glance or expression of judgment invokes torment and judgment. There is no fight or flight options for those attending IRS, as it is a legally sanctioned institution implemented by governing authorities. Parents, governments, officials and the public have all sanctioned this institution under a misrepresented guise of tutelage, education and "integration", (Milloy, 1999, Logan 2010). Whom could a victim turn for help? There was no negotiation with a colonial mindset begging for mercy, no passionate reasoning to stop the abuse. Children simply had to endure and survive the nature of en masse Canadian psychopathy. Research shows learned helplessness and hopelessness result from an inability to escape abuse. The research indicates Canadian attitude toward Aboriginal identities remain stubbornly rooted in racism. Justice Sinclair reinforces this notion in an interview revealing the Canadian public education system teaches racist ideology throughout the IRS era. Sinclair wants Canadians to understand their education of Aboriginal people was incorrect and deliberate in serving Canadian colonization.

Dr. Vaknin provides an online sample of his book, Malignant Self Love; The Psychology of Torture (1999). "There is one place in which one's privacy, intimacy, integrity and inviolability are guaranteed – one's body, a unique temple and a familiar territory of sense and personal history. The torturer invades, defiles and desecrates this shrine. He does so publicly, deliberately, repeatedly and, often, sadistically and sexually, with undisguised pleasure. Hence the all-pervasive, long-lasting, and, frequently, irreversible effects and outcomes of torture.

In a way, the torture victim's own body is rendered his worse enemy. It is corporeal agony that compels the sufferer to mutate, his identity to fragment, his ideals and principles to crumble. The body becomes an accomplice of the tormentor, an uninterruptible channel of communication, a treasonous, poisoned territory.

It fosters a humiliating dependency of the abused on the perpetrator. Bodily needs denied – sleep, toilet, food, water – are wrongly perceived by the victim as the direct causes of his degradation and dehumanization. As he sees it, he is rendered bestial not by the sadistic bullies around him but by his own flesh.

The concept of "body" has transferable qualities to "family", or "home". Torture is often applied to kin and kith, compatriots, or colleagues. This intends to disrupt the continuity of "surroundings, habits, appearance, relations with others", as the CIA put it in one of its manuals. A sense of cohesive self-identity depends crucially on the familiar and the continuous. By attacking both one's biological body and one's "social body", the victim's psyche is strained to the point of dissociation.

Beatrice Patsalides describes this transmogrification thus in "Ethics of the Unspeakable: Torture Survivors in Psychoanalytic Treatment":

"As the gap between the 'I' and the 'me' deepens, dissociation and alienation increase. The subject that, under torture, was forced into the position of pure object has lost his or her sense of interiority, intimacy, and privacy…Thoughts and dreams attack the mind and invade the body as if the protective skin that normally contains our thoughts, gives us space to breathe in between the thought and the thing being thought about, and separates between inside and outside, past and present, me and you, was lost."

Torture robs the victim of the most basic modes of relating to reality and, thus, is the equivalent of cognitive death. Space and time are warped by sleep deprivation. The self ("I") is shattered. The tortured have nothing familiar to hold on to: family, home, personal belongings, loved ones, language, name. Gradually, they lose their mental resilience and sense of freedom. They feel alien – unable to communicate, relate, attach, or empathize with others.

Torture splinters early childhood grandiose narcissistic fantasies of uniqueness, omnipotence, invulnerability, and impenetrability. But it enhances the fantasy of merger with an idealized and omnipotent (though not benign) other – the inflicter of agony. The twin processes of individuation and separation are reversed.

Torture is the ultimate act of perverted intimacy. The torturer invades the victim's body, pervades his psyche, and possesses his mind. Deprived of contact with others and starved for human interactions, the prey bonds with the predator. "Traumatic bonding", akin to the Stockholm Syndrome, is about hope and the search for meaning in the brutal and indifferent and nightmarish universe of the torture cell.

The abuser becomes the black hole at the center of the victim's surrealistic galaxy, sucking in the sufferer's universal need for solace. The victim tries to "control" his tormentor by becoming one with him (introjecting him) and by appealing to the monster's presumably dormant humanity and empathy.

This bonding is especially strong when the torturer and the tortured form a dyad and "collaborate" in the rituals and acts of torture (for instance, when the victim is coerced into selecting the torture implements and the types of torment to be inflicted, or to choose between two evils).

The psychologist Shirley Spitz offers this powerful overview of the contradictory nature of torture in a seminar titled "The Psychology of Torture" (1989):

"Torture is an obscenity in that it joins what is most private with what is most public. Torture entails all the isolation and extreme solitude of privacy with none of the usual security embodied therein... Torture entails at the same time all the self-exposure of the utterly public with none of its possibilities for camaraderie or shared experience. (The presence of an all powerful other with whom to merge, without the security of the other's benign intentions.)

Torture combines complete humiliating exposure with utter devastating isolation. The final products and outcome of torture are a scarred and often shattered victim and an empty display of the fiction of power."

Obsessed by endless ruminations, demented by pain and a continuum of sleeplessness – the victim regresses, shedding all but the most primitive defense mechanisms: splitting, narcissism, dissociation, Projective Identification, introjection, and cognitive dissonance. The victim constructs an alternative world, often suffering from depersonalization and derealization, hallucinations, ideas of reference, delusions, and psychotic episodes.

Sometimes the victim comes to crave pain – very much as self-mutilators do – because it is a proof and a reminder of his individuated existence otherwise blurred by the incessant torture. Pain shields the sufferer from disintegration and capitulation. It preserves the veracity of his unthinkable and unspeakable experiences.

This dual process of the victim's alienation and addiction to anguish complements the perpetrator's view of his quarry as "inhuman", or "subhuman". The torturer assumes the position of the sole authority, the exclusive fount of meaning and interpretation, the source of both evil and good.

Torture is about reprogramming the victim to succumb to an alternative exegesis of the world, proffered by the abuser. It is an act of deep, indelible, traumatic indoctrination. The abused also swallows whole and assimilates the torturer's negative view of him and often, as a result, is rendered suicidal, self-destructive, or self-defeating.

Thus, torture has no cut-off date. The sounds, the voices, the smells, the sensations reverberate long after the episode has ended – both in nightmares and in waking moments. The victim's ability to trust other people – i.e., to assume that their motives are at least rational, if not necessarily benign – has been irrevocably undermined. Social institutions are perceived as precariously poised on the verge of an ominous, Kafkaesque mutation. Nothing is either safe, or credible anymore.

Victims typically react by undulating between emotional numbing and increased arousal: insomnia, irritability, restlessness, and attention deficits. Recollections of the traumatic events intrude in the form of dreams, night terrors, flashbacks, and distressing associations.

The tortured develop compulsive rituals to fend off obsessive thoughts. Other psychological sequelae reported include cognitive impairment, reduced capacity to learn, memory disorders, sexual dysfunction, social withdrawal, inability to maintain long-term relationships, or even mere intimacy, phobias, ideas of reference and superstitions, delusions, hallucinations, psychotic microepisodes, and emotional flatness.

Depression and anxiety are very common. These are forms and manifestations of self-directed aggression. The sufferer rages at his own victimhood and resulting multiple dysfunction. He feels shamed by his new disabilities and responsible, or even guilty, somehow, for his predicament and the dire consequences borne by his nearest and dearest. His sense of self-worth and self-esteem are crippled.

In a nutshell, torture victims suffer from a Post-Traumatic Stress Disorder (PTSD). Their strong feelings of anxiety, guilt, and shame are also typical of victims of childhood abuse, domestic violence, and rape. They feel anxious because the perpetrator's behavior is seemingly arbitrary and unpredictable – or mechanically and inhumanly regular.

They feel guilty and disgraced because, to restore a semblance of order to their shattered world and a modicum of dominion over their chaotic life, they need to transform themselves into the cause of their own degradation and the accomplices of their tormentors". (http://samvak.tripod.com/torturepsychology.html)

Barnes, Josefowitz and Cole (2008) have analyzed the academic outcomes of students attending IRS. They say there is no evidence suggesting Aboriginal people suffered from mental health issues historically. The result of attending IRS not only created poor academic outcomes but also created a legacy of poor mental health issues for Aboriginal people.

Chronic underfunding of these schools created poor diet and living conditions such as low or no heated classrooms and overcrowding. The author's state because the policy of assimilation is rooted in racism, discrimination, racial denigration occurred, and abuse widespread. These environments targeted identity and created low or no self-esteem, low self-concepts, low self-efficacy none of which promote health and wellbeing necessary for education. This produces low academic performance, resulting in low employment prospects and overall poverty. Under funded environments with malnourishment, under-education, abuse and neglect were inhumane institutions of torture. This contributes to students developing severe personality and anxiety based disorders with no access to mental health or medical attention for several generations. Metis people would survive these institutions of torture only to live the remainder of their lives in torment (Vaknin 1999, Menzies 2006, Barnes et al.2006, Blackstock et al.2004, Kirmeyer et al.2000).

One pop psychologist coined the term "inner child" describing the internalization of abuse that interrupts childhood development. Bradshaw describes shame and guilt associated with the abuse children experience. In his book, *Healing the Shame that Binds Us*, Bradshaw describes eloquently, the process of abuse, torture and neglect and the influences on personal development and behavior.

When these shame based children grow into adulthood, many are unaware of the challenges they face in attempting to raise a family. In her book *Toxic Parents: Overcoming Their Hurtful Legacy and Reclaiming Your Life,* Dr. Susan Forward describes parents who were abusive toward their children and how children inherit a legacy of abuse only to repeat the cycle. Clearly, abused children model what they have learned from their environments as Menzies (2006, 2007) described in his study of intergenerational trauma from a Social Work perspective.

Intergenerational effects of IRS abuses are real and occurring presently. Individuals often survive while others died or disappeared. Some were assimilated, others suffered the fate of their resistance living emotionally and psychologically scarred. Many survivors developed personality and anxiety disorders like Post-Traumatic Stress Disorder (PTSD) while other cases could result in anti-social personality disorder and sexual offences (Rojas, Gretton 2007). The research link individuals developing in chaotic and volatile environments exhibit behavioral problems often resulting in conflict with the law, incarceration and institutionalization. Menzies, suggests that a diagnosis of PTSD undermines the extent of the damage as it encompasses a person entirely in a tormented state of anomie or homelessness. For Menzies, some survivors of IRS are not just acting out their abuse they *are* their abuse. The abuse left them homeless and alienated in their own body. Karl Marx would describe this as alienation in his Economic and Philosophical Manuscripts of 1844 by the way.

Menzies shares a participants experience with the intergenerational effect of IRS. This participant describes the absence of his mother during childhood. He said he saw shows like *Leave it to Beaver*, where children present as happy and excitedly run to hug their parents lovingly and dramatically. He said he decided to try that with his mother. He describes his mother not knowing how to react to his display of affection so he decided to shut himself off from her at that point. Presumably, he felt rejected.

Attachment is primary in human experience and our first introduction to social relations. If attachment with our caregivers is interrupted, the damaging effects go beyond one generation

(Henley, 2005). This person could not attach to his mother properly or attachment barely occurred and so how could he transfer this knowledge if he never experienced it and attach to anyone. Its impossible! Menzies participants offer these scenarios to explain why they are maladjusted. "I have no one really to get close to. That's been a problem for me...When things are really doing good, I feel I really don't deserve this. Even relationships – you try to be there for them but you never could be".

Blackstock, Trocmé, Bennett, (2004) follow Aboriginal children including Metis children in the Canadian childcare system. They compare their situation with non-Aboriginal children in care. These children were apprehended due to alleged child maltreatment. The authors say present estimates of child apprehension are three times higher than that of the IRS era. More than one-half of all cases are substantiated as child abuse. The authors find that Aboriginal families do not have stability needed to raise a healthy family. The levels of substance abuse and family dysfunction, abuse and neglect are factors in child maltreatment and indicate a relation with IRS history. Is it possible Aboriginal population growth exacerbated mental health issues through transference of children of survivors because intergenerational effects remain unaddressed?

These findings agree with Barnes, Josefowitz and Cole in terms of academic outcomes and employment potential as well as Menzies discussion on alienation and homelessness. IRS created profound dysfunction in survivors and transference occurs in successive generations creating a legacy of abuse and dysfunction.

Barnes and Vulcano studied non-Aboriginal students, Aboriginal students including First Nation and Metis and compared the three group's academic performance in comparison to non-Aboriginal students. They wanted to know what academic outcomes could occur based on school self-acceptance concepts or identity. They suggest that if Aboriginal people are considered "profane" by mainstream society then those suffering the most would be those who are least acculturated or assimilated. Their findings suggest that Metis children resemble First Nations children in school self-acceptance measures or identity in comparison to the "mainstream". This study reveals Metis students acculturated more to "mainstream" than First Nations children in terms of material possessions. That is, they have televisions at home and other markers of assimilation compared to First Nations children who do not own these possessions at the time. "White" children, considered the normative in this study thus represent the standard to which Metis and First Nation children should acculturate. Metis children have lower self-concepts than "whites" do while First Nations Children have the lowest school self-concept scores. This results in lower academic performance based on ethnicity and level of assimilation. This study is reminiscent of Porter's, The Vertical Mosaic: An Analysis of Social Class and Power in Canada (1965). Porter reveals Canadian society is racially structured. The normative standard, British imperialists, occupy the most powerful segments of Canadian society, while the least acculturated ethnicities descend accordingly to the least powerful.

Rojas and Gretton (2007) observe the history and characteristics of Aboriginal youth sexual offenders. Mental health issues such as Fetal Alcohol Spectrum Disorder are more prevalent in Aboriginal youth offenders. There is a milieu of social characteristics and demographic dynamics contributing to sexual offending. This includes a history of violence and victimization with instability in the environment. Instability includes poverty, family dysfunction such as, co-dependency and abnormal personality, abnormal behavior, and substance abuse is apparent. Young males age 13 to 17 are at the highest risk for sexual offending behavior. Recidivism is likelier to occur in Aboriginal youth offenders. Overall, the home environment is replete with mental health issues and coping is difficult with overwhelming conditions to adapt. The consequences contribute to further social disruption and it is important to intervene in the cycle of violence early say the authors.

Weiman (2006) points out the Royal Commission on Aboriginal Peoples have long since passed and very little of its recommendations implemented. This article suggests an unwillingness to address the issues facing Aboriginal people in Canada. She points out that all necessary research is done and the time to implement and address solutions is now. Aboriginal youth have the highest rates of suicide in Canada and yet little is done to address the situation. Weiman points out that youth are willing to be a part of the solution and not a part of the problem. She encourages stakeholders to listen to what youth have to say about the current challenges they face and to include Aboriginal youth in the solution process.

Lavallee and Poole (2010) point out that Western approaches have dominated the area of psychological treatment of mental health issues. They point out traditional western approaches misunderstood and undervalued indigenous knowledge base treatment. The authors suggest that Indigenous knowledge can augment treatment in addressing intergenerational effects of IRS.

Stewart (2008) reinforce Lavallee and Poole, that Western approaches do not do as well on their own in treating Aboriginal mental health issues resulting from intergenerational effects of IRS. Stewart believes that integrating indigenous models of healing and traditional knowledge augments contemporary approaches facilitating the healing process. Several themes developed. *Community* needs consideration when healing while respecting the diversity within the community. *Cultural Identity* considers the persons self-concept holistically within the world. Without this awareness, ones healing journey will be difficult. Incorporating cultural practice into healing is imperative to the healing journey. *Holistic Approach* is the spiritual, cultural and traditional aspect toward healing. This includes feasts, ceremony and elders. Mental health focus should include these areas to develop a balanced healing journey. *Interdependence* refers to reinforcement between the healthy and the un-healthy. The healthier can always lend a helping hand.

In sum, implementing these themes will help a person and their community to heal from the effects of colonization.

The present status of Metis people's mental health issues is clear in *The Profile of Metis Health Status and Healthcare Access Utilization in Manitoba; A Population Based Study* (Martens, et al. 2010). This complex study provides a broad overview of the situation Metis people face in terms of health and wellbeing considering Diabetes and Metis Psychology. Succinctly,

"Provincially, Metis have a significantly higher prevalence of diabetes compared to all other Manitobans (11.8% vs. 8.8%). There is also a steep gradient of diabetes prevalence with PMR, with the least healthy regions having the highest prevalence". Diabetes and the effects of this disease on mental health are discussed. For this research document, Diabetes directly affects cognitive function negatively. Balancing health and well-being, facing Diabetes as a family member or as a diagnosed person is a massive undertaking. It reflects the sentiments expressed on the government of Manitoba website concerning mental health and caregivers. These types of diseases and mental health issues affect relationships and ability to function and challenge the ability to cope under these conditions.

Bruce (2000) concurs with these assessments regarding Diabetes among Metis. These limitations affect almost all areas of living including relationships. This has a detrimental effect on quality of life. If quality of life is affected then coping with limitations suggests psychology may be affected. In the conclusion, the author calls upon the need for psychological studies on Metis people with Diabetes to determine the effects on Metis psychology.

Kirmeyer, Brass and Taite (2000) in their study of mental health issues reveal Aboriginal people have higher rates of mental health problems compared to the general population in Canada. Suicide, attempted suicide, substance abuse, abuse and violence are all indications of mental health problems in the home and community. The evidence shows that cultural discontinuity such as assimilation, IRS, and racism are causes of increased mental health problems. Their research reveals Aboriginal mental health is underreported.

Indices of poor mental health such as suicide and others are related to individual perceptions of self and identity and are generally regarded negatively. Low self-esteem and self-perception, helplessness and hopelessness are likelier to occur among Aboriginal populations due to a continuum of factors already discussed in detail.

Additionally, "Eurocentric gazing" of Aboriginal identity and culture tends to "otherize" Aboriginal people and leads to racist ideology. Perhaps the best description of Eurocentric gazing is discussed in Said's, Orientalism where Said goes to great length describing the development of the Occident, the place in which European's *otherize* the Orient. This is a dysfunctional cognitive behavior that Said reveals in his literature review throughout antiquity to the present. "Eurocentric gazing" and Aboriginal self-perception leads to reciprocating, self-fulfilling prophecies leading to behavior reinforcing perceptions within the context of colonial power dynamics. Barnes, Josefowitz and Cole (2008) reveal in their analysis that low expectations of Aboriginal academic outcomes produce expected results.

Barnes, Josefowitz and Cole say Metis have undergone a century of cultural ambivalence due to racism, assimilation and IRS. Metis people presently define their ethnicity in the context of colonialism. The authors suggest this will likely continue under these conditions. Canadian racism and oppression is lifting its repressive power allowing Metis identity to flourish and improve mental health. Cultural control and self-determination assist in the overall mental well-being of Metis people. Finally, the authors agree with other assessments on treatment for survivors of IRS. They agree that psychiatric practice must be culturally relevant.

These discussions described Metis people and their history including colonization, corruption, racism and assimilation. These include a legacy of severe inhumane treatment over Metis identity and land base. The consequences of Canadian colonization and Imperialism including corruption through racist ideology, patriarchy and religious ideals imposed on Metis people resulted in multi-generational torment. The consequences remain with us presently due to transference of dysfunction, which then transfers to family and community. Metis youth are subjected to diverse forms of abuse and neglect and consequently self-concepts, academic performance, employment rates and ability to function in a healthy manner are all adversely affected. This transfers and reinforces dysfunctional family settings to new generations of Metis children. This recycling, reciprocating transference and exchange doctrine is likely to continue unless intervention is timely and effective. Metis youth are ready for positive change. This includes developing solutions, integrating a model of health care that is culturally relevant and changing how Canadians view Metis people. Though many would view the situation too complex, that redress appear impossible, the solution is simple. Mutual respect and equal access to wealth and power are the only solutions, it is simple as that and it is all Metis have ever asked of Canada.

In analyzing the history of this reciprocating madness one must wonder, from whence this madness came? How did it all begin? It has been shown that Aboriginal people, including Metis have never historically shown any evidence of mental health issues as seen in the legacy of IRS. After IRS, mental health issues are clearly seen. So how is it that suddenly mental health issues become prevalent post IRS? In analyzing the literature on the effects of torture and other abuses, it is known the victims of abuse alienate themselves, dissociate, alienate from others and attach to their tormentors in a dysfunctional attempt to cope with the pain and humiliation. Herein lays the assimilation process. Finally, this document indicated colonial bullies exploit the vulnerable and manipulate the variables to create a vulnerable situation. This dysfunction is seen throughout history in dysfunctional human relations between empires and nations. It is seen in other situations of colonization, imperialism and nation building. Denying this reveals a dysfunctional personal relationship with oneself and community. The abuser in their narcissistic isolation is compelled by insecurity to control others and a maniacal megalomaniac ritual of abuse ensues when exploiter meets vulnerable. Predatory rape, abuse, neglect and torture are all elements of a sick need for control stemming from insecurity, or a feeling of a loss of control. This is the dysfunctional relationship that we understand as Psychopathic and has transferable qualities in Canadian Empire. Canadian colonizers and settlers experienced their own horrific colonial histories, in the European, the Middle Eastern, Near and Far Eastern and African theatres. All of which include multiple traumatic events similar to the Metis experience. Some were and are worse. Canadians must consider this fact as a part of their identity in order for us all to heal otherwise the corruption will remain. The Canadians that remain and those who are newcomers must identify and resist corruption from their own colonial experiences, intergenerational effects and personal and familial dysfunction including; alcoholism, incest, family violence, sports fanaticism, child neglect and over and under involved parenting among other indicators of dysfunction. Canadians must become aware and admit they too are assimilated, alienated, tormented and homeless.

When Canadians admit they are homeless, inside and out, that they have no business here presently then they are ready to renegotiate the terms of Canadian expansion with a new vision. That is the only business that remains in our relationship. It is unfinished business. It is better late than never. Metis people have been under the thumb of colonial control for many generations resisting. In spite of multi-generational abuse and torment, Metis people refuse to accommodate dysfunction inherent in the totality of colonialism. Metis people refused the tenets proffered by their tormentors, those agents of abuse and their bystanders who sanction institutionalized torture in Canada. No one knows the Metis experience in war and atrocity better than the Metis, except others who no longer are in denial of their own experiences. In sum, Metis people state undeniably, "We are a nation, a people united in family and community. We believe in ourselves and we accept nothing less than a united community, healthy and whole complete with mutual respect and determination".

"Theoretically there is a perfect possibility of happiness: believing in the indestructible element in oneself and not striving towards it". Franz Kafka".

Then the Lone Wolf Warrior offered a list of references for anyone who wishes to check the work. Then the wolf sat down.

Chapter 7

THE BEAST

The Elders murmured with each other and then one got up to speak into the microphone.

We have heard your words and they are strong! We have considered them very carefully. We will now reveal to you this night terror that haunts your dreams.

You have spoken of many great and terrible deeds. Feminism, capitalism, classism, and patriarchy, religion you say? These are all very good observations. Very evil things are afoot!

THE TORMENTOR

You have described eloquently the psychopath, the authoritarian personality type. This is a person who is unreasonable you say, a dangerous person. Then you describe a tormentor that tortures people. It seems you are saying this tormentor is a psychopath. You tell us that something happened ten thousand years ago that brought about the coming of the great corruption. Somehow, somewhere, someone lost their way you say, that they lost faith. You say they suddenly got control issues. You say they have entitlement issues. You say they are selfish and have no self-respect. You tell us this tormentor, this psychopath who was once whole and is now wholly corrupted, gave birth to the great corruption. It sounds like you are describing someone who took control of the people and forced them into their will by oppressing them with many lies. In twisting the truth, they made the people feel insecure and so the people were won over and eventually took to attacking others. Apparently, this group was never satisfied and they just kept taking. We have many legends that tell us about this person. But we will come back to that later or one of the other Elders can tell us more. Whatever it was that happened, you seem to be telling us that a great corruption became an Empire. Throughout history, there were many Empires? They were all competing for supremacy?

Yes, that is all correct answered a few of the Rainbow Warriors.

And what of this corporation you speak of, asked one of the Elders.

The corporation was once an office, it was once a bureaucracy filled with administrators who oversaw the business at hand. Several laws were made to make the corporation have the same legal rights as a real person. Someone did a study and found the corporation, being a giant person had all the characteristics of a psychopath. Corporations only care about making a profit. That is their only mandate.

Mandate, yes we understand mandate, said the Elders.

Yes, their mandate is selfish, self-centered, and the corporation has no regard for you, me, our children's inheritance of the world we live in, it only cares about profit. It does not consider its consumption of resources, fairness or equity. The corporation only cares about profit. It is full of authoritarian leaders and followers. It is hierarchically stratified based in racism. It requires all employees to tow the party line whether they like it or not.

They are actually quite stupid, interrupted another. All of these major corporations that stubbornly maintained white supremacy, catering to white people, preferring to do business with whites only are now all going out of business. When you target a single group, you have marginalized all other groups. It is delusional to think the marginalized are not aware of your preference to white people. Safeway, Sears, Eaton's and the great and magnificent Hudson's Bay Company are all claiming bankruptcy or are totally out of business. They have shot themselves in the head and killed their profitability.

Is that why you believe that capitalism is problematic asked the Elder?

Yes.

Is that it replied the Elder?

Yes. Well, there are the other considerations, the feminist perspective, Marxism and the like.

It would appear you are describing assimilation throughout the ancient civilizations, tribes, city-states, Empires, nations, nation building, throughout cultures. At one time, we governed ourselves collectively. We were like this corporation but not exactly in some ways. We had our traditions and teachings similar to the ancient ones. So it would have been as though a psychopath would have twisted our teachings, assimilating one person at a time, twisting them, corrupting them in our group.

The great beast would know they are different and in order to feel safe and secure, they would prefer to blend in with the people. Blending in is a way of hiding anonymously. Since our old societies would have discovered a corrupted person immediately, the authoritarian as Dr. Bob Altemeyer would describe them, as well as Noam Chomsky and others, we have described them as at worst psychopaths or at least disciples. These individuals would have to create their own society, by assimilating, empire building so they can remain anonymous among an Empire of dysfunction. They would appear normal.

In the ancient times, we would have that happen now and then. The Warriors would discover their dysfunction and they would talk with the person for many days, years! If the person could not or would not be corrected and if they were not a danger, we would just watch over them. We had no prisons or concepts of prisons so we assigned a group of Warriors to watch over the person. If they would not behave and became dangerous, we would banish them.

Some of you young ones might be thinking, big deal if I was banished, I would just go live somewhere else! That's your individualism thinking, you learned that from watching too much TV. To be banished was like a death sentence. It was very difficult to survive on your own. You were sure to die. But at the same time, other groups may find you wandering alone and they would have been told you were coming as the *Scouts* would share news through the moccasin telegraph. Many often tried lying about their predicament but that gets them nowhere as news travels very fast that someone corrupted is out and about.

The other group could offer to take them but they would have to work with the people in camp, cleaning, sewing, tanning that sort of thing. This is how they earn their keep. I'm not sure who it was that said this was women's work, as if this work is disparaging even as they devalue women with such talk. Whomever it was that said this knows nothing about the Way of the Warrior, but rather it speaks volumes about where they originate.

But again, if they are too dangerous to keep around the Warriors will just kill them to protect the children and our Elders. These psychopaths often go after the sick, the young and the Elderly. They never go after someone who will give them too much of a hard time. It's not worth their effort, as they don't like work.

We see this behavior in bullies. In the old days, a bully would have been a person who thinks highly of himself or herself and no one else is as important. This is contrary to the Way of the Warrior. Now you listen carefully, said the Elder. My friend will now approach the microphone and tell you a story.

An Elder approached the microphone and began to talk about the sacred fire, which are the children of the Earth. They are our future. This is why we are a child-centered community and people! This is why we always think in terms of seven generations for the sake of the children. Every generation must think like that so that the children of the earth have an earth to be born into. We have lost that when your great corruption arrived. Nowadays people can only think about themselves and what they can get out of life today. They tell us this is the only life they have left and so they want to party all the time, go on vacation all the time. They say they are tired. Well I guess so eh!

If the Warriors are born into this world and are attacked, even before they are born and they are engaged with the enemy all these years, it is no surprise they would be battle fatigued.

Even the feminists agree that men oppress the women! Women give birth now under unnatural conditions and so even before the children are even born, a woman who is affected by the great corruption oppresses the child in the womb! Even as the children develop in their mother's womb, they are cut out by agents of the great corruption in barbaric acts recorded throughout history you tell us. Why would Warriors do such horrific things?

It was under great torment and dysfunctional environments that caused the parents to turn on their own children and children to rise up against their own families and parents. They consume each other now, clawing, biting and tearing at each other. With an I'll show them attitude they commit suicide. Sometimes they display their suicide online and many come to watch? What manner of mental illness is this, what sickness what depravity? Many are now engaged in a co-dependent relationship, dysfunctional and unhealthy they are in relations with each other based on selfish needs rather than self and mutual respect, balanced by sacred law and medicine wheel technology.

All the people wept for themselves and their children and their was a great and sorrowful moaning that could be heard. Many remembered family and friends consumed and fallen in battle against the great corruption, in Indian Residential Schools, in the streets of Winnipeg and the racism in the public education systems and justice systems. They recalled the missing and murdered women and the senseless violence they face everyday. There were many deaths of children while in care with the Authority and many that go unnoticed because the government hides it, justified by law. Thousands upon thousands of children are apprehended. As many families that are tormented by these conditions of white supremacy in Canada. Even as they count the number if dead and dying Aboriginal children they count the money they will make off the survivors who are likelier to over-represent in the justice system and child welfare systems. Many jobs will be created and taxes will be collected through this oppressive system. There was heartfelt sorrow and regret over all they had done and experienced. They were grieving and sad, confused and angry. Many crying had cried out silently. There was no sound, as they held their breath as if to cry out instead a great and tumultuous trembling, wholly consumed in emotion they were like a rattle as their eyes watered silently. They sounded without making a sound. Others hysterical or were horrified and terrified by this great corruption, many crying screamed in fright.

Suddenly, all heard a scream shriller and more piercing than all others did and many snapped to attention! There was another great and piercing cry heard from on high! Many kept crying not knowing what to do many fell to their knees. Others looked around at each other and great wonder was in their eyes. Then again, it could be heard loudly as it was now amplified over the sound systems. The cameras pointed upward searching and so to did many people, and now there was no mistake. A great and magnificent Eagle was circling above! And they saw it scream!

LOOK! THERE ARE MORE COMING FROM THE EAST someone cried! There were now four massive Eagles circling above the people. They were greater in stature than anyone had ever seen before in their lives with a wingspan wider than highway six on the way up to Thompson, Manitoba. The Eagles were Taller than the tallest Warrior! Only the very old Elders could recall seeing Eagles so magnificent, they are rare to see now. The wind could be heard rushing beneath their wings when they all suddenly dropped from great heights toward the crowd gathered outside. Screaming, they swooped only a few feet over the heads of the people. As if in slow motion, everyone heard the wings, FWOOM! FWOOM! FWOOM! Just then it circled back and up again but not before each one touched the building with their great talons where all the Elders had gathered. Many said they could feel its body heat as it flew overhead. Others said they were instantaneously comforted. What a sight to behold! It was unforgettable!

The Elder spoke into the microphone, "SEMAH"!

And people reached into their pockets and purses and threw Tobacco into the sacred fire that was set by the Helpers earlier. They were saying thank you and offered many prayers.

WEENDIGO

The Elder continued, the signs and wonders have arrived and the prophecies are fulfilled. You are the Rainbow Warriors! We have told stories about a great beast we learned about as children. Its name was not allowed to be said. It was *Weendigo*! That is what the Medicine people would have diagnosed our bullies with in the old days, we would have said, that one is Weendigo. When the Roman Catholic took our children away to be educated in France ages and ages ago it seems. Our children returned changed. Their behavior was Weendigo. That's how we said it. We said they have become Weendigo!

There was a great stir among the people and many began shouting angrily.

Weendigo was the great beast that roamed all over searching for children to eat. It feeds off our children. We always told the people to keep a close eye on our purpose in life, the sacred fire and to tend to it always. We understood that we were not the top of the food chain. We too feared a great predator. And so we lived our lives in balance and harmony and for many generations we were free from this great corruption. It was our teachings, our traditional and healing ways that kept the great beast away from the children of the earth and all of us were aware of it. We maintained equality, respected diversity, we never took more than what is necessary to live, we respected all our relations and we were in total balance, equilibrium with our environment. It was for the sake of the children, for seven generations. But the great corruption has come to feast on our children, to possess them and control them.

We were overwhelmed with these Weendigo people that came to us long ago. It swallowed up everything in its path, the birds could not even get away from its power. It was like a black hole that sucked everything in, not even light could escape! All the animals ran away, the trees and forests were made into deserts overnight!

The great dust bowl they called it. It was a very sad thing to watch. It almost appeared that the end of the world was occurring before our very eyes! This Weendigo, it cannot be reasoned with, there is no bargaining, you cannot negotiate with it, you cannot trust it. It tells only lies and half truths always twisting and contorting things. It is quite the charmer!

Sexy, an Elder shouted!

It would appear we have been inundated with agents of the great corruption said another Elder. It would appear someone in the ancient villages managed to get control of the people even as the Weendigo was able to gain control over the German nation and made many Germans Weendigo!

Another Elder spoke up saying, I remember when the whole world was at war against the power of this great beast. The German nation was reduced to nothing after the First World War. The people were miserable and starving. They were very hard pressed. We are seeing it now in the news.

Greece and other European countries are hard pressed against extremist groups who promise to deliver the people from hard times.

We have seen it in Canada when the conservatives exploited a Weendigo summer to their advantage. They promised to deliver a tough on crime mandate. They have delivered their own paternalistic, patriarchal, hierarchical, authoritarian version but not until all social program budgets were cut and slashed. Now civil liberties are being slashed, scientists are silenced, racism is rampant, and children are dying more than ever or will have to develop in even worse situations of poverty. The Weendigo reigns ever since Weendigo summer. More and more people join the ranks of these extremists to topple properly elected governments.

So long as they were properly elected and weren't lying, cheating or stealing votes with Robocalls, circumvention of election finance rules the Elders said laughing.

Well that's the thing of it eh, said the Elder after a good laugh. We have to trust them to do what they say they are going to do!

Well I don't, said one Elder. I don't vote, never have, never will. Why? Why should I? So they can keep stealing money and do whatever they want? And they are all the same. They all say the same thing, how they will save the people from corruption and they end up more corrupt than the last.

When I was a youth, I could see the hypocrisy of democracy! Why would I go in for that? This is what I am talking about, right here, right now, what we are doing here today. I am hoping for a revolution!

Yes, you have told us about your political views and we respect them replied another Elder.

And I also told you to read the book, *We Were Not The Savages by Daniel Paul*.

Is that the one where he shows how the British constantly talked about how barbaric we Indians are, how savage and blood thirsty, when in fact the British engaged in campaigns of genocide, wiping out the Beothuk, paying five dollars a scalp, indiscriminately murdering women and children and the Elderly?

That'd be the one! It got so bad, blond and ginger scalps were being turned in for the bounty replied the other Elder! They said we were savages, unchristianized and uncivilized. Self-righteousness corrupted beliefs founded in their religions that advocate for the destruction of the infidel and the sinner. At first, I thought it was not the religions that were to be blamed, but rather it was all these insecure unstable people. But their religious writings also advise their followers to aggress against sinners and infidels invigorated by their fervent beliefs.

It is confusing to respect these religions that proselytize and assimilate aggressively after all we have been through. I guess I have to draw my healthy boundary and leave it at that.

Make no mistake though I am not a racist! I am an ethnologist....hahhh I'm just kidding!

But seriously though my challenge is to clarify the teachings of these religions in a respectful way that honors the Way of the Warrior, our sacred teachings which we have carried intergenerationally since time immemorial. At least we are aware of the Weendigo. Some of these religions have been Weendigo for over ten thousand years.

The Church of England and other protestant churches of the reformation resulted in support for the horrors and atrocities. The Spanish used to smash our babies heads against the rocks! To this day, the Roman Catholic Church will not apologize for their part in the Indian Residential Schools.

A ho shouted many Elders! All the Elders understood and it was indeed a difficult mystery to understand. All agreed to live and let live, without prejudice and with respect. Though many feelings were excited one Elder burned *sweetgrass* which brought healing to the group.

In the old days, when the colonization of Turtle Island began, the British Empire was expanding. They had teachings that convinced them they were superior to all other people in the world. But when they came here, they quickly realized they were powerless by our sheer numbers for we numbered in the millions upon millions. We respected diversity and we lived in relative peace compared to what was going on in Europe and the Middle East. But now Canada wants this same diversity for themselves but they never think to ask us how we managed diversity when we number among millions and we had abundance!

They were only a few dozen scattered here and there at first. One of their ships could only carry so many at one time. At first, they came and set up their forts and they traded with us. But they did not know how to survive the winter. And we shared with them generously. They cut down all the trees, our relations and they chased away many four legged's and those that fly, they made many fires stupidly.

Then one of the young Elders laughingly quoted a line from the movie Avatar, "your like a baybee, making noise, don't know what to do". Everyone laughed.

They needed our help and so we helped them, we fed them and gave them medicine. They survived and they wanted to trade.

But their ways were not the same as ours and many of us would not trade with them. They were too Weendigo. For one thing, they were very dirty and they spread disease, which nearly wiped us all out. Apparently, they got those diseases from living among swine and chickens. You can read all about that in *Guns, Germs, and Steel,* by *Jared Diamond.*

Then the British came to understand they had to learn from us or die. And even as they received letters from their Kingdom far away advising them to be superior and to take everything, many knew they were powerless to do so. They tried to corrupt our chiefs by offering many valuable gifts but our Chiefs simply gave them away to the people. Then they tried to turn one tribe against another, typical of the great beast to divide and conquer. They tried to take our Warriors as their slaves but our Warriors saw no honor in the way they practiced their form of slavery. Our Warriors would escape rather than remain with the Weendigo's. Finally, the British men of the forts began losing their own Warriors to come live with us, the people. Many of their Warriors preferred our life as it was a true expression of freedom.

No taxes, said an Elder!

No taxes replied the Elder speaking. But the British forts had teachings that many believed to their deaths and many could not or would not see that our ways were beneficial in harmony and peace. Many of them were very difficult, stubborn and obstinate with fervent belief in loyalty to the crown and white supremacist thinking.

I guess that kind of thinking is that authoritarianism you and Bob describe eh? Anyway….

It was the French who faired better than the British did. The French who would escape their oppressive Empires and mental slavery running to our people, learned that the most profitable thing to do was marry into the Children of the Earth.

And so they *married up*! I read about that in a book called *A Fair Country, Telling Truths about Canada by John Ralston Saul*. This established vast and mighty trade networks and those they married were key players in their trading systems. When the French learned this method, many French participated. The British believed they were too superior and believed they did not need to marry. Perhaps it was their authoritarian personalities and their belief in white supremacy but they tried to maintain their systems. So they stayed in their forts but they were losing more British solders to straying away. Many years later, the British finally saw that in order to survive they would have to allow themselves to become assimilated to our ways and they finally took to marrying. This was very profitable for the British. But the British would require of those they married to lose their identity and become totally British. While the French preferred to be assimilated into the Way of the Warrior. That is when a new nation was born.

BIRTH OF A NEW NATION

So we do not disrespect by telling the story wrong, we will ask our Metis Elders to come and share with us.

And so a Metis Elder approached the microphone.

Jacques would marry into the Children of the Earth and live with the people. Jacques would speak of their savior Jesus and god and all them 'postles. But many preferred spiritual philosophy over religion. Those they married would teach them the ways and this benefitted the French traders in their relations with many of our people.

Today, we would call it *Cultural Competency* or *Cultural Proficiency* and it made relations amenable. The French did not take the same perspective as the British. And so the French enjoyed prosperity as we worked together often as equals, recognizing mutual respect for each others ways.

Not so with the British traders.

New Children of the Earth came because of these friendlier relations with the French.

Children with the British came as well but racism was rampant by that time. These children were not the same as the Children of the Earth. It was the British insistence they were superior to the Children of the Earth and so they raised their children to be British and these children maintained a British identity for many years along with white supremacy ideology, patriarchy, paternalism, hierarchical stratifications based in racism, authoritarianism.

Jacques' children would grow up in the traditional and healing ways of the Children of the Earth and they would take these teachings to heart. They would be raised in medicine wheel technology, peace, harmony, and prosperity. They would appear almost no different than other Ojibway save for being of mixed descent, culturally these were First Nation children. They would begin to number among many with our people and they would marry. They would have children and those children would marry each other, a process referred to as "endogamy".

Little Pierre, son of Jacque would be trained to trade along the river ways and waterways of Turtle Island. Every Spring Pierre would help his father to trade and set up depots, which sometimes held trade goods over a season. It is important to note that this was not a paternalistic, patriarchal, hierarchical, authoritarian system at this point. That did not come until later. At this point, these original Metis children were virtually identical to Ojibway.

Eventually when Jacque passed on Pierre would inherit the family business. Pierre would marry Marie, one of the daughters of another Metis family, these marriages, having a firm establishment in trading routes would become profitable, and they would move away from the First Nation family groups and establish year round depots along the rivers. They would have children who would now be raised among other families of mixed descent. This is where the birth of a new nation occurs at these depots along rivers and lakes.

The children of Pierre and Marie would now live along the river ways and waterways, along the great lakes and their communities would become profitable trading posts where French traders would come. It makes sense this would happen as the children of Pierre and Marie would speak many languages having been raised among so many different cultures, they would be able to communicate effectively, powerfully and would become well-respected people.

This would prove to be very profitable for these communities. These communities would grow in power and influence and the children of this new nation would rise up to become one of the most powerful nations among the people. They were the full expression of what should have happened in our relations with the newcomers. But this was not meant to be. We would have to endure many years with the British.

They would come and cut down all the trees and leave everything in waste. They would bring their priests from Catholic and Anglican faiths, which would introduce patriarchy, paternalism, hierarchy and authoritarianism. The egalitarian or communitarian ways, the devaluation of women and their important roles, the child-centered community would be discouraged even repressed by the Catholics as they meddled in the affairs of Metis. They would now be in a position to exploit the Metis made vulnerable especially after the Riel Resistances. In order for the Metis to qualify for their charity the Metis must recant the Way of the Warrior, they would have to confess!

But we are a little ahead of ourselves in the story.

Some of those trading posts became great American cities like Chicago and Detroit. And so those communities were sprinkled across the Midwest up to Red River and a little beyond. They were so powerful they controlled trading prices by manipulating one company against another. The powerful Hudson's Bay Company went to war against the Northwest Company. The Metis had a part to play as well as they did not like the idea of a monopoly growing in their territory. So if the prices were not good at the Hudson's Bay Company, they would go to the Northwest Company and if not good there, they went to the States. Even when the Hudson's Bay Company won their monopoly, the Metis would undermine their monopoly by trading elsewhere. This was illegal but unenforceable for many years.

It was Riel and the Metis who would stand up and resist the great corruption and they negotiated the terms of treaty with the British establishment of the day. It was pointless, as we have said, we knew all along that you couldn't bargain with Weendigo, there is no negotiating, you cannot reason with it. We did not know that Weendigo was already possessing much of Europe with this Empire building and nation building business of enslaving the people of those lands, encroaching, terrorizing, raping, murdering, destroying all that is sacred.

Many of those children fled the oppressions, which is common to Weendigo, to capture and to control, to enslave and that is how the British behaved in Red River in those days.

In 1870, the Metis were numbering a great and magnificent number! We had our own language and spiritual philosophy, culture and teachings. We numbered nearly ten thousand strong and we could muster a massive army within an hour, faster than any European muster. We were a powerful nation, the only one daring enough to stand up to the mighty Sioux nations! Many respected the Metis.

Many would not encroach on our territory and they respected us for a long time. It was the great corruption that came to change our relations with the Metis. When land, hunting and furs became scarce, then there were wars. It is when resources become scarce, the game is no more, and we must compete for food, clothing and other trade goods we are hard pressed to share everything.

But even with the strength of the Metis, the massive immigration waves of those Europeans trying to escape the power of Weendigo already in Europe, came to Turtle Island. Many of them were now Weendigo. They came in the thousands upon thousands, equinox to equinox. We were inundated. What were we to do? We were perished from their diseases and corruption, we would perish and our ways would be lost forever and we would all be enslaved by Weendigo. So we negotiated with that which cannot be negotiated with and look at us now. Even as we resist the assimilation programs that were imposed upon us, we are losing many children to the Weendigo. Even some of those people who became agents of the great corruption only fool themselves. To be in league with this beast is not the path of wisdom. It is foolishness. It is the dark side of contrary!

Even the beautiful Metis and First Nation wives the British had married and their beautiful children, being raised British, to think British, they thought they were in fact British and they had nothing to do with Metis identity and culture! How embarrassing it must have been, how sad and unfair it must have felt when actual British women began to arrive.

The British women would laugh and scoff at the Metis wives who thought they were British. Pffft, the white women would say, please! The British Hudson's Bay Company men would abandon their wives and children, kicking them out of the Forts. These women and children were no longer British but were now called *half-breed*! In a racist system, one dominated by the British, meant that even your children could be rejected and that's just what those men did!

That is how the British children of Hudson's Bay Company men were identified, half-breed. Half-breed is not how Metis identify. Soon thousands upon thousands of British and other European groups would arrive to inundate the Metis.

There are stories of half-breed Metis who struggled under the new system. Just a few years before the children of Hudson's Bay

Company men were the elite upper class, now they were no different from Metis people. Humble pie was served as these children previously thought themselves superior to Metis and would not join them during the Riel Resistance. So many having been served their humble pie then joined the ranks of Metis as they were too Weendigo to be among First Nation groups, they were not white so the Metis took them in and showed them what it meant to be Metis. There is still division among our ranks due to this racism and the Catholic and Christian religions.

After the great Diaspora of the Metis occurred, many fleeing as far away as the Yukon, the Metis were forced from their homes, land stolen, some racist British simply arrived to Metis homes, told them to leave but not before raping and in some cases murdering. Or Metis would arrive to find someone else living in their homes and they would be forced to relocate if they could get away without being raped and murdered.

As for the scrip system, the Supreme Court of Canada agrees that delays and other insidious methods corrupted the process, cheating Metis out of their land. While the population of Winnipeg ballooned as immigrants flowed in, Metis were being bullied and harassed, raped, disappeared and murdered. Under conditions of duress Metis who had scrip sold it for a pittance and attempted to get away. Many speculators argued with Metis saying they may as well sell it now, as it is apparent they won't keep their land even if they got it. The Orangemen would come and kick them out. Sell now and get out. Thomas Flanagan figures this was a fair deal. This was scandalous! It was robbery, theft, burglary, blackmail, embezzlement and extortion, fraud, false pretenses, larceny and currently Canadians are in possession of stolen goods.

Now many were staving on the roadsides with their families as they attempted to run away from the Weendigo's. For many years, Metis were non-citizens. They were not on the voter registry lists and thus could not attend public schools, buy and sell, work and vote. They were simply left to die an act of genocide.

In order to eat they had to rely on the church who would take up collections. They would attempt to hunt game but all game was gone. They ate crows, muskrat and other scavengers. But many

Metis had to confess the words of death before they could get any charity. Thus many Metis were converted to Catholicism.

Culturally they had to abandon and put away all sense of what it meant to be Metis. That is how Catholicism came to the Metis. It was not really present before but now it was introduced in such a way as to convert under conditions of duress. That is how the Catholic faith came to the Metis.

That is how Weendigo came to Red River.

And so we are here to tell you that it is not religion, capitalism, feminism, classism, Imperialism, or any other ism. It is Weendigo, and we have always known this! It is not the oppression of women, oppression of races, classes or empires. IT IS THE OPPRESSION OF CHILDREN!

There was a great stir among the people watching and listening. Many began to speak out of turn and chaos was the result. Many began to shout profanities and others wept.

HEY HEY HEY! Cried a great Elder! YOU ARE ALL HURTING MY EARS!

Yes, said one of the Rainbow Warriors. Statistics are empirical! Children, all over the world are oppressed with the highest levels of death, suicide, and poor mental and physical health, highest levels of poverty, lowest education rates, highest incarceration rates, highest apprehension rates...

The list could go on, interrupted the Elder.

The Rainbow Warrior sat down knowing they had spoken without holding the talking stick.

When the Canadians came, they too were losing their children. Those who strike treaty with the great beast, in Europe and then here on Turtle Island, are delusional if they think they have any control in the great corruption.

A spouse believes they can manage the abuse they get when in an abusive relationship. They will do everything they can to assuage the rage of an abusive spouse. They will have the house spotless, slippers will be ready for the arrival of the abuser, dinner will be ready emphasizing meal preferences, the paper will be made ready, the remote controls placed conveniently, the lighting is arranged, not a speck of dust to complain about, everything must be perfect. And still the abuser attacks and beats the spouse down as nothing will stop the mood swing, nothing can be done. And so the spouse begins to think they did something, it must be them and so they try to behave themselves in a vain attempt to make the relationship work. It is a cycle of dysfunction that wears the spouse down until they are severely beaten into submission and become an abusers punching bag or they are murdered or they escape. You cant negotiate with this thing, it doesn't bargain, it cant be reasoned with, you do not have control.

Empires negotiating terms with the great beast is an exercise in futility! Weendigo will colonize your mind and your souls all are nearly helpless against demonic possession. Your soul is clasped in chains, placed behind apparition bars in a phantom prison, located in the furthest regions of your medicine wheel, a deep dark dungeon hidden away in the back of your mind, left there like an afterthought. There, you will become like a wee small voice. Your sacred self can only cry from within, through your dreams your inner child. The soul held prisoner, speaks to the children of the earth in their dreams. Children are being given over to the beast and are raised among lies of white supremacy. This is a great abomination! Children are memorizing and the reciting the words of death as if they were the words of life. The Children of the Earth are controlled, like husks, by husks, enslaved to serve the master. What manner of devilry is this? Are Christians devil worshippers? Have they got it all backwards thinking they are worshipping god, when in fact they are worshipping the devil?

You have all spoken well in identifying why Canadians were bystanders to the destruction of our children. All of our teachings are child centered. Everything about us, our lifestyles, ways, our psychology too you say eh? It is all child centered. We always thought of our children first. But they passed laws and forbid us from passing on our teachings to our children. They passed more laws, namely the Indian Act, which forbid us from speaking our languages, and took away our children into these Indian

Residential Schools to assimilate them and make them into agents of the great beast as if they could bargain with Weendigo!

We saw how changed our children were when they came back from these schools. We saw that Weendigo had corrupted their minds with many false teachings and our own children were disrespectful of our ways! They said we practiced WITCHCRAFT! They shook in their pants, wetting themselves for fear of consequence they would face upon their return to the Indian Residential Schools. They ran away from us terrified and afraid. They did not want to visit with many of their grandparents. We were not even allowed to heal our children with ceremony as we once did and they refused it anyway. Many of us were helpless. Helpless, we could only stand and watch as the Weendigo's took our sacred fire away from us, to be eaten alive from the outside in and then, from the inside out. It was vey sad to witness the terrible destruction of their souls. But we had to remain strong for the sake of the children for seven generations as we knew a time would come when the Rainbow Warriors would rise up in resistance to the great corruption. But when the children grew up among the Weendigo's learning their ways, they would have children and do to their own children, what happened to them in those institutions of torture. Indian residential schools, public education schools, child and family services, justice, racism in the Weendigo cities and towns, exercise with all authority and public sanction the breaking down of our identities. Just like your dreams, we now wander among the living dead, the husks who search for our souls to imprison and consume us for eternity.

Have we created industries of torture? Public education, children's hospitals, social services, policing and the like are now institutions of corruption. Do we now objectify our children seeing them as an opportunity for industry? Are we failing in our fiduciary duty, duty to care and standard of care as we would rather protect our careers and incomes rather than protect our sacred fires? Has racism allowed us to dehumanize our children, to objectify them and to use them to enhance our careers? Is our self-loathing and self-destruction so bad we are now turning on our own children? Are we harvesting ourselves so this beast can continue to consume us, the same way we harvest chickens? Have we mass produced children of the earth to offer to this great beast? Have we developed intricate and detailed self-destruction and are we now sharing these devilish teachings to the young people, all for a mere night's pleasure and entertainment in honor of this thing? Do we morally justify these actions for the sake of our own children over and above other people's children in favoritism? Do we look upon our children as industry?

All were quiet now. There was a growing wind. Night was coming.

In return, the Weendigo has over many centuries, given its slaves material things satisfying lies of materialism, wealth, status and power, all delusions of the mind proliferated by Weendigo culture. And so, with these cultural constructions that value *SEXUAL INTERCOURSE*, gold, oil and other resources produced industries, manufacturing and production all in pursuit of these delusions. Some get more, others get less and it is a sin to have sex so they control that too. In the old days, we used to have no shame in the act of sexual intercourse nor did we have any gender issues nor were oppressive towards other choices people made for themselves in these regards. All were sacred. Today, they use shame and guilt, primary motivators to control everyone and many hide in a closet. Meanwhile anyone who has dealings with priests and nuns as children knows how sick they can be.

Weendigo culture is a culture of lies and delusions. It is a culture of slaves and they are seeking to enslave and devour.

Many tears were now raining down the onlookers cheeks. They understood everything, making all the connections, and were horrified at the precision of Weendigo. They listened hoping for a cure. Many wondered if all was lost.

Of course, if the beast runs out of children to eat, what then? The Beast will starve! But that does not mean we implement whole nations and empires with many stories and complex cultural constructions so that we can harvest and offer our children in sacrifice to this thing! Does it?

I am from the Weendigo's said the foolish one feeling great remorse, sadness in his heart, grieving over all that has been done. My Elder told me I am Weendigo Kahn.

Eh? What's that said an Elder?

It's true, I was told my medicine was very powerful. I was told I am a contrary spirit. I was told I am Weendigo Kahn.

Then many burst out laughing as if fresh rain had fallen and they were coming out of a draught.

No you are not Weendigo, said the Elder. The Weendigo is also contrary. But it is the most contrary thing one could meet. It is the coldest of the cold, the hottest of the hot, the brightest of the bright, the darkest of all darkness. It is pure evil.

It's true you are *Weendigo Kahn* but that is not the same as Weendigo.

Weendigo is the great beast that eats children it is contrary.

We have teachings about contrary people. It does not mean they are Weendigo. It means they come from that same place in the great mystery where everything is different, backwards, but contrary spirit is very sacred. Even this teaching about fate that we heard today from the Rainbow Warriors is contrary. How can one be happy when bad luck happens? Yet, the strange thing about fate is that in the end, you really would not want it any other way. We do not wish for sickness to bring about contentment. That is silly. And yet, it is a great mystery that sometimes we are made whole by the power of the contrary spirit. You my young contrary are called foolish one because you are silly and like to play jokes. But that is a good thing! Have you ever heard the phrase laughter is the best medicine? You are our icebreaker! You are our hero! You bring us healing. Your medicine is very powerful indeed! So don't be too hard on yourself. We are not talking about you little one. You are our only hope in this great mystery!

The young Rainbow Warrior smiled a bright and happy smile!

Chapter 8

EPIPHANIES

All my life I was afraid. I was afraid of the dark. I was afraid of my parents. I was afraid of my teachers. I was afraid of what people would think of me. I was afraid I was ugly. I was sure I was ugly. But the truth is there is no reason to be afraid of anything. Fear as we know it is dysfunctional. It is just that we are trained to believe in what these cultures have told us to believe in.

I grew up with Vampires that lived in the night and slept in the daytime, surely these were contraries. These Vampires sucked the blood of people and they lived on them like parasites. I have seen many movies about Vampires. How they turned people against themselves so they are totally possessed by these demons. I grew up on Werewolves that would kill you and leave you undead. Not able to pass on. You would be alive but not alive. You would be like a ghost, adrift in between both worlds.

Kind'a like a crackhead the Weendigo Kahn asked?

Everyone laughed.

Not quite, interjected a Metis Psychologist. Addicts are lost but they are not wholly lost. They can be recovered if that is what they want. I was talking about the horror stories of Werewolves and how I would dream of them calling out to each other searching for me, to possess my soul.

Oh that dream, the sacred clown said. I heard them too.

Yes, it was as if the whole city was turned and we had no place to hide so we hid in plain site. All we could do was walk past them as they searched and searched hungry for bloodshed. How frightened I was as I walked down those cold, wet, lonely streets with no place to hide. How hopeless I felt. I was worried to death. I may as well have been one of them.

Then when I saw the Zombie movies, I could see the pattern. I saw that I was running, hiding, trying to be free from the evil that hunted for me. I was trying not to be turned.

I thought about my sexual abusers and how they would creep up on me and I had no one to turn to for help. I guess that's how those IRS survivors felt eh, cold and alone with no one to help you? There must be so many kids like that out there even right now! Oh how I wish I could just take them all in and save them.

Those sexual abusers are like this psychopath I guess eh, said another?

DYSFUNCTION, CO-DEPENDENT RELATIONS AND PROJECTION

No, said the Metis psychologist, they are not quite like a psychopath. They are having a type of psychotic episode but they know better, they could have stopped themselves long before they came to abuse. They often have excuses like, that one seduced me or, I couldn't help myself they say. The truth is, they knew it was wrong. They just didn't ask for help. They tried to resist alone if they tried at all. They were too prideful. They are sick people that need help.

A young person said, I was physically abused, rejected and I was molested, sexually abused by some of my family, my aunts, my uncles. My dad put me out to work on the street. I don't know why they did that. I was little and I am ashamed about the whole affair. I tried to ask for help but no one listened. They said I was making trouble. One said I was sexy, I was attractive to them I guess, if that's even possible. I felt special, I wanted that relationship because the other was violent and abusive. Sometimes, I think the violence is preferable. I feel ashamed of myself because of these feelings and thoughts.

What you don't understand is that it's not whether or not you were attractive or what you may or may not have done to arouse someone, all rape and sexual abuse are about control. Abusers don't care about you. They objectify you like a predator that preys on its victim all they care about is what they get in the end. It's not about you, it's about them. They think they love you but it's a corrupted form, delusional and they will say many sweet things to get what they want. They often don't even know why they behave like this or where it comes from. Sometimes they don't even know they have a problem. They just feel entitled. They crave control.

Not everyone who has control issues is a rapist either, but if we are talking about sexual abuse and sexual violence, these insidious control issues are distinct from other types of control issues.

For example, some people will just keep their home clean while others are workaholics or get into professions that allow them opportunity to control others. So it's important to make that distinction and it's important to get help before things get unmanageable.

Bullies and abusers, sexual and other forms of abuse that develop with the person, into a personality are attracted to victims. Victims often behave in just such a way that attracts bullies and bullies behave in just such a way as to attract victims. Both tear at each other until they complete the ritual. It is like a ritual both engage to fulfill their dysfunctional desires. Both are victims of course and both need help and support.

The bully is a coward, insecure with insecure attachment styles in their personality development. They never attract a stronger person they prefer vulnerable people. Victims don't feel like they deserve anything better than abuse so they are also insecure. It is nothing inherent with them as people, it is just how they were raised in the land of Weendigo.

Just then, another Rainbow Warrior said, I guess that's all it is then, sickness. For a long time I was afraid to go to the mall. I hated crowded places. I just knew they were thinking things about me.

How did you know they were thinking things about you, asked the Elder?

Oh I knew it, I could see it in their faces, how they looked at me and they stared so rudely! They thought I was a dirty Indian! They talked to each other when I walked by and they would whisper it! When I turn around they would just stare at me.

Okay, but did you actually hear them saying something about you? That you were a dirty Indian?

No, but I knew they were thinking it. I saw it in their eyes!

The Metis psychologist asked the young person if they were a mind reader because if they were, they were the first mind readers they had ever met. The psychologist didn't mean to sound offensive but to point something out.

Well, what are you trying to say?

You don't really know what people are thinking. You can't possibly know. You might be able to surmise what another is thinking but there is no way you could know anyone's thoughts.

Yah but I know that "white" people are racist against Indians and so when I see them, they judge me, they think of all the stereotypes! That's how I know what they're thinking! It's in the research! Walk down any street downtown or turn the channel on any television station anywhere in Canada and you will see image upon white supremacist image of the superiority of white people, and that black people and Mexicans can do well too if they just become white. White people are racists!

The Elders looked on this discussion, which had everyone enthralled!

Okay, there is research that suggest SOME white people are racists but do you believe that ALL "white" people are racists?

Well, no, not all of them. That would make me racist. But most of them!

Okay so what makes you think every white person you see in the mall is racist and is thinking racist things about you?

Hmmmm. Okay, I see what your saying. You're saying that I am projecting.

Projecting? What's that, asked the psychologist already knowing the answer.

Projecting is when I think all white people are racist, they are thinking racist things about me, and when I go out to the mall, every white person I see must be thinking racist things about me. Your right, I don't really know what they are thinking. But my mind is trained to be ready for anything and so I trained my mind to anticipate what is out there. In this case, white people, and they must be thinking racist things about me. So I project that out to white people, mentally I push these ideas onto the people I see out there and so I see them as if they really are thinking racist things about me. So when I see that being projected back at me, I assume they really are thinking racist things about me. AM I REALLY DOING THAT?

Yes, you are!

Wow. I had no idea. I'M THE RACIST ONE?

Yes, you are! Well, we don't really know if all white people are racist or rely on stereotypes. It may be that some do, but not all and it's not fair to put everyone into one basket. It can't be that all white people are racist but some may be. If they are, then that is their problem. We do not know what is driving them to behave like that. It may be an authoritarian personality type, some type of aggressive personality, perhaps they too were abused as a child. Maybe their marriage is breaking up. Maybe they're poorly educated. We don't know. It could even be something really sad, like maybe their child is dying of cancer at home or they lost a child or loved one and it's making them miserable. If they are being racist, that is their problem. We do not have to let it bother us by taking it personal.

Whoa, said the Rainbow Warrior.

And the young Rainbow Warrior had a sudden realization, an epiphany. The Rainbow Warrior understood they too were assimilated, Christianized, civilized even though they did everything to resist corruption.

You may want to take some time with that one and process it for a while, alone, in private. Don't be too hard on yourself. You will find, it's not your fault. Most business are owned by white people and they assume the only people in the world who have money are white people. So they advertise only to white people using white supremacist images. No doubt you're triggered by all these images as they inflect white supremacy transferring to you inferiority.

So our insecurities, our fears and anxieties are all culturally constructed, asked an Elder?

SOCIOLOGY, PATRIARCHY, CULTURE AND GENDER ISSUES

It would appear so said a sociologist in the room.

Once you realize that all of this, our entire world as we understand it is not real, it is not what we think it is, it is not the truth. Our world was built on lies, all lies, which it is all in our head. When we realize this, we will never be afraid of the dark ever again. Our nightmares will cease to have the effect that it once did. We will be able to throw off the oppressive regimes in our lives and live free and emancipated from the fears that haunt our darkest nightmares.

Are shame and guilt the same asked a young Rainbow Warrior?

Why not? We are taught to feel ashamed by teachings of righteousness and evil, good and bad. These cultural constructions are not the same when compared across time in history and across cultures around the world. These constructions are simply reinforced negatively or positively with pain or reward. Should we do something that our society says is wrong it may not be the same for another society. What is shameful for us is not shameful for others.

It is important to realize that our current culture as dysfunctional as it is requires us to obey laws that are consistent with the dominant culture. We would never say that it is okay to do some of the things we once did, as that would be advocating anti-social behavior. Some things we once did included marrying at the age of nine or practicing polygamy. Both are in fact illegal nowadays. We used to beat our children and the Mennonites in Manitoba have been in the news concerning their cultural and traditional practices that are now deemed criminal.

We have seen our Aboriginal children apprehended from Aboriginal homes and they have been fostered out to Hutterite and Mennonite cultures where the children are now raised, Christianized and assimilated. We have seen over a dozen Aboriginal children with Hutterites and Mennonites at Wal-Mart dressed in Hutterite and Mennonite traditional clothing speaking German. It looked like an abomination to witness this first hand. But upon closer examination you can count the dollars. At approximately $3,000.00 a month per child, we were looking at

$45,000.00 a month worth of kids! How one established social norm is culturally appropriate and the other is not, appears as though we have entered the surreal.

Consider gender issues, continued the sociologist. In our dominant Judeo-Christianized culture, we have a nuclear family that consists of a mother, father and two children. This is called the nuclear family. I don't think it has anything to do with nuclear war or anything like that.

Anyways, this cultural phenomenon emphasizes gender roles based in patriarchy, where a man is the head of the house and a woman is a slave. The children are slaves too. This started when men discovered they could have many slaves, umm errr, children by fathering many children by having many wives. The children are then subjected to the rule of the father's house. That is where we get the phrase *children of Abraham* or *Children of Israel*. A single man could effectively father hundreds of children in one life and have total ownership over the wives and children. That is an opportunity to build a powerful workforce, army, tribe and so that is what the children did, they worked with their mothers in the fields, hunting and gathering, fighting enemies, enslaving and assimilating. That is how patriarchy began eons and eons ago.

It is important to note that this is not said so that we are to blame Jewish people for the problems we face today. This was an established cultural norm and the Jewish people had no part to play in how other groups adopted patriarchy and used it to their advantage in social control and resource gathering whether insidious or not. It is just that from a religious perspective in relation to the Talmud, Torah, Tanahk and the Holy Bible our sources for history of Western "civilization", this is the most familiar resource to understand patriarchal origins which we all experience today.

Patriarchy permeates our social values so much that we take it for granted that this is a normal function of human living. Meanwhile, we have failed to appreciate the diversity of human existence. We have failed to analyze critically the institutions we have established as normal. We are sorry that we have empowered some of those institutions through social consent. Some of us do not want to rock the boat *a metaphor for established cultural norms and practices*, or to bring trouble to loved ones or ourselves. However, some of us do.

Some Warriors have resisted the great corruption and they now identify as allies with the gay community. They have challenged the status quo and have accepted that some people do not ascribe to the Judeo-Christian norms, which forbid and outlaw homosexuality, transgender and bisexuality.

We were born into this culture and so it appears normal, as if this is the way we are supposed to live. It appears so normal anything else looks weird, foreign and we can even become xenophobic.

I guess that's why we need to educate ourselves better, so that we can tell for ourselves what is corrupt, asked one close by?

Education is a great start! It is important to question introspectively. *The unexamined life is not worth living Socrates* said. It is best to look at where we came from, what our history is. Therapy helps. Both are the path of wisdom. Warriors must be open to new teachings, new ways while maintaining balance with the medicine wheel.

Just then, another joined in with a story. That's very interesting, they said. I have an aunt who being the eldest in a family that is mostly sisters with two very young brothers was raised to hunt, fish and do all the work that men do. She was not gay but she had to wear men's cloths and do men's work and so many thought she was an *abomination in eyes of the Lord*! She faced open ridicule, harassment and abuse from the church, community and other family. But there were no men in the family and she being the Eldest of the girls, took the responsibility, she cared for her family as if she were a man and only because society imposed these established norms upon her and her family!

The sociologist continued, this used to happen a lot with the children of the earth in the old days. Women would take over men's roles. Men sometimes took over women's roles. Sometimes things would change and so the people had to adjust.

It may seem strange to consider when you come from a patriarchal system that trains you to see these situations as abnormal but in the indigenous world there were no genders. Many believed spirit has no gender. So there may be no ridicule. It was understood as a necessity rather than an abomination. But not all indigenous societies were so accommodating. Some were patriarchal even before the introduction of Judeo-Christian religions replied the sociologist.

Finally, said the sociologist. It may be difficult for many to understand being born into a patriarchal system that some people are women when they have boy parts or they are men when they have girl parts. There are those who are born with both sexual parts and they were considered very sacred people in many indigenous societies.

Patriarchy and its systems of power do not allow us to consider these issues. You would be viscerally rejected from your family and community if you ever considered these issues. You would not be able to buy or sell, you would be ostracized and you would have to leave your community to start over somewhere else. That is the power of patriarchy. Most people would rather not think about these issues. But things are changing and youth are leading the way.

I have these dreams, entered another. My teeth are breaking like glass in my mouth. I am spitting them out on the floor. I am horrified. I don't understand what is happening. I think I am done, but teeth keep falling out. It never ends.

I think I know what your dream means, replied another. In World War Two, many Europeans were severely malnourished as they were very badly treated. Many died. They lay starving in the street and other healthier nourished people actually stepped over them casually as if they were dead animals. The survivors, suffering from malnutrition causes their teeth to become brittle and they literally break like glass. Apparently, there is some link to malnutrition and oral health and oral health to better nutrition. It is a type of interdependent relationship where one affects the other. Anyways, many Europeans came to Canada to escape the holocaust, Holodomor, and the horrors of war and aggression. When they arrived, many found their teeth would break like glass in their mouth. Even worse, this effect was intergenerational! It carried on two or three generations and we still do not know when or if the consequence of malnutrition will end for some as their teeth continue to break off in shards.

I wonder what kind of consequence we Aboriginal people will face having faced our own instances of malnutrition experiments as we were the guinea pigs for nutrition scientists. They knowingly subjected the children to malnutrition just to compare with healthy well-nourished kids.

Boy, talk about *relative deprivation*, said another!

What's that, they asked?

Relative deprivation is a type of torment. It happens when people compare their situation with others who have more. They experience relative deprivation a sense of not having what others have and they long for it, pining, another answered.

Is relative deprivation like inequality, a few asked.

Yes. Inequality is the apparent and physical difference between the have's and the have not's. Relative deprivation is the sensation we experience when we have not, and we see that others have.

Did you know that the Canadian government admitted they harmed Aboriginal people with *Indian Residential Schools* and then offered therapy and access to psychological services for survivors and their children?

No!

Many became intrigued at this latest question.

Well they did! And now they want to end the funding that allows access psychological services. They were very quiet about the whole affair. Almost everyone I spoke with told me they had no idea psychological services were available. And it's not available to the children of children of survivors either! It only goes to survivors and their children. So because I was a child of survivors, I can get help, but my kids can't. They even covered the cost of mileage to and from your home and the psychologist's office. They even fly you in and out! It's all ending now. They say they have fulfilled their legal obligations according to their five-year mandate to heal over a century of genocide. I guess they think transference only goes so far intergenerationally. Apparently, we're all automatically cured after five years.

There was much stirring among the hundreds of people present because they were all offended that they were not made aware that psychological services were available to them.

It is up to us children of children of survivors to demand this help! What logic is this that we are all healed from this great multi-generational and dominating Weendigo cultural imposition of racism and trauma?

Many agreed!

I was told they changed their policy, that they would cover the children of children of survivors for therapy. So I called on behalf of my kids. I was told, yes, in some certain cases, the grandchildren, brothers or sisters or any other family member or spouse that had contact with a survivor, could access a psychologist. Then they called me back and said my kids would not qualify. That really pissed me off! You don't tell me bullshit and then tell me more bullshit! I got all triggered up! So I called them back to appeal it. They told me there was nothing to appeal because my kids were supposed to make an appointment with the psychologist and the psychologist was supposed to come up with a care plan. Then they would consider the care plan and decide at that point if they would approve the claim or not. So, that's what your supposed to do if you need help for your grandkids.

What a fucken runaround eh, many murmured.

I called them one time! I submitted all my mileage forms to them. They asked for my Social Insurance Number and other ID. I gave it to them trusting I was giving this sensitive information to the right people. So when I thought of it later, I called them back. They were very rude! Then they said they would punish me for my insolence by making all possible, legal delays in providing me with payment. How dare I question them it seemed!

I get that when I go collect my social assistance.

Welfare, said another!

Farewell, another said laughing.

I get that when I call the doctors office and when I get there to talk to one of the nurses.

I get that when I talk to people at the Employment Insurance offices.

Are you referring to all the white people who occupy the best employment positions in Canada?

They always present like they have no soul and I guess it's true, they really don't if they have been given over wholly to this great beast. They must be husks, empty, soulless, shallow people who lack all depth.

You can't expect compassion from such a thing said another.

I don't anymore! I always assume they are husks unless they can prove to me otherwise. If they get all authoritarian on me, I treat them as they treat me. The only difference is I know I have rights and I don't take no shit from them. I don't expect such a thing to be reasonable so I resist their judgmentalism and prejudice.

The thing to think about, said the Metis psychologist who had no idea psychological services were available, is that when we encounter these agents of the great beast, we must understand they are very sick people. *They need compassion, not judgmentalism.*

I don't have any respect for a child abuser said one of the people in the audience! And one that would sexually abuse a child is a monster!

That's your cultural ways and teachings you have learned from Weendigo talking, the Elder said. The teachings of right and wrong, justice, reprisal and revenge have deluded many in thinking they are justified by self-righteous indignation to aggress against others with a "burn the witch" attitude! That kind of thinking is not your fault, you were born into a world that thinks this way. It is only natural to want to defend yourself from aggressive people. Blaming is futile.

It's true said one of the Rainbow Warriors. If Weendigo came to the Children of the Earth eons and eons ago to find our children to feast upon them, and Weendigo has been capturing, enslaving and assimilating many nations to do its bidding then you would have to go all they way back to the beginning to find your blame. It is Weendigo that has corrupted the minds of many generations of people. The great corruption came to my parents and took them to the IRS to be tortured, Christianized, civilized and assimilated, their identities broken down and they were made to confess! While there they were subject to many tortures and much cruelty. Even if they made it all the way home, their parents would fear reprisal from the priests, nuns, police and government officials like Indian agents, social workers of the dreaded children's aid society and they would beat the little urchin all the way back to the institution of torture. It was horrific for them as there was no escape though some tried it killed them.

Much like the Warriors of old, who would rather die than to be a slave, asked one?

They died in honor, said the Elder and many agreed with much murmuring and talk.

They were forced to witness the sexual, physical, mental and emotional abuses and even engage in them forced into that by the priests and nuns! They were told that it was all for their own good because they were the spawn of Satan! There was no one to come help them. The priests who had full control over the post offices and postal workers who likely went to church every Sunday intercepted the resistance letters they sent. Even the police at the time were Christianized in the same way would bring the children back to the schools to be returned to their torture and horror. There was no escape for them. They resisted as best they could but they were just children!

They could not understand what was happening. They were helpless. And so they were corrupted and everything became backwards and twisted for them. Soon, they negotiated the terms of surrender with Weendigo and they became agents of the great corruption, enslaved. When they came out of those places, they were not the same!

Then they had ME! Before I was even born, I was already under attack in the spirit world as they tried to kill me before I could even be born! The hospital lied to my mother and told her she needed to have her tubes tied and would never again be able to give birth. They called this practice eugenics, compulsory or forced sterilization of men and women.

This is now known as a crime against humanity. It is clearly a practice of ethnic cleansing and genocide. Mother nearly gave in but my father intervened only just in time! The procedure was cancelled. But that was not the end of it. They would get me, sooner or later. Weendigo had everything in place. My mother was affected by the torture and she was alienated from herself, as she learned in the day schools that she was nothing but a dirty Indian, they said. They tortured her and tormented her. They turned her against herself and made her dysfunctional. She hated herself and thought herself worthless and undeserving. But how could you stop a pregnancy?

So I was born and while I came from the spirit world and was being made in the womb, in that secret place where I was fashioned together by the Creators loving tenderness, I was under constant attack. Alcohol came in, dope came in, diseases, the smoke of "white" man's Tobacco, and the self-loathing and fits of rage my mother would engage in nearly had me aborted anyways! Mother's hatred of herself and others fueled passionate and tumultuous hormones and I was being made in a cesspool of great and terrific rage, even as my mother fought and resisted Weendigo. The war that she waged against the great corruption was indeed very powerful! But I was born! Out I came, pissed right off in an instant of taking my first breath!

There I remained, pissed off for 38 more years! And like many of you, I had nightmares! Like many of you, I resisted as a Warrior, but I was ineffective in many ways, I was dysfunctional! Eventually, I would make my way here even as I am now.

It was not until the time the Canadian government came to admit these terrible things really did occur and apologized for it. This is when I realized that these horrors are indeed true and my life was changed. All that we have heard today is no longer being repressed and it is real and tangible and cannot be denied any longer.

Though many are still in denial of it.

Then my father came to me one day and said nonchalantly, that he just got back from the lawyers office. He had given his statement regarding his treatment at one of these IRS, speaking as if he was unaffected. Then suddenly, and without warning, he broke down and collapsed right in front of me and he wept a thick guttural hoarse weeping and I watched every fiber of his being twist and turn inside out, as he cried out in full view of all his work comrades. Oh, how he wept in a great and terrible display of heartfelt sorrow from deep within his soul, his spirit wept. It was nothing like I had ever seen before!

I had to help him up, so I picked up my old father and carried him to his cubicle where he transformed before my very eyes into a child of about the age of seven or eight.

Before me was someone I had never met! A small child that suddenly giggled and talked about his experiences. He showed me a photo of him at the school and he was the smallest, clearly a result of malnutrition, deprivation dwarfism they call it. The other boys towered over him by about four feet. Such a small lad. You know how we treat the small kids in school today. We bully them! Well you can imagine my dad had nothing going for him being Metis, small, dark skinned and talked with a funny accent, saying "tings" like "over dare" pointing with his lips. How they would have tortured him in addition to the sexual, physical, mental and emotional abuses that he would have endured. They would break him.

And so my parents having no understanding of what is occurring in their lives would grow and develop into adulthood trying to forget *everting lie dat der eh*! They would try to live their lives as if *nutting* happened to them. Their minds would be twisted. Their souls tormented. Then they would meet each other and see something in each other, whether it is twisted, corrupted or whether it was special, holy and sacred I do not know and now I care not!

In a co-dependent relationship, my parents met. Father being broken psychologically and assimilated into a white, patriarchal, paternalistic, hierarchical, authoritarian system by Indian Residential School, same with mother. Both came together perhaps thinking they would find comfort, love and care, safety, security and stability. Instead, they used each other. They objectified each other. Twisted and corrupted beliefs would conflict with each other and they would tear at each other, confused they would bite at each other and loath each other. They thought they would fix their relationship if they had kids and so they kept having kids. In a cycle of abuse where both were engaged, making it chaotic and unpredictable for us to survive, they were volatile. At any moment, they could go off into a vicious and violent tangent. Then when they were done and we kids were left to witness the whole event wide eyed and terrified, we became objectified as they projected their self-loathing, hatred of each other blaming their shitty abusive co-dependent relationship on us kids. We then got the living shit beaten out of us and we became their punching bags, objects of their hatred.

They never loved themselves not each other, they never loved us. They objectified everything.

Dad used us as his excuse to head to the racetrack, pool halls and bars. While we dressed in rags and second hand cloths he dressed in the finest cloths justified by his authority and as the breadwinner, he needed to present dignified to others. Mom supported this bullshit for years. He believed that as head of the household he should be afforded every luxury to ensure he would be around to care for the family.

Mother in her self-loathing felt like she was honored to be with father as he came from good stock. He was wealthier than her family group. But she found out what a disappointment he was. She hated the fact that she had to remain with him for us kids as she put it. She had to endure his control over her and his abuse of power. He could cheat on her but she could not unless he could watch. She felt like a whore.

What did they want to get from each other? Control, power, prestige, wealth. She was his ornament to adorn his shoulder when they went out. He was her ornament and she derived a sense of worth, while they were out among other women. She had a role and so did he. They both romanticized each other and they beat each other. Both were insecure, tormented and twisted inside. Both were selfish, fixated on themselves trying to find reprieve from the mental anguish of childhood among the priests and nuns. Both felt they deserved each other, this was as good as it gets, this was the best they could do. The grass looked greener on the other side of the fence. They justified their infidelity. Both, in the end had used each other up. Both were deluded.

Both thought they could control the others madness. They hid their dysfunction from themselves and from others he the alcoholic drug user, she the child abuser. They were blind to their own madness.

Just like treaty relationships, Metis land claims, in Canada. Just like abusive relationships in families, just like families who hide the shame of child molesters and abusers. Dysfunctional relationships we think we can control, we think we can keep hidden by not airing our dirty laundry. This dysfunctional thinking that we can control our enemies by keeping them closer, our child abusers and wife beaters deluded with thoughts we can make them behave. We are deluded in thinking we have control. We don't.

But the great corruption would have its way, one way or another. Their relationship would not be based on healthy boundaries and self and mutual respect but rather based in dysfunction. They would engage in co-dependency. Eventually this co-dependency would run its course and when the relationship no longer served one another, they would end it violently and in great chaos.

Meanwhile we children would be subjected to the same torments they received in IRS. We would develop amidst great corruption, in our society, cities, public education institutions, prisons both real and imagined, beaten and rejected, violence and instability with many mood swings as triggers would torment us. Then we became the parents.

Everyone listened with great intensity and they hung on every word bringing them to the edge of their seats!

We never knew when our how they would strike or what new mind games they would play. And so we grew up this way, always on edge, hypervigilant, developing our minds, learning dysfunction, we became dysfunctional.

Our minds were always ruminating in thoughts flashes of depressing, distressing images would invade and intrude throughout the day, always at the level of my subconscious. Pow, pow, pow! Invasive thoughts of me locked in the basement for weeks on end, dismissed, shamed, abused, shunned by our parents and family. Bang, bang, bang! Flashbacks of beatings anger and rage. All day long, every day all my life a steady assault in my mind, mental torment and anguish as if I were reliving it all. Thump, thump, thump, went my bed at night and long into adulthood.

They offered me chocolate and to this day, I still get a hard on when I smell chocolate.

I too was insecure, and it seems like it's just a word now when I say it, but with all of this new meaning I can see that this word, insecure, has more depth to it than I first thought! I had no idea it meant self-loathing, no self-respect, low or no self-esteem and how these would cripple me in my ability to function at home, in relationships, at work.

I had no idea I was ruminating on negative dysfunctional thought process that led to poor coping methods such as addictive behavior as subtle as staying up late, resulting in me sleeping in and missing appointments, chasing neon rainbows, always trying to have fun. I had no idea I was motivated to avoid distressing thoughts. Later on in life, upon waking from a horrible sleep, a normal thing for me, I would go, go, go, sleep deprived.

I had no idea I was doing it to avoid distressing thoughts of child abuse and insecurity. I would pack my day full of responsibilities just to run, run, run away from my thoughts! I can't take comfort in the fact that at least I didn't drink because my unaddressed insecurities left my family with an absent parent projecting my fears onto my children. I had no idea it was a seven-generation thing, intergenerational. I thought I was normal!

Tears were very apparent now.

And so Weendigo Kahn, sacred clown, your humor is like the tarpaulin that opened when the Elder called DOOR and the light shines in. I was blinking trying to adjust to the light. You are like fresh summer rain and it is indeed powerful! Meegwetch! I can now learn to laugh again and I look forward to my future.

I can forgive myself and I can revisit many times in my life that tormented me and I can discover the truth of what is so disturbing and I know that I will find most of it was none of my doing. I can let myself enjoy all of those things that were forbidden because of Weendigo culture. I can live emancipated! Those low frequency pulse charges that would force me to remember what I was trying desperately to forget, pulsating just below consciousness had become a way of life. I had no idea this is what was happening.

So this was my minds way of protecting me from further abuse and harm. I was remembering what was happening to me so that I could prevent it from ever happening again. That is where my never again attitude developed in my life. That is where I became insecure! NEVER AGAIN!

Now that I was old enough to stop abusers from harming me, I said NEVER AGAIN! I saw everyone as potential abusers. I projected that insecurity on them and assumed they could not be trusted. NEVER AGAIN! I hated them for their stereotypes and racism. I shut myself off from them and I would push their buttons to see if they were going to reject me and when they finally had enough of me pushing them away, they would leave. I would say, see, you left everyone leaves. People hate me. I am despicable, repulsive and disgusting. I must be because no one ever accepts me. I hated myself for doing that. I hated myself for lying to myself about these things. And yet, I had to protect myself from the liars and cheaters, hypocrites. I had a NEVER AGAIN attitude! Angry! Anger! Fear! Resentment! Hate and suffering!

Sobbing and sniffling could be heard.

When I think about it, I cannot really blame my parents or those who are corrupted for how I was raised and the sufferings I endured. They only did what was taught to them and what was right in their eyes. Just like that white man who was yelling at his four year old calling him a fag and a sissy, teaching his son to hate and devalue women, teaching him to hate his own mother.

I spoke with my grandmother about these things and she told me she was hard on her children because she knew the world was a cruel and mean place and she believed you needed to be tough to survive. So she was distant and unapproachable to her children and she would not offer sympathy or empathy. She presented as cold. Her children were the same. They believed they were doing us a favor raising us in these dysfunctional culturally imposed ways.

So I wondered about her parents and those before her. I looked into the history books and I discovered the further we go back in *Western* history, the harder it was for children. Half of all children were stillborn. The half that survived never made it past the age of two or three. The next half never had a teen life, they were simply children and then adults by the time they were nine.

Teenagers are a relatively new phenomenon. It is only recently that a person would be a child up to the age of nine and then instantly be ready for marriage. This was a common practice even up to about 1930.

One researcher showed that a German teacher proudly and accurately kept records of all the corporal punishments they administered to students. In other words, all of the physical abuse was recorded and we can access these records today. There were entire empires that physically abused children. And so you can imagine the affects that would have on childhood, personality and psychological and perceptual developments. Recent research indicates increased likelihood of anxiety disorder in children subjected to corporal punishment. So we have nations of anxiety ridden people. The latest show 1 in 6 Winnipeggers have a mental health issue but when you break the numbers down it's more like 1 in 2 because of the lack of supports available for mental health in Manitoba.

So I dug further and found it was a common thing to sodomize children and keep them for sex slaves during the time of the Roman Empire. Going even further into ancient history the suffering many children endured and then grew to have children of their own to mistreat, means that all of these generations of poor abused souls had no idea they were hurting themselves, turning against themselves and each other. They sometimes call it the Devil. We now understand the Elders call it Weendigo!

So if you want to blame someone, you have to go back to the beginning. I cannot hold my parents accountable. But I have learned to draw a healthy boundary and if those who cannot or will not see their dysfunction must not cross my healthy boundary! I must insist on it! I must not cross my healthy boundary either, to compromise my dignity and newly discovered self-respect! So I do not visit those who remain ignorant. I have separated myself from them. Someday, when they are ready, I too will be ready but not one damn minute sooner! Why you might ask? Because I have children, it is for the sake of the children, seven generations! I do not want to risk the children exposure to dysfunction and they would be if I was among dysfunction, was triggered by it and then brought that back home. At present, I am not strong enough for that yet and I recognize that I need help with this and I am getting help. *For the sake of the children, seven generations.*

That's how I knew there was something wrong. Although, all this dysfunction in my life seemed normal, survivable, acceptable, I could not escape the reality that not only was this lifestyle unhealthy, but I could not possibly be healthy. I realized that if my grandparents and parents, aunts, uncles, cousins, brothers and sisters endured these repeated and traumatic abuses, I can't be unaffected. There must be something terribly wrong and I knew I could not see it I needed help! That's why I called the Indian Residential School Crisis Line and they set me up with access to a psychologist. I guess it was worse than I thought. But I have to tell you it has been enormously helpful. I am not the same insecure person. It is a work in progress. We all are. I understand that now. I can live and let live. I can find peace and serenity whenever I want. Life is entirely different, healthier, and happier. I can't tell you enough what a relief it has been to let go many issues that caused me to be unwell. I am not entirely healed and have a way to go yet but I am committed as I am aware of the gravity of the situation.

A ho! A ho! Many replied!

An Elder replied, social workers and foster care providers are not allowed to form attachments to the children they care for because the attachments compromise the quality of care. Social workers and foster care providers can end up being over invested in one child, perhaps favoring or advocating in a different manner than they would for others. Often attachments in these cases are not about the child but rather about the social worker or care provider and what they get out of the relationship. Likewise, the child may not understand the complex dynamics of relationships, often with a childlike sense of wonder they process behavior of adults and others from a vulnerable position. Some children will exploit this position to their advantage while others learn from the role modeling made available to them from agents of the systems.

If social workers and agents such as foster care providers behave indifferent, separated and without proper healthy attachment styles toward children in care, then those children will role model behavior. Being raised in environments lacking a loving environment, where everything is clinical, policy and procedure, caregivers are distant, working with limited resources, forces children to grow up fast. Children in care may learn to see others as objects that serve them or not. Many children will become self-centered, indifferent, detached from others. They become survivors of grave indignity, which often becomes problematic for them later in life. As always, there are exceptions to these scenarios. The point is that many children are victims of a grave indignity that occurs presently and has occurred for seven generations.

In our Western culture, attachment occurs with parents who provide a safe, secure, stable and loving environment. In such cases, children may develop into healthy functional adults. While in others, even with all the right stuff children will learn through role modeling and other cognitive processes how to behave in the world. They could be problematic and dysfunctional as well. You see a child requires attachment to parents and caregivers to facilitate a healthy, loving bond. It would appear there are various culturally based attachment styles and various factors, beliefs, perceptions, interactions between child and caregiver that produce different kinds of bonds. Some are about as healthy as we can imagine is healthy from our perceptions while others are not.

One mother developed a severe dysfunctional relationship with her children. All of them were affected. Because the mother was raised in a cold, detached, abusive environment made hostile by colonization, white supremacist, religious ideology, patriarchy, paternalism, race based hierarchical structures that are stratified, the Riel Resistances, xenophobia, hatred and a cold, indifferent, detached Children's Aid Society, police, government, social services network, all cold and distant, herself raised by equally hostile parents.

This little girl was raised in unimaginable poverty, racism and hatred. The repeated abuse that came from her parents and society helped develop the personality of a women that reflected her insecure childhood and attachment styles. This personality would become a reflection of her cognitive processes and personal development. If all she ever knew were hostility, punishment and open ridicule that was projected on her by family and Canadian society, would be how she viewed herself. She learned it. If Canadian society thought she was a thing, a dirty filthy thing not worth saving, similar to animals who should be put down, then she would come to believe those very same principles in her development.

She would vow not to repeat the same treatment she received as a little girl to her own children if she was to have any. She would have understood how it made her feel and that it is not good. But the damage is done, she would have developed an insecure attachment style, becoming insecure in a hostile world she would have to survive. She would not be aware of the belief systems that would have developed in a dysfunctional way within her psyche and personality. Her survival instincts would have been sharpened to a swift and powerful reaction with a never again attitude at the slightest threat. Similar to war veterans who would quickly learn how to survive combat or perish she would value those perceptions that have ensured her survival of a cold and hostile world that is careless toward her person.

Then at age 12 after a rape she would have become pregnant. But no less than two years later she would become pregnant again but this time she would have a partner who would help raise their daughter. Then another child would come shortly thereafter. Then more children.

The mother would both love and hate all of her children even as she both loves and hates herself.

Later, like her mother, the daughter would be raped at a young age. The daughter would have been born into a cold, hostile, uncaring environment. Like her mother, she would have been blamed for bringing the rape on herself in a twisted, sick illogical reasoning that at age 11 she seduced the man who raped her. How is it that an 11-year-old girl in her pre-pubescent years be remotely sexy to any right thinking man? But that was the thinking of the day that men were animalistic, they could not control their urges and if they were seduced by an 11 year old girl it was not the man's fault, it was the child's. So in addition to being raped this little girl was beaten for her bewitching seduction on an innocent man and the child was demonized by the family. If it were a different religion or time, the girl would have been discarded or murdered in an honor killing it would seem, if she were not married off by then.

In a twisted and corrupted way, the mother would hate her daughter, envious perhaps of the young girl's beauty and attention from men. The mother would teach her daughter to marry-up. At the same time, having the same experience would have regret and turmoil over what her daughter went through. But the time and culture of society would never allow any grieving or healing and the man would remain in the family's daily life, a reminder of the abuse of power. The humility, powerlessness, guilt, shame, resentment over what occurred could never be resolved in a healthy way. In those days, all they had for mental health issues were the priests and nuns. The last thing you want to do is visit the clergy for these issues. You're better off managing these things on your own. Still, in another twisted and corrupted way, the mother would have justified her emotions, conclusions and processing of the event dismissively, she went through it she got over it. Such contradictions in belief systems, all dysfunctional processes would produce a dysfunctional relationship between her daughter and herself.

The young girl would develop among the hostile, twisted, sordid environments that are not of their own making, but rather come from a dominating culture and society, from colonization. The young girl would learn of her mother's confusion and to exploit it for personal gain. The young girl would learn that the world she lives in values materialism, that material things could be adorned upon their bodies and derive a sense of self-esteem, worth and personhood. As for her own personhood, her true identity, her true sense of self, that was beaten down so badly that a sick, twisted, corrupted version developed which now presents itself to a cruel and hostile world. Having been deprived of many material things that would have been good for healthy development in a different situation, poverty made them necessary, seen as objects that bring a false sense of self-worth. In childhood, other children would have teased the poor girl for being poor and deprived, she would be ostracized by other kids. She would then learn that if she had what they had, she could fit in. Then looking at the vulnerable position her mother was in, she would use guilt and shame to acquire materialism for self-worth.

In a twisted process, both mother and daughter would become engaged in a dysfunctional process of button pushing, abuse and punishment. Both would use their relationship against each other to gain power and control. The young girl would learn to exploit the environment, seeing the hypocrisy and yet participating in the abuse at times. The mother would learn to exploit her daughter, using approval and dysfunction to her advantage. Infidelity, sexuality, immediate gratification, risky lifestyles and the like would become a pursuit of happiness. However, neither would be happy as these behaviors only resolved their issues for a short term. This would become a relationship based on guilt and shame, abuse and perversion. Both would be morally justified, both would have dirt on the other.

As the daughter develops under these compromised predicaments, she too has a daughter. It is a sad story that repeats itself in the life of this innocent child who had nothing to do with the great corruption that came upon their family. The child is an infant, helpless save for the crying that tells whomever the caregiver is that something is wrong. But the child learns that crying is useless after a while. There is only soft whimpering that is left and then later, sadness. Deep inhumane sadness and grief that consumes the identity of the infant who becomes a toddler.

Happiness is often brief and momentary as a very sick mother who screams and yells at her child whenever frustration and lack of patience is available to the mother raises the poor child. "I FUCKEN TOLD YOU TO GO TO YOUR ROOM FOR FUCK SAKES, FUCK ARE YOU EVER STUPID," she screams at her daughter knowing no one can hear the verbal abuse. The mother thinks the child should know how to behave, she thinks the child is capable and fully developed cognitively. The mother thinks the child is a fully-grown adult, but is still a child, a toddler. Not once ever does the mother reflect back at the small child and see how she processed things at that age in attempt to understand the child's seeming incompetent behavior. The mother does not know the child is still developing. The child is helpless and confused forced to process things faster or suffer abuse. The beatings and the neglect the cold hostile environment inundate the little girl with profundities she cannot possibly understand except that she did something wrong, she must be bad.

That is how the little girl grows and develops. She must try to appease her abuser. She must try to redirect violent mood swings from her mother. She must attempt to control her environment. Even as a toddler at the age of 4 the small child begins to show signs of survivalism. The talk is very mature for her age. The behavior very mature and under strict control of the mother, the child must behave in just such a way as to avoid and prevent verbal, physical, emotional abuse and turmoil.

The mother warns her daughter of the cruel and hostile world of men. She warns her child of good touch and bad touch. In a sincere effort to protect her child from the horror of her life she over invests in her child by being too protective, too controlling. The glares, the stares, the beatings and the berating's to the little girl's personhood causes the child to develop an insecure attachment style, dysfunctional personality and a poor perception of reality. The mother genderizes the little girl who prefers to be a boy. She emphasizes girl toys and says cars are for boys in a swift and virulent admonishment of hatred and self-loathing.

Now age 8 the little girl is soft spoken and broken hearted. It is clear that she is very sad. She is beyond sad, she is locked away in a prison, hidden deep within her psyche in a cold dark place where she remains damaged, broken and dejected. No one wants her. She has become dead. She is emotionally flat. She wants to escape but she can't. Where can she escape to? Grandmother? Hardly. Grandfather? For god sakes no! She is held captive by her mother and there she must remain to be subjected to indignity for her entire life. The only escape is the prison she is forced to flee.

There is one other alternative. It is the Family Services system, but it is just as dysfunctional as the family she lives with presently. A child must choose between the lesser of two evils.

The story books, the libraries, the worksheets at school, television, and commercials even other children present as healthy, stable and loved. But not her, she is violated, abused and tormented with intergenerational abuse developing in hostility. She can tell she is deprived but she does not understand how it came to be this way. She only knows that not once, ever in her life did she feel loved and so she feels worthless and has lost all hope. Soon, the pattern will repeat itself in the small child's life only because she was born into a cruel, indifferent world and she is guilty only because she was born into this family. This is a family that is targeted for assimilation by the great corruption that imposes itself upon them. The great corruption has trained its agents well, to hate the children of the earth and so they hated them most grievously even justifiably from their own sick sordid perception of justice. And so this little girl is trained to hate herself just for being herself even as her mother was trained to hate herself and her grandmother before her.

The child is now a teenager who is near completely dysfunctional with poor attachment styles and coping methods. In spite of all her mother's fears and worries projected onto her she could not escape the sexual abuse that came. So she says, "fuck it". She becomes exactly what her mother and grandmothers does not want her to be as if she can own her identity with empowerment. It is delusional. Soon she will drop out of school, as useless as public education has become anyways she works the streets, hustling trying to make a life for herself. It is a violent, harsh, cruel unrelenting battery of abuse, self-abuse and morbid reflection. The hell and the horror remains with solutions from white supremacists. She knows better. What the fuck do white people know anyway? They are the ones that stole the land, they are the ones that raped, and they are the ones that are racist. Now they set themselves up as gods who know what is best and they have all the answers. The now arrive in droves to fix the problem they created with their solutions. So fuck them! Fuck them all to hell!

Her mother is now old and grown into a terrible raging alcoholic still engaged in a twisted, sick, dysfunctional relationship with her grandmother. There is three generations of horrific abuse and all they have is each other. They are totally unaware that anything is wrong and anyone who judges can go fuck themselves. They are surviving amid great horror and corruption that is not of their own making, but rather is a system of cold indifference toward them for being born of Aboriginal descent. They are not husks, they are simply locked away fearing for their safety. They are dysfunctional only because of their history, intergenerational effects of the great corruption. When Canada invaded Red River, when they killed, raped, murdered and pillaged Metis homes, dismissing them as retarded savages, objectifying them, projecting these insecurities on them they relegated them to horrific conditions to develop in. It is a great and terrible crime against humanity and Canada should be ashamed of themselves for the horrors and the indignity. But they're not. They're proud of it, proud of the country they built for themselves!

And for years they come to grandma's house, to eat her food, to drink and use and to fuck. Parties and drunkenness, vulnerable everyone comes to exploit them. But they don't mind so long as they get something in return, like capitalists, buyers and sellers. Then the social workers come to repeat their white supremacy, even if they are devolved into Aboriginal managed agencies, white supremacy and its ideology of patriarchy, paternalism, hierarchy and authoritarianism all of which comes from religions. This is a story that is ten thousand years or more, old. It is your story and it is ours. No one has been spared its insidious nature. Not one, ever.

And only now, you say, the Canadian government has allocated funds to help this family to access a psychologist and other cultural supports like ceremony and Elders? But it's all very hush-hush? Maybe they realize the magnitude of the damage they have done to people, families and children. The cost could be astronomical but they are legally obligated to provide the service for those who need it. I just hope they are respectful in providing the service, not the empty husks you have described at the employment insurance, farewell offices.

CAME TO BELIEVE

I should like to entitle this talk *Came to Believe* the Elder continued. Came to believe means that we came to believe in whatever it was that we were taught to believe. Whether that is god or some spiritual belief for some, or whether it was the social order we live which may be racist for some or you do not believe in such nonsense. The point is that we all came to believe.

I have been studying the phenomenon of dysfunction since I was born because I was born into it, but more technically in the last 13 years as a scholar. In sum, I will be happy to provide a written bibliography for anyone who requests it.

My fascination with chaos comes from my own experiences of hypocrisy within an overly religious home that was obviously dysfunctional. Although I never knew it at the time, many of the behaviors written in the news seemed totally normal and not dysfunctional. A shooting or stabbing, a preventable death or by accident or suicide was commonplace. The conditions that I grew up in were normal for me. The fact that I could see my Polish and Ukrainian friends living differently, in loving homes where food was abundant, privileged to wear the latest fashions with an abundance of toys made no difference. That was the way the white man lived and how we lived was our lot. They had their role and we had ours. It was accepted. In many cases, I was not allowed to be friends with some and that was more common later in my teen years. There was nothing we could do about it and many of us did not even try. If we got a little ahead, that was fine and dandy but to push forward with more ambition, with dreams and plans was sometimes not even considered. To many of us, such behavior brought unwanted attention to the rest of our family. And the family would shut someone down for rocking the boat. The fear of losing our welfare or having social services snoop around was ever present.

I could see something wrong with this kind of thinking as a child but being born into this mess made it difficult to pinpoint exactly. The mental trap was puzzling, twisting, winding with many barriers. In order to successfully navigate this psychological maze one must have be totally honest with oneself and at the same time completely secretive. You could not lie to yourself to hold on to a belief system that would prevent you from the truth later on. Also, because of the support system style that was available and also rooted in dysfunction, you could not openly resist your reality. One must question everything and remain open to new ideas in the face of strict dogma and authoritarianism. It takes courage to stand up to the might of ideology. The prayer meetings followed by the sexual and physical abuses did not match up. I had to know if this was god's doing, the Devil's, or ours. So my academics started out by reading the Bible and studying what it had to say and how we attempted to live it. If it was not Christianity, it was our own traditional Elders who were hypocrites.

After being pushed out of high school by embedded racial ignorance therein, I too like many other young men and women came to believe that my only future was as a gangster. Teachers were taught we "Indians" were inferior, unteachable and disruptive in class. Back then, they did not know that disruptive behavior was an indication of an unstable home. But even if they did know it, they did not know why the home was disruptive. It was just assumed and taken for granted that teachers should not invest too much time in us "natives". The lack of education, but not for a lack of many of us kids trying to get educated, resulted in being pushed out of a hostile and racist institution. This meant we had no qualifications for above minimum wage jobs. So the quick easy money the constable described did provide incentive. However, I had to try other things first, to be sure that I was not undermining my own success, I honestly had to be sure. So I tried to work and gain experience towards a career. It was most frustrating. Consider rent and other bills that needed paying on top of dysfunctional beliefs. The constant frustration is maddening. So I returned to school as a last desperate effort.

I later focused on psychology and history in my education experience. Soon, I became aware that something was amiss and I had to know what was wrong. Obsessively I poured over books and through the tombs in search of the truth.

When I signed on for the Gang Awareness Training session with the WPS, I was hoping to learn something new about the paradigm of dysfunction. I was hoping to learn something about safety for staff and participants. I hoped that I would learn more about the conditions that create gangs and how perhaps the police can assist in changing those conditions so this is not an option for people. Did the police have an alternative solution for people? Could they identify helpful factors? What I mean by that has nothing to do with arresting and charging offenders, which is what police currently do. I was hoping for something positive. I wanted to know what the police know about gangs and how they can help people after all, "service", is in their name. I hoped that I would see how the police would advocate on behalf of offenders. Instead, I saw the opposite. WPS's official position is that gangs and gangsters are destructive, volatile people who cannot be reasoned with, cannot be bargained with, there is no negotiating or rationalizing with them. They must be stopped! I do not disagree entirely but if I understand things correctly, to take a narrow approach with little more information to justify this behavior is disagreeable.

Admittedly the constable said gangs develop in any ethnicity. However my problem with the presentation we witnessed was clearly the work of propaganda that is as old as Canada itself. We saw moving emotional video clippings and then we saw pictures of "Indians". Canadians throughout history have been taught that the "Indian" is inferior to all other ethnicities or races. This presentation was rife with propaganda. Let me show you how.

Admittedly we saw some images of white kids beating each other as a gang initiation. The majority of the images we saw were people of Indigenous descent. Admittedly many of the gangs in Winnipeg have names associated with Indigenous people. The Native Syndicate, The Indian Posse, The Manitoba Warriors are among the names given. The Main Street Rattlers and Deuce were non-associative except that we know who frequents the Main Street area and we know that Deuce is predominantly comprised of Indigenous people when they were around. However, there was no mention of the fact that these gangs do not represent the Indigenous population to be sure. Thus, we were left with the impression that our gang problem lays with the "Indian" problem. It is "common knowledge" that a majority of criminal acts occur among Indigenous populations, our prisons and social services are over representing Indigenous people. The media loves a good story and thus without the full story, or with what our propaganda machine dictates to us, the mind may conclude that the "Indian" problem is still with us. In this case, I believe the information we were shown was misrepresentative. Indigenous people are aware of our socio-economic disparity, poverty and dysfunction. We have been raising awareness to it for over a hundred years. However, what we have found is that the "Indian" problem is not our problem, it's an imaginary problem in the mindset of non-Indigenous people who came to believe in the images of the "Indian". Of course, we have been mentioning this, but we found that most people are not ready to hear these kinds of things. It simply does not make sense to many and they do not really care to investigate further. Instead, we found that consistently people rely on availability heuristics, schematics, "common knowledge" and many other cognitive shortcuts. The term, cognitive miser comes to mind. But not everyone engages in this manner of thinking, just some. It is important to create more awareness so that change can occur.

There was no scientific basis for almost anything we saw. We saw no statistical evidence that was relevant. Nothing was backed by any credible research. Much of the discussion was based on case study, which as we know is non-representative. We could have learned this material by watching the evening news.

We were given a profile that identifies a gangster. We may as well have been shown a cartoon character of a short, fat, unshaven fellow with a black mask tied around his eyes. There is no data available that would corroborate with the constables profile of a gangster unless we rely on prejudice. There is plenty of research on prejudice and profiling based on racism or discrimination. Even a quick internet search would provide better information than what the WPS presented in their Gang Awareness Training session. From what I understand, the WPS relies on prejudice and we should too because when moved emotionally by the images and video clippings we saw should justify our hasty judgments. The profile we saw showed the attire of the vast majority of every kids worldwide, even some adults. Sometimes when I roll my sleeves up, the other will fall down part of the way before the other does. Does that mean that I am a gangster? The point is that being poor and dispossessed does not mean that you are a gangster and you do not have to be poor to dress like a gangster. But I think the hidden message that only our subconscious would pick up is the racial profiling, it sways us because we have been bombarded with propaganda since birth.

While it was not explicitly said, it was implied throughout the presentation that the police are the good guys and gangsters are bad and here is how we identify gangsters. The images of the "Indian" both historical and contemporary have always dehumanized and demonized. The research on this is empirical. Make no mistake; we are conditioned to prejudice the "Indian". Only recently, have we begun to make efforts in dissuading ourselves from the stereotypes of the "Indian". The reason why I mention the "Indian" so much is because this image encompasses entire groups of people. Today, the contemporary term we use, that we think is appropriate, is "Aboriginal". The "Indian" term tends to encompass diverse groups of First Nations, Métis and Innu people.

IMAGES OF THE INDIAN FROM A EUROPEAN PERSPECTIVE

Images of the Indian started shortly after contact in 1492. Columbus sent back letters describing the people he encountered. He said that these people have no concept of god or Jesus, go about naked and other descriptions. Shortly after that letter was received the Bishops and Cardinals of the church met to decide if these people were even human. The idea that someone would be naked in their daily activities was a deplorable notion. The fact they knew nothing of Jesus the Christ meant they had a lot of work to do. The understanding was that these were pagan, barbarian, savages in need of Christianizing, civilizing and assimilating, to enslave.

CLASSICAL CONDITIONING

In this case, we were shown images and video clippings that produced an emotional response. We were then shown images of Indigenous people. The consequence is that we learn to be emotionally charged when we see Indigenous people. It was repetitive. Along with these emotions comes harsh judgmentalism that is also paired with the images of Indigenous people. Emotional images prompting judgmentalism followed by images of "Indians" in need of Christianizing, civilizing, and assimilation and if they resist, we will punish them severely. This occurs on a daily basis in the two conservative presses we are privileged to read. One that is more conservative than the other.

MISREPRESENTATION

The Granny and her grandson image created shock and horror. We do not really know what we saw in that image. We are told that if grandparents are gangsters, then children are gangsters and eventually the grandchildren are destined to become gangsters. Earlier we were told of a story about how one person was telling their kids that it won't be long before they get a ride in a police cruiser. Yet the constable presented himself in a favorable and rational fashion saying that there are other reasons for a ride in a cruiser other than the fact that they are children of gangsters, perhaps they were enjoying a sit in the back seat at a fair with the lights on? Yet in this startling image, we are told that this is a grandma proud of her grandchild sporting gang colors. Of course, the grandma was a kokum, a person of Indigenous descent. Perhaps the bandana was for spiritual or ceremonial purposes. We do not really know what the situation is and this grandmother should be consulted, as it may be that this picture was taken and presented out of context.

In the vision quest ceremony, I was given a red bandana to represent the strength and courage of the spiritual journey. The color red, black, white and yellow are sacred colors of the medicine wheel.

Admittedly, I personally know of dysfunctional individuals, grandmothers and grandfathers, parents who will exploit their own children. But knowing this and judging this situation is easy complete with catharsis when you are not aware of all the facts and that is what propagandists consider ideal. They hope to sway their audience with only half-truths. In doing so they get the support they need to carry out their mission. What we were meant to see was a sick person devoid of all morality, a hopeless case who should not have rights or access to her grandchildren. That is all we were meant to see. That is all they want us to see. It validates their work, why they should be there, it recruits social workers to police work, it validates the need to apprehend children to their so called family services agencies, their ideology, their oppression, should we agree with the tenets proffered. It is a white supremacist ideal.

DEMONIZING AND DEHUMANIZING

Demonizing and dehumanizing the outgroup makes it easier to oppress and or annihilate because the process changes how we perceive the people targeted for oppression.

The constable was correct in that gangs began to appear in the 1980's with the Main Street Rattlers and they were barely or loosely organized "thugs". Then in the late 1980's early 1990's the Deuce and the Indian Posse street gangs developed. I can tell you from my own experiences that the other criminal elements less visible were the Chinese and the Italians. That part corroborates with my own knowledge of gangs. In the later summer of 1994 the Manitoba Warrior's organized. These were not youth but grown men with connections to political leaders, it was similar to the U.S. American Indian Movement, something that was meant to be helpful to the people. As dysfunction operates, they probably truly believed they were helping the people. But to do so, they had to beat the people into submission. The very model used one the white supremacists by the Italians or Roman Empire.

What was missing from the information was the fact that at that time in Manitoba the prison system overrepresented Indigenous people with over 81 percent of those incarcerated. Also missing is that the vast majority of gangs expand into corporate and political atmospheres governed mostly by non-Indigenous people. Yet most of the images we saw were people of Indigenous descent or immigrants. The police are focused on these groups and place our attention here. Why? Perhaps it is easier to show results with this group of gangsters rather than the other groups of gangsters like Rob Ford and his brother or the corruption with the Quebec Mafia. The Indigenous and the immigrants are scapegoats. Further to what is missing is that these developments occur because of the oppression the dominant state implemented on the Indigenous population. Overrepresentation in the prison systems creates resentment within the ranks of the oppressed. Specifically, the Indigenous populations.

RESENTMENT

Consider that in WW2 the Germans under a Nazi regime consider the Polish barely human and sought to enslave them. "Germany invaded the Soviet Union on June 22, 1941. Of the three million Soviets troops taken prisoner in the invasion, two million were dead within nine months, either shot, starved, or worked to death" (http://www.pbs.org/auschwitz/learning/guides/episode_1.html).
The Soviets gave as much back as they got or more, they are still arguing about it in history books. The point here is that resentment, a memory of a traumatic event or unresolved emotional issue will fuel the fire of hate, a very powerful emotion of anger. Indigenous people have developed with death, hunger and disease in abundance for generations. They are not strangers to suffering. One can imagine the level of resentment that remains embedded in psychology. It plays itself out in daily rituals of dysfunctional behaviors. If the situation does not change soon, with an exploding Indigenous population that continues to be oppressed, gangs will not be the only problem we face in the future. But maybe that is why the police are starting up a campaign of propaganda as we have witnessed, to drum up support for what they are about to do. The new laws that are being considered, the systems coming

together to identify at-risk families, to ban alcohol from homes present as insidious in nature, discriminatory and oppressive.

EMOTION

On emotion, Paul Ekman describes a state of mind where rational information is blocked from entering the mind of the emotionalist. Ekman calls this the "refractory period", where the only information that enters the emotionalists mind is that which justifies the emotion. So if you are talking to an angry person while they are angry and you are finding it difficult to reach them, this is the reason why. At this point, there is no negotiating, you cannot bargain with the person, you cannot reason, the refractory period only allows justification of emotion. In this case, I agree with the constable. People who are in a constant state of emotion, such as the oppressed and recently arrived immigrants, may be susceptible to criminal behavior or commit a violent crime. However, I do not think arresting and charging is the end of the story. It may be a part of the services our society provides among other supports, but we should not rely on it as a final solution.

The presentation we saw was loaded with emotional material that angered us, disgusted us, saddened us, we were afraid, and surprised us. All of these emotions were primed by material that was taken out of context and without scientific basis. We were then guided toward a convenient set of principles and moral justifications for a harder stance against people who qualify under the criminal code as gangsters. Again, while I agree that in some cases we do need to have justice for criminal offences, further support for such individuals may be necessary as opposed to locking them up and throwing away the key. Consider the sons and daughters and or other family members who have lost someone to an oppressive regime, which clearly has its own set of problems. Rehabilitation and preventive measures seem more appropriate not just for victims of crime but also for families. It may cost more but in the long run it will be far cheaper to manage crime this way rather than creating resentment, closed ranks and biased information processing. This presentation offers a program of punishment and the children who are also victims of oppression are not even considered by WPS propaganda.

Oppression is a system of cruelty implemented on people, usually in totalitarian states. However, we know that oppression can occur anywhere at any time given the right circumstances. In our case as Canadians, the state is currently in an oppressive mode towards Indigenous people also known as Aboriginal people, First Nations, Innu and Métis people. The purpose of oppression is to press down on people, to hold them back from flourishing. Why do we need to oppress the Indigenous?

COMPETITION AND COLONIZATION

Competition for scarce resources is the primary reason. Canada wants access to natural resource, to exploit them and to profit. Canada does not want to share those profits even though legally, Indigenous people have a right to share in the profits as equals. Sharing equally is not as profitable as keeping all shares to oneself. The spirit and intent of the treaties were to negotiate on a nation-to-nation basis, as equals in the development of Canada. But those in power, mostly of British descent would not, could not come to believe that sharing as equals with "pagan, barbarian, savages" was possible. If profit would not allow it, racist ideology would not allow it.

During colonization processes, the French lost the war of 1812 on the Plains of Abraham to the British. The French abandoned those early francophone colonists who then developed into their own French Canadian community we know today as the Quebecoise. The British being in the business of colonization for hundreds of years already sought to exploit what we know today as Canada for its natural resources. Enter Sir John A. McDonald and Canadian expansion vis a vis the development of the Canadian National Railway. The only thing that stood in the way were the Metis here in Winnipeg. The Metis resisted Canadian expansion unless treaties could be negotiated on a nation-to-nation basis allowing for the equal participation in Canadian expansion. MacDonald planned to build a Railway connecting the East Coast to the West Coast. On the West, Canada would connect to the East India Trading Company, a British owned company, and the East Coast would be connected to Europe.

The Battle of Batoche resulting in the absolute surrender of the Metis resistance and its primary leader, Louis Riel. Consequently, the East was now connected with the West coast and Canada was formed. The purpose of expansion is profit. Who profits? In this case, mostly the British. Other Europeans like the Polish and Ukrainians came after the Metis resistances but only because Britons did not want to immigrate to Canada, they were happy where they were. Ukrainians and Polish people on the other hand were engaged in the nation building process in Europe, which included bloodshed in civil wars, including genocide, ethnic cleansing, raping's, murders, and other heinous acts. So, many Ukrainians and Polish and other Europeans were happy to immigrate. The chance for a new life, land and opportunity awaited them here in Canada and it was free! The only thing in the way of this expansion was the Indian problem. So after suppressing the Metis, the Canadian government sought to resettle the Indians off the land and placed into reserves to keep them away from newcomers. The land promised to the "Slavic" people as the British called them, was consistently second grade to the land given to the British. The best and most favorable land was saved for British immigrants. The Ukrainians, Polish and the Icelandic immigrants among other groups were given the worst land which often had large boulders pitted in them. You could remove them once a year but in the next, new ones would surface. This is not good for agriculture. Indians got the worst land of all, Metis lost everything.

THE RESERVES

Meanwhile, the racism that occurred on a daily basis in "civilized" society, other oppressive measures were being taken on the reserves.

The British believed they were superior to everyone as racism privileged them as the white race. This superiority complex contributed to the dehumanization process of primarily the Indigenous groups, but the "Slavic" people too were considered less than human, including the Portuguese, Spanish, Germans, Greeks, Turks, Italians and we can follow from East to West on the European map down south to the African nations. The racist ideology justified most of history's most notorious and most heinous acts including genocide and ethnic cleansing in Canada. The Metis were ethnically cleansed from Manitoba, genocide occurred in the form of neglect, Canada hoped Metis would die off, the British believed the Metis would simply disappear in time, a form of slow deliberate genocide. The Beothuk, a First Nation group was permanently exterminated in 1829. The reserve system is a form of ethnic cleansing as it removes a population away so that a new population can inhabit the land base. Some Indians did not make it to many of the signing of the treaties and thus still being Indigenous are not recognized as Indians under the Indian Act and do not benefit from the treaties. These are known as non-status Indians.

THE INDIAN AGENT

The Indian Agent in charge of administering treaty rights deliberately withheld food rations in order to oppress the people, to control them and eventually to break them into submission. Under these conditions the development of collaborators occurred, where people collaborated with the oppressor to benefit for the sake of food. This created insecurity and divided the people. Duncan Campbell Scott in charge of the Department of Indian Affairs advocated for the assimilation of Indian people. However assimilation programs were already well underway long before the Battle of the Plains of Abraham. Missionaries came to Christianize the Indigenous. This is where Scott and others learned that the resistance to previous assimilation attempts causing failure was due to the preservation of language. Scott believed that if you take away the language, the culture would soon fall. Then the Indian Residential School (IRS) systems developed under the sanction of the church and state. Around the same time, farming programs kept parents and grandparents busy on the reserve farms while the children were away at the IRS. Children were taken away and often times forcibly to the IRS where the survival rate was 50/50. These actions separated Indigenous people from the rest of Canada, isolating them from newly arrived immigrants. Meanwhile the campaign of propaganda concerning the "Indian" was implemented in mainstream Canadian society creating distrust, and disinformation about Indigenous people. Together, the Reserve system, assimilation, the ethnic cleansing and campaign of propaganda directed against Indigenous people culminated in a dysfunctional relationship between Canadians and Indigenous people. IRS beside the aftermath of colonization is considered the most direct historical event that contributed to the severe dysfunction we know today. However, the abuses that occurred under these circumstances are not what the Indigenous requested for themselves in the treaty processes. These impositions came from Canadians as bystanders, the Canadian government. What we see today is not consequential to being "Indian", it is directly related to a horrific and racist history.

Children were brought to these schools, born in these schools, they were killed in these schools.

Those who survived were made dysfunctional. The legacy of IRS is now known as family dysfunction or inter-generational affects that imposed themselves upon the children of the survivors. Both my parents attended IRS and I am a second generational survivor of IRS. I will tell you what that means momentarily.

The Indian Agent had total control over the lives of those families on reserves. Food rations were dispensed or withheld for punishment and positive reinforcement for sharing information. The Indian could not buy or sell any livestock they owned or wanted to own without permission from the Indian Agent. The Indian could not leave the reserve without written permission. If an Indian wanted to live in the city, they could do so but they had to give up status as an Indian, becoming totally assimilated. Indians could not join the great wars unless they gave up their status as Indians to serve. Nevertheless, many Indians gave it up for an opportunity to serve Canada. Nevertheless, even after serving in the great wars Indians were still not allowed to drink in a public bar, it was illegal.

THE METIS

As for the Metis, Canada totally ignored them, as they were not Indian and they were not Canadian, they had no rights to land or property. Not being Canadian meant you were not on the voters registry and therefore ineligible for education. Although, the church often took Metis students into the Indian Residential Schools and the Day Schools, this was the only alternative available for Metis children to get education. Not being Canadian, Metis did not have the credentials like a Social Insurance Number to work or pay taxes and so could not buy or sell anything. Having been ethnically cleansed from their homeland, their land and wealth absconded largely by The Orangemen the British/Canadian answer to the Ku Klux Klan would simply take a person's home, kicking them out of it without warning.

The conflict between the Orangemen and the Catholics is a conflict between two religious orders. This conflict is most noticeable within the borders of Ireland. However, the conflict plays itself out within Canadian borders as well. The Orangemen came from the East representing British white supremacy to undermine the Catholic missions in the West in Canada dominated by Metis who only had partial relationships with Catholics.

These Metis in a great Diaspora moved westward in hopes of a new beginning. But that was soon washed away by the flood of immigrants that came after them only to repeat the process. If any Metis were caught camped out on land, the police would arrest them for squatting. Soon, public outcry for the government to do something about the Metis situation caused the government to act. The government in its great wisdom and generosity allowed the Metis to live within a couple hundred feet of government roads and railways. This is how the Metis became known as the Road Allowance People. My father was born and raised in such a settlement. The province of Alberta is the only province in Canada that have given the Metis a land base of their own.

Why did the public cry out? It was because they could not stand to see ragged and starved to death people and their ragged poor children wandering in an out of town sites begging for food. Crow and Muskrat were staple diets. It was the recently arrived immigrants, Ukrainian and Polish people who cried out advocating for better living conditions, which allowed the road allowances to occur. Here the Metis could settle and begin small farms, which they did. Both my parents tell me fond stories of their poverty-ridden childhood. But was it enough?

We know today that the heinous nature of the IRS era is the root of the challenges we face today with regard to Indigenous involvement in gangs. We know that inter-generational effects of IRS develops into family dysfunction described by the constable. The constable did not spend nearly enough time on the dynamics of dysfunction and was almost dismissive as a convenient excuse for savage, barbaric behavior and how it develops for one reason or another. However, I will share in depth so that you can understand and comprehend fully digesting the meaning of dysfunction, family dysfunction and inter-generational effects.

INDIAN RESIDENTIAL SCHOOLS AND THE PROGRAM OF ASSIMILATION

On Wednesday June 11, 2008 at 3:00 p.m. (Eastern Daylight Time), the Prime Minister of Canada, the Right Honourable Stephen Harper, made a Statement of Apology to former students of Indian Residential Schools, on behalf of the Government of Canada.

On February 24, 2012, the TRC Commissioners tabled a 40-page Interim Report with 20 recommendations. This Interim Report includes information on the activities of the Commission from its appointment until June 30, 2011.

The following is a brief summary of the Interim Report's Findings, Recommendations and Conclusions.

Summary of Findings

Through its work, the Commission has reached certain conclusions about the residential school system. The Commission has concluded that:

· Residential schools constituted an assault on Aboriginal children.

· Residential schools constituted an assault on Aboriginal families.

· Residential schools constituted an assault on Aboriginal culture.

· Residential schools constituted an assault on self-governing and self-sustaining Aboriginal nations.

· The impacts of the residential school system were immediate, and have been ongoing since the earliest years of the schools.

· Canadians have been denied a full and proper education as to the nature of Aboriginal societies, and the history of the relationship between Aboriginal and non-Aboriginal peoples.

· It will take time and commitment to reverse this legacy. The schools operated in Canada for well over a century. In the same way, the reconciliation process will have to span generations. It will take time to re-establish respect.

· Effective reconciliation will see Aboriginal people regaining their sense of self-respect, and the development of relations of mutual respect between Aboriginal and non-Aboriginal people.

· In future reports, the Truth and Reconciliation Commission will be making specific recommendations as to how reconciliation can be furthered.

The survival rate was 50 percent. Severe underfunding created poor living conditions. Underfunding meant poor nutrition and health care, which meant diseases were rampant. We understand that in many cases, there was no education, instead there was a lot of work or slave labor. Children were beaten if they spoke their languages but that is an understatement in itself. If what I got was anything like what my parents got as seen in the inter-generational effects if Indian Residential School legacy, then I can tell you with great certainty, it is an understatement. The beatings were fierce and terrifying inasmuch as it was to witness beatings or sexual abuses, even murders. The deplorable living and severely violent conditions, the objectification affected the mental health and development of these children. If we look at the present situation with what we know in sociology, psychology, medicine and health, we can understand what the survivors of Indian Residential School had to endure. We have a notion of what their experience was. It's like moving backwards using what we know and then moving forwards again to understand the totality of totalities.

FAMILY DYSFUNCTION AND INTER-GENERATIONAL EFFECTS

Being born into family dysfunction means, that child will develop among family dysfunction. Dysfunctional caregivers with a history of IRS experiences will role model dysfunctional behavior to children. Information such as belief systems, perception, and ideology, the objectification will be transferred to the children. German people mentioned that they truly believed the source of their problems were resulting from being cheated by the Jewish community. This was taught in public schools. Being born and raised in an environment of racially charged hate will develop belief systems congruent with hate towards the outgroups. Similarly, Canadian children were taught they were superior to "Indians" in public education settings. Many Canadian parents resisted teaching this to their children while many came to believe they were superior to "Indians".

This does not charge the current religious, patriarchal, paternalistic, race based, hierarchical authoritarian regimes of white supremacy to lead indigenous people out of dysfunction. If that were so, it would truly be the blind leading the blind. White people don't know everything!

Post-Traumatic Stress Disorder and other anxiety related mental health issues like panic attacks, flash backs are among the dysfunctional products of horrific childhood experiences. Triggering events would cause a caregiver to suddenly change behavior resembling the fear and anxiety of childhood events. They might suddenly become irritated and agitated or suddenly blue. Moodiness and under reacted emotions or over reacted emotions meant that people around the dysfunctional person was volatile, unpredictable and dangerous. The intensity and seriousness of childhood experiences would play itself out in ritualistic fashion as the person attempts to resolve inner conflict. They were never allowed to tell their story because of the sanctimony of religious and government authority meant one would experience serious fallout for opening up. Also, people would never believe it. No support would be available and so, the expression of pent up unresolved emotional issues would find their way in the lives of community members. Explosive and violent acts of behavior would cause further disruption for the children of survivors. The effects would produce a seriously undermined community replete with dysfunction such as corruption, suspicion, anxiety, abuses with instability. All of which contributes to dysfunctional belief systems passed on inter-generationally. For example, one grandmother believed that she was doing her kids a favor by mistreating them, beating them as she thought she was toughening them up. Then the children became parents and this belief system was passed on to the next generation. And then the dysfunctional belief system found its way into the grandchildren.

Have you ever wondered why a person in an abusive relationship does not leave the abuser? Among other reasons, the cycle of abuse, the living conditions, the suffering the person is conditioned through a series of belief systems that begin early in childhood. Among these belief systems are insecurity and self-loathing, the person may come to believe they deserve the abuse. Later they came to believe they were not worth anything better and would not find anything better for themselves. They come to believe that they must rely totally on the abuser. Escape seems impossible. The constant state of negative emotion either generated by the victim or the abuser meant hopelessness and despair. Recall the roommate torture situation where a very large and strong man became the victim of his tormentor who was half his size. While I do not know all the details of the case it does appear that the cycle of abuse may have played a role, decreasing the victim's ability to judge the situation resulting in severe conditions of abuse. Above all, the victim stated that he endured his abuse because he wanted to prove that he was not a "sissy". Disfigured, brutalized, emaciated and near death, the victim endured suffering to the very end because he came to believe that he needed to prove his worth. He felt worthless. This situation is no different in gangland where the initiate must prove to the full patch member they are worth membership. The entire scenario begins with the victim feeling a sense of worthlessness but all they have to do is prove to themselves, to someone and they will be accepted. The need here is acceptance because it may be that they never felt accepted before, especially if they were raised in an abusive atmosphere where attachment did not occur or was dysfunctional.

People talk about bullies gravitating towards victims. Have you ever wondered why that is? The ritual of behavior brings the dynamics together. The Bully has a need for control or has control issues, seeks to exploit the vulnerable to satisfy his need for control. Usually when the bully feels a loss of control in their life they seek to balance the equation by taking control. The victim behaves in ways the bully can identify and then exploit. Bullies rarely go after people who will challenge them. Bullies prefer easy victims. In the case of gang initiation, the victim has a need for acceptance among other reasons for participating in gang activity. The needs will prevail over any sort of rationalization because the distress of being alone is emotionally charged and the only information available will be the one to justify the behavior.

In a way, the entire initiation ritual we witnessed that was emotionally disturbing is a form of assimilation consistent with torture. Torture not only breaks down identity but it successfully gets the victim to participate in the ritual of abuse. That is what we saw when the initiate allowed people to beat her until in addition to proving herself, the full participation in self-mutilation.

Because the environments these children are developing in are volatile, unstable, abusive environments, children may develop or under develop emotionally. Post-Traumatic Stress Disorder may be prevalent among other mental health issues such as FASD. These developments will affect a person's belief systems about reality and influence their perception of the world. This perception will influence decision-making ability and judgments. The severe conditions which these kids develop under, such as, daily hunger, violence and abuses, by caregivers, parents and family members who take advantage of the vulnerable situations these kids are in; produce a fatigued individual who must remain alert at all times in readiness to cope with the next abuse ritual, hunger, pain and suffering. In order to be on the edge where they need to be, they may likely subconsciously ruminate on negative events keeping themselves emotional to justify and maintain hyper vigilance. I have seen parents using their children to sell drugs believing that like swearing, it is inevitable. I have known parents sexually exploit their children forcing their daughters into prostitution. Many do not make it. Suicide is the only way out. The agony and the pain of this suffering affects ones thought processes so that it becomes difficult to be positive about anything, to judge or assess rationally. The sense of hopelessness and despair increases and the heart begins to harden as emotions begin to turn off or switch on with inappropriate intensity. One becomes indifferent towards others under these conditions. They may begin to see others as objects for their own gratification and develop psychopathic tendencies. Under these situations, all people are objectified, based on egocentric hedonism. Even in an abusive relationship where one is undermined and abused, the relationship itself is a source of gratification for what its worth for the victim. They come to believe that they are loved and this is what it means to be loved. This may have been role modeled to them. Some kids have told me of their version of playing house where they trash the furniture and beat each other up, as this is what they know of relationships and family. Perhaps some kids could not even imagine what "house" is all about so they do not play it. The sexually abused child will defend their abusive parents believing their parents love them. The constant and ongoing disruption to safety, security, love and stability make life volatile, perception is off center and belief systems become dysfunctional. Even if a true love was found, it is likely to be rejected or sabotaged because it is foreign. As for safety, it may become unbearable to feel safe, as that is unfamiliar. Security is especially difficult as many develop the feeling that they deserve the abuse; they come to believe they deserve nothing better. The learned helplessness is so deeply ensconced that the idea of anything better is virtually non-existent. The possibility of positive direction is undermined by dysfunctional belief systems and reinforced by role models, dysfunctional relationships, family and friends. Escape is not even in the mindset, escape from what? They come to believe that this reality they exist in, is all they can look forward, for the rest of their lives. They are caught in a state of learned helplessness, a belief that nothing they do will ever change their situation so they do not even try. If they see someone trying to "better" themselves, they scoff and say things like, "who do you think you are"? They attempt to bring them back down for among other reasons, they are afraid to lose a friend, they must continue to see that their reality is truly the only reality they have. Witnessing someone escape their reality does not fit with their constructions of reality, what they have come to know and accept, that this is all they have. Alternatively, it reinforces the notions of abandonment, that people cannot be trusted or reliable. However, some come to believe that a better life is possible and they will take steps toward "bettering" themselves.

Such people come to a point of readiness for change. They are open. They have what the alcoholics refer to as a moment of clarity. It takes hold and is fruitful enough to produce steps toward emancipation. The scoffers will scoff and the naysayers will harp but if they ignore all this, they may make enough strides to leave this group entirely. However, they will find themselves in new territory, unfamiliar territory and they will not have much support. They may look back and be tempted to go back to the places of familiarity. Being in new territory, they may see that they are now small fish in a bigger pond and that may be unsettling. They may be tempted to go back to being a big fish in a small pond.

RELATIONSHIPS

Gang awareness is about being aware of relationships. Poor kids who come from these violent and dysfunctional homes are the most vulnerable to influences of gang families. For one thing, the gang makes sense under these conditions. There is safety in numbers. There is acceptance no matter how dysfunctional, it is what it is. These kids have come to believe this is all they have to look forward to in their lives. Having experienced severe abuse in the home, in the schools, in the streets, in social services and the like, there is no safer place than taking direct control by making this choice. An abusive relationship in many ways is all about control. The sense of hopelessness and helplessness becomes so pervasive that any small act is meaningful enough to feel a sense of control. Control is found to be one of the most influential factors in rape. Rape is the ritual of control over the vulnerable and in a way, it is the ritualistic expression of the loss of control in the perpetrators life when they were a victim. The ritual does not have to be about rape either. It could be about homelessness, sexuality and masturbation, manipulation of others and the like. These can be often be the expression of the victim's experiences of abuse. One scholar believes that homelessness is the theme of the victims of IRS abuse because they never experienced a home life as children and they were punished for being Indian or Metis or Innu to the point that they are not even at home in their own skin. This theme plays itself out every day in the lives of many of the homeless people he works. In psychology, we understand these issues among others as insecure attachment or anxious ambivalent attachments styles, attachment disorder. Relationships are wrought with dysfunction because of early life experiences and later life reinforcements.

COGNITIVE DIVERSITY

It was not until I began to work social services where I became truly acquainted with the diversity of cognitive ability. It was here that I realized that every person is unique in their own cognitive development while appearing to blend in with what we understand as normal cognitive and human behavior. Every person's experience teaches each person a unique pattern of understanding.

NEUROBEHAVIORAL DEVELOPMENT

Throughout our lives, we are constantly learning new things about reality and behavior. We have seen in imagery the development of neural connections, which facilitate learning. The neurons literally reach out to each other connecting and storing in memory the learned information. Over time, these connections thicken and cause learning to be further ensconced. Whenever we are faced with a stimulus, our information receptors like the eyes and the ears carry information to our brains and stimulate certain regions recalling memories and through a series of bio-chemical changes in the body, this helps us to prepare for whatever stimulus we face. The sight of a gun pointed at our face is sure to produce the appropriate responses. However, consider the person who has grown and developed in the severest conditions of human depravity such as the legacy of Indian Residential School. The neurons have reached out to each other and made their connections producing learned behavior and memory.

COGNITIVE BEHAVIORAL THERAPY

CBT seeks to assist a person with identifying dysfunctional belief systems and their roots, which are often early in childhood and often among major themes such as fear, anger, and other emotions. So that through analyses once can change into more functional belief systems that help with a realistic, balanced and harmonious life. However, therapists agree that this cannot happen unless a person is ready for change. Readiness for change is the pinnacle for successful therapy. In the past, judges used to force people to attend therapy but that is less common on account of the understanding that if a person is not ready for change, change is not likely to happen. Permanently deleting learned behavior or memories may never be available or possible. However, with help, people can change their beliefs, emotional experiences and behavior from dysfunctional ones to healthier ones with time and repeated attempts. In the very least, with help, one can change the level of intensity of an emotional response so that the distress one experiences is appropriate to the event they face. Help, can improve the lives of individuals by changing perception to one that is balanced and reality based rather than imagined. But as we know, it is a long and difficult road to be able to face ones past and discover the meanings of those horrific events. While some events are more tolerable than others, some will never be approached unless one is ready.

TORTURE

The IRS experience is consistent with torture. The purpose of torture is to break down identity to produce a new one. The process and rituals of abuse are the method to re-education. The purpose of assimilation has always been to kill the Indian in the child and produce a white person. Outwardly, these people would look Indian but would behave white. The purpose is to produce a citizen that can be inserted into the capitalistic system and taxed while they give up legal right to the land base, including any revenue from natural resources. Again, there is not enough profit in sharing profit. The torture that many children experienced was malnutrition, sleep deprivation, sickness and disease, beatings for speaking their language, sexual abuses and the like. These experiences occurred daily for years. The consequence was the development of dysfunctional belief system about identity skewing perception toward an unsafe worldview to say the least.

These developed beliefs are biologically ensconced and to disconnect the neurons in developing new beliefs takes time and repetition with sincere motivation. Pulling up ones socks and getting a little elbow grease toward a positive work ethic is a lot harder than it looks. The barriers to health and wellbeing are a near permanently frustrating process. Anyone who attempts this kind of monumental change should be honored and respected. Plus, having to change friends and separate oneself from dysfunctional family and other distractions is beyond difficult. It requires faith when ones has no faith. It requires trust where one has never trusted before. It requires hope to those who never learned to hope or abandoned all hope. How does one behave in a way they have never learned to behave? How does one love when one has never experienced love? These challenges face both the oppressor and the oppressed. It will require respect for each other's ways of managing their own affairs, to trust in the others solutions, to challenge each other in a healthy way ensuring a healthy relationship is maintained for the sake of the children for seven generations.

THE IMAGES OF THE GRANDMOTHER AND GRANDCHILD AND OTHER INDIGENOUS PEOPLE

I saw the misrepresentation of the truth of this image by the constable. The constable implied that gangsters, the enemy of society, of Indigenous descent, Asian, Italian ethnicity are not trustworthy, do not love their children, and deserve to be punished with harsher sentences. The idea that media such as hip hop or rap music, movies, glorifying gang activity is a main influential factor is not correct. While these may have some influence in the same way the culture influences our behavior, it is not the full story. In fact it is a shortcut to thinking that redirects our attention from the truth. The truth I have shared with you already as to what truly influences behavior. In comparison, the things the constable produced as evidence to the development of gangs in Winnipeg dwarf what was presented. In consideration of the terms family dysfunction and inter-generational effects of gang life, I hope that you are more familiar with the dynamics of where dysfunction occurs and how it relates to people's lives. If the history that occurred did not occur, we would not have seen these developments today. Admittedly, I personally know grandparents in the throes of family dysfunction support their children and grandchildren's choices. For them, they are displaying the only kind of love and affection they know as they are within a system of thinking, a paradigm a mindset. They were conditioned to behave in these ways by external factors foreign to their natural ways. The internalized factors are consequential to their experiences. Those who resisted assimilation did so at great cost to themselves and their families as the scars of their resistance remains psychologically embedded in Post-Traumatic Stress Disorder and other mental health illnesses.

We can change our perceptions and our beliefs if we are ready for that. While I recognize that, the emotions we experienced when we saw the image of the young man who was gunned down in the streets because of a gangland shootout was intense. I believe the purpose of that display was to prime us for the next images we saw of "Indians" complete with shock and horror towards the Indigenous replete with already presented prejudices. This maneuver will get those who are sitting on the fence of racism to get off the fence towards discrimination. It is no different from when the Nazi regime presented images of vermin and cockroaches flooding German homes and then presenting images of Jewish people. However, if we know this is a possibility, that propaganda may have presented itself before us; we can now choose whether or not we want to believe it. Should we not consider the true influences on human behavior or should we just focus on behavior and punish without considering all the fact, to be prejudiced, hoping the behavior will go away. We would really need to exercise faith because the research does not support the belief that stiffer punishments will change behavior. But you can believe it if you want.

We Indigenous have never accepted this life, we have always resisted the systems of oppression as insidious as they are and we continue today. The gangster never really chose that life, it was presented as the only option available, one that they were born into, lived, survived and resist. To expect people to simply make the right choice, a rational one is simply an irrational expectation. But to expect you and others to believe me is also irrational. Unless you are ready to accept the truth, ready for change, everything I have told you makes no sense.

This is also true for me too. I was raised to hate white man from town. I was raised to believe this world is unsafe, that I am despicable and horrific to look upon. I came to believe that I was worthless. Moreover, I found reasons to continue to believe this daily. Like the police, I stayed in a constant state of emotion, only allowing that information which justified emotion. I was putting out a fire with gasoline, as is the case in all conflicts. Today, I have over years of therapy under me and my life is positively changing. I hope that yours changes positively too.

And that's why we need to be compassionate with others who are disturbed. They need reinforcement and help.
They are like us, lost, said another Rainbow Warrior.

It is like the blind, leading the blind cried another. Is there any hope?

There may be, replied an Elder. There may be.

Another Rainbow Warrior spoke up as well. They said they were always afraid to speak their mind and when they did, they waited for the other shoe to drop. They said they felt great emotional torment and shame for speaking their mind. For days, they would hide from everyone believing they did a very shameful thing by speaking up, speaking out. They understood now that it is okay to talk and share. They understood that it was now safe for them to speak the talk medicine and that it is healthy to do so. Those who would try to shut them up are the ones who have the problem, not them! They understood that anyone who would try to shame them for speaking were doing so out of that history of violence, hatred, self-loathing and assimilation. They are to be pitied and not judged. In talking and sharing, we have nothing to be ashamed, we have done nothing wrong they said. The Sharing Circle was always a sacred healing path. We are more than our talk and our thoughts, we are deeper and wider that what we see or hear and feel. We are perfect!

Another Rainbow Warrior encouraged all the others saying, what we are feeling inside is not what we perceive on the outside. Projecting our dysfunctional thoughts onto others is not wise. People are not our abusers. They are products of their culture. We can't blame them, judge them, punish them, or correct them. They are oblivious to what has happened to them, which has made them the way they are. Remember your compassion!

Just then another spoke up saying, remember to enjoy the moment. Come back to her, drift not away. The war is over. All we have is today, one day at a time.

Another Rainbow Warrior spoke saying, slow down, and take it easy. There are fires out there, but they are not yours to put out. Martyrdom is not necessary. You don't have to represent others, especially if they do not ask you!

And another Rainbow Warrior spoke saying, Many have their own problems they are not even remotely aware of, there is no point in judging them. If they are not ready for your talk medicine, then there is no reasoning with them, or being angry with them as you cannot bargain with them, they will not negotiate.

When they attack you or criticize you it is important to realize their anger and their crazy eyes are not about YOU, said another Rainbow Warrior! It is about them! Whatever happened to them in their life, whatever history they have with the great corruption and the beast, which is trying to possess them, is driving them mad! Everyone has their own perceptions, opinions, understandings, from whatever culture they come from, whatever history they have. Right or wrong, if they attack, it's not about YOU, it's about them! You don't need to take it personally.

They are not your abusers, oppressors, ultimate criminals, psychopaths, sociopaths, anti-socials, Nazi's, Stalinists, torturer nor tormentor and they needn't be given the same level of historical importance. We do not scream at the top of our lungs, "WHITE MAN FROM TOWN" in hatred, judgment and loathing as if Adolf Hitler himself was in your presence. No, calm down and see it for what it is. It is just ignorance and remember your compassion.

Then another Rainbow Warrior approached the microphone and began to speak. Accept yourself and let go the need to prove yourself to yourself and to others. The thing about racism is that you can be a racist if you want, but you will always have to prove your self worth to others and they don't accept anyone except for their own. If they are not ready to accept you, then nothing you do or say will convince them you are worth it, that you deserve respect, that you are a person. Remember to love yourself, even as you always have, as you show this in your resistance against the great beast all these years.

Remember your compassion and be patient with yourself and others. We are all a work in progress. Forgive yourself when you make mistakes and stay committed to living excellent!

Be a part of the solution and not the problem a very young Rainbow Warrior said. Live and let live. You deserve goodness, wholesome happiness and peace. You are worthy of love.

Have faith, said another Rainbow Warrior. Extend your faith to trust. Sometimes that means taking a leap of faith. Take a leap of faith when some ignorant white supremacist offends you, recognize your anger and theirs and know that when they are angry, you cannot reason with them, they will not negotiate, there is no bargaining. Walk away from the angry person and manage the situation from a distance, with reinforcement, perhaps submit a grievance through the appropriate channels. Have faith in your use of instrumental aggression, it is more powerful than you think. It is more powerful than hostile aggression which does nothing for the situation we all face. Have faith, extend your faith to trust.

Its okay to be angry said another Rainbow Warrior, so long as our anger is used wisely. We don't project and attack out of delusions, we empower ourselves with courage to make changes. There is a difference between *hostile* aggression and *instrumental* aggression. If you find that your are becoming hostile recognize the signs and wonders that occur throughout your body and do no go with your first instinct which is to attack. Wait, stop yourself, as angry as you are and have faith that you can manage yourself to behave yourself. It's what you do with your anger that makes all the difference. Remember your wolf. Your anger is like a wolf or bear that is protecting a cub. You must go to it, comfort it, like it was a *baybee* and to caress it and care for it like a *baybee*. Only then can your anger be comforted by your actions of self-love and respect. And when your anger is comforted, you may be able to extend your inner peace to others. Therefore, remember your wolf, your spirit guide and protector.

And give yourself credit said another Rainbow Warrior to the people. Be good to yourself, you are not in denial anymore. You are open and awake! You have courage! You loved yourself respectfully all these long years through many dark times, trials and tribulations you have preserved that sacred part of who you truly are. You have done well for yourself!

Another Rainbow Warrior said, mistakes will happen. Don't beat yourself up too much over them. Do not be too hard on yourself. We learn from our mistakes. Don't allow yourself a victim role and deny yourself the abuser role, neither are healthy and you are more than these roles. Have faith and remember to be in the moment. In the moment there are no fiery darts thrown at you. In the moment, in the here and now, this very moment. You are safe, secure, stable and loved. Remind yourself of that often! The war is over now. This is a time of peace and healing! So don't worry so much anymore. Let your cares and worries go. They cannot help you. So it is important to recognize the abundant peace, love, serenity and harmony that is all around us. We can tap into that at any time even as great clashes and calamities happen, we can always reach out and grasp the truth, that is, that there is abundant peace all around us. There is plenty for everyone! We all deserve this peace and harmony. You deserve this you are worthy!

Take some time each day and practice all you have learned. Meditate. Practice sitting in the moment to experience all she has to offer and absorb it into every fiber of your being. With practice it gets better, it really does.

Finally, the last Rainbow Warrior spoke, don't think you are, know you are!

The Elders replied.

Now more than any other time, our children are apprehended at rate three or four times higher than the old 60's scoop. Now more than ever our children are involved with the justice systems. Now more than ever, our children are in poverty, suffer illnesses, are abused and more than ever, no one listens to them. Everyone dismisses them, judges them and they tell the children that they bring trouble upon themselves. The oppression of children is clearly apparent. Everyone is too focused on the fathers who have their own worries they care for from a patriarchal perspective.

Young people are aware there is a problem with the world we live in today. They understand they do not want to hear about our sanctimony, our religions, and our hypocrisy. They understand that what we often offer them is not the solution as it is a part of the problem, for some reason young people know this. That is why they have stopped talking to us, they have stopped listening to our words. It is time to present the Sharing Circle, talk medicine back into our lives. We must talk to each other with respect. We were all children once too and in many ways, many of us still are, for better or for worse. But the smokescreens and the lies are too much for us to try and understand all things. This at least we know, that our children are being produced and manufactured to be eaten by the great beast and many people have attempted to negotiate with this abomination. In negotiating with this abomination, they have become agents of this abomination. But not all of them are, many resist!

There are social workers, police, probation, justices, health services and teachers and all of those professions have great warriors within them who are trying to change the system from within. They are trying, but they do not have all the answers and they are burned out. They are inundated with too much Weendigo and they says things like, "the system is broken and we don't know how to fix it". When we bring back the Sharing Circle, talk medicine, and we become a child-centered society once again with respect to our traditional and healing ways, we will do much to fix the broken system.

Young people know who are there to help and who are not wholly corrupted. As for those who are agents of abomination, we must remember our compassion and accept them for what they are. Our caring spirit to the thing that should not be will go a long way to healing the possessed person. This is very difficult to do when you are angry. In the same way, we remember our wolf and we practice self-love and respect, we acknowledge the wolf in others, even if they are possessed, assimilated and psychopathic. They were not always this way. Nor are they hopeless. So we accept things for what they are and we have the courage to change what we can.

The system, as broken as it is can be our powerful ally. We have resisted its totalitarianism and have ensured the proper procedures are in place to protect the children of the earth. These protections are there and have some good Warriors working in them and some maybe not so good.

The Canadian Constitution is the highest law in which all other laws must be consistent. The Constitution, these systems consist of our human rights, treaty rights, Aboriginal rights. We have a right to be treated fairly in every situation, education, justice, employment and the like. There is due process, protocol established in all these situations that are there to assure us fair and respectful treatment. If the *bosses* do not want to treat us fairly, we can exercise our rights by filing grievances, complaints, claims against our bosses in case they need reminding that they are required by law to be respectful. Though some of you may scoff at the grievance procedures, that you have rights, you must remember that laws, even the highest one at the level of the Supreme Court of Canada, which ensure our rights are protected in our Constitution, protect these rights and grievance procedures. Many fought and died to bring you this gift. You do not just *have a right to remain silent*!

So it is important to recognize that you can grieve through these procedures and force the corrupt to change and it is well within your right to do so, so feel free and at liberty to do that. You are not doing anything wrong for speaking your mind. That is why we have the Manitoba Human Rights Commission, The Manitoba Ombudsman, The Manitoba Appeals Commission, the Workers Advisors Office, The Children's Advocate, and the like who have many good warriors and maybe some not so good ones, but they are there, charged with the duty to represent, a duty to care and they have a standard of care which by law, they must enact on your behalf. So the system, as broken as it is, at times it seems we need to be saved from the system, it is there for YOU! Why? Because you deserve it! You are worthy! You are a valuable person for our society.

And I would encourage all the children who have been apprehended by these child and family services, I would encourage all the parents of children who have been apprehended to learn the system and justice systems and make it work for you. They will help you and are very eager to make sure the system is working properly. But they will never know if you do not speak! All citizens must throw off the smokescreen that tells them one person will never make a difference. When citizens take action, one becomes thousands and public outcry demands changes!

Then the Weendigo Kahn said, You gotta fight! For your right! And everyone, even the Elders joined in, TO PAAAAARTAYYYY!

With that the Elder said laughing, lets feast!

Afterword

INDIANS

In a course with *Dr. Emma LaRocque* entitled, *Images of First Nation People from a European Perspective*, I was asked what comes to mind when I hear the word, *Indian*. I was then challenged with imaginations of the Indian, what had come to my mind. Along with friends and relatives, I also saw drunks on main and I recalled images if bloodthirsty savages with their war clubs, bowing knives and tomahawks for scalping I learned in grade six social studies in 1983. I had to withdraw from the course but I did retake it the next year with Dr. Peter Kulchyski and did very well in it.

I learned about this European gaze that *Edward Said* describes in his book *Orientalism* and later in *Imperialism*. This European gaze has transferable characteristics when the European gaze is turned toward the Indian. Succinctly put, the European gaze is an ethnocentric gaze that perceives others from a superior position, judging others, dismissing them, dehumanizing them all of which serves to exploit them for profiteering. I would strongly encourage anyone to read about this phenomenon to get a clear understanding of all the facets related to this issue. It affects us all and is a crucial step towards world peace.

We learned about white supremacy, which is not in doubt. Though many white people will say they are not racist, this book has attempted to show how white people are born into privilege, supremacy, power, status and wealth. Not all white people are privileged, but overall, the statistics show that white people do better than any other ethnic group in Canada. This makes sense when you apply the principle of discrimination and if you have power, you are likelier to help one of your own rather than others. There is a plethora of belief systems that are utilized to make this happen and it can get pretty bad, as bad as pushing bodies alive or dead, children or adults into ovens. No one, not one single person can argue that white people are not the most privileged in Canada, the research is repeatedly peer reviewed worldwide and this makes it empirical.

Now that we have established the existence of white supremacy and that most would like to believe it no longer exists let's show you that it in fact does exist.

We have already described *The Invention of the White Race* by *Theodore. W. Allen*. We know about *Porter's Vertical Mosaic*. We are aware of the role and influence of the Catholic and Protestant churches during colonization. Finally, we have seen how Dr. Bob Altemeyer and others work has shown how specifically white supremacy and the dehumanization process works. All of this is irrefutable.

Culture plays a significant role too. We have described that history records the role of the church where we have for thousands of years, received hierarchical, patriarchal, paternalistic, authoritarian morality and ethics. Any review of history will point out the hypocrisy of the church very quickly, and this is where we got our teachings. Nevertheless, the church taught people how to govern themselves morally. Kingdoms, not Queendoms used the pattern of the church fathers as the model for governance. Along with this transferable role modeling of the church, came the corruption inherent in it. So you have what we have today. A government that is based in hierarchical, patriarchal, paternalistic, authoritarian style of corrupt rulership. It doesn't matter if women are elected we are still utilizing this model.

Our church, governance, history have provided us with the basis for culture and it is a culture based in hierarchical, patriarchal, paternalistic, authoritarian style of corrupt rulership. From the constitution all the way down to the child, every government office, department, private corporation, education, private or public, social service, private or public, utilizes, hierarchical, patriarchal, paternalistic, authoritarian style of corrupt rulership.

We learn about it in our children's storybooks at our schools, library's and from our teachers. We learn about it in our television shows, cartoons, and the like. Long before we are born, we are subjected to it. Boys wear blue and girls wear pink. We are gendered. Every aspect of our perception, understanding comprehension, belief systems, and psychology is formulated by hierarchical, patriarchal, paternalistic, authoritarian style of corrupt rulership. It permeates every aspect of our lives. Our cultures, no matter where they come from around the world have this model influencing their ways of doing things.

If this is the world we are born into and develop in then we are products of culture and not the people we think we are. We are trained to think what the culture has us thinking and we are hard pressed to think outside the box. I believe that it is youth are the only ones capable of doing thinking outside the box but they are persecuted, dismissed, dehumanized, relegated as wards of the parents, the father mostly or if without parents, wards of the state. We cannot or will not appreciate the gift young people bring to our societies.

Let's focus a little more on the psychology of dehumanization. On the extreme end, we have described psychopathic behavior citing work from Dr.'s Babiak and Hare as well as Vaknin. There are others however you can find them in any first year Social Psychology text book. They describe the processes that are used by people when dehumanizing.

I could describe in great detail how specifically we learn but that would require chapters and chapters to be written and it would have to be most academic. That is beyond the scope of this book. There are behavior modification techniques such as positive and negative reinforcement, intervals of rewards and punishment, socialization methods, indoctrination and the like that all play a role in what you come to believe about your reality.

Even mystics can't get away from culture. They described mystical experiences as god experiences. Why god? Why can't it be something else? Why does god have to be a white man with a white beard sitting on a throne in the sky rewarding and punishing people? Why not an elephant or a snake?

It's because that's not a part of our constructions of reality. We cannot or will not imagine anything other than what we have been taught, familiar with, have accepted as a universal truth. We say its common sense or that it's the way it's always been or worse, that there is nothing we can do about it so we may as well accept it, the problem is too big.

Such thinking has enslaved people to do and say things that have resulted in genocide, oppression, colonization and the like. And it's all righteous according to those who bought into the message. Some colonized are even grateful for the great corruption to have come and saved them from the pagan, barbaric ways and they thank god for sending these missionaries to save them. Utter nonsense.

The Eurocentric gaze or the white perspective comes from a place of supremacy, superiority justified by god as god does for those who do for themselves and punishes the unrighteous heathen who would not be converted. Many a righteous zealot has turned into a bloodthirsty savage in the name of god or their sports team.

Dehumanization is the process, which we look at a race of people, and our white supremacy, our superior sense of entitlement affords us the opportunity to place judgment. Even many assimilated ethnicities not white ascribe to a white supremacy belief system sometimes as if they are white. We look at the other and we do not understand them or their ways as it is different from ours. We have been told by the church fathers they are heathens, unchristian, pagan, barbarian, savages. If they will not convert to Christianity, Islam, or other religions, they remain heathens, infidels, unchristian, pagan, barbarian, savages. They do not know what is good for them we think and when we discuss this with other like-minded individuals, we are positively reinforced for thinking like this. We feel a sense of camaraderie, brotherhood. It is us, against them.

These thought processes develop into stereotypes about others. We say things like, nigger, kike, wop, and frog. For a complete listing of racist terms that refer to various ethnic groups, see wikipedia (http://en.wikipedia.org/wiki/List_of_ethnic_slurs). We all know what these racist slurs mean and we all know how it makes us feel.

We feel objectified, dehumanized, and we become insecure and for very good reasons. When we dehumanize other people and groups, we threaten them with genocide. We know from history that dehumanization has led to ethnic cleansing, genocide, holocaust, assimilation programs, concentration camps, force labor camps, re-education camps, Indian Residential Schools where indigenous languages were forbidden, practicing traditional and cultural ways forbidden, disappeared people, firing squads, maiming, beheading and scalping.

Scalping is not an Indian thing by they way, it originates with other ethnic groups and there has been no evidence it was practiced by the people of Turtle Island prior to colonization. However, scalping is associated with bloodthirsty savages as a barbaric act. The truth is this is projected on Indians by settlers in ignorance, which then justifies further retaliation by white settlers in visceral hate filled revenge. Meanwhile, it was a practice originating with Europeans not Indians. Indigenous people eventually practiced scalping, not all practiced this nor did it originate with *natives*.

Returning to the course I took with Dr. Peter Kulchyski at the University of Manitoba and others, I learned that Europeans look at Indians in a dehumanizing manner. We used a book by *Daniel Francis* called T*he Imaginary Indian* which presented Eurocentric imaginations of the Indian. The term Indian elicits images and imagination of a bloodthirsty savage, a heathen that monstrously murders settler children and peaceful priests and nuns. Careless and witless these murderous monsters, barbarian, savages, without feeling, remorse, guilt or shame, unabashedly kill, kill, kill! They are *wagon burners* and *spear chucker's*. Clearly, this is a projection from a European perspective a practice that many Europeans may feel shame and guilt over but rather than accept responsibility for their barbarism they project it onto Indians.

The other image of the Indian is one that childishly mimics the good qualities of the white man. The noble savage is the Indian that has likeable even noble characteristics that are admirable from a European perspective. There is a hint of humanity in these imaginations and images of the noble savage. They almost appear civilized. The noble savage has super human qualities like characters in James Fennimore Cooper's Last of the Mohican's and are super sexualized like Pocahontas. Both had their day in the universe and they are part of the vanishing Indian tale.

The vanishing Indian story as seen in movies and storybooks show the progress and development of civilized society entering the wild and untamed world of savages in either Africa, India, Indonesia or

North America. This is a natural progress, as civilization is understood to advance and move forward. The savage, pagan, barbarian or noble savage, must make way to progress and civilization and so we see them as vanishing into the twilight to disappear forever. But they have these noble qualities and still they disappear as they stubbornly maintain their traditional and cultural antichrist ways have no place with civilization. It is as if these stories and movies prepare the viewers for the annihilation and destruction of the Indian and is morally justified with belief systems of civilization and progress.

Characters are created from these European perspectives of the pagan, barbarian savage or the noble savage. They are implemented in stories told from a European perspective. Sorry son, we had to kill the Indian, they would not see to reason. They brought it on themselves. They are stupid people, ignorant, stubborn in their ways. They insist on living as *hunter-gatherers*, insist on scalping. We can't have that kind of barbarian living in our neighborhoods son, they must go. And so you see son, they deserve what they get, they bring it on themselves. We can't have backward savages among us. They don't want to live by the rules, the rule of law son, we can't have such barbarism among us. They must vanish.

So let's name our sports teams after these noble savages, let's utilize the savagery of these barbarians, projecting these constructions of reality onto our teams.

Where once we used these images to justify our torture, murder, killings, genocides, women, children, smashing their babies heads against rocks, cutting them out of their mothers wombs, cutting mothers breasts so they cannot breast-feed their babies, let us now use these images to super impose on our sports teams son!

Let's reduce these barbarians to characters, caricaturizing them, minimizing them to suit our fanciful needs of white supremacy. After all, we are superior to them. Let's call our hockey teams the Chicago Blackhawks, let's name our baseball teams the Cleveland Indians and let's pretend our hands are tomahawks where we scalp the other team like those bloodthirsty savages did to our settlers.

Let's imagine that we are bloodthirsty savages and take that to the visiting team!

Heck son, they should be happy we now admire these pagan, barbarian savages! Their courage, tenacious characters in spite of all the abuse torment and murder that we gave to them, they are still here! Those Indians are tough sons of bitches! Kinda like us son, but we can kick their ass anyday son!

It's such an admirable thing for a man to sow many oats. We are the head of household's son! We rule this world! We deserve to fuck these Indians good just like we fuck women all over the world. So let's put Pocahontas on a pedestal son, let's beautify her, sexualize her and let's fuck her like the bitch she is son. Even our white women can see the sexual qualities of Pocahontas. She is a wild one, hot, spicy and wet. She'll fuck anyone and she deserves it the slut!

Oh what's that son? Can you hear it? Indians are offended that we still look at them with these imaginations? How can they be offended? What's so offensive about these images? We are honoring *OUR* Indian people, these noble savages. I say *ours* because we own these people son, we have taken everything from them and placed them on reserves and we own the rights. We dominate them in every way son and we should! They don't know what's good for them. They are like children who don't know what's best. Don't be offended by that son, I wasn't talking about you I was talking about these pierogi and cabbage eaters. They need to be managed like we manage our women son. Women have their place and why would women think their place in the kitchen and laundry rooms are sexist? A good woman would never think such a thing!

So that's our job son and don't ever be ashamed of it.

Objectification is the process where we no longer see a person, we see an object. We objectify women. We sexualize them. We see them in pieces rather than the whole. We see tits and ass, legs and feet. We do not see them as a whole. We manage them and we rule over them. We do this throughout every facet of society and we capitalize off it. I am no feminist but I can see that in every image, billboard advertisements place women as a sexual object and many women play into this role themselves. But I am not judging here, I am pointing out how far objectification of people can dehumanize to the point women will collaborate with the great corruption. Indians are no different and I use this word Indian to include Metis and Innu people as the term Indian is projected onto us by white people.

The objectification of the Indian is offensive because it is a critical component to dehumanization of indigenous people of Turtle Island. You can't kill an Indian if you see them as you see your own white supremacist self, a Campbell's soup kid or other imagination you choose for yourself, Christianized, civilized, normal. The two programs are not compatible, murder is not compatible with one who values the human family. Such an individual that murders is considered a monster in the white world. So it is much easier to kill an Indian, there is honor in killing a *brave* or a *buck* even if they are small, cute cuddly little children. Why not rape a hot, spicy, Pocahontas (who was about 12 years old by the way) bitch? It is even justifiable to rape, kill, torment, Indians and to smash their baby's heads against rocks by swinging those little savages over head by their infant legs. You would never do this to a human but an Indian, well you're doing them a favor from your white supremacist mindset. It's morally and justifiably acceptable when utilizing racist ideology and white supremacy.

Oh c'mon now, your saying, that's not what we are doing when we name our teams like that. It's all in fun! It's about team spirit! We don't really believe in these racist things. We're just having fun.

At whose expense?

Oh c'mon now, *you people* are being too sensitive.

You people....

When we maintain these racist beliefs, minimizing their effects as if we don't secretly admire our superiority and ownership over people as if we don't feel safer and secure that we control people, managing them, we perpetuate intergenerational white supremacy. It is no different from raising children among the Ku Klux Klan whose children are born into families of white supremacist and white supremacy cultures. When I say we *maintain* racism, I mean we literally maintain it. We care for it. We make sure it keeps working in our psyche's our lifestyles and culture. It literally takes work to maintain and perpetuate white supremacy. Cognitive energy is spent daily to twist truths into lies, corrupting what we experience. It requires a massive amount of energy to do that and yet even though cancer is on the rise along with other diseases, we stubbornly maintain these beliefs unquestionably to fit our constructions of reality to the detriment of our health through wasted energy spent on dysfunctional racist beliefs.

It would be stupid if we Indians made a team for ourselves and called it, *White Do-Gooder's*, The Great White Sharks/Fathers, The White Child Molesters, The Greedy Land Grabbers, The Raper's, well hell, that's overtly racist! Let's superimpose a white babies head on a soccer ball and kick that around the field. Let's toss a white mans balls around a football field. Let's pretend a hockey puck is a frozen penis. Let's justify the rape of white women even if they are only twelve in our stories.

We would never mean to be derogatory with these imaginations. We would never intend to harm white people with these insensitive imaginations. Surely, you wouldn't be offended by these constructions of reality. Surely, you're not that sensitive.

These stupid racist, patriarchal, paternalistic, hierarchical authoritarian psychological constructions clearly reach for moral justification and racism. White people would react to these with visceral hatred and a *burn the witch* mentality.

But we're not racist, you're still saying.

Why is it not racist for white people to create these imaginary images and it's racist if we Indians make a team called *White Do-Gooder's*? It's hypocrisy and it's racist.

Some of you may be saying that's not how my mind works. But if you still do not understand why objectifying and dehumanizing indigenous people is immoral, after all you have read and the monumental research then you need help for whatever it was that turned you into the violent corrupted person you are. You are Weendigo.

Bibliographical References

1. Aboriginal Healing Foundation, (2004) Historic Trauma and Aboriginal Healing Ottawa: Aboriginal Healing Foundation,

2. Adams, Howard. (1999) Tortured People. Penticton: Theytus,

3. Allen Theodore, W. (1997). The Invention of the White Race; The Origins of Racial Oppression in Anglo-America, Vol. 2, Verso.

4. Altemeyer, Bob, (2006) The Authoritarians. http://home.cc.umanitoba.ca/~altemey/

5. Babiak, Paul Ph. D. & Hare, Robert D. Ph. D. (2006) Snakes in Suits; When Psychopaths go to Work. Harper Collins.

6. Barnes, Gordon E. And Vulcano, Brent A. (1982) School Self-acceptance Among Canadian Indian, White and Metis Children, University of Manitoba CANAD. J. BEHAV. SCI./REV. CANAD. SCI.COMP., 14(1)

7. Barnes, Josefowitz, Cole, (2006) Residential Schools: Impact on Aboriginal Students' Academic and Cognitive Development; Ester Cole Canadian Journal of School Psychology; 2006; 21, 1/2; CBCA Complete pg. 18

8. Bruce, Sharon G. (2000) Ethnicity & Health; 5(1): 47–57 The Impact of Diabetes Mellitus Among the Metis of Western Canada Manitoba Centre for Health Policy and Evaluation, University of Manitoba, Canada

9. Blackstock, Trocmé, Bennett, (2004) Domestic Violence and Child Welfare Child Maltreatment Investigations Among Aboriginal and Non-Aboriginal Families in Canada VIOLENCE AGAINST WOMEN, Vol. 10 No. 8, August 2004 901-916 DOI: 10.1177/1077801204266312 © Sage Publications

10. Chartrand, Paul, (1991).Manitoba's Metis Settlement Scheme of 1870. Native Law Centre, University of Saskatchewan., Saskatoon.

11. Chomksy, Noam. (2003) Hegemony or Survival: America's Quest for Global Dominance. Henry Holt and Company

12. Darley, J. M. & Latané, B. (1968). "Bystander intervention in emergencies: Diffusion of responsibility". Journal of Personality and Social Psychology 8: 377–383.

13. Diamond, Jared. (1999) Guns, Germsm and Steel: The Fate of Human Societies, Norton.

14. Dyck, Noel (1991) What is the Indian "problem" : tutelage and resistance in Canadian Indian administration. St. John's : Memorial University of Newfoundland, Institute of Social and Economic Research, c1991.

15. Flanagan, Thomas "The Case Against Metis Aboriginal Rights," Canadian Public Policy, Volume 9, Number 1 (March, 1983), p. 14.

16. Fleras, Augie and Kunz, Jean Lock (2001) Media and Minorities; Representing Diversity in a multicultural Canada; Thompson Educational Publishing Inc.

17. Forward, Susan, (1989) Toxic Parents: Overcoming Their Hurtful Legacy and Reclaiming Your Life, Bantam Books

18. Gourluck, Russ, (2010) The Mosaic Village; An Illustrated History of Winnipeg of the North End, Great Plains Publications

19. Gutsch, William A. Jr. Ph. D. (1998) 1001 Things Everyone Should Know about the Universe. Doubleday Dell Publishing Group, Inc.

20. Hanh, Thich, Nhat. ((2004) Taming the Tiger Within: Meditations on Transforming Difficult Emotions. The Berkley Publishing Group.

21. Harris, Sam. (2004) The End of Faith: Religion, Terror, and the Future of Reason. Norton

22. Harris, Sam. (2010) The Moral Landscape: How Science can Determine Human Values. Free Press, a division of Simon and Schuster, Inc.

23. Hatt, Ken, (1985) Ethnic Discourse in Alberta: Land and the Metis in the Ewing Commission, Canadian Ethnic Studies/Etudes ethniques au Canada, 17:2 p.64

24. Heffernan, Margaret. (2011) Willful Blindness: Why we ignore the obvious at our own peril, Anchor Canada.

25. Henley, David. (2005) Attachment disorders in post-institutionalized adopted children: art therapy approaches to reactivity and detachment, Long Island University, C.W. Post Campus

26. Keith, Anita L. (2006) For Our Children, Our Sacred Beings Healing the Land Publications

27. Kirmayer, J, Brass, Gregory M, Tait, Caroline L, (2000) The Mental Health of Aboriginal Peoples: Transformations of Identity and Community Laurence (Can J Psychiatry 2000;45:607-616)

28. Lavallee Lynn F. & Poole, Jennifer M. (2010) Beyond Recovery: Colonization, Health and Healing for Indigenous People in Canada Received: 18 May 2009 / Accepted: 5 August 2009 / Published online: 18 August 2009 # Springer Science + Business Media, LLC 2009. Int J Ment Health Addiction (2010) 8:271–281 DOI 10.1007/s11469-009-9239-8

29. Logan, Tricia, Elizabeth. (2007) We Were Outsiders: The Metis and Residential Schools, Thesis, University of Manitoba, Department of Native Studies.

30. Martens PJ, Bartlett J, Burland E, Prior H, Burchill C, Huq, S, Romphf L, Sanguins, J, Carter S, Bailly A. Profi le of Metis Health Status and Healthcare Utilization in Manitoba: A Population Based Study. Winnipeg, MB: Manitoba Centre for Health Policy, June 2010.

31. Menzies, Peter (2007) Understanding Aboriginal Intergeneration Trauma from a Social Work Perspective The Canadian Journal of Native Studies; 2007; 27, 2; CBCA Complete pg. 367

32. Menzies, Peter (2006) Intergenerational Trauma and Homeless Aboriginal Men, Canadian Review of Social Policy; 2006; 58; CBCA Complete pg. 1

33. Milne, Brad. (1995) "The Historiography of Metis Land Dispersal, 1870-1890". Manitoba History, Issue 30, (Fall), 1995, pp 30-41.

34. Milloy, John S., A National Crime, Winnipeg: University of Manitoba Press, 1999

35. Paul, Daniel, N. (2006) First Nations History, We Were Not The Savages: Collision Between European and Native American Civilizations. 3rd Ed. Fernwood Publishing Company.

36. Porter, John (1965) The Vertical Mosaic: An Analysis of Social Class and Power in Canada, University of Toronto Press

37. Rojas and Gretton, (2007) Background, Offence Characteristics, and Criminal Outcomes of Aboriginal Youth Who Sexually Offend: A Closer Look at Aboriginal Youth Intervention Needs Sex Abuse 2007 19: 257 DOI: 10.1177/107906320701900306

38. Royal Commission on Aboriginal Peoples (RCAP), Chapter 10: Looking Forward, Looking Back, 1996

39. Saul, John Raulston. (2008) A Fair Country; Telling Truths About Canada, Viking Canada, Penguin Group

40. Sawchuk, Joe (2001) Negotiating an Identity: Metis Political Organizations, the Canadian Government, and Competing Concepts of Aboriginality The American Indian Quarterly, Volume 25, Number 1, Winter 2001, pp. 73-92 (Article) Published by University of Nebraska Press DOI: 10.1353/aiq.2001.0012

41. Said, Edward W. (1978). Orientalism, A Division of Random House, New York

42. Said, Edward W. (1993). Culture and Imperialism, A Division of Random House, New York

43. Sealey, Bruce and Antoine Lussier, The Metis Canada's Forgotten People, Winnipeg: Pemmican, 1975

44. Shore, Fred. "The Emergence of the Metis Nation in Manitoba" in Metis Legacy Eds. Lawrence Barkwell, Leah Dorian and Darren Prefontaine. Winnipeg: Pemmican, (2001). P.71-78

45. Shore, Fred and Lawrence Barkwell, Past Reflects the Present, The Metis Elders Conference, (Winnipeg: MMF), 1997

46. Sprague, D.N. "Government Lawlessness in the Administration of Manitoba Land Claims, 1870-1887", Manitoba Law Journal, 10 (4), 1988:

47. Sprague , D.N. and R.P. Frye, The Genealogy of the First Metis Nation: The Development and Dispersal of the Red River Settlement, 1820-1900. Winnipeg: Pemmican Publications, 1983

48. Sprague, D. N. (1992). Metis land claims. In K. Coates (Ed.) Aboriginal land claims in Canada: A regional perspective, (pp. 195-213). Toronto: Copp Clark Pitman Ltd.

49. Stewart, Suzanne, (2008). International Journal of Health Promotion and Education. Vol. 46 Number 2, 2008 49-56

50. Weiman, Cornelia, 2006, Improving the Mental Health Status of Canada's Aboriginal Youth, Journal Canadian Acad. Child Adolescent Psychiatry 15:4 November 2006

Internet Sources:

1. (http://www.survivorsoftorture.org/survivors/torture/what.html- last accessed February 21, 2005)

2. (http://members.lycos.co.uk/trilby/generaleffects.html last accessed February, 21 2005)

3. (http://samvak.tripod.com/torturepsychology.html)

4. http://www.tvo.org/TVO/WebObjects/TVO.woa?videoid%3F90 1719363001

5. Jane Elliot, A Class Divided; available on the internet, a PBS Frontline Production. http://www.pbs.org/wgbh/pages/frontline/shows/divided/etc/view. html

6. http://www.cic.gc.ca/english/pdf/research-stats/facts2010.pdf

7. (http://www.gangstersout.com/registry.htm)

8. (http://en.wikipedia.org/wiki/Gangs_in_Canada)

9. (http://markosun.wordpress.com/2010/10/17/winnipeg-criminal-gangs/)

10.   http://www.cccb.ca/site/eng/media-room/files/2630-apology-on-residential-schools-by-the-catholic-church

Manitoba Population and Mental Health Statistics:

1. http://www.gov.mb.ca/health/mh/index.html
2. http://www.gov.mb.ca/health/annstats/as0910.pdf
3. http://www.gov.mb.ca/health/population/pr2010.pdf

THE WAY OF THE WARRIOR
RAINBOW WARRIORS

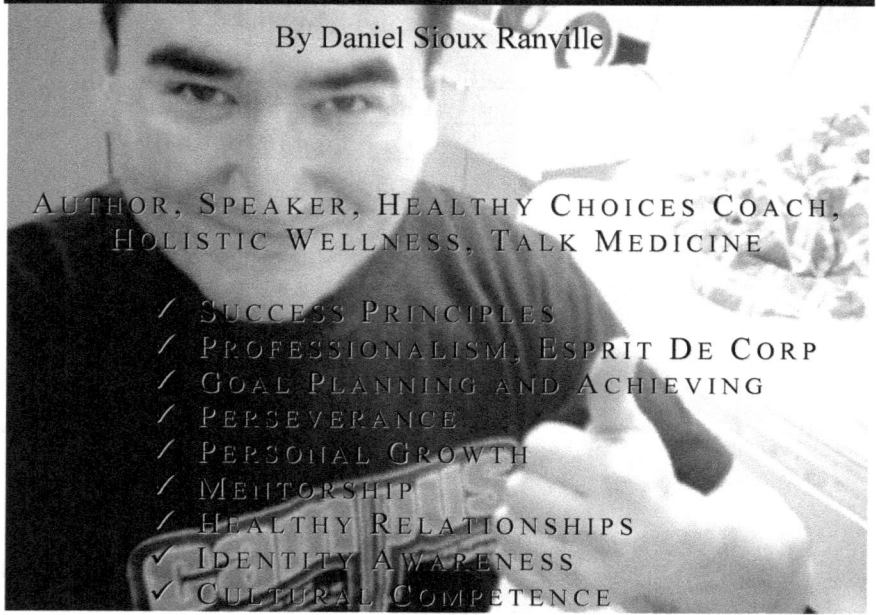

By Daniel Sioux Ranville

AUTHOR, SPEAKER, HEALTHY CHOICES COACH,
HOLISTIC WELLNESS, TALK MEDICINE

✓ SUCCESS PRINCIPLES
✓ PROFESSIONALISM, ESPRIT DE CORP
✓ GOAL PLANNING AND ACHIEVING
✓ PERSEVERANCE
✓ PERSONAL GROWTH
✓ MENTORSHIP
✓ HEALTHY RELATIONSHIPS
✓ IDENTITY AWARENESS
✓ CULTURAL COMPETENCE

Contact Daniel Sioux Ranville for your next event

Warchief Publishing
586 Lansdowne Avenue
Winnipeg Manitoba, Canada
R2W0H6
www.warchief.biz
Email: saintsioux@hotmail.com

www.ingramcontent.com/pod-product-compliance
Lightning Source LLC
Chambersburg PA
CBHW071311170626
46809CB00001B/397